IMAGE COMICS

PRESENTS

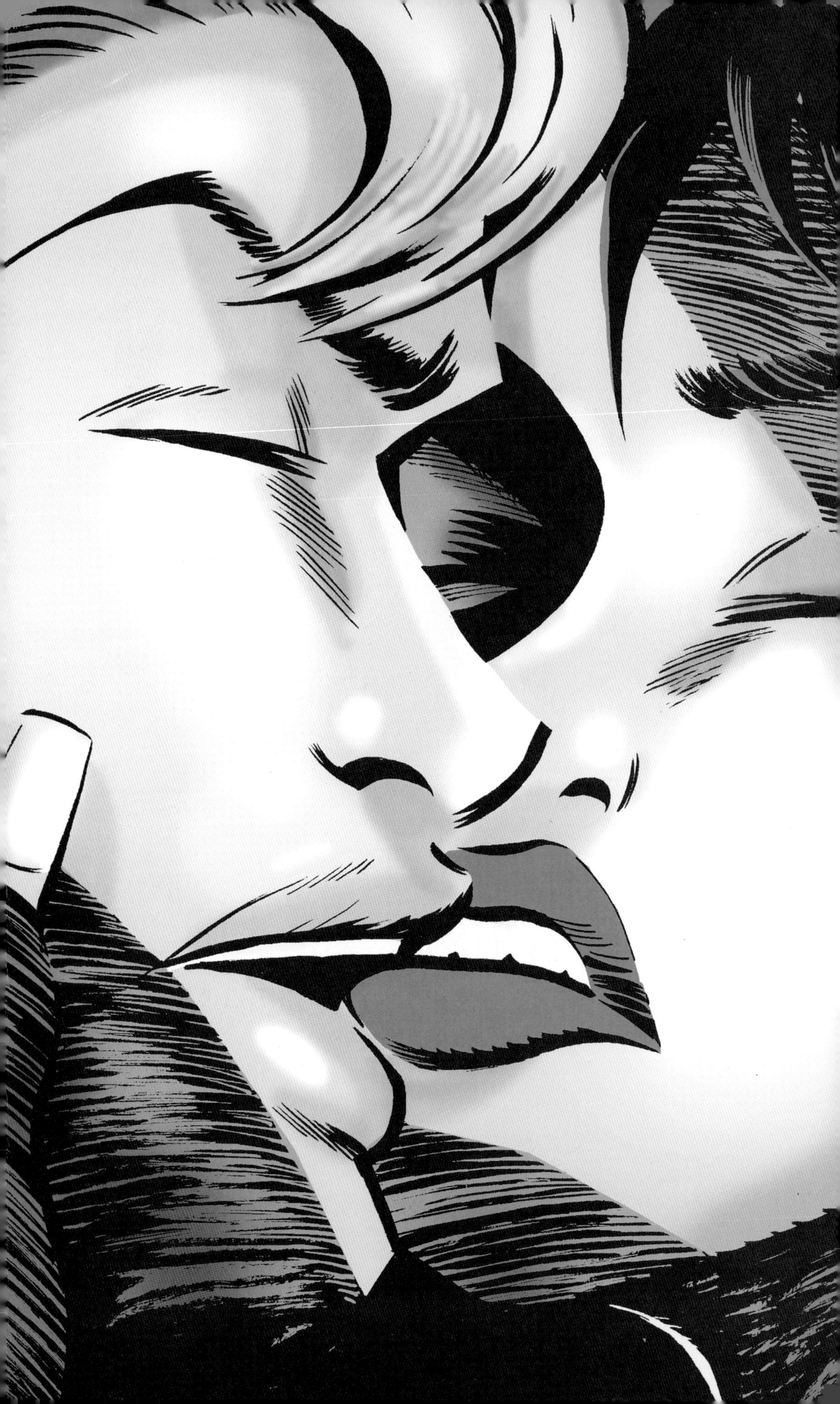

VIOLENT LOVE

VIOLENT LOVE
VOLUME TWO
"HEARTS ON FIRE"

WRITTEN BY **FRANK J. BARBIERE**   ART BY **VICTOR SANTOS**
DESIGN BY **DYLAN TODD**

image

FRANK
TO VICTOR, AND ALL MY
ARTISTIC COLLABORATORS.

YOU TURN DREAMS INTO ART.

VICTOR
TO MY BROTHERS,
RAÚL AND SERGIO.

VIOLENT LOVE, VOLUME 2: HEARTS ON FIRE First printing. January 2018. Published by Image Comics, Inc. Office of publication: 2701 NW Vaughn St., Suite 780, Portland, OR 97210. Copyright © 2018 Frank J. Barbiere & Victor Santos. All rights reserved. Contains material originally published in single magazine form as VIOLENT LOVE #6–10. "Violent Love," its logos, and the likenesses of all characters herein are trademarks of Frank J. Barbiere & Victor Santos, unless otherwise noted. "Image" and the Image Comics logos are registered trademarks of Image Comics, Inc. No part of this publication may be reproduced or transmitted, in any form or by any means (except for short excerpts for journalistic or review purposes), without the express written permission of Frank J. Barbiere, Victor Santos, or Image Comics, Inc. All names, characters, events, and locales in this publication are entirely fictional. Any resemblance to actual persons (living or dead), events, or places, without satiric intent, is coincidental. Printed in the USA. For information regarding the CPSIA on this printed material call: 203-595-3636 and provide reference #RICH–773932. For international rights, contact: foreignlicensing@imagecomics.com. ISBN: 978-1-5343-0478-9.

PUBLISHED BY IMAGE COMICS, INC

ROBERT KIRKMAN CHIEF OPERATING OFFICER   ERIK LARSEN CHIEF FINANCIAL OFFICER   TODD MCFARLANE PRESIDENT   MARC SILVESTRI CHIEF EXECUTIVE OFFICER
JIM VALENTINO VICE PRESIDENT   ERIC STEPHENSON PUBLISHER   COREY HART DIRECTOR OF SALES   JEFF BOISON DIRECTOR OF PUBLISHING PLANNING & BOOK TRADE SALES
CHRIS ROSS DIRECTOR OF DIGITAL SALES   JEFF STANG DIRECTOR OF SPECIALTY SALES   KAT SALAZAR DIRECTOR OF PR & MARKETING   DREW GILL ART DIRECTOR
HEATHER DOORNINK PRODUCTION DIRECTOR   BRANWYN BIGGLESTONE CONTROLLER

IMAGECOMICS.COM

"Now all these tastes improve
Through the view that comes with you
Like they handed me my life
for the first time it felt worth it
Like I deserved it."

JETS TO BRAZIL

CHAPTER SIX

"BASTARDS OF YOUNG"

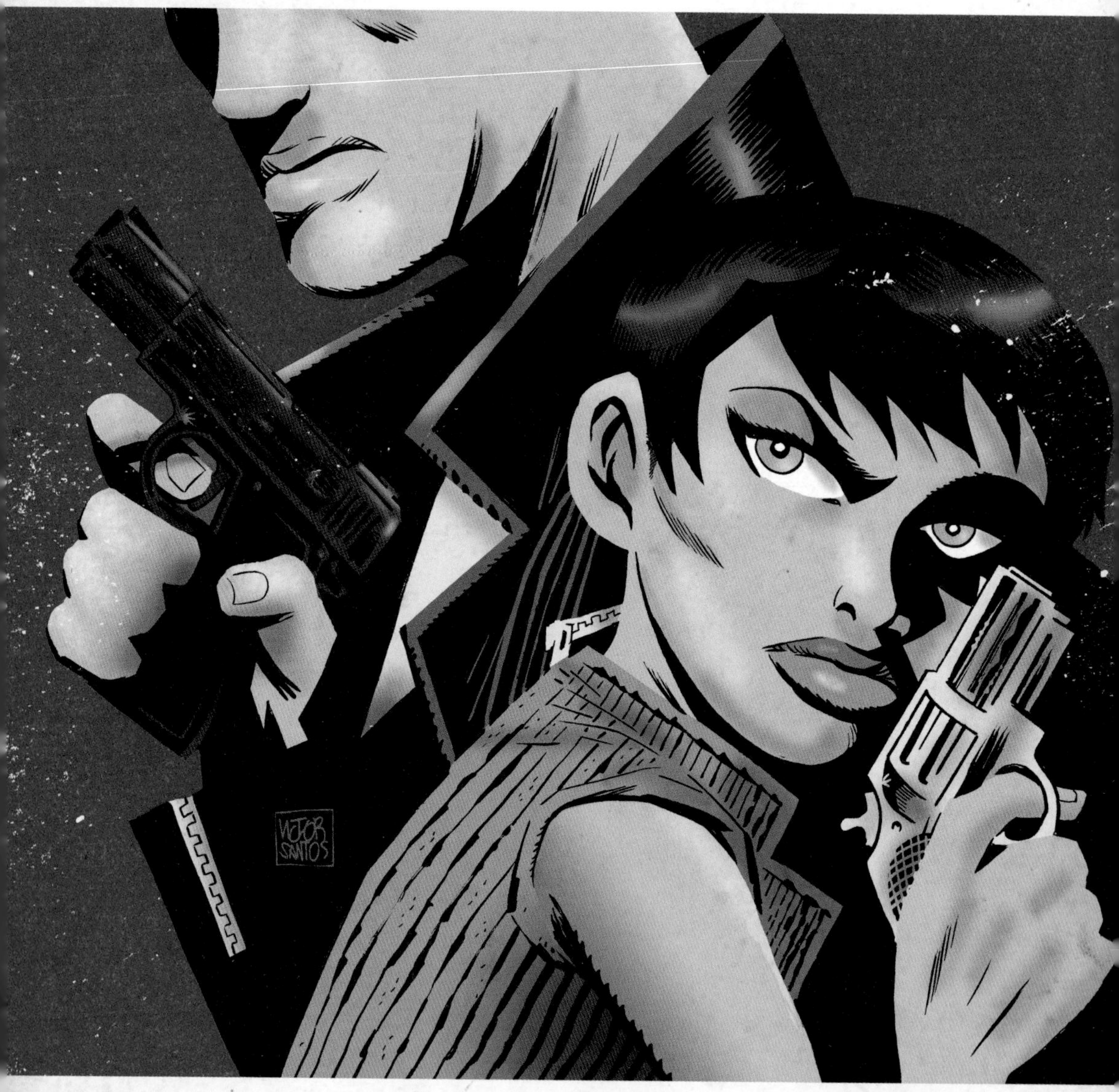

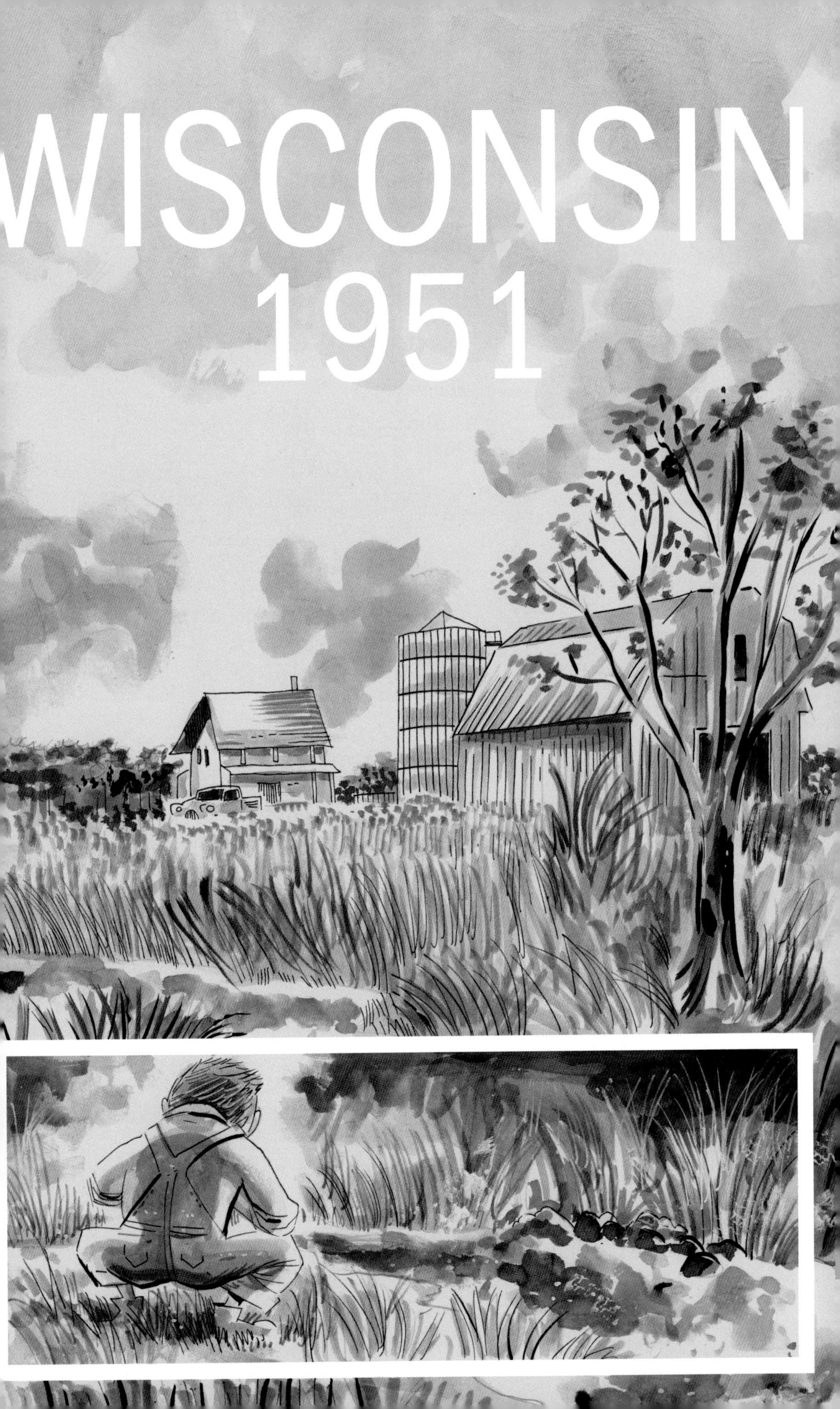
WISCONSIN
1951

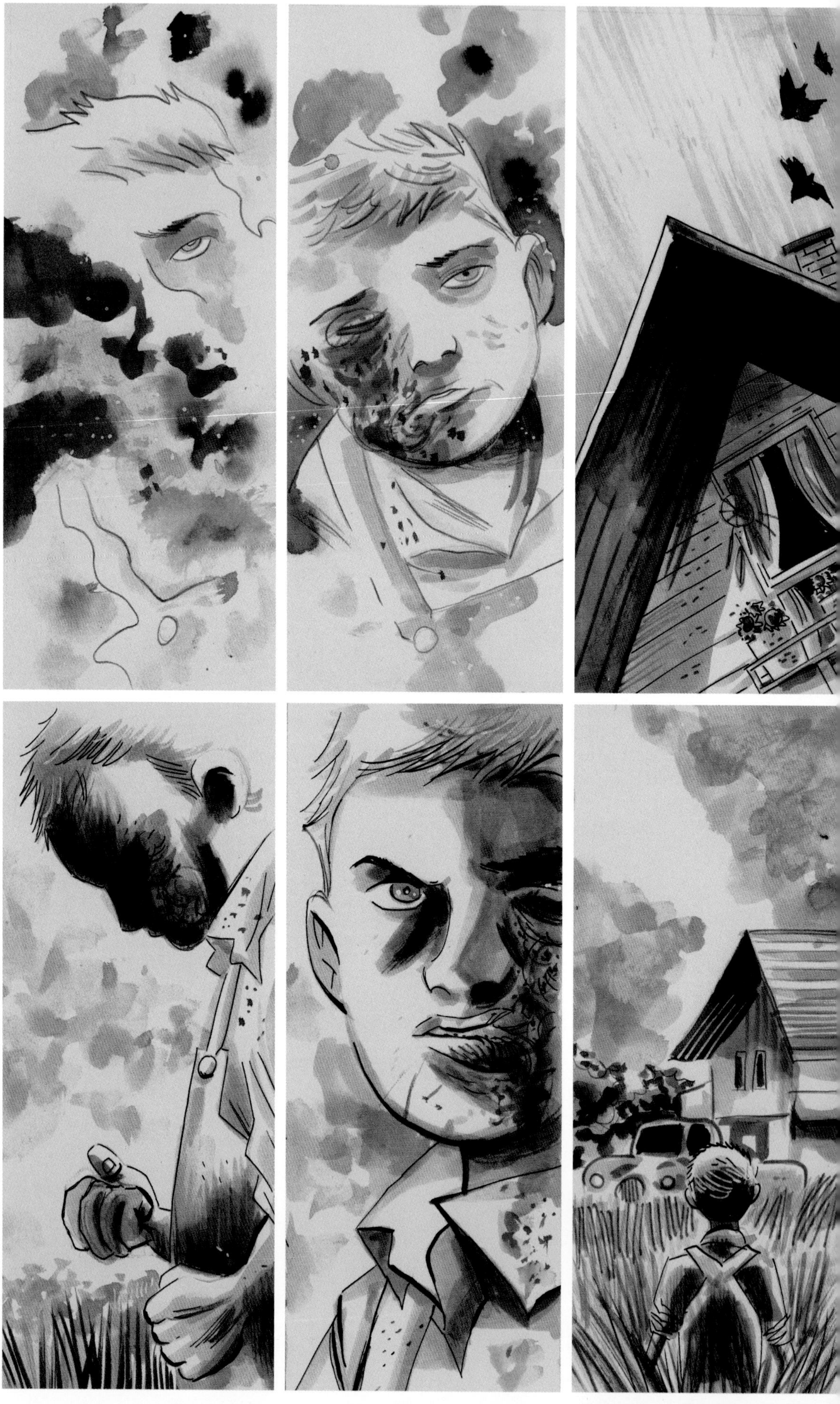

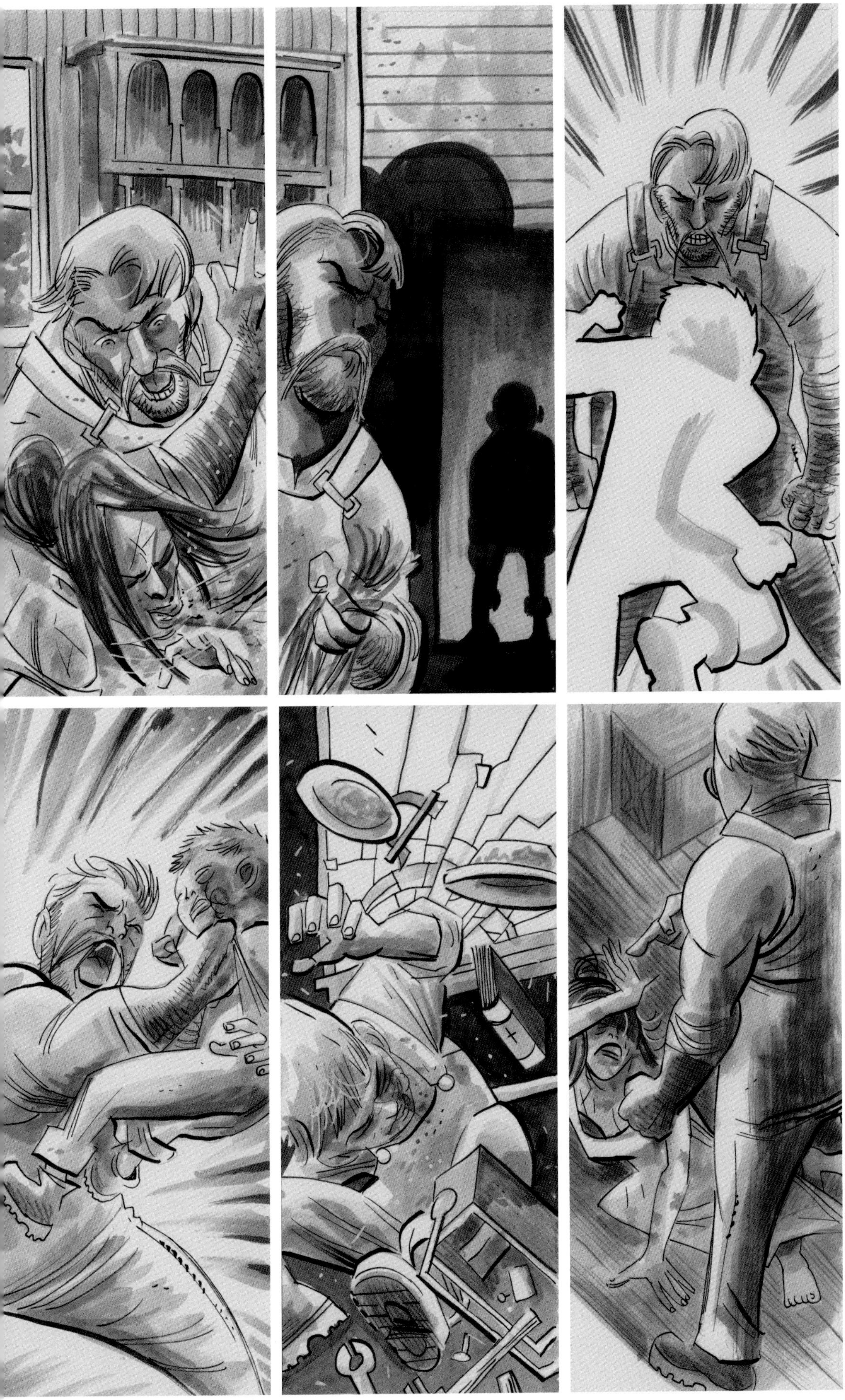

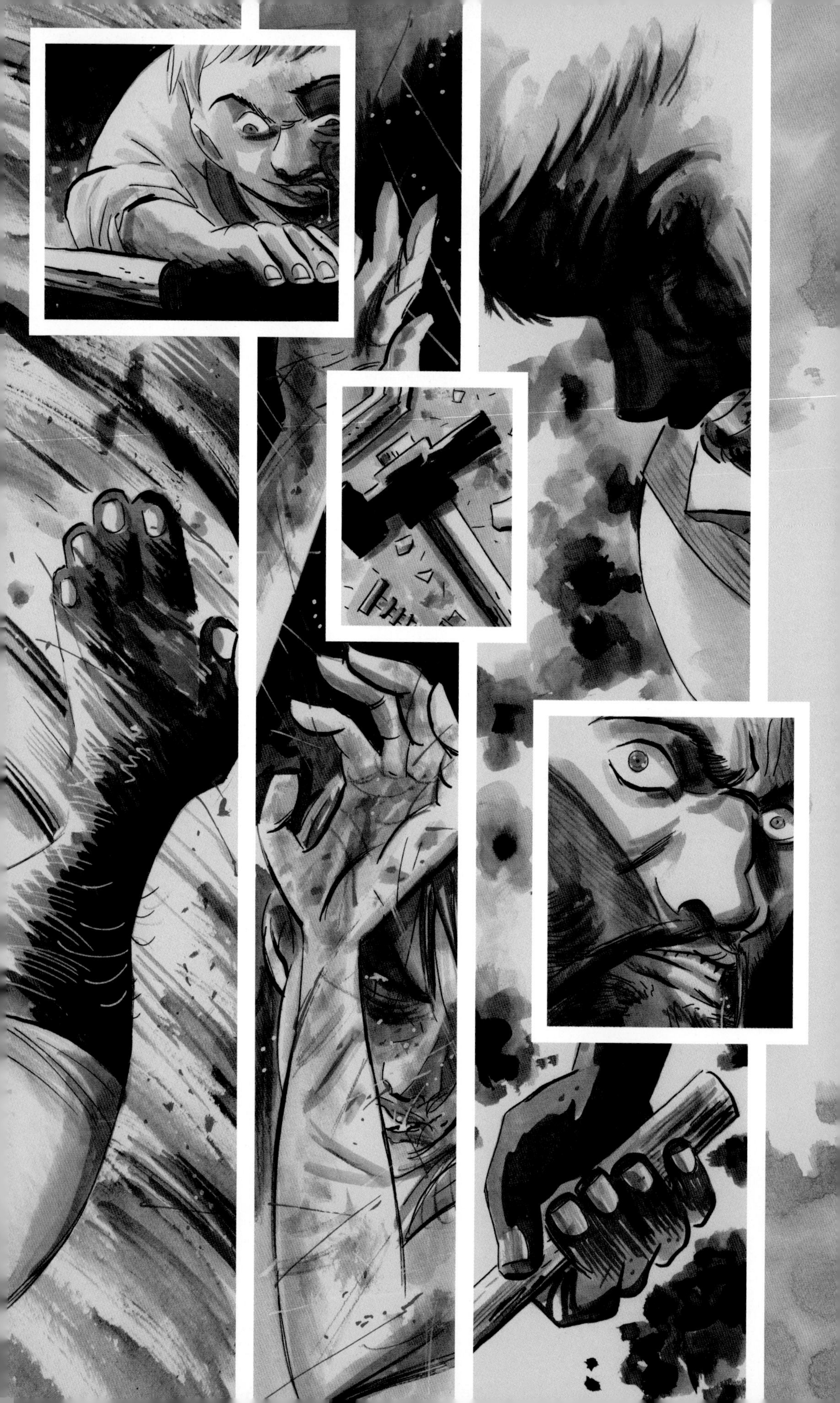

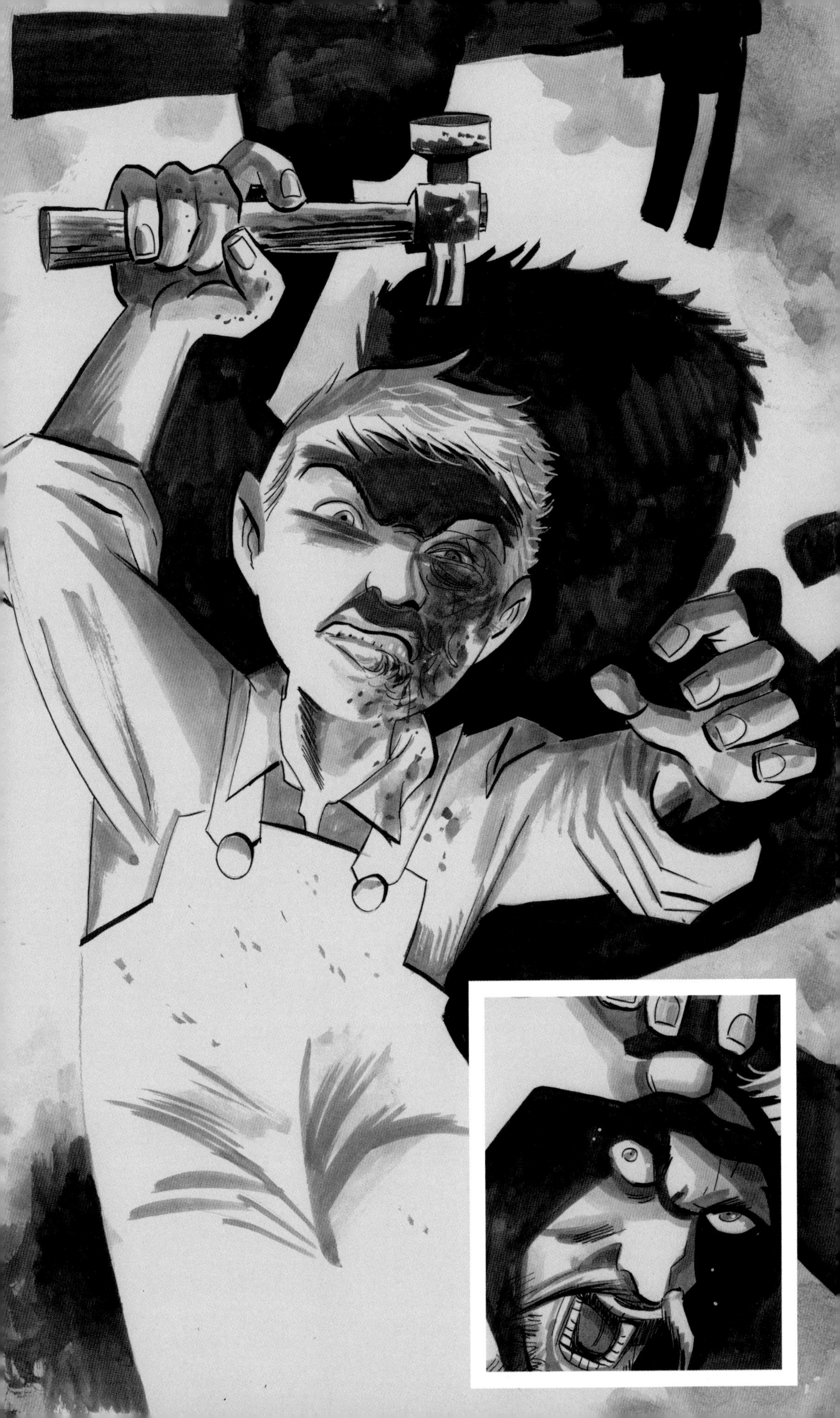

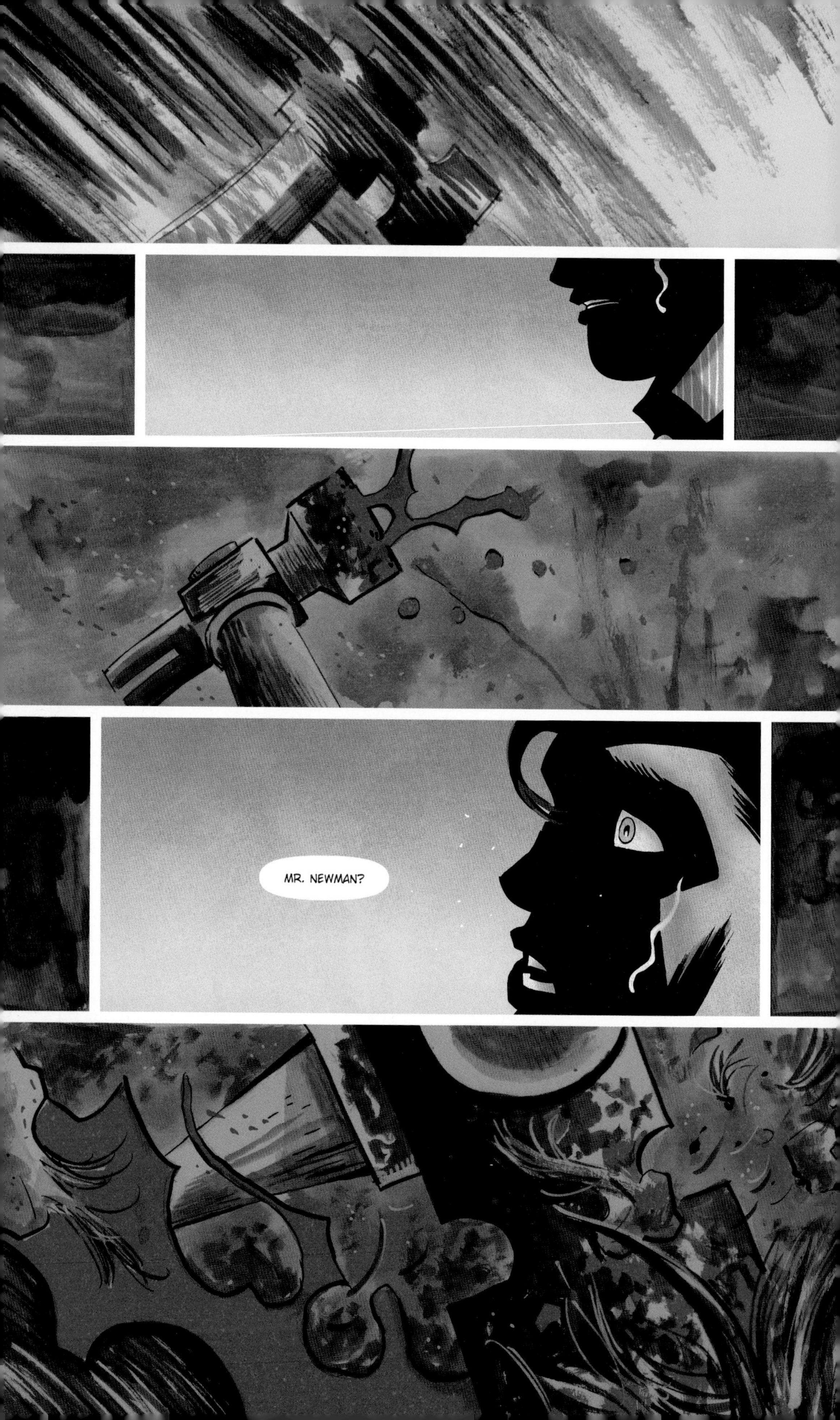
MR. NEWMAN?

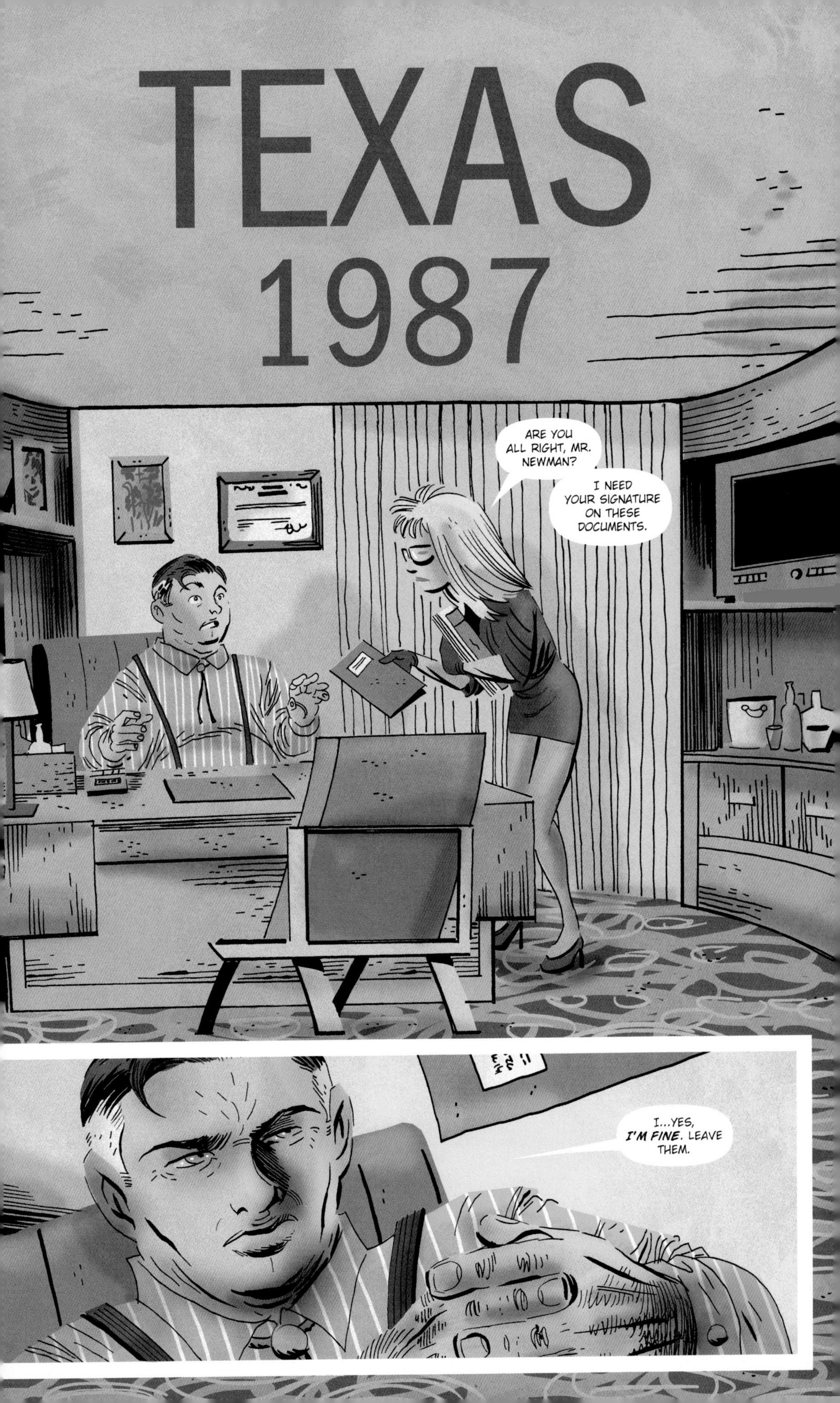
TEXAS
1987
ARE YOU ALL RIGHT, MR. NEWMAN?
I NEED YOUR SIGNATURE ON THESE DOCUMENTS.
I...YES, *I'M FINE*. LEAVE THEM.

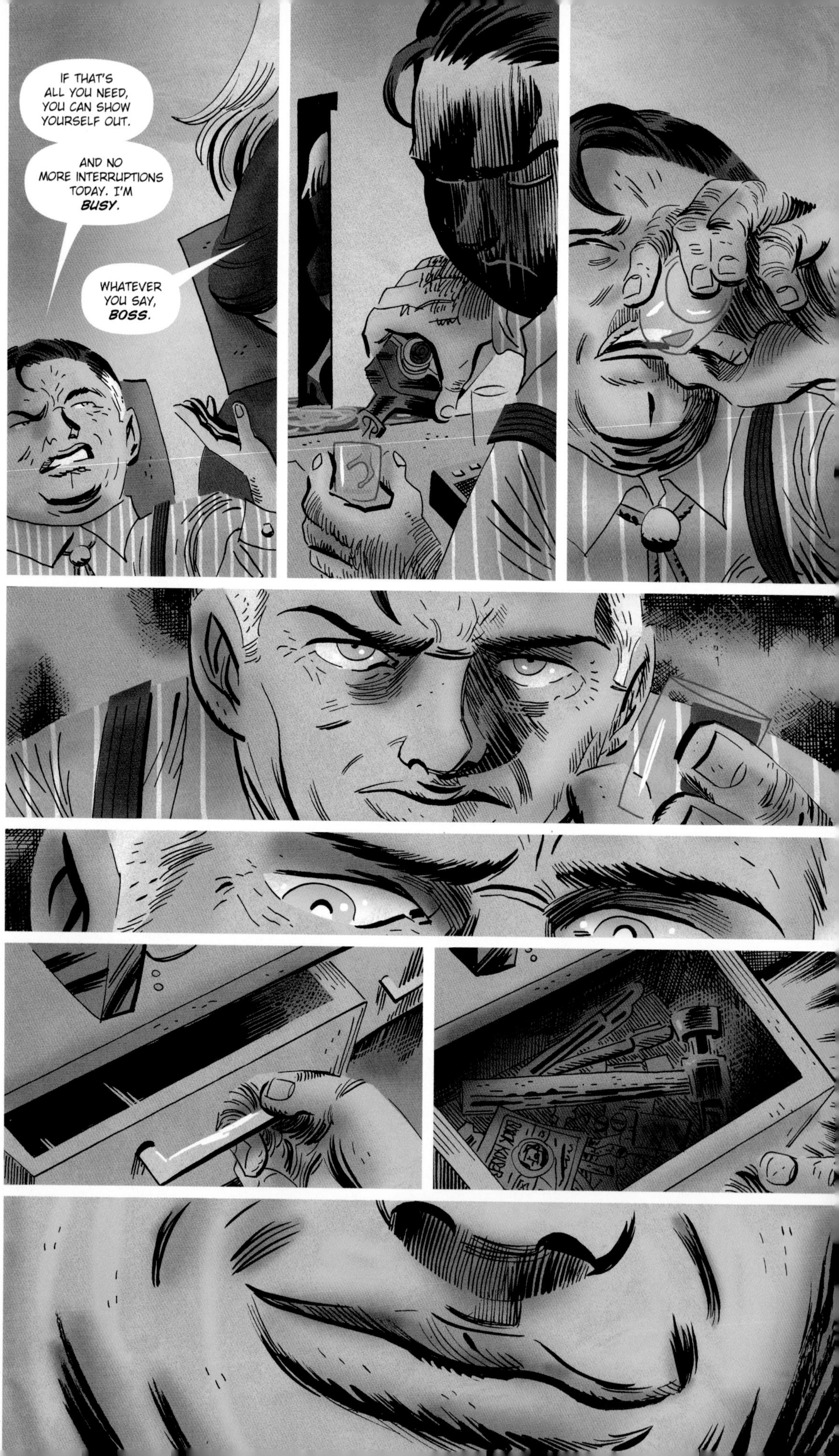
IF THAT'S ALL YOU NEED, YOU CAN SHOW YOURSELF OUT.
AND NO MORE INTERRUPTIONS TODAY. I'M **BUSY**.
WHATEVER YOU SAY, **BOSS**.

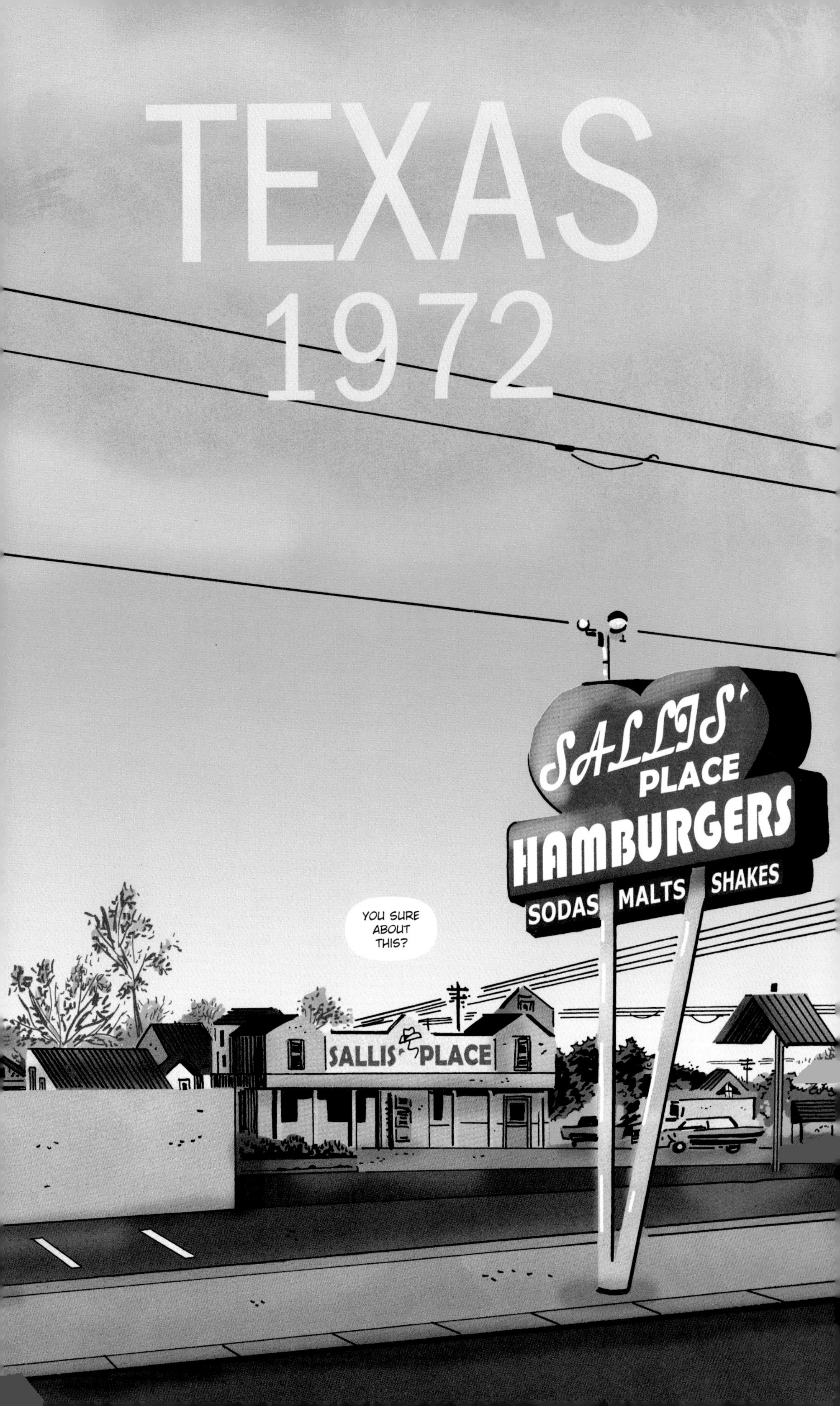
TEXAS
1972
SALLIS' PLACE
HAMBURGERS
SODAS MALTS SHAKES
YOU SURE ABOUT THIS?
SALLIS' PLACE

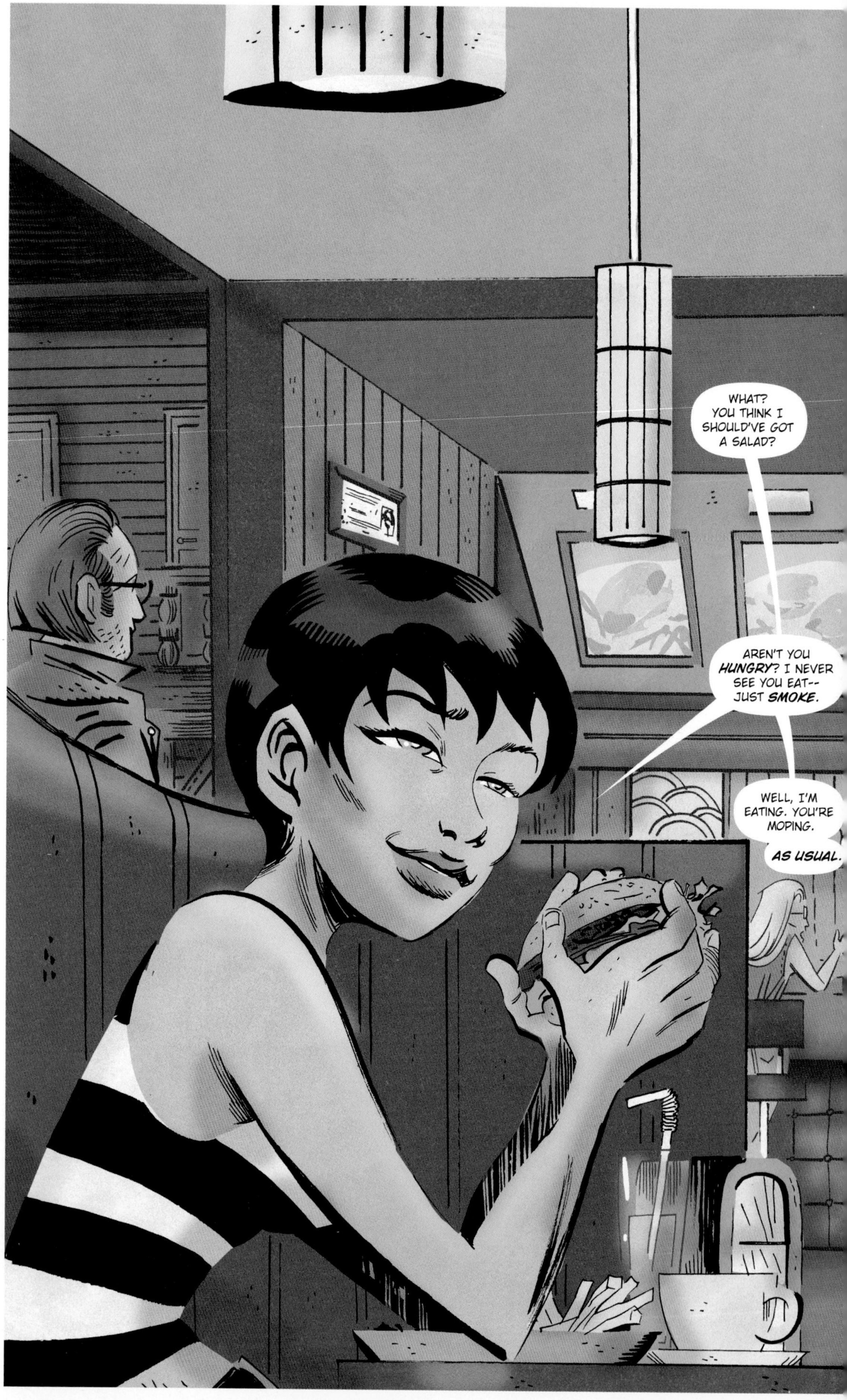
WHAT? YOU THINK I SHOULD'VE GOT A SALAD?
AREN'T YOU *HUNGRY*? I NEVER SEE YOU EAT-- JUST *SMOKE.*
WELL, I'M EATING. YOU'RE MOPING.
AS USUAL.

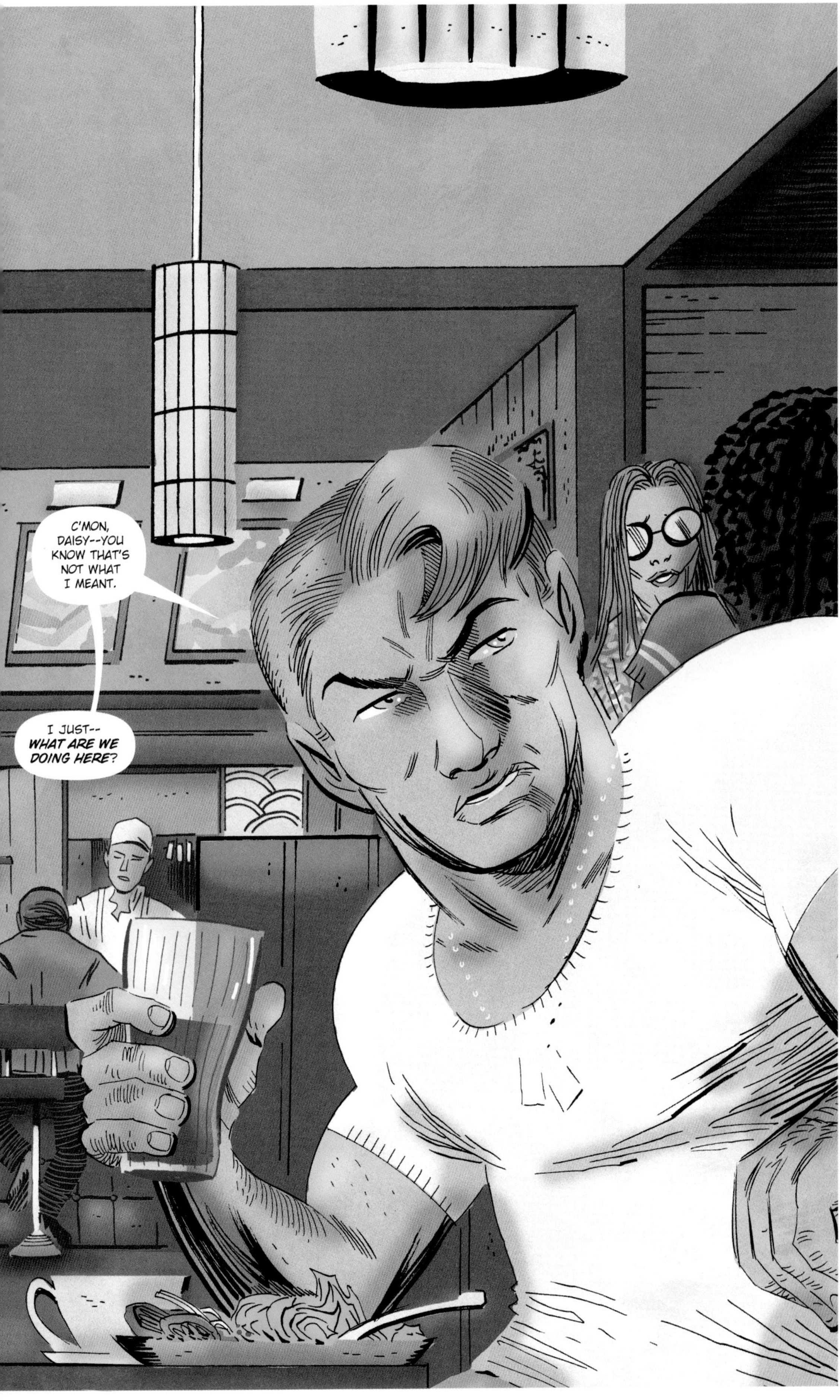
C'MON, DAISY--YOU KNOW THAT'S NOT WHAT I MEANT.
I JUST-- **WHAT ARE WE DOING HERE?**

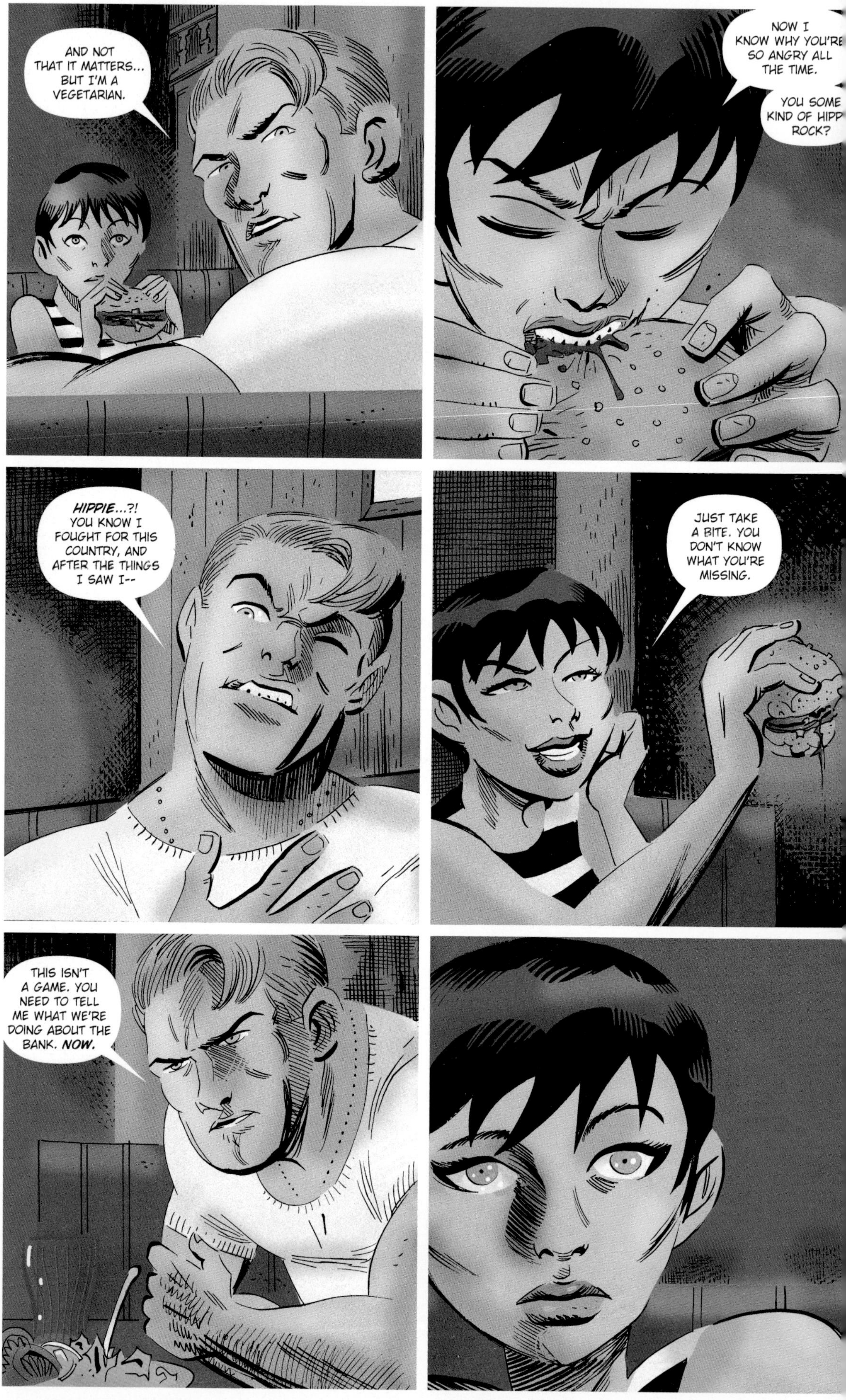
AND NOT THAT IT MATTERS... BUT I'M A VEGETARIAN.
NOW I KNOW WHY YOU'RE SO ANGRY ALL THE TIME.
YOU SOME KIND OF HIPP ROCK?
HIPPIE...?! YOU KNOW I FOUGHT FOR THIS COUNTRY, AND AFTER THE THINGS I SAW I--
JUST TAKE A BITE. YOU DON'T KNOW WHAT YOU'RE MISSING.
THIS ISN'T A GAME. YOU NEED TO TELL ME WHAT WE'RE DOING ABOUT THE BANK. NOW.

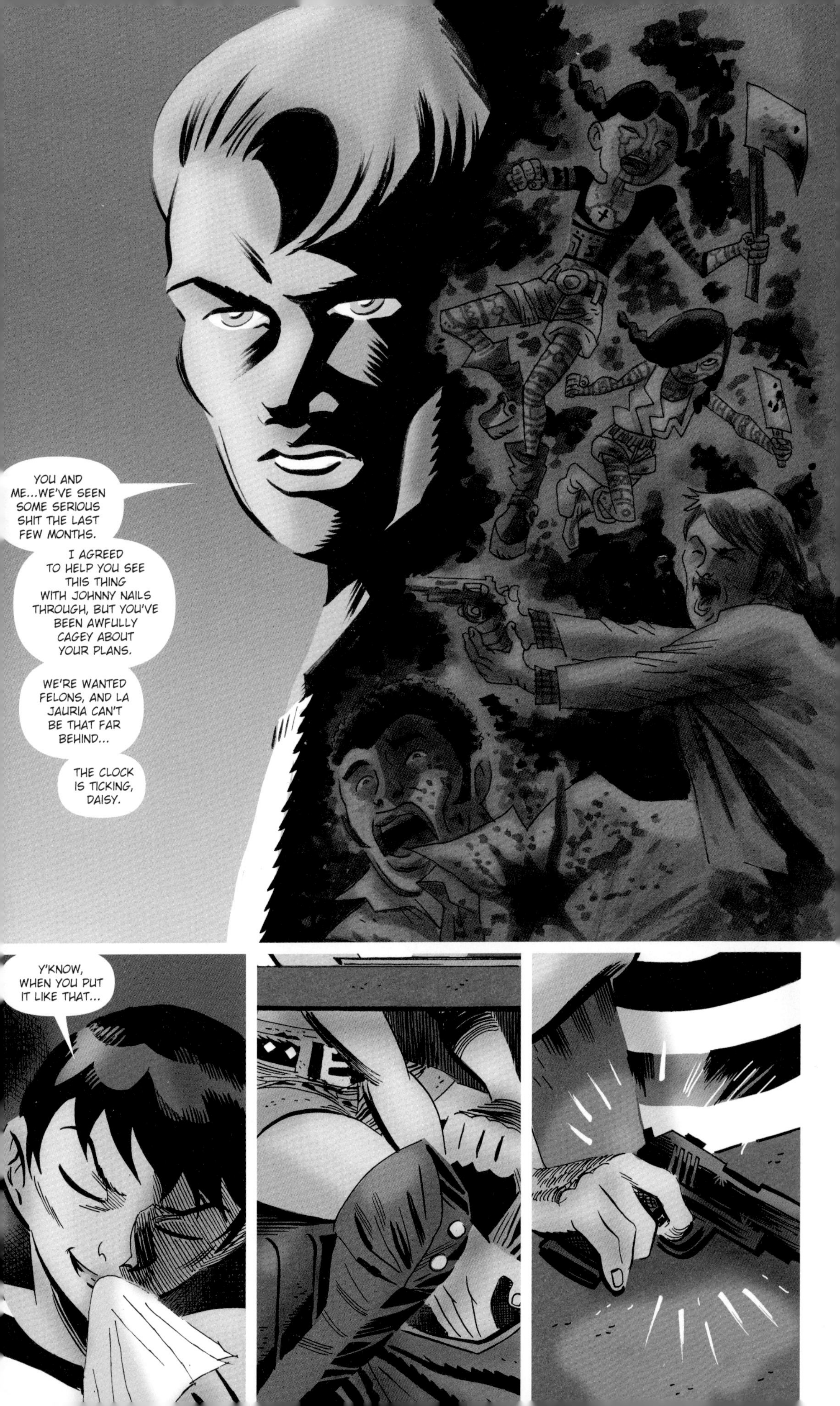
YOU AND ME...WE'VE SEEN SOME SERIOUS SHIT THE LAST FEW MONTHS.
I AGREED TO HELP YOU SEE THIS THING WITH JOHNNY NAILS THROUGH, BUT YOU'VE BEEN AWFULLY CAGEY ABOUT YOUR PLANS.
WE'RE WANTED FELONS, AND LA JAURIA CAN'T BE THAT FAR BEHIND...
THE CLOCK IS TICKING, DAISY.
Y'KNOW, WHEN YOU PUT IT LIKE THAT...

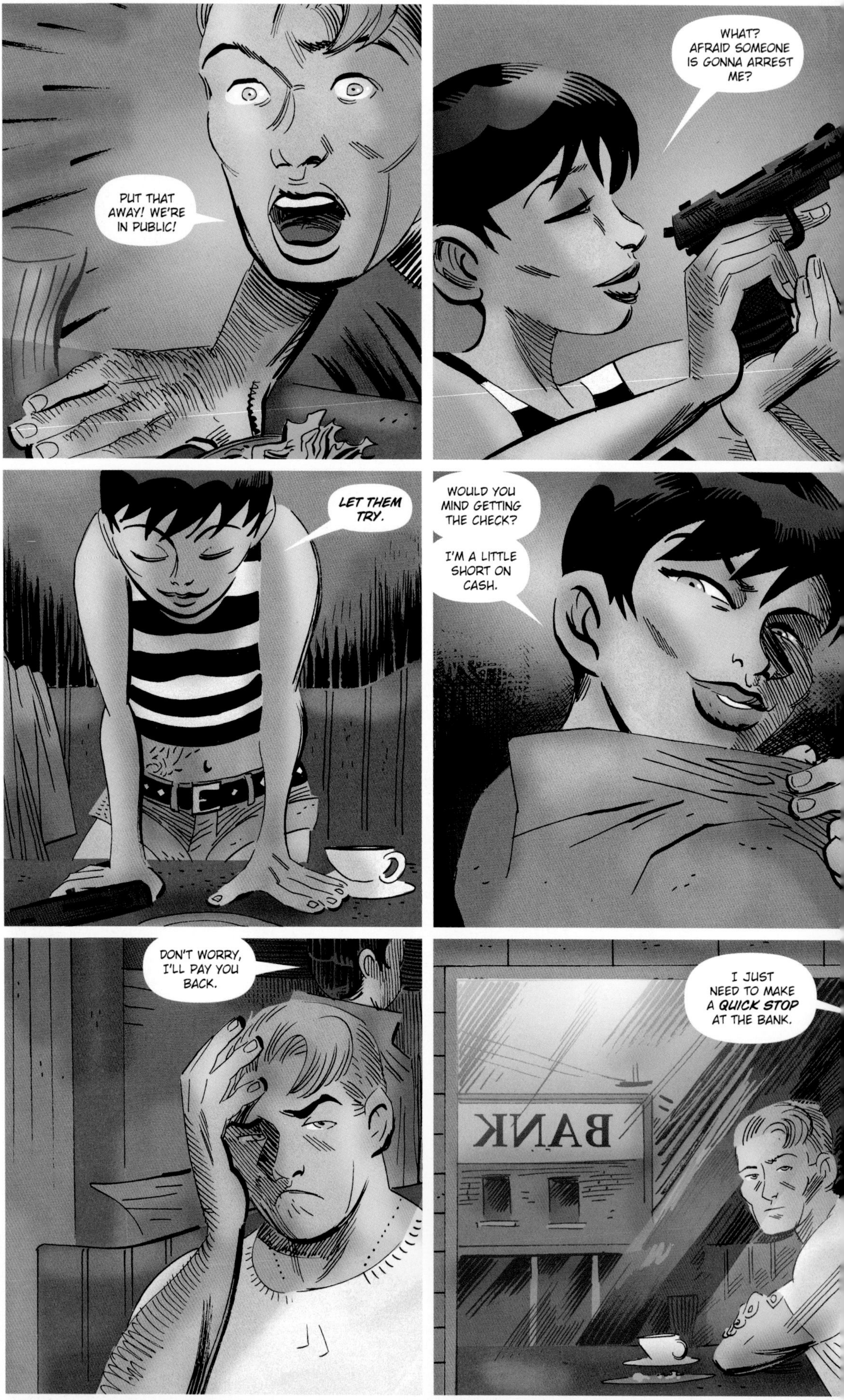
PUT THAT AWAY! WE'RE IN PUBLIC!
WHAT? AFRAID SOMEONE IS GONNA ARREST ME?
LET THEM TRY.
WOULD YOU MIND GETTING THE CHECK?
I'M A LITTLE SHORT ON CASH.
DON'T WORRY, I'LL PAY YOU BACK.
I JUST NEED TO MAKE A QUICK STOP AT THE BANK.
BANK

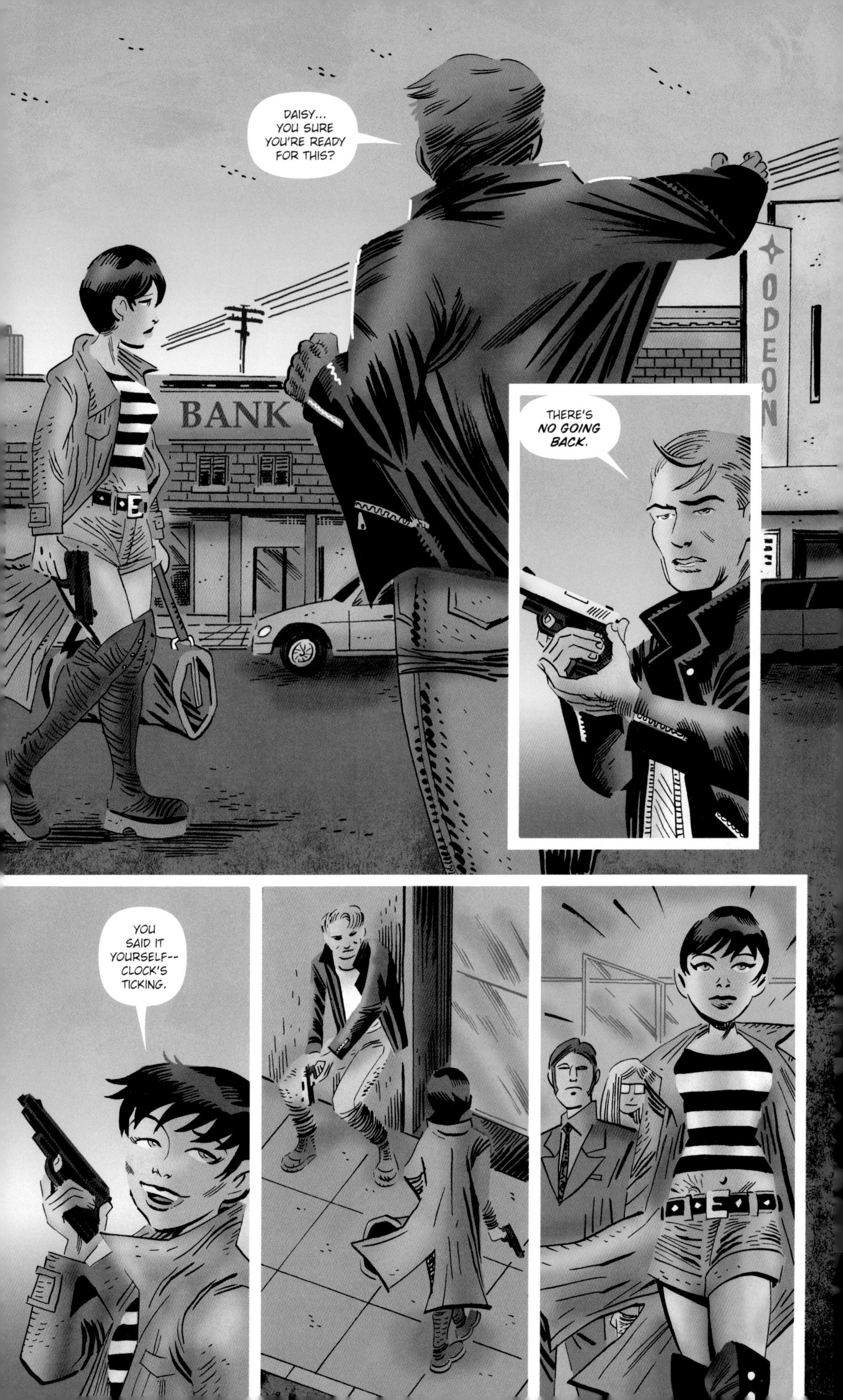

DAISY... YOU SURE YOU'RE READY FOR THIS?
BANK
ODEON
THERE'S NO GOING BACK.
YOU SAID IT YOURSELF--CLOCK'S TICKING.

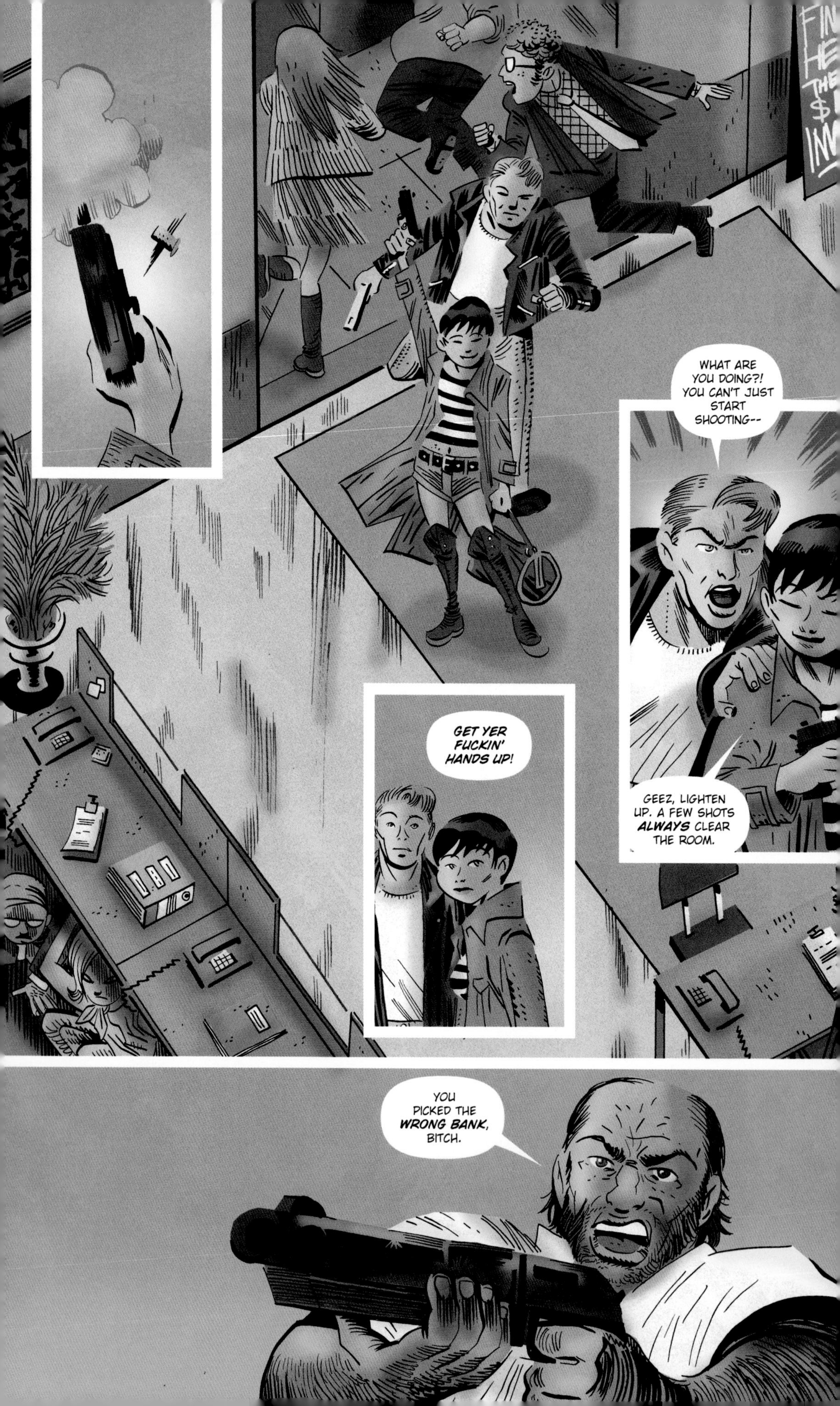
WHAT ARE YOU DOING?! YOU CAN'T JUST START SHOOTING--
GEEZ, LIGHTEN UP. A FEW SHOTS ALWAYS CLEAR THE ROOM.
GET YER FUCKIN' HANDS UP!
YOU PICKED THE WRONG BANK, BITCH.

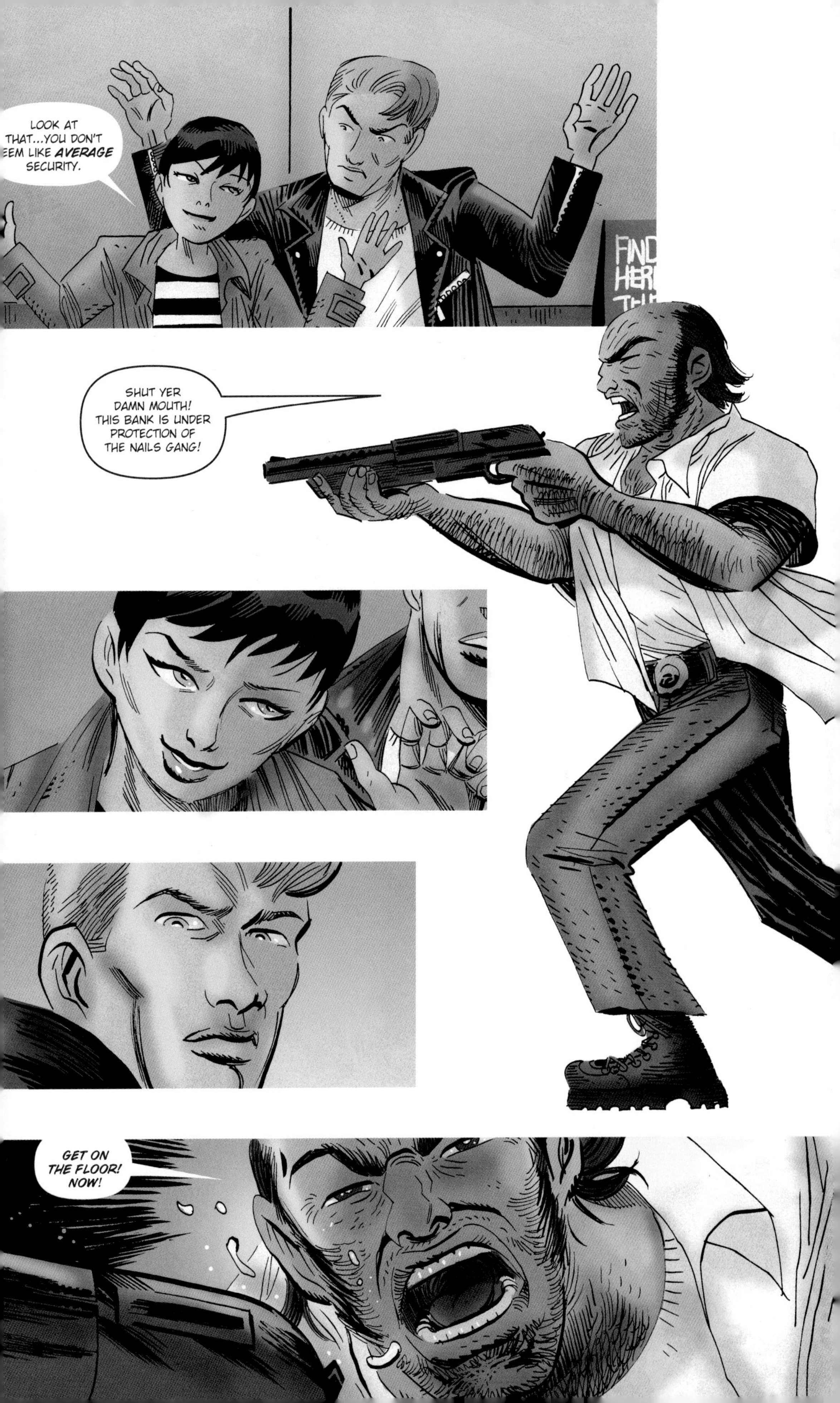
LOOK AT THAT...YOU DON'T SEEM LIKE *AVERAGE* SECURITY.
FIND HERE
SHUT YER DAMN MOUTH! THIS BANK IS UNDER PROTECTION OF THE NAILS GANG!
GET ON THE FLOOR! NOW!

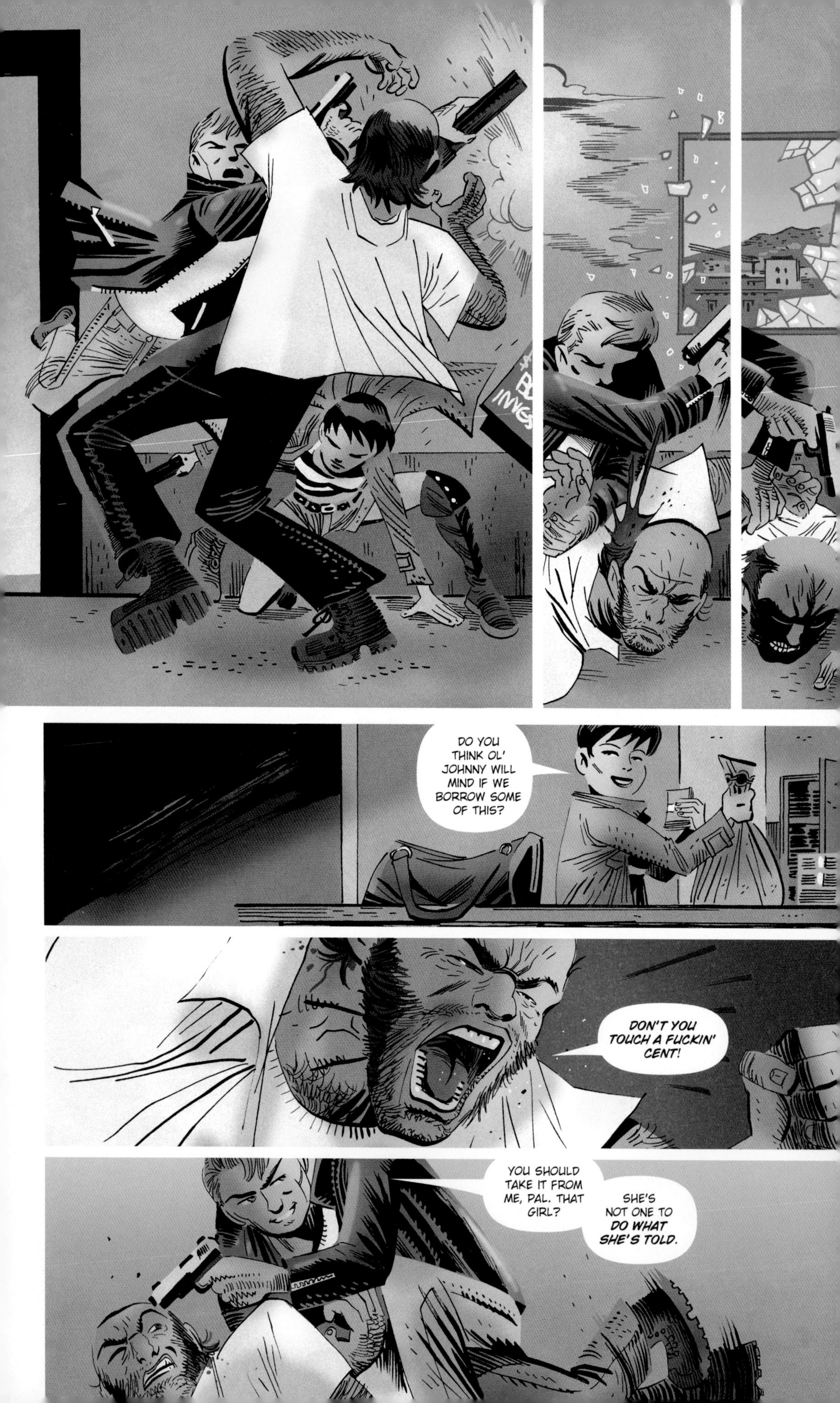
DO YOU THINK OL' JOHNNY WILL MIND IF WE BORROW SOME OF THIS?
DON'T YOU TOUCH A FUCKIN' CENT!
YOU SHOULD TAKE IT FROM ME, PAL. THAT GIRL?
SHE'S NOT ONE TO DO WHAT SHE'S TOLD.

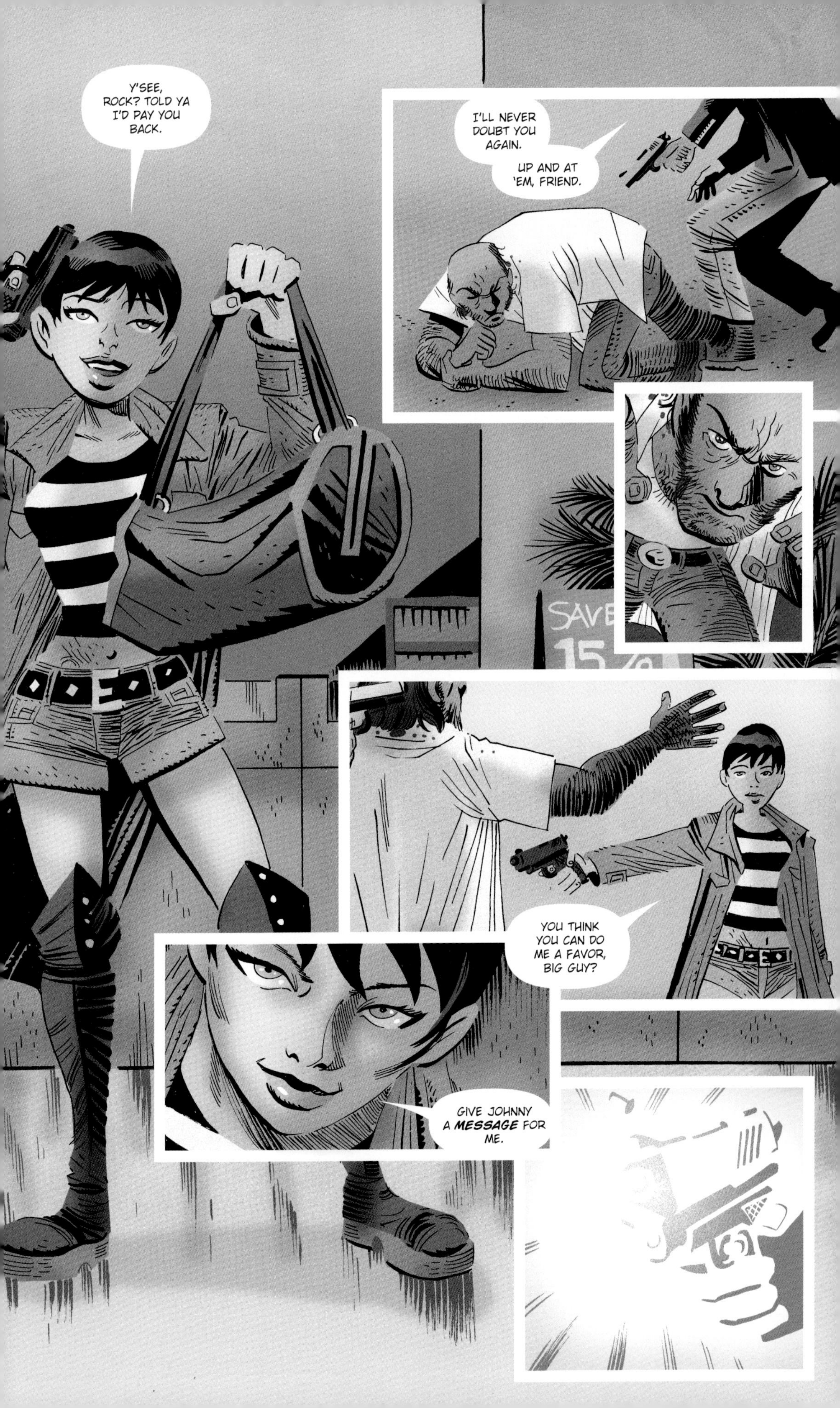
Y'SEE, ROCK? TOLD YA I'D PAY YOU BACK.
I'LL NEVER DOUBT YOU AGAIN.
UP AND AT 'EM, FRIEND.
SAVE 15
YOU THINK YOU CAN DO ME A FAVOR, BIG GUY?
GIVE JOHNNY A ***MESSAGE*** FOR ME.

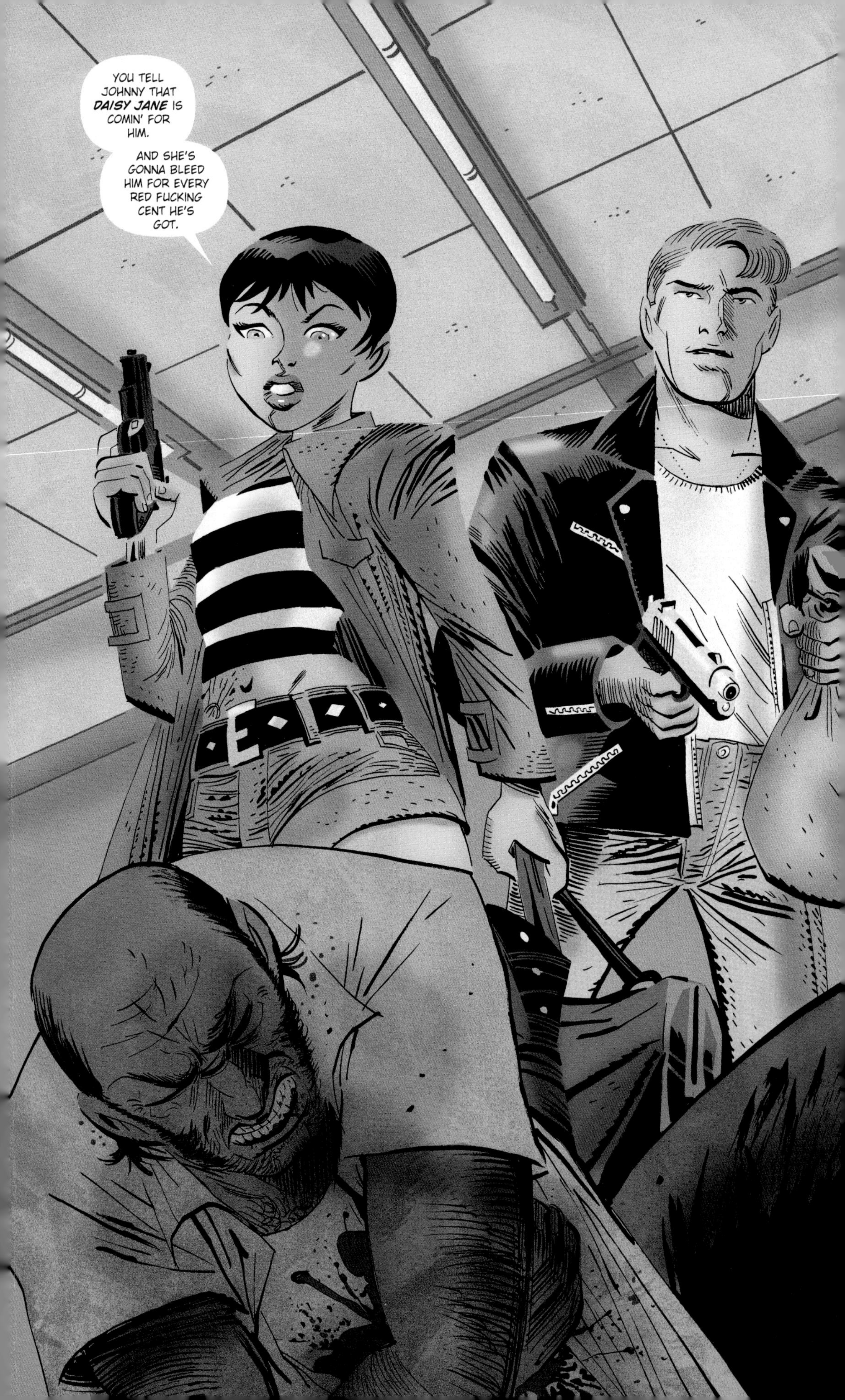
YOU TELL JOHNNY THAT DAISY JANE IS COMIN' FOR HIM.
AND SHE'S GONNA BLEED HIM FOR EVERY RED FUCKING CENT HE'S GOT.

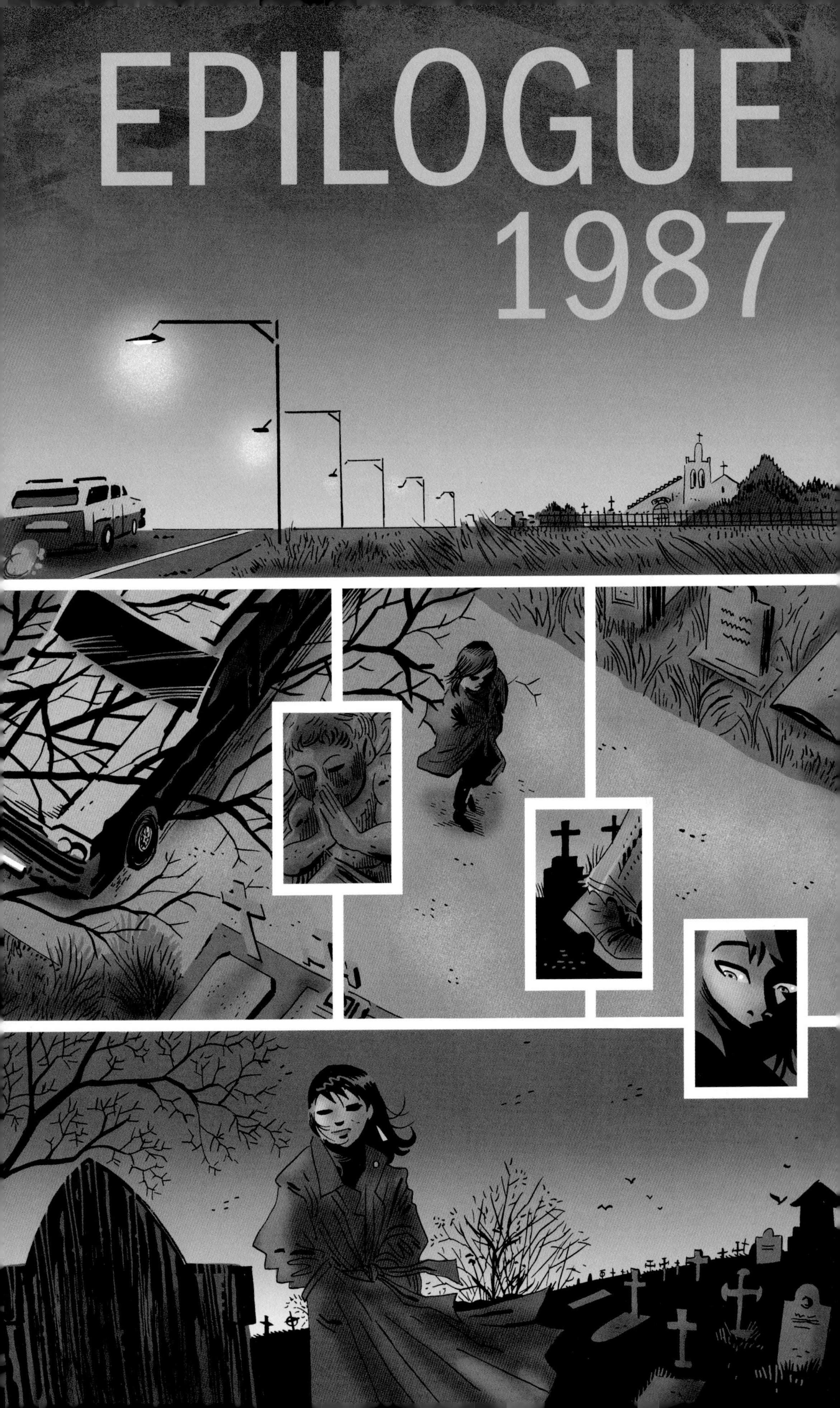
EPILOGUE
1987

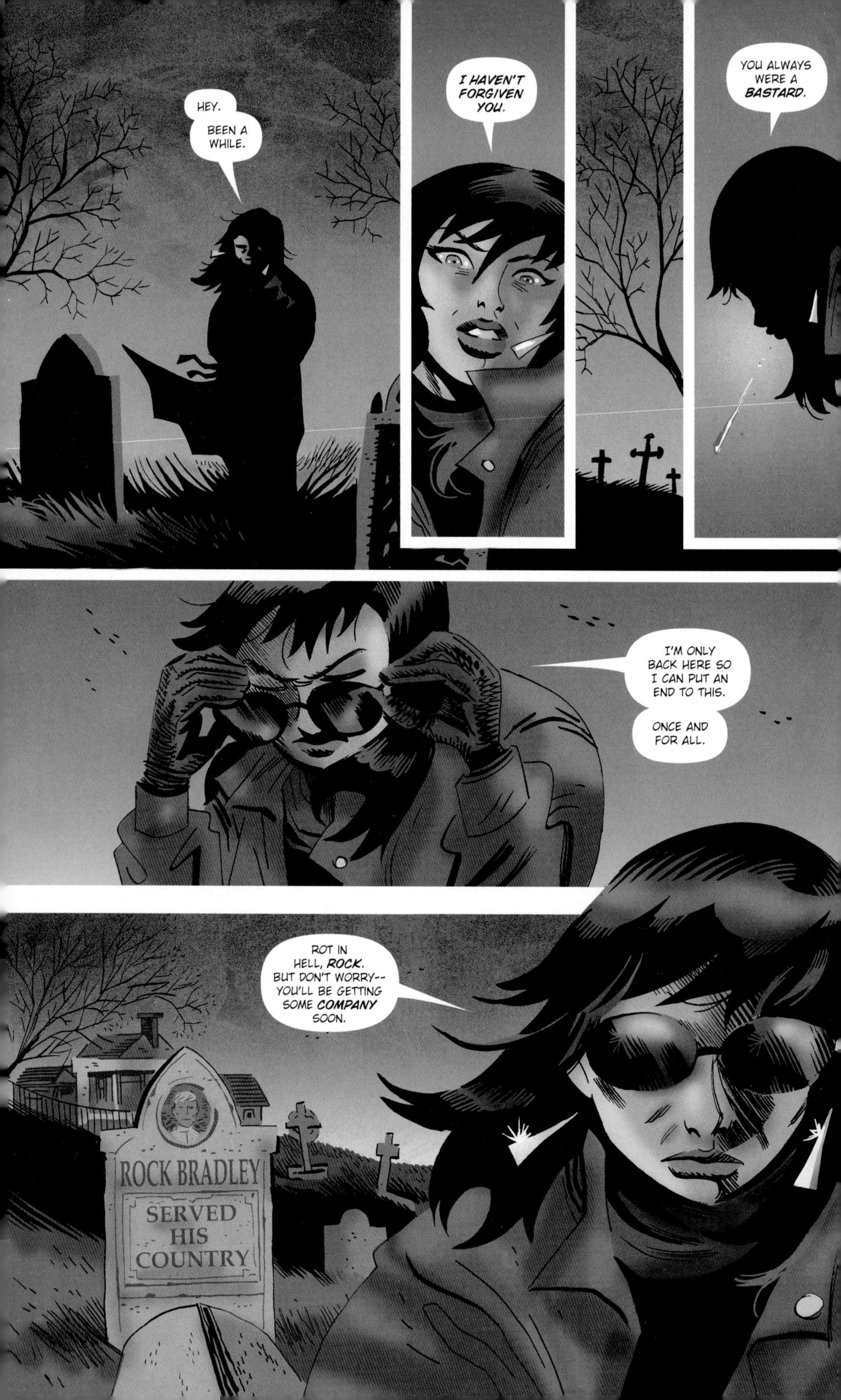
HEY.
BEEN A WHILE.
I HAVEN'T FORGIVEN YOU.
YOU ALWAYS WERE A BASTARD.
I'M ONLY BACK HERE SO I CAN PUT AN END TO THIS.
ONCE AND FOR ALL.
ROT IN HELL, ROCK. BUT DON'T WORRY-- YOU'LL BE GETTING SOME COMPANY SOON.
ROCK BRADLEY
SERVED HIS COUNTRY

CHAPTER SEVEN

"SUNDAY MORNING COMING DOWN"

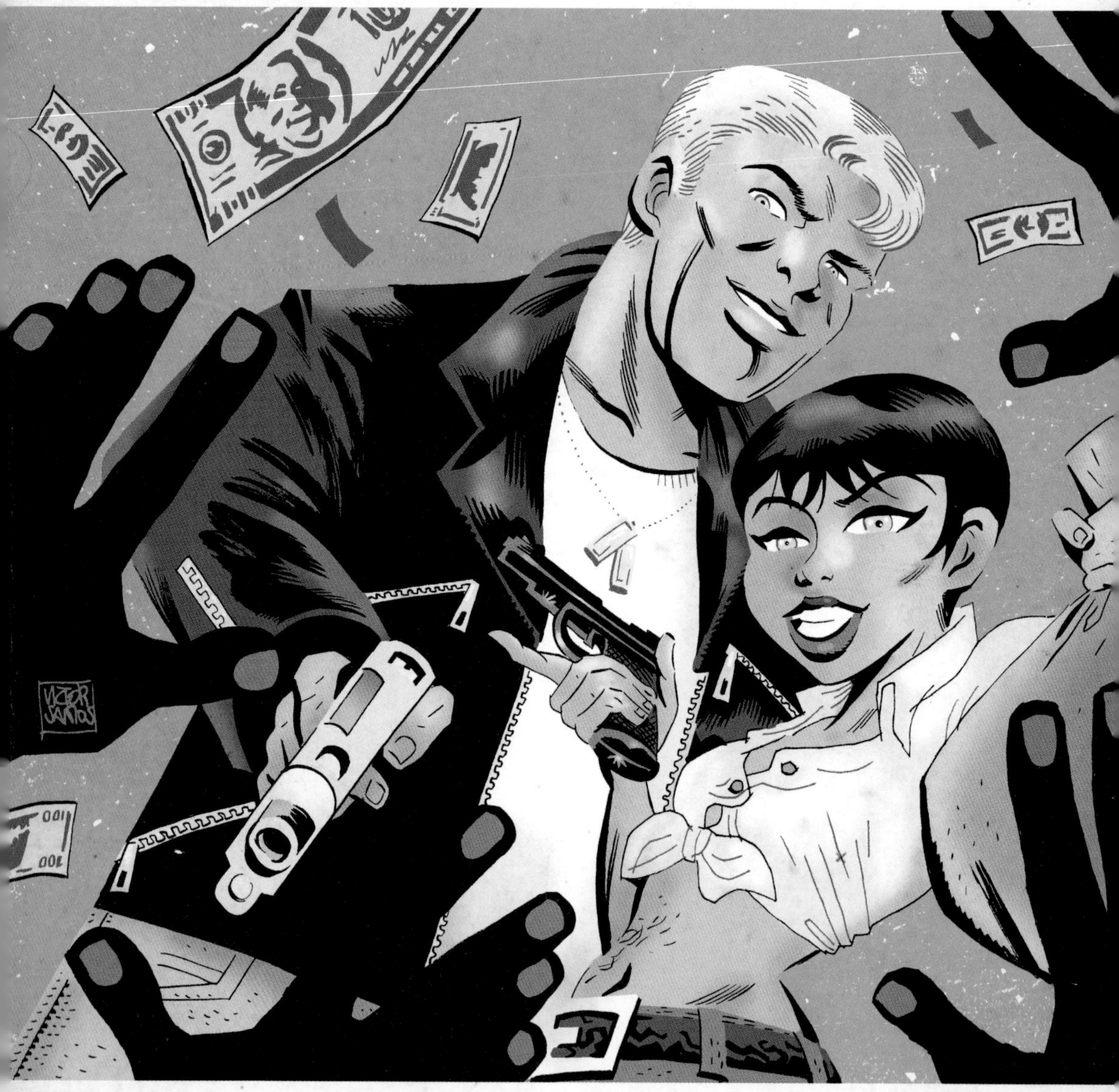

VICTOR SANTOS

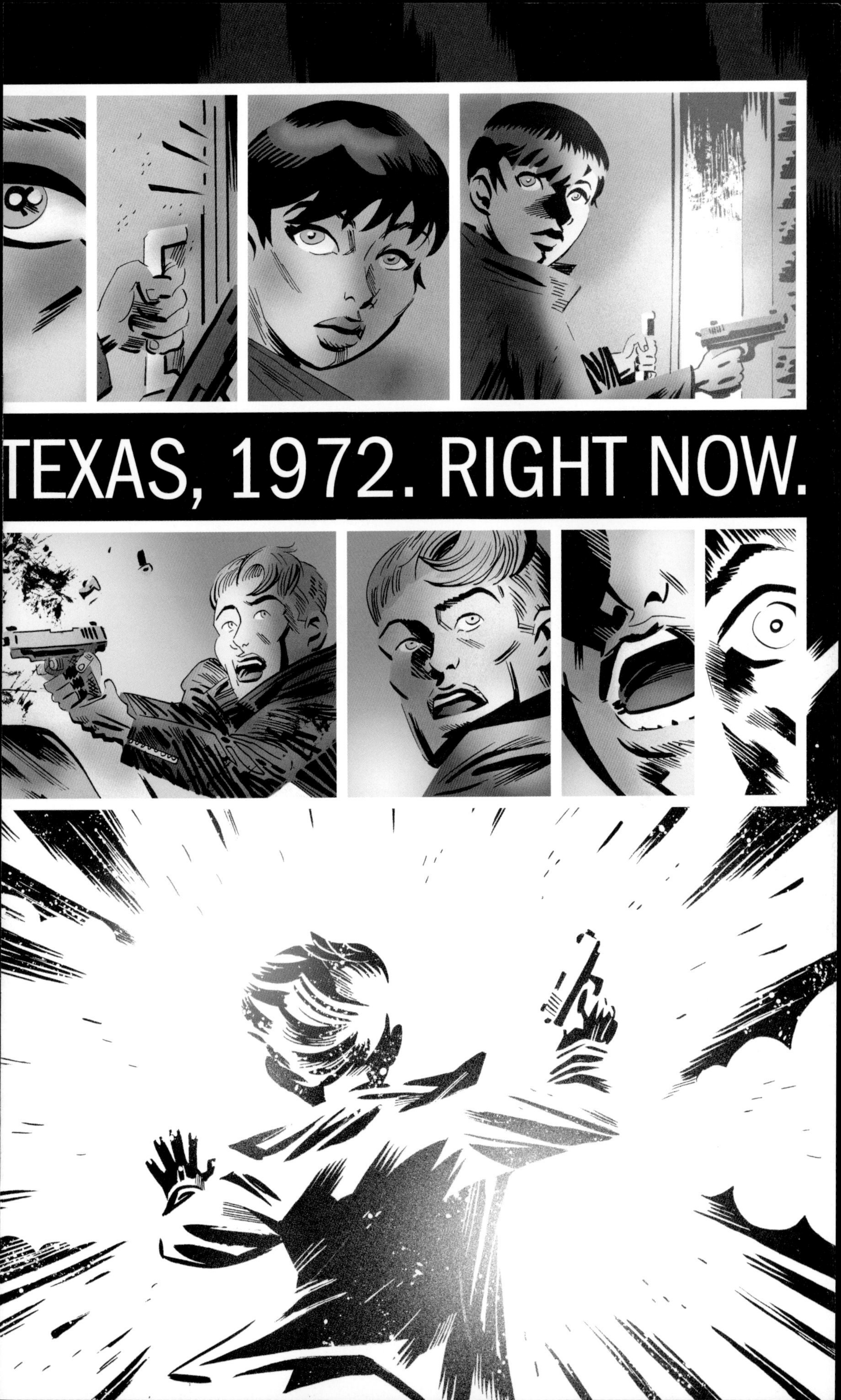
TEXAS, 1972. RIGHT NOW.

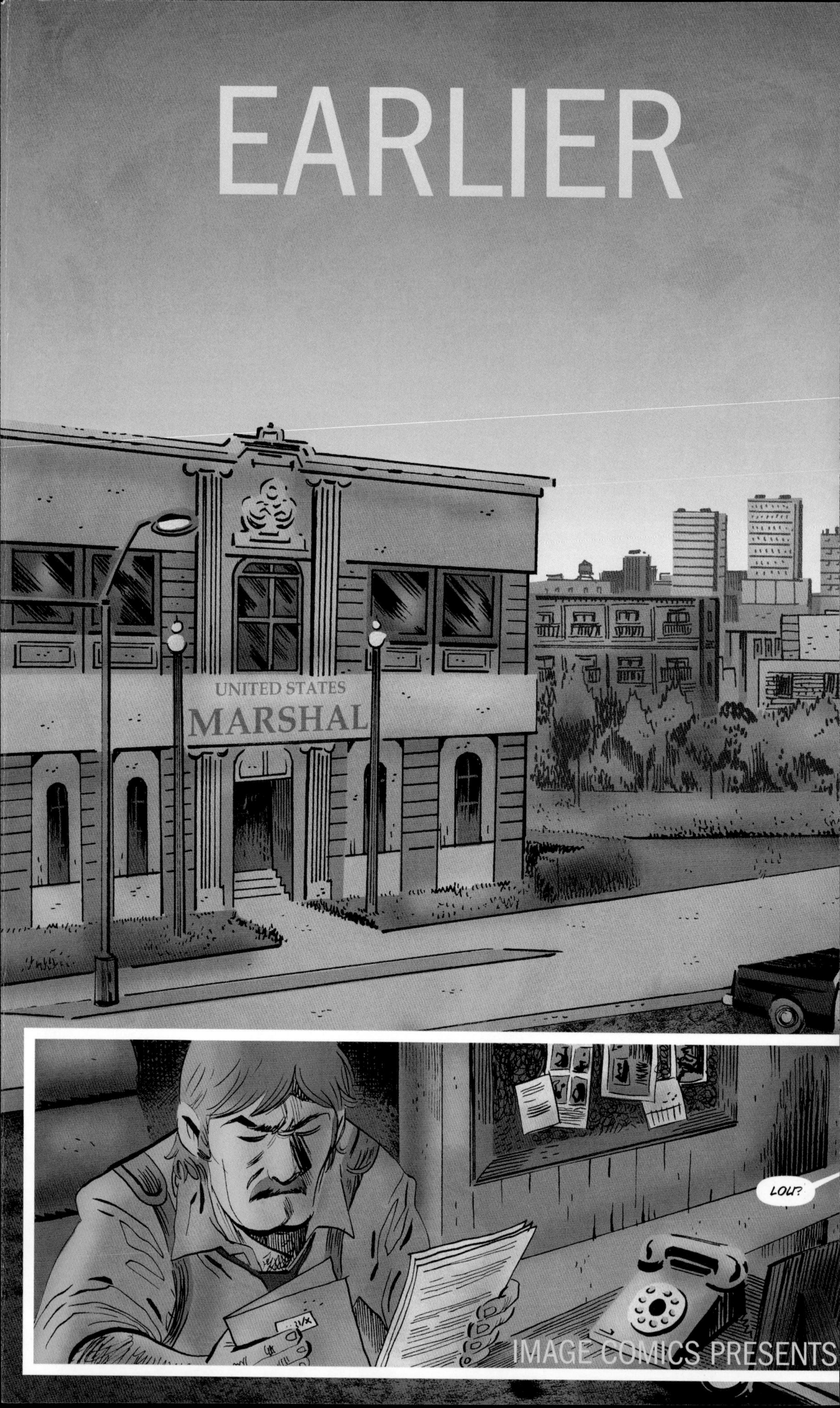
EARLIER
UNITED STATES
MARSHAL
LOU?
IMAGE COMICS PRESENTS

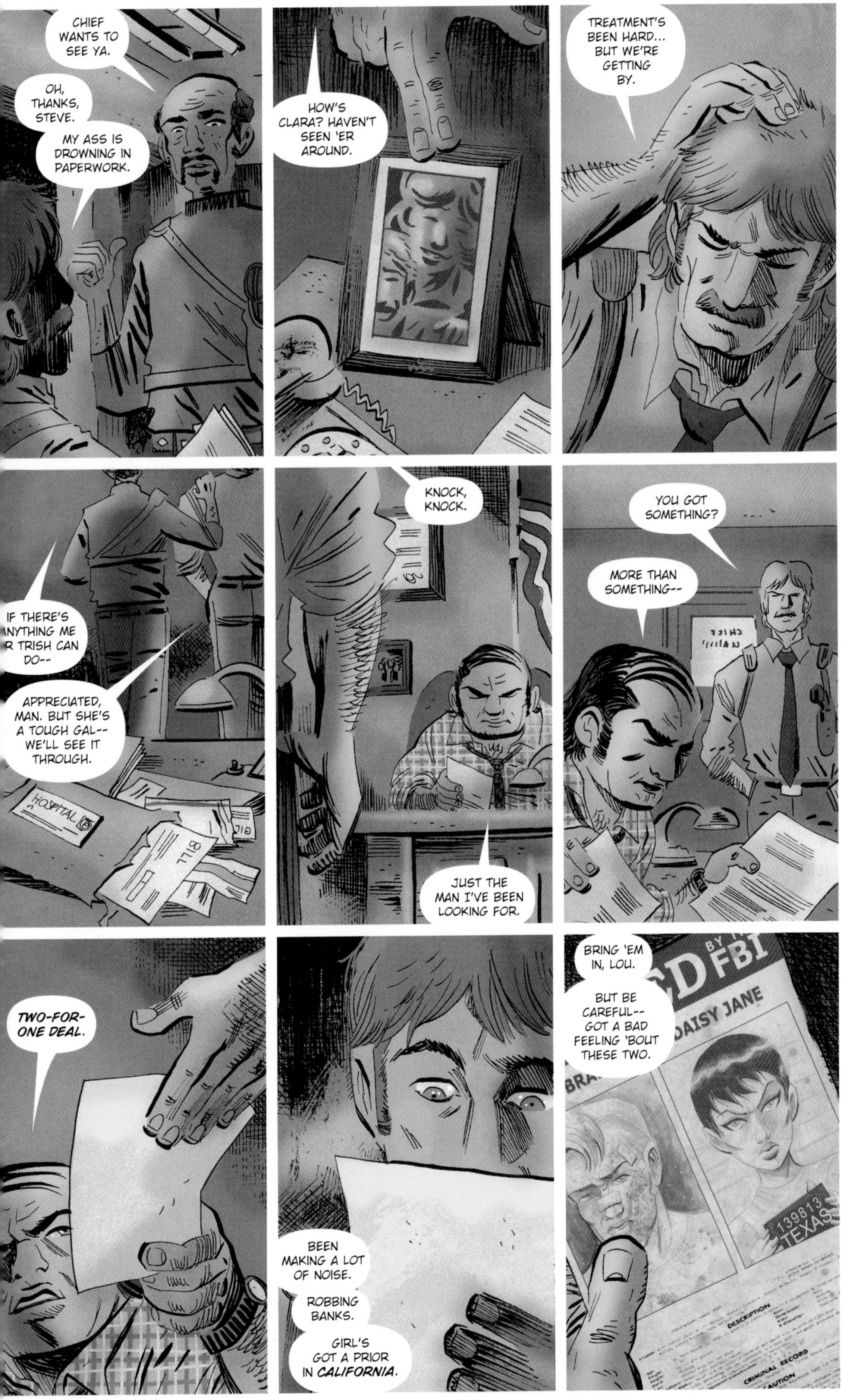
CHIEF WANTS TO SEE YA.
OH, THANKS, STEVE.
MY ASS IS DROWNING IN PAPERWORK.
HOW'S CLARA? HAVEN'T SEEN 'ER AROUND.
TREATMENT'S BEEN HARD... BUT WE'RE GETTING BY.
IF THERE'S ANYTHING ME OR TRISH CAN DO--
APPRECIATED, MAN. BUT SHE'S A TOUGH GAL-- WE'LL SEE IT THROUGH.
HOSPITAL
BILL
KNOCK, KNOCK.
JUST THE MAN I'VE BEEN LOOKING FOR.
YOU GOT SOMETHING?
MORE THAN SOMETHING--
CHIEF
TWO-FOR-ONE DEAL.
BEEN MAKING A LOT OF NOISE.
ROBBING BANKS.
GIRL'S GOT A PRIOR IN *CALIFORNIA*.
BRING 'EM IN, LOU.
BUT BE CAREFUL-- GOT A BAD FEELING 'BOUT THESE TWO.
BY THE FBI
DAISY JANE
139813 TEXAS
DESCRIPTION
CRIMINAL RECORD
CAUTION

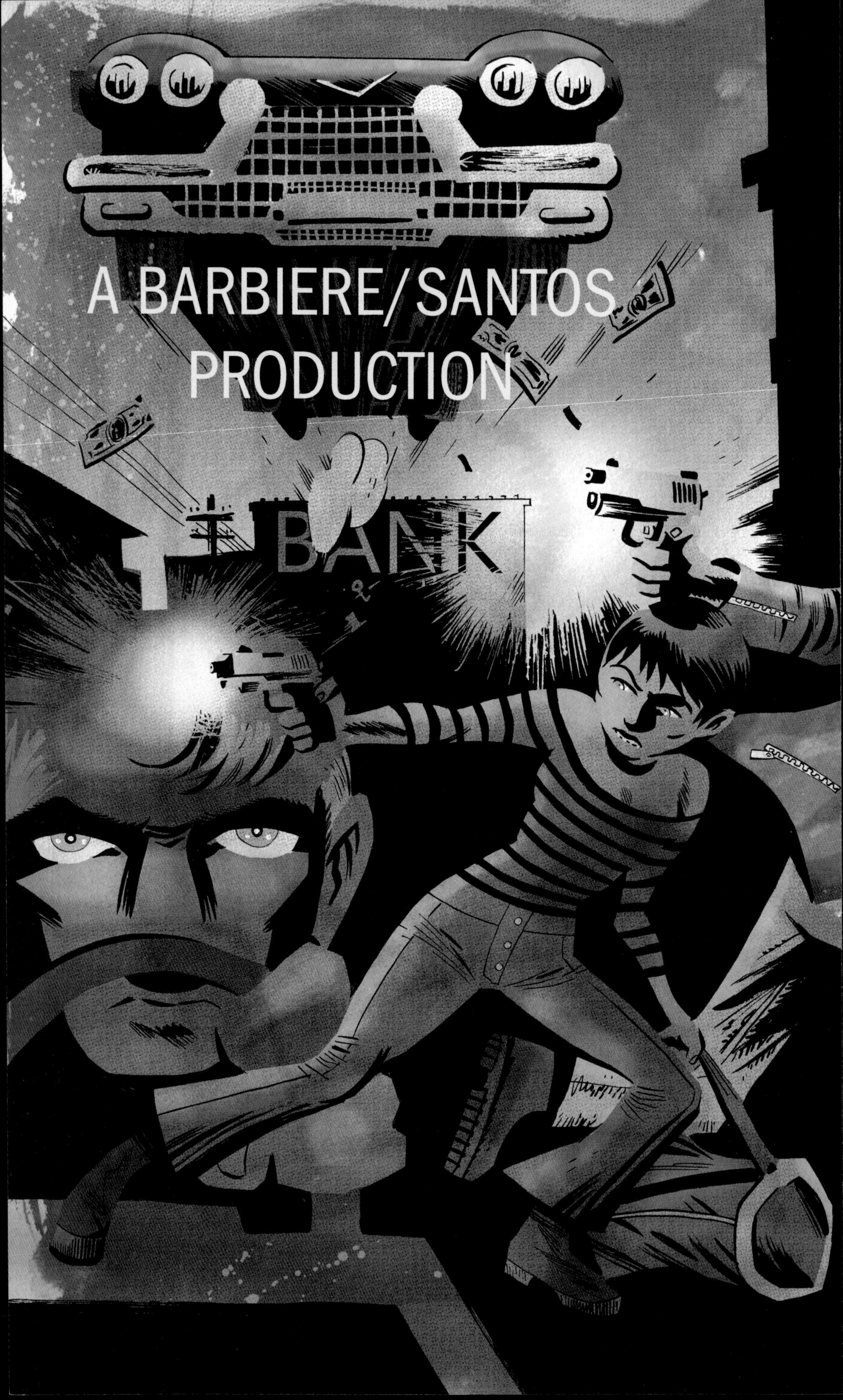
A BARBIERE/SANTOS
PRODUCTION
BANK

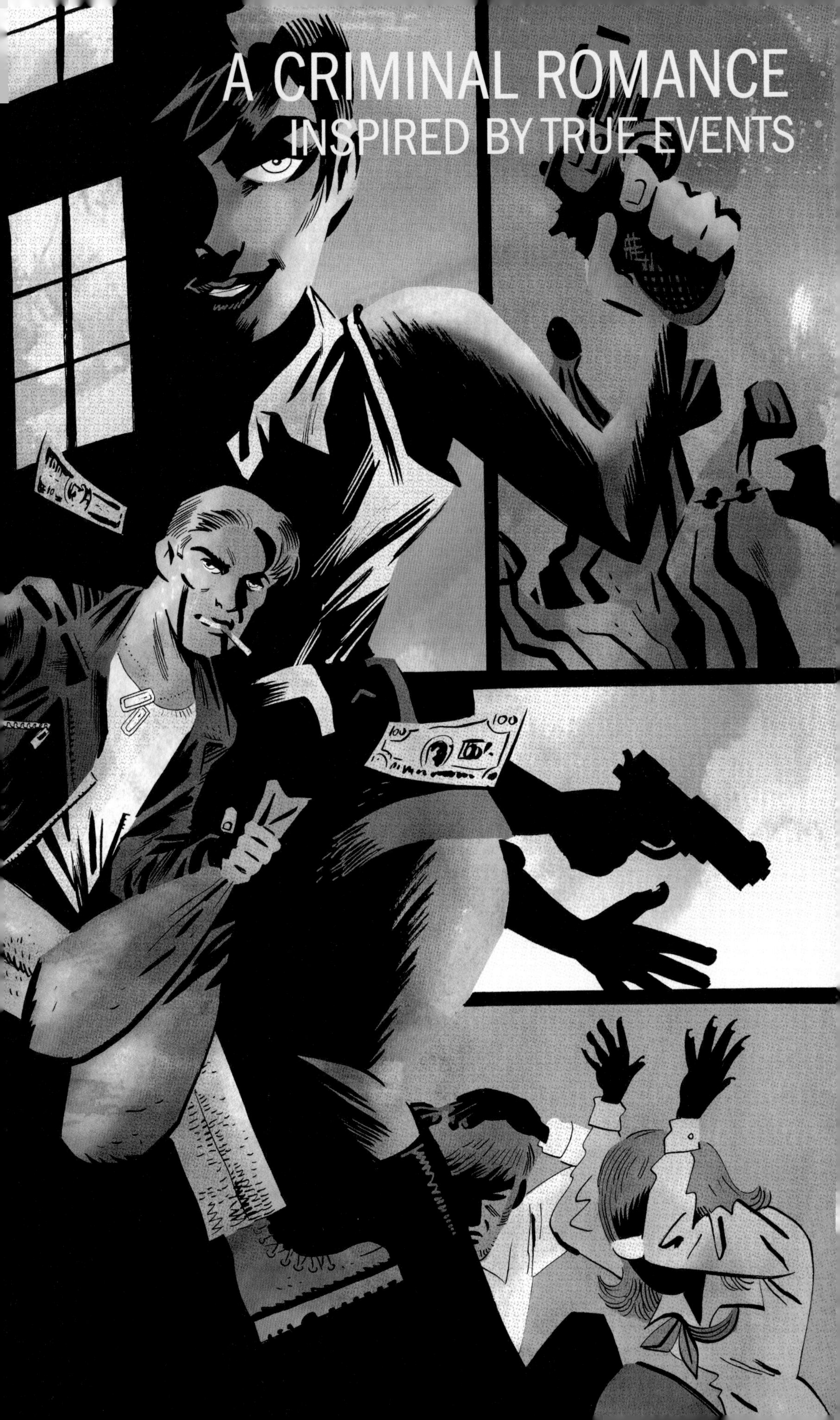
A CRIMINAL ROMANCE
INSPIRED BY TRUE EVENTS

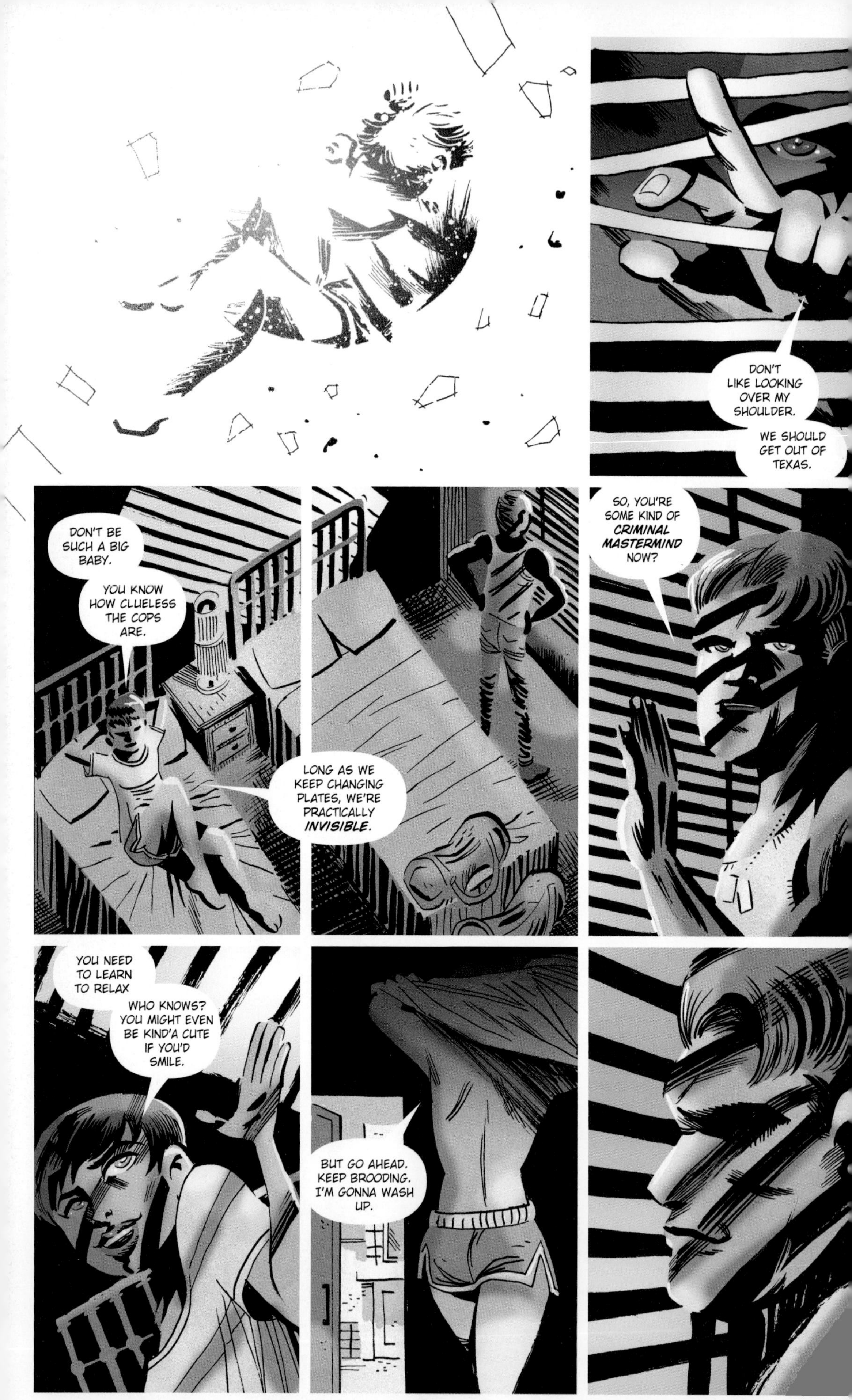
DON'T LIKE LOOKING OVER MY SHOULDER.
WE SHOULD GET OUT OF TEXAS.
DON'T BE SUCH A BIG BABY.
YOU KNOW HOW CLUELESS THE COPS ARE.
LONG AS WE KEEP CHANGING PLATES, WE'RE PRACTICALLY INVISIBLE.
SO, YOU'RE SOME KIND OF CRIMINAL MASTERMIND NOW?
YOU NEED TO LEARN TO RELAX
WHO KNOWS? YOU MIGHT EVEN BE KIND'A CUTE IF YOU'D SMILE.
BUT GO AHEAD. KEEP BROODING. I'M GONNA WASH UP.

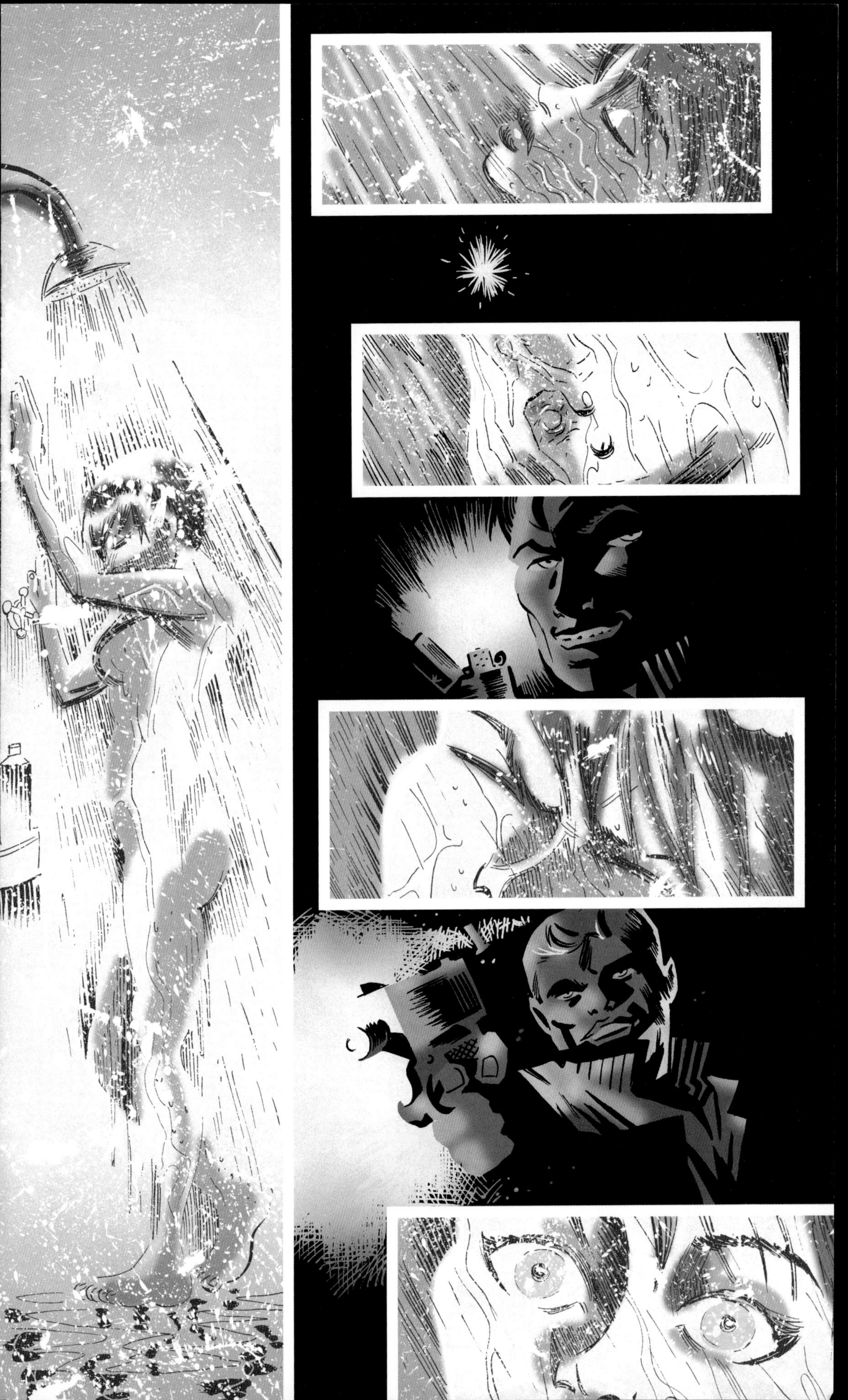

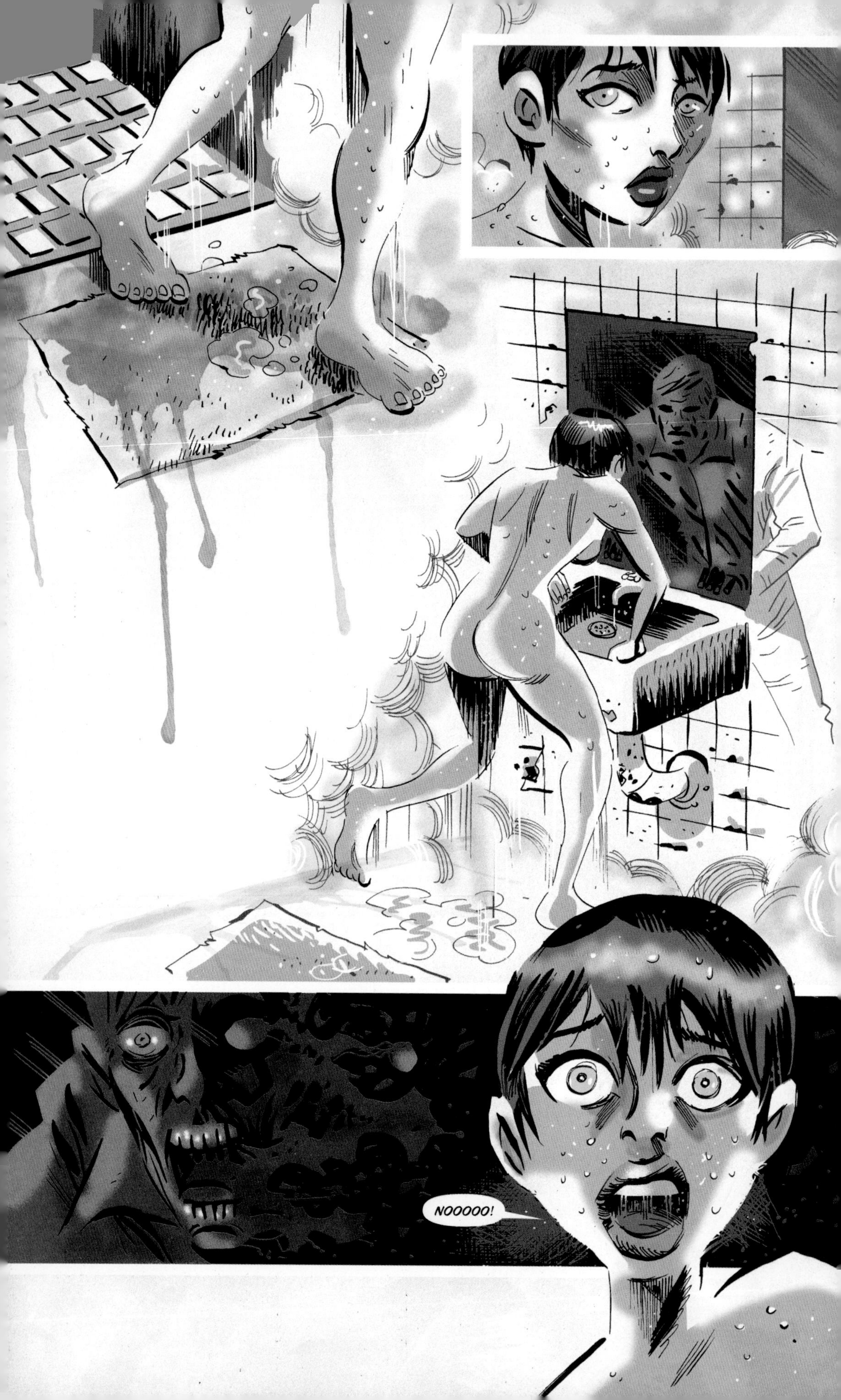
NOOOOO!

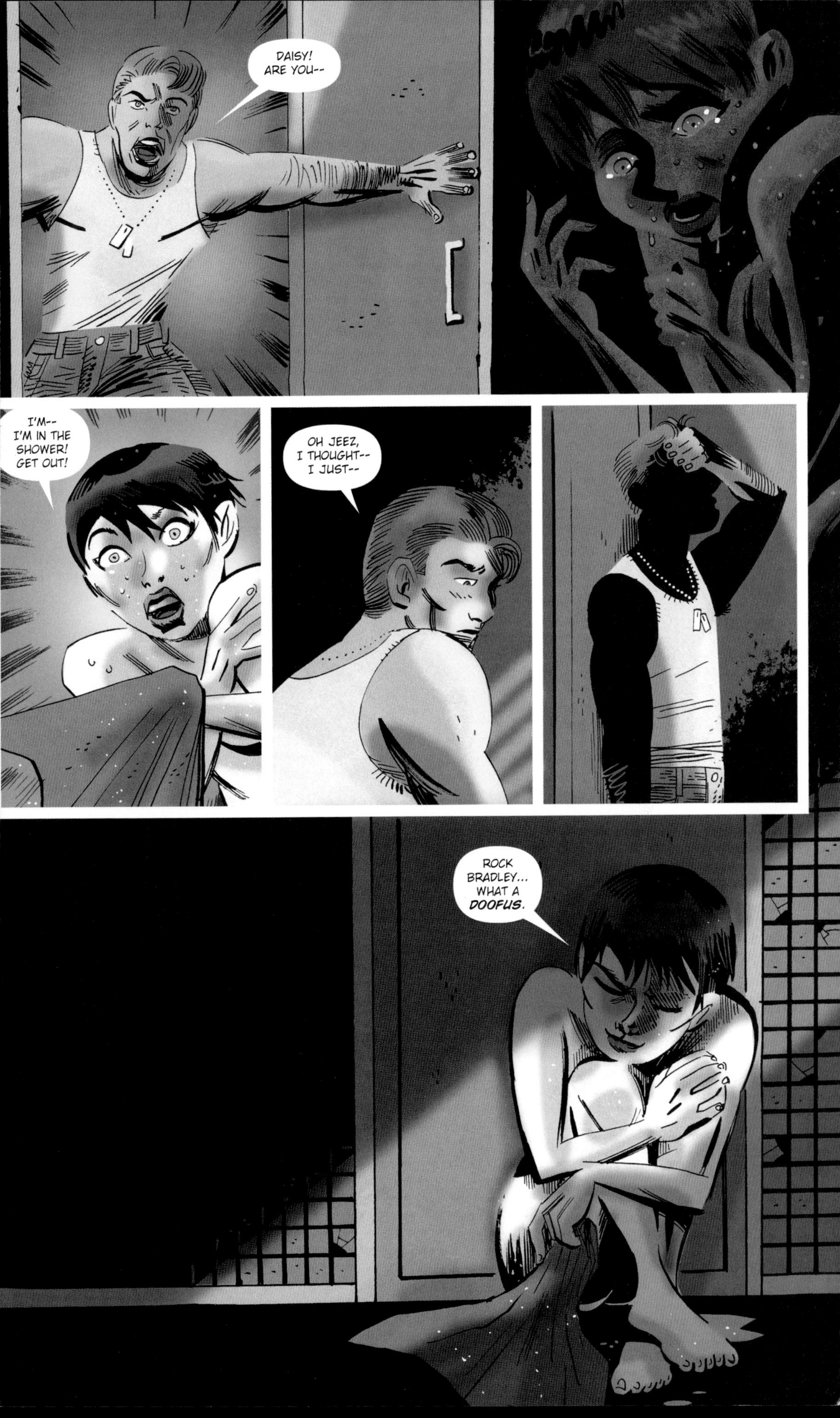
DAISY! ARE YOU--
I'M-- I'M IN THE SHOWER! GET OUT!
OH JEEZ, I THOUGHT-- I JUST--
ROCK BRADLEY... WHAT A DOOFUS.

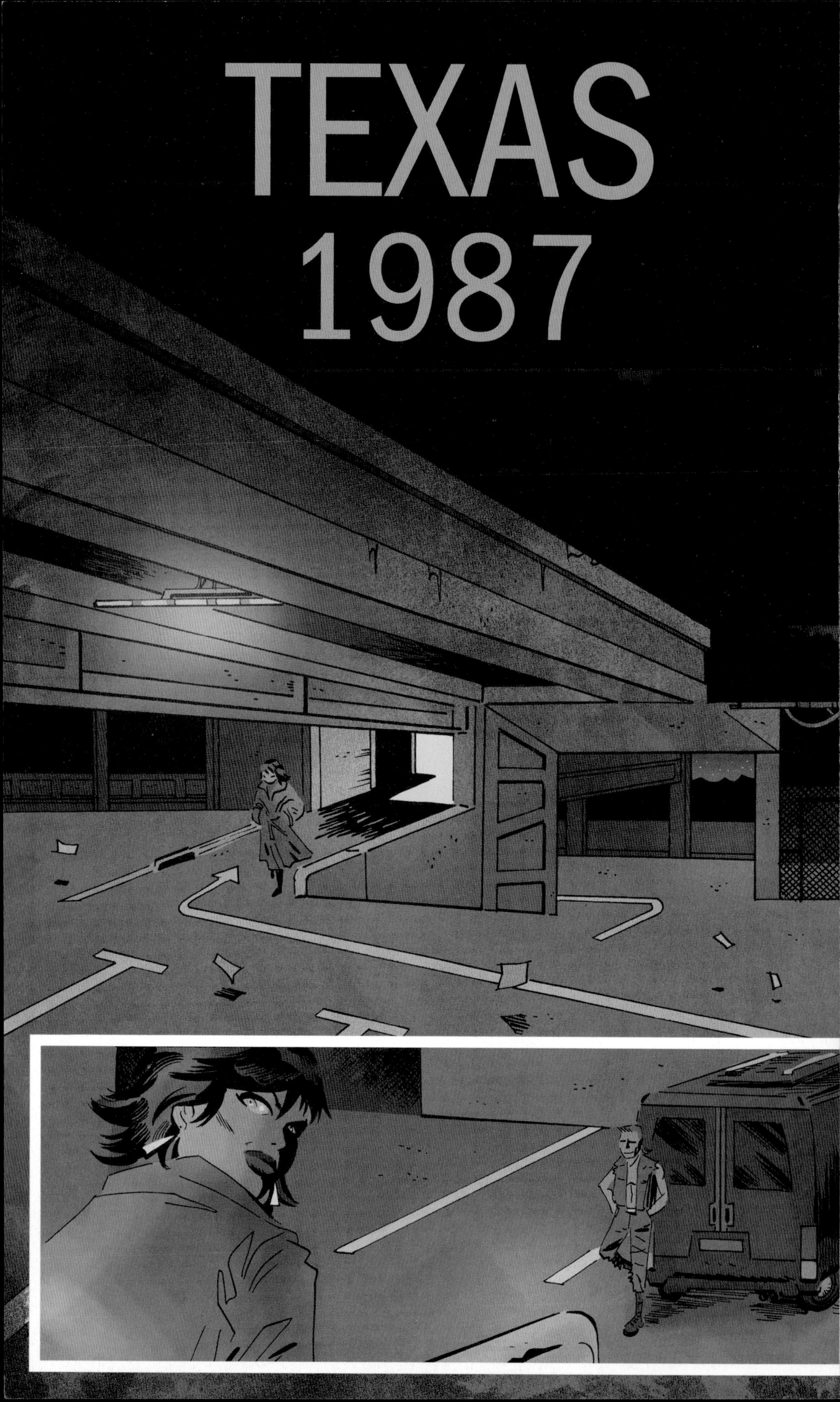
TEXAS
1987

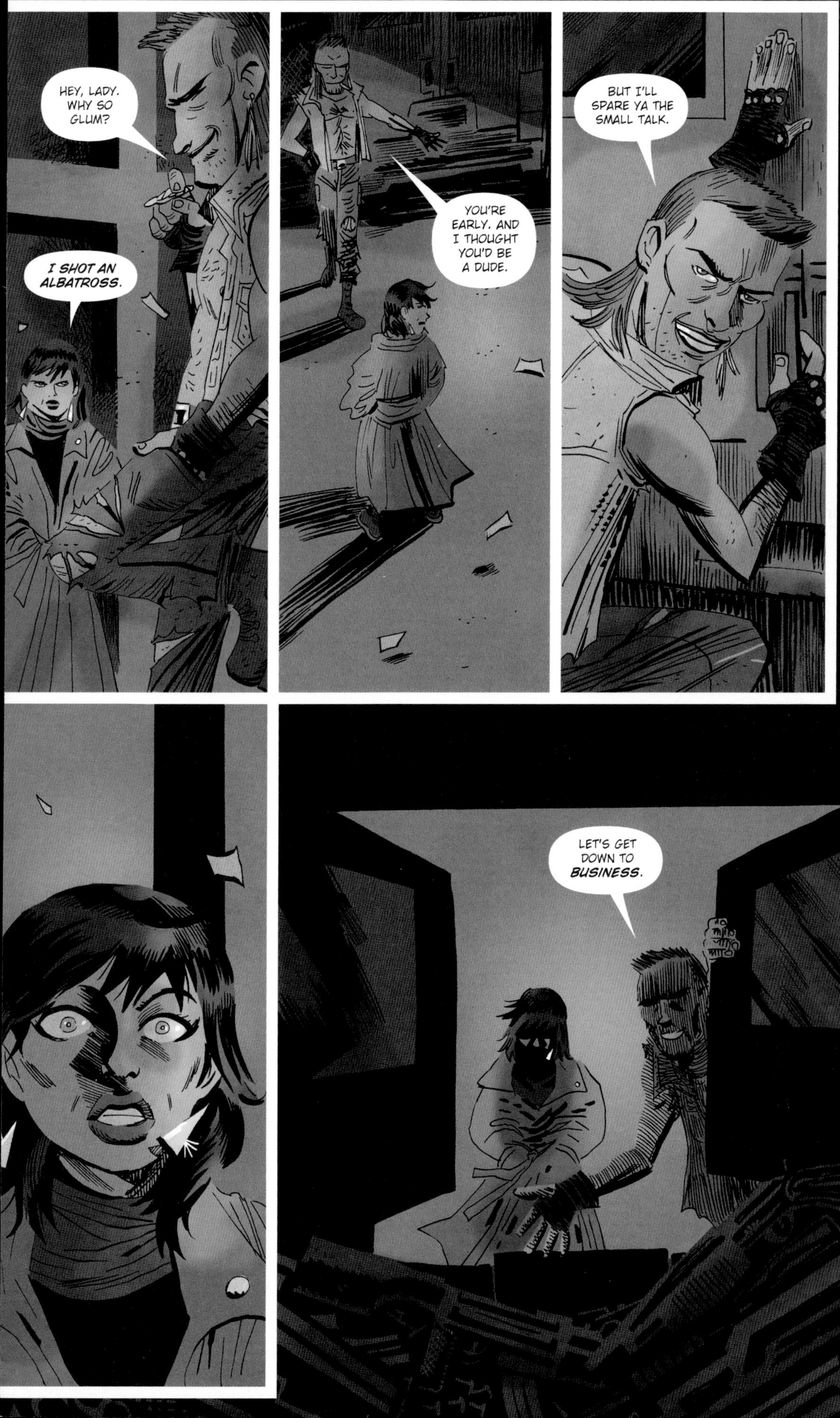
HEY, LADY. WHY SO GLUM?
I SHOT AN ALBATROSS.
YOU'RE EARLY. AND I THOUGHT YOU'D BE A DUDE.
BUT I'LL SPARE YA THE SMALL TALK.
LET'S GET DOWN TO BUSINESS.

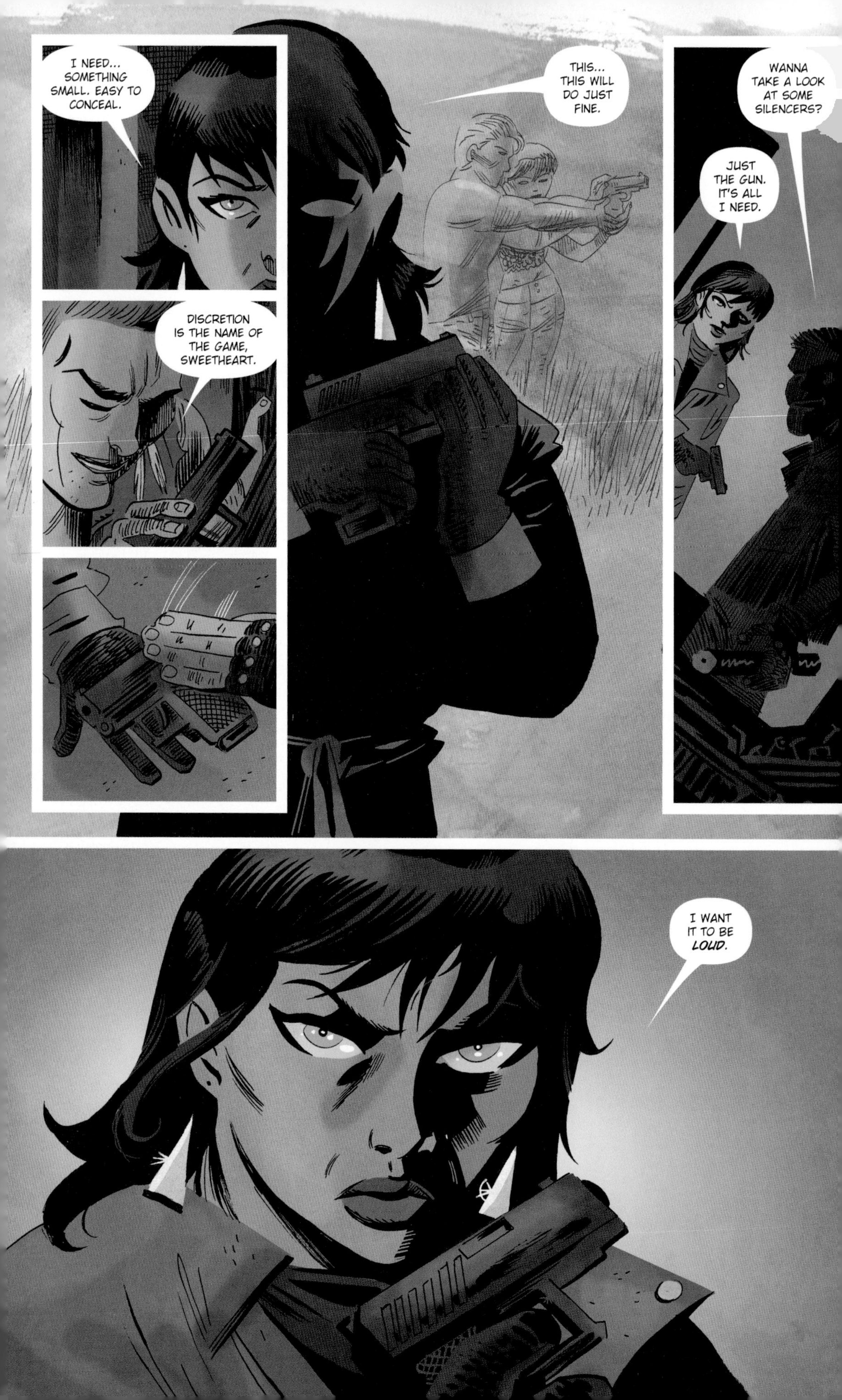

I NEED... SOMETHING SMALL. EASY TO CONCEAL.
DISCRETION IS THE NAME OF THE GAME, SWEETHEART.
THIS... THIS WILL DO JUST FINE.
WANNA TAKE A LOOK AT SOME SILENCERS?
JUST THE GUN. IT'S ALL I NEED.
I WANT IT TO BE *LOUD*.

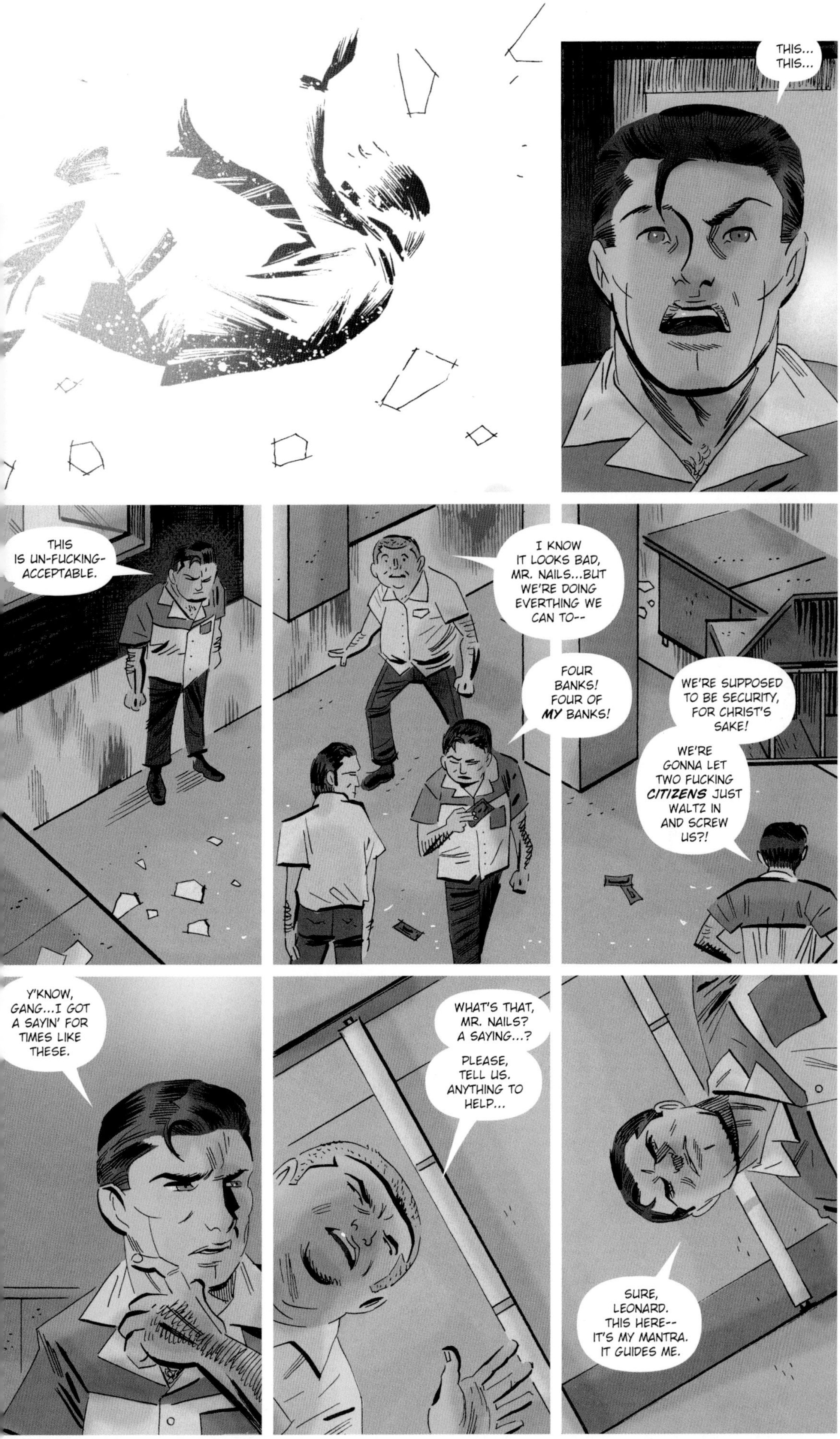
THIS... THIS...
THIS IS UN-FUCKING-ACCEPTABLE.
I KNOW IT LOOKS BAD, MR. NAILS...BUT WE'RE DOING EVERTHING WE CAN TO--
FOUR BANKS! FOUR OF *MY* BANKS!
WE'RE SUPPOSED TO BE SECURITY, FOR CHRIST'S SAKE!
WE'RE GONNA LET TWO FUCKING *CITIZENS* JUST WALTZ IN AND SCREW US?!
Y'KNOW, GANG...I GOT A SAYIN' FOR TIMES LIKE THESE.
WHAT'S THAT, MR. NAILS? A SAYING...?
PLEASE, TELL US. ANYTHING TO HELP...
SURE, LEONARD. THIS HERE-- IT'S MY MANTRA. IT GUIDES ME.

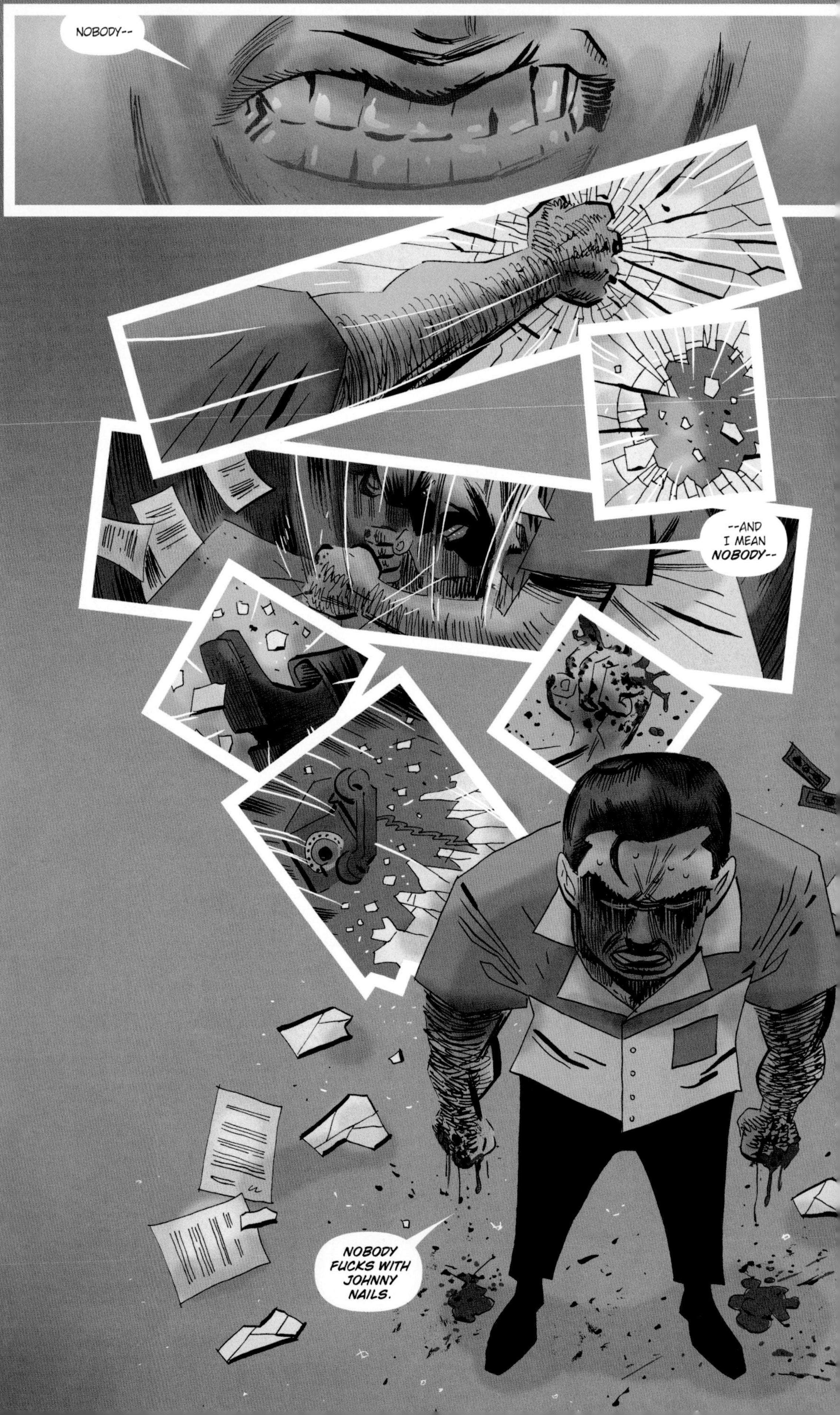
NOBODY--
--AND I MEAN NOBODY--
NOBODY FUCKS WITH JOHNNY NAILS.

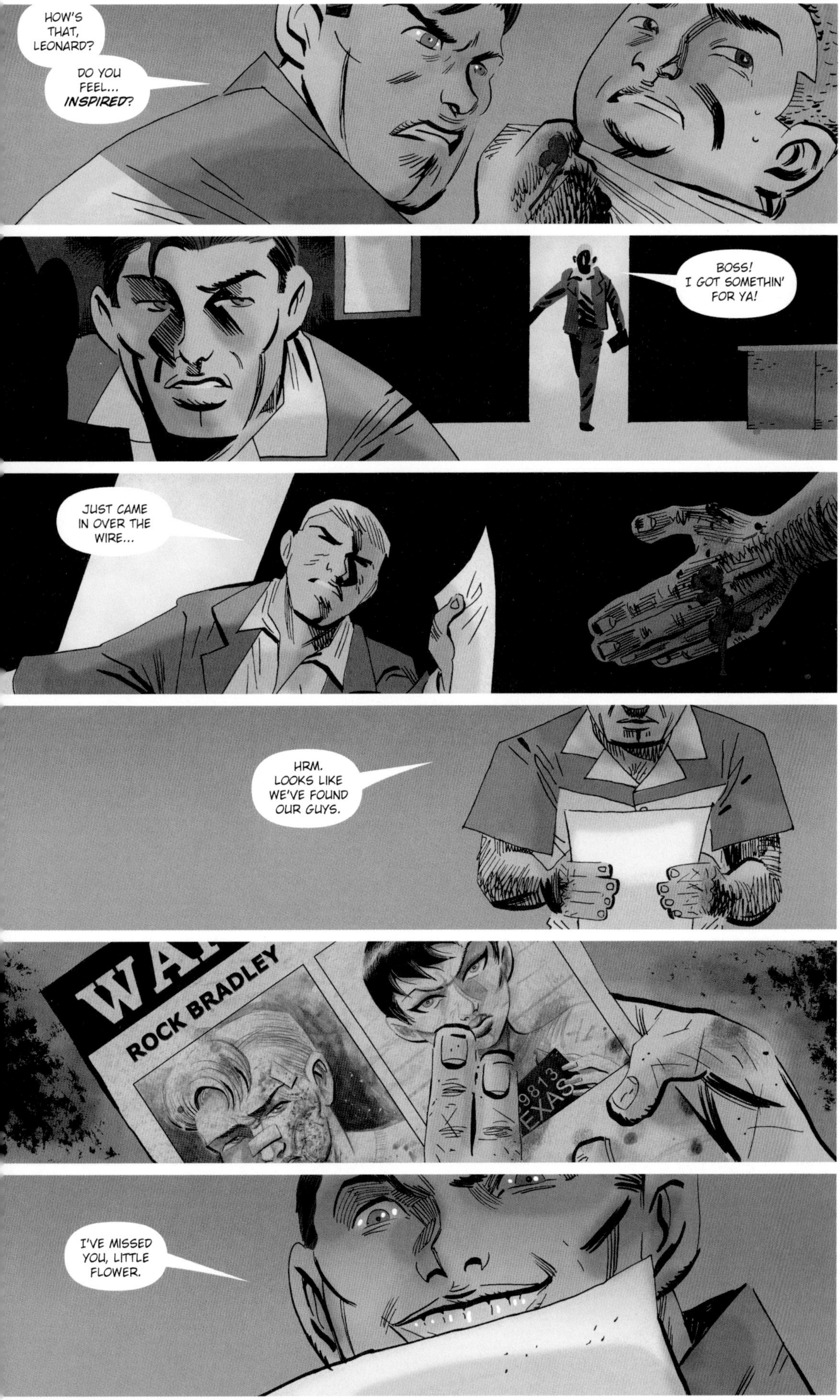
HOW'S THAT, LEONARD?
DO YOU FEEL... *INSPIRED?*
BOSS! I GOT SOMETHIN' FOR YA!
JUST CAME IN OVER THE WIRE...
HRM. LOOKS LIKE WE'VE FOUND OUR GUYS.
WA
ROCK BRADLEY
I'VE MISSED YOU, LITTLE FLOWER.

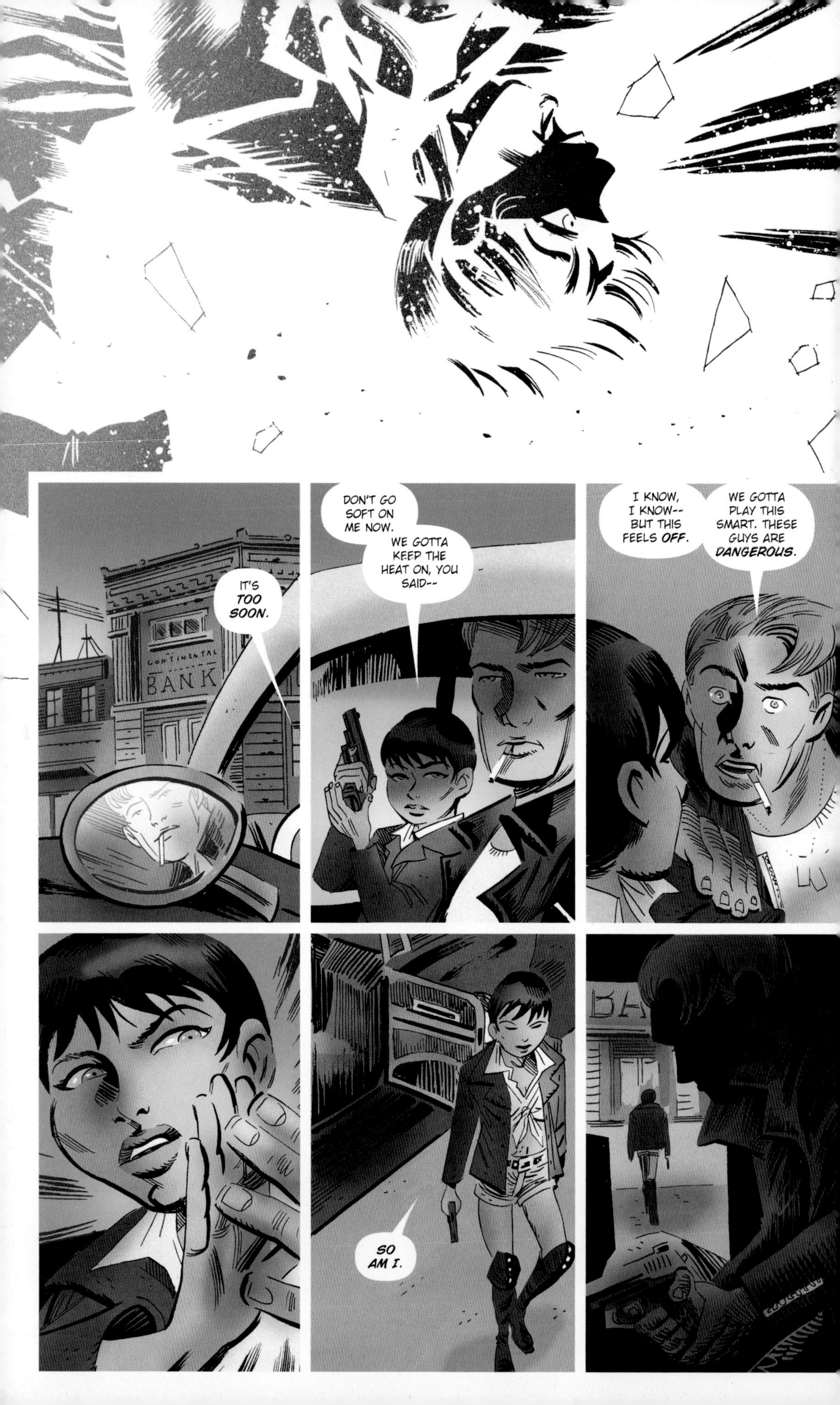

CONTINENTAL
BANK
IT'S TOO SOON.
DON'T GO SOFT ON ME NOW.
WE GOTTA KEEP THE HEAT ON, YOU SAID--
I KNOW, I KNOW-- BUT THIS FEELS OFF.
WE GOTTA PLAY THIS SMART. THESE GUYS ARE DANGEROUS.
SO AM I.

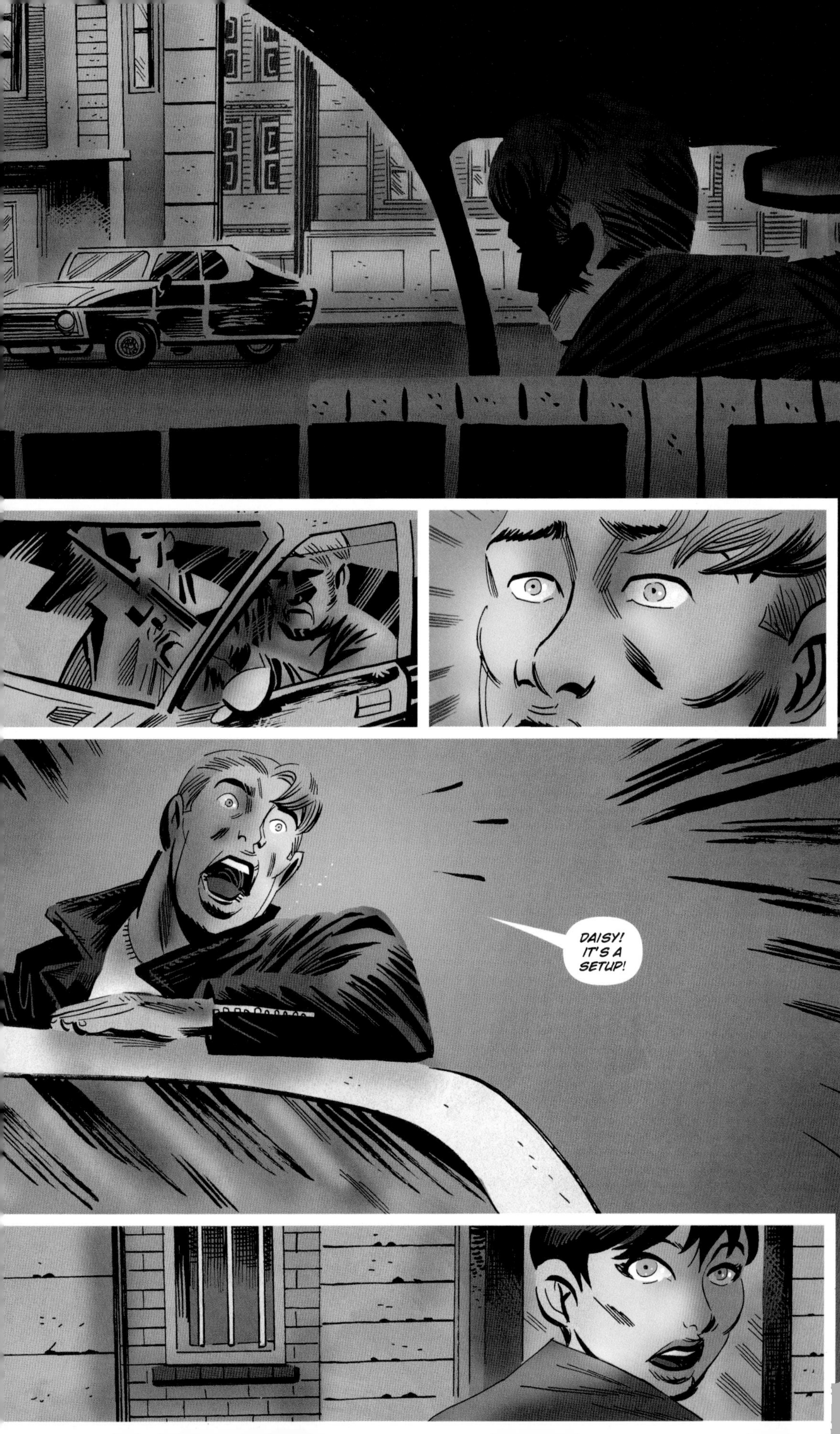
DAISY! IT'S A SETUP!

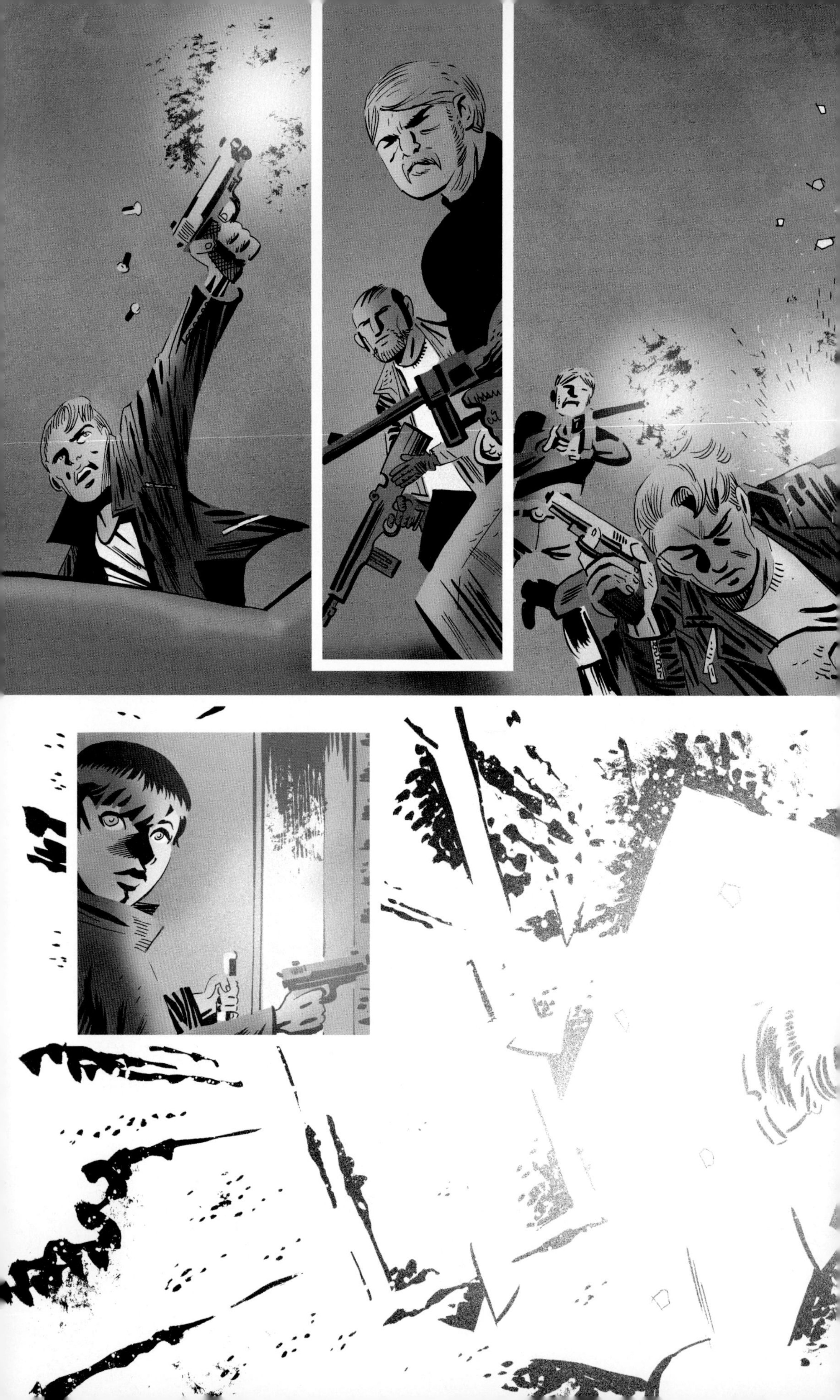

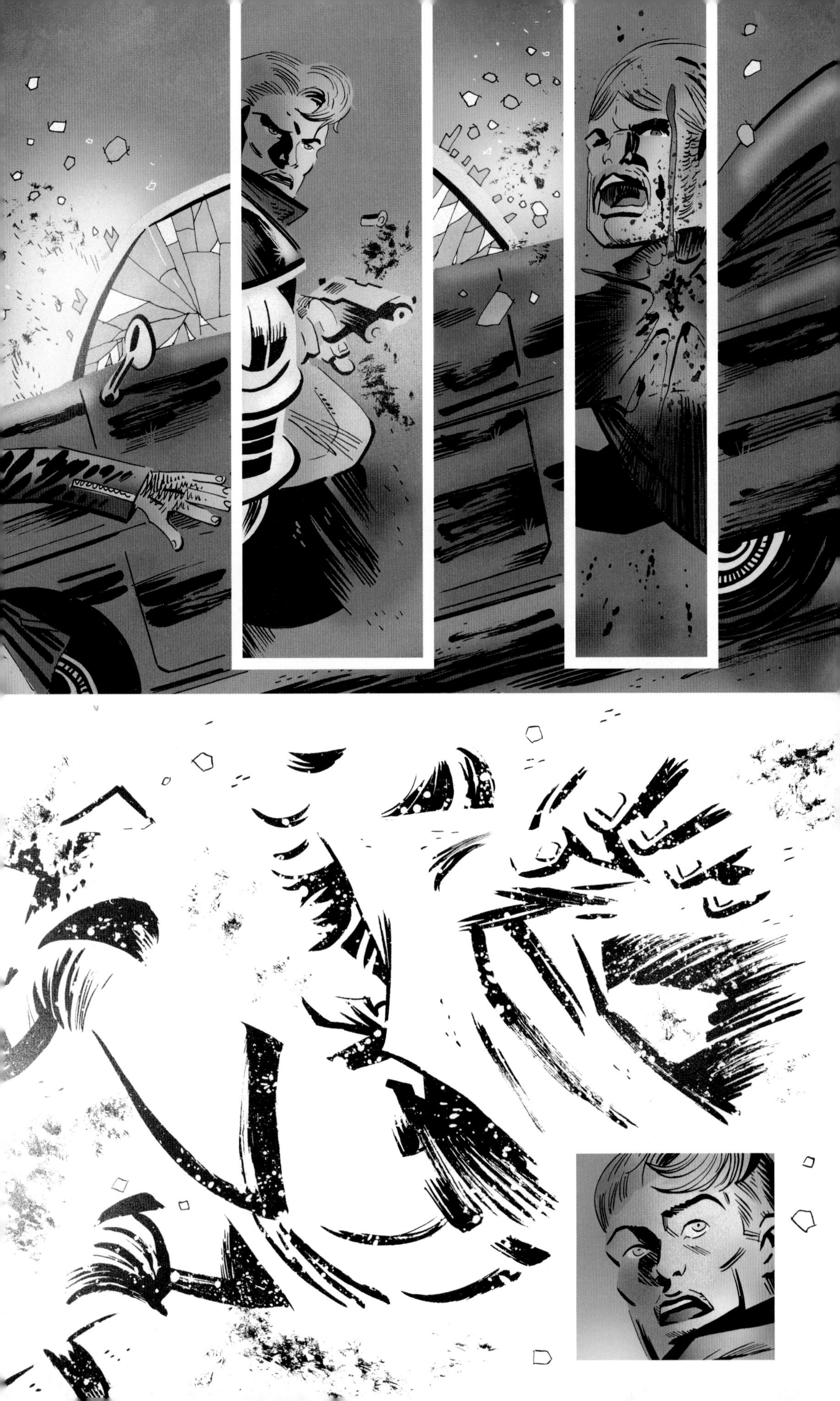

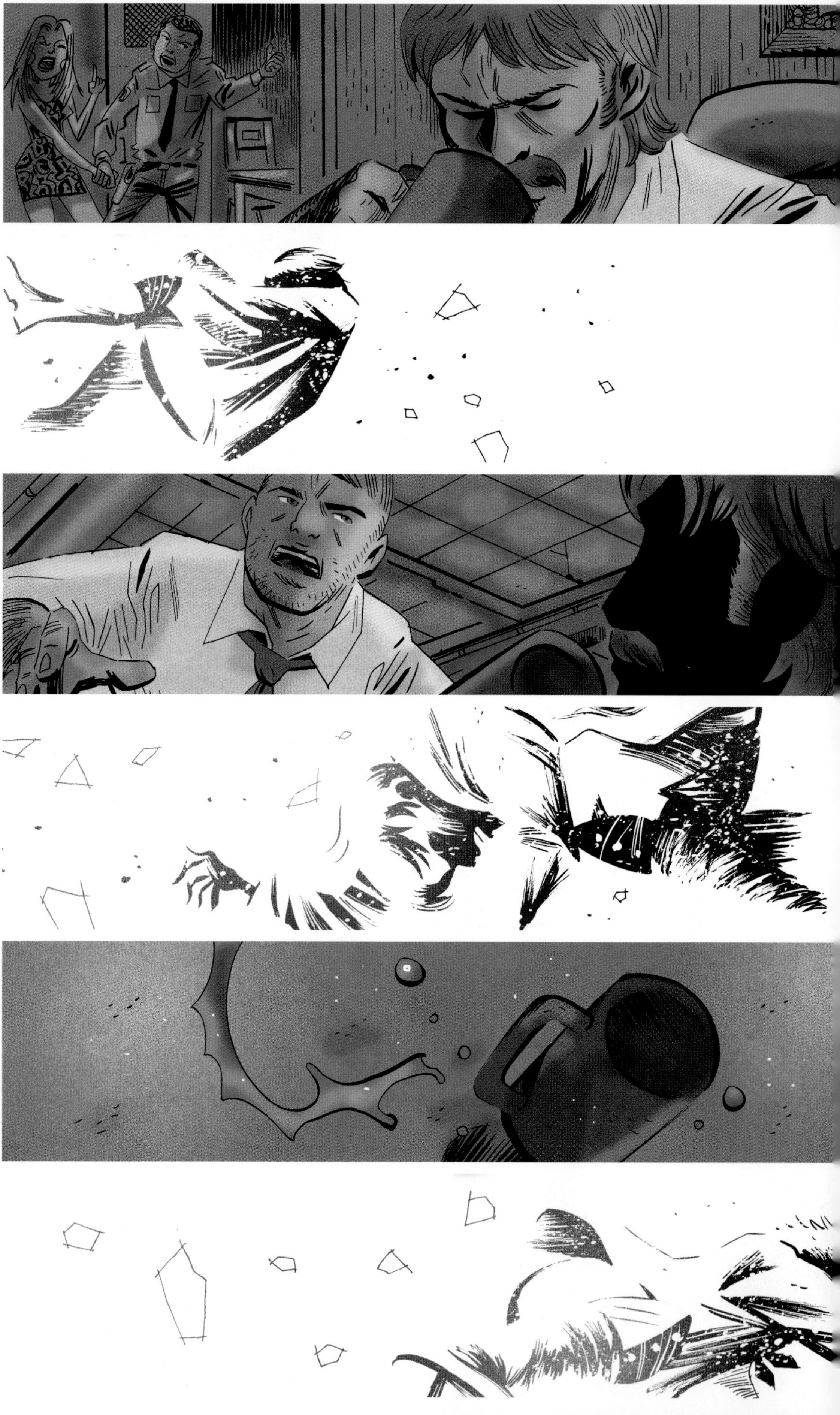

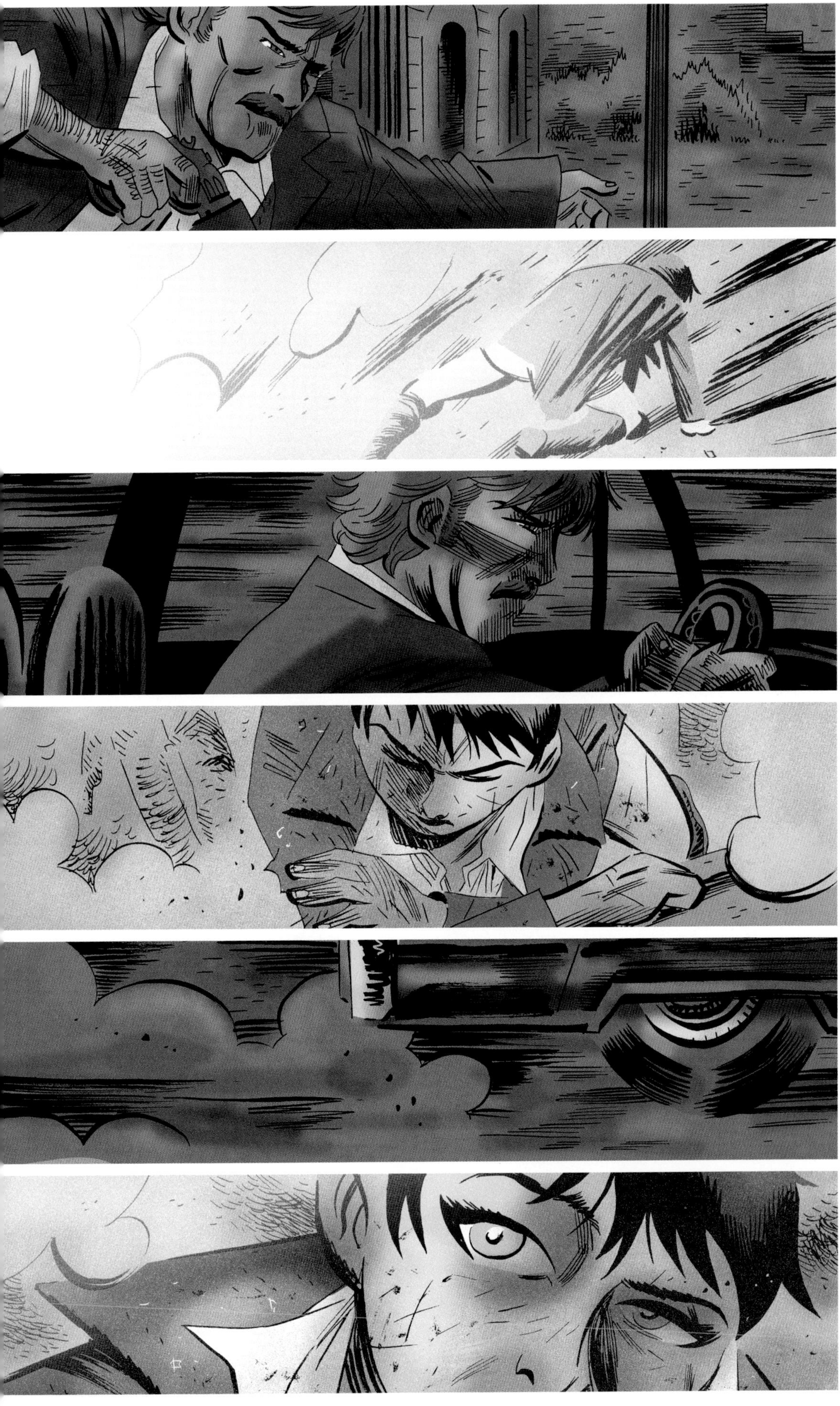

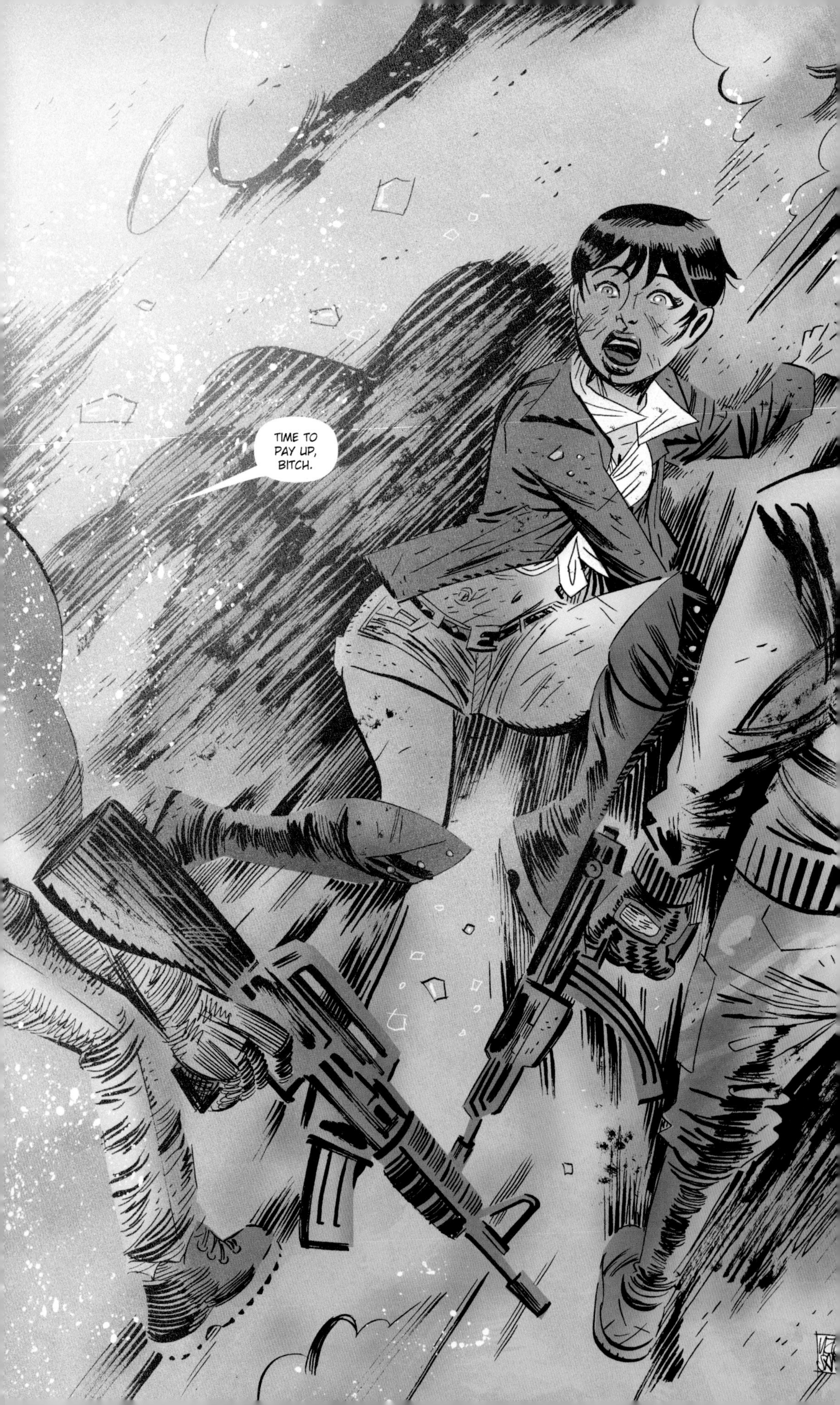
TIME TO PAY UP, BITCH.

CHAPTER EIGHT

"HEARTS ON FIRE"

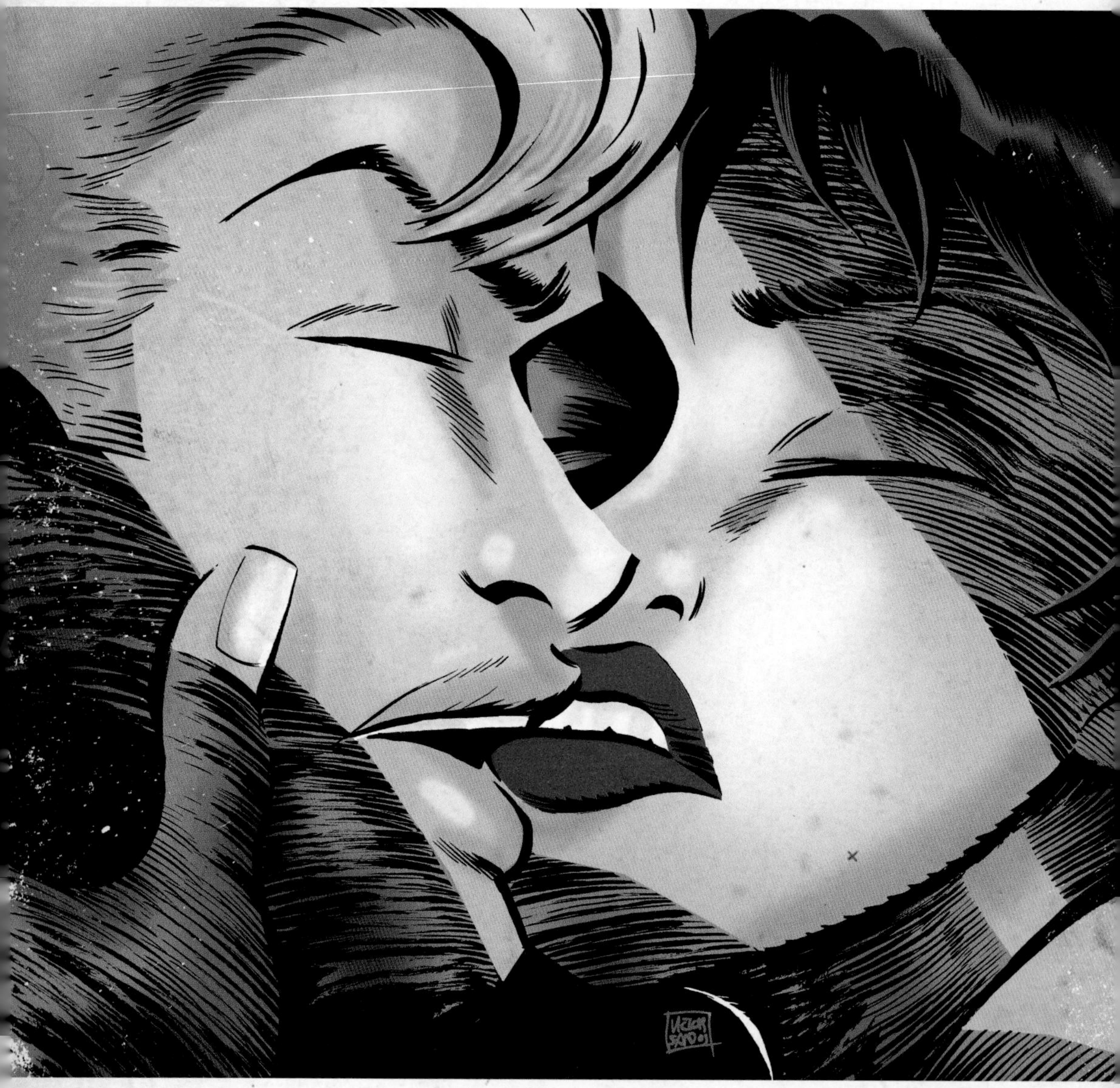

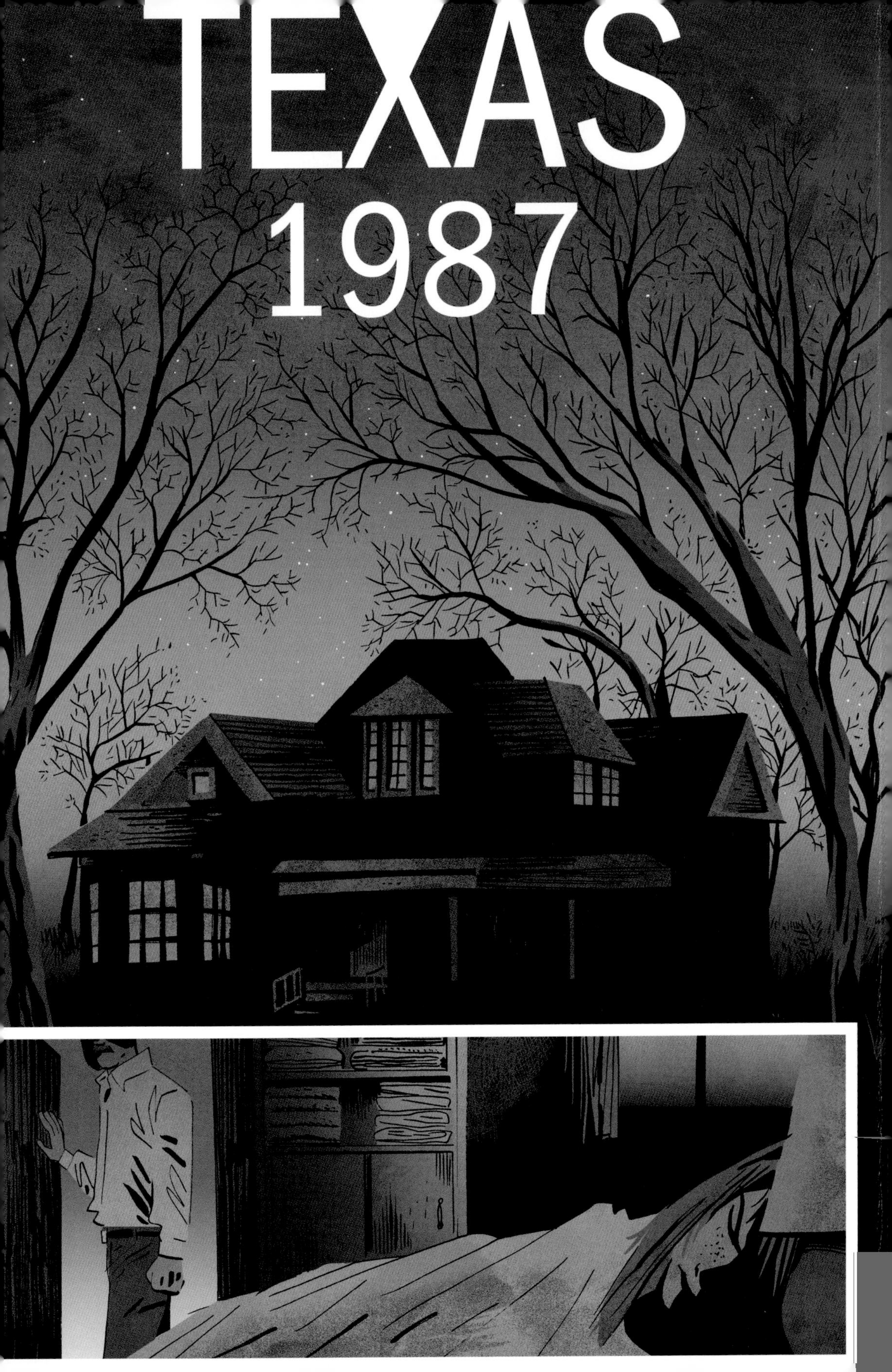
TEXAS
1987

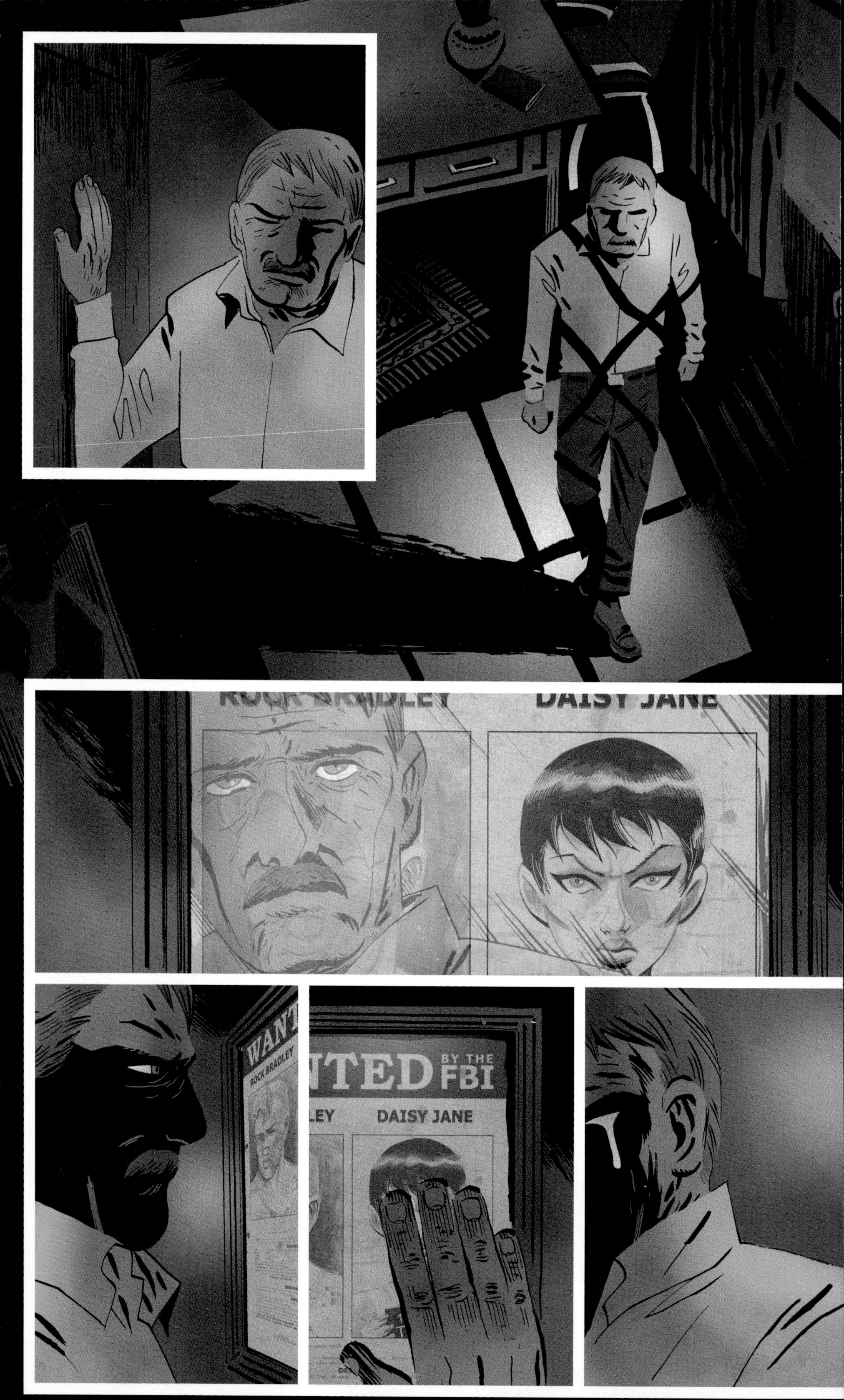
DAISY JANE
ROCK BRADLEY
NTED BY THE FBI
LEY
DAISY JANE

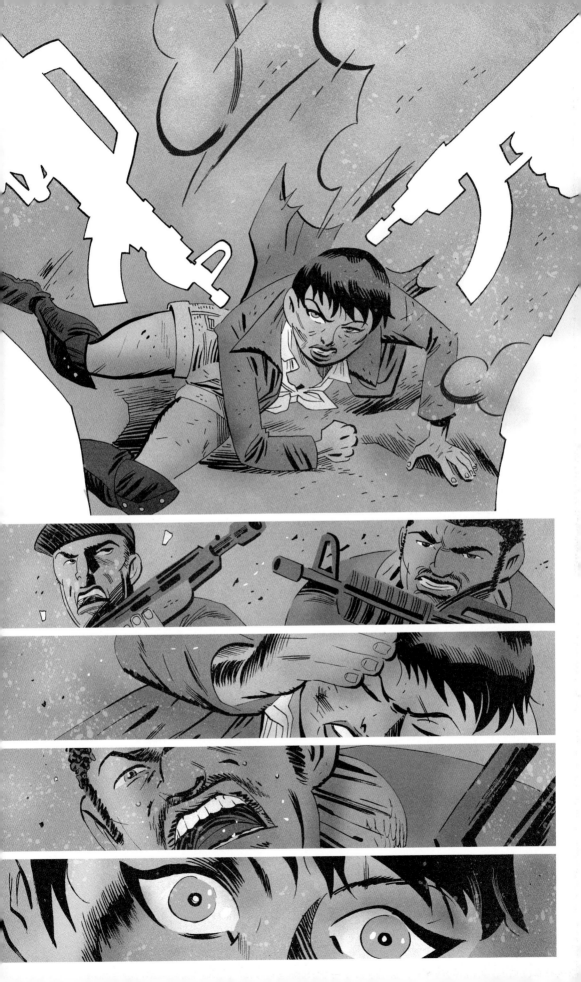

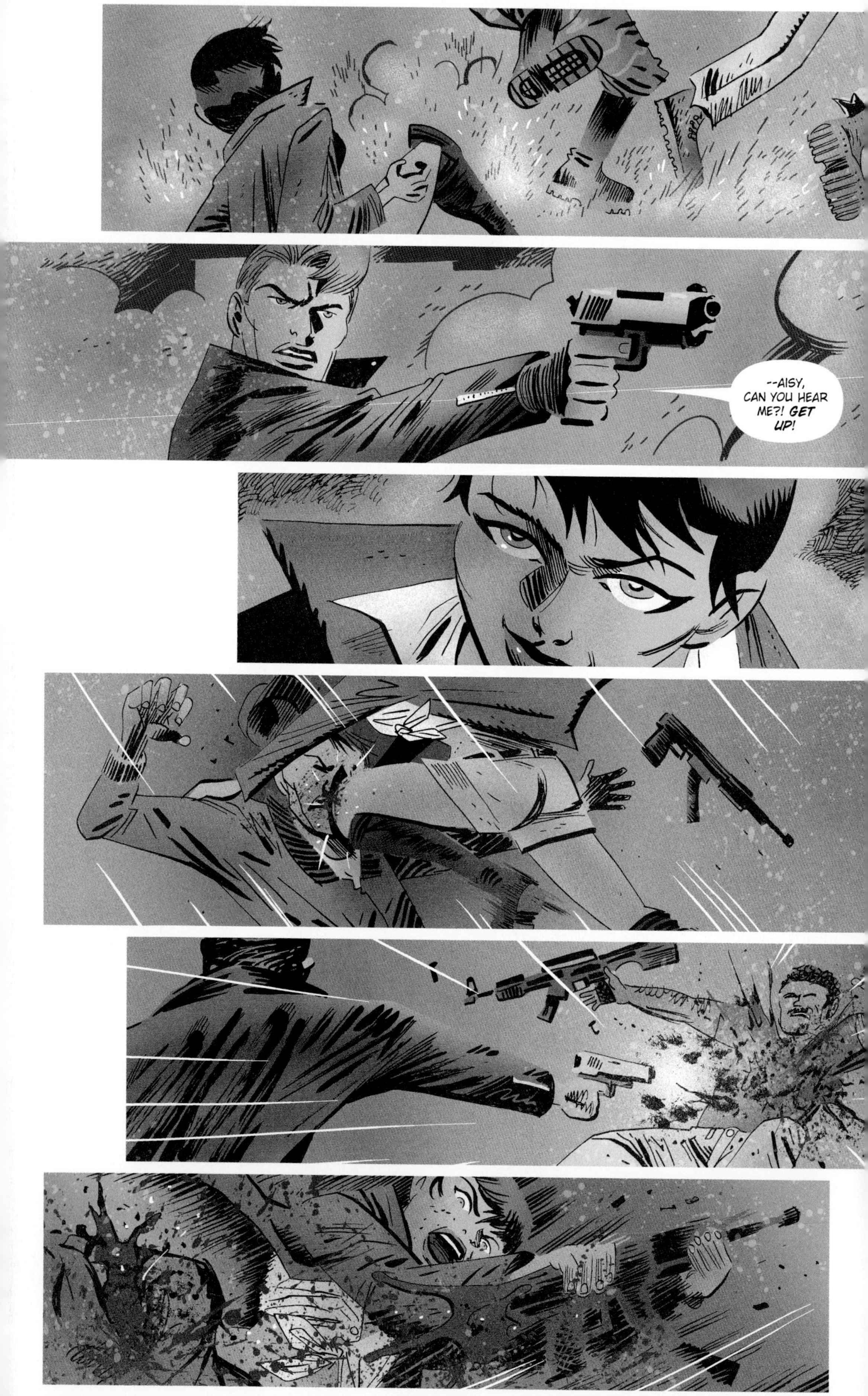
--AISY, CAN YOU HEAR ME?! **GET UP!**

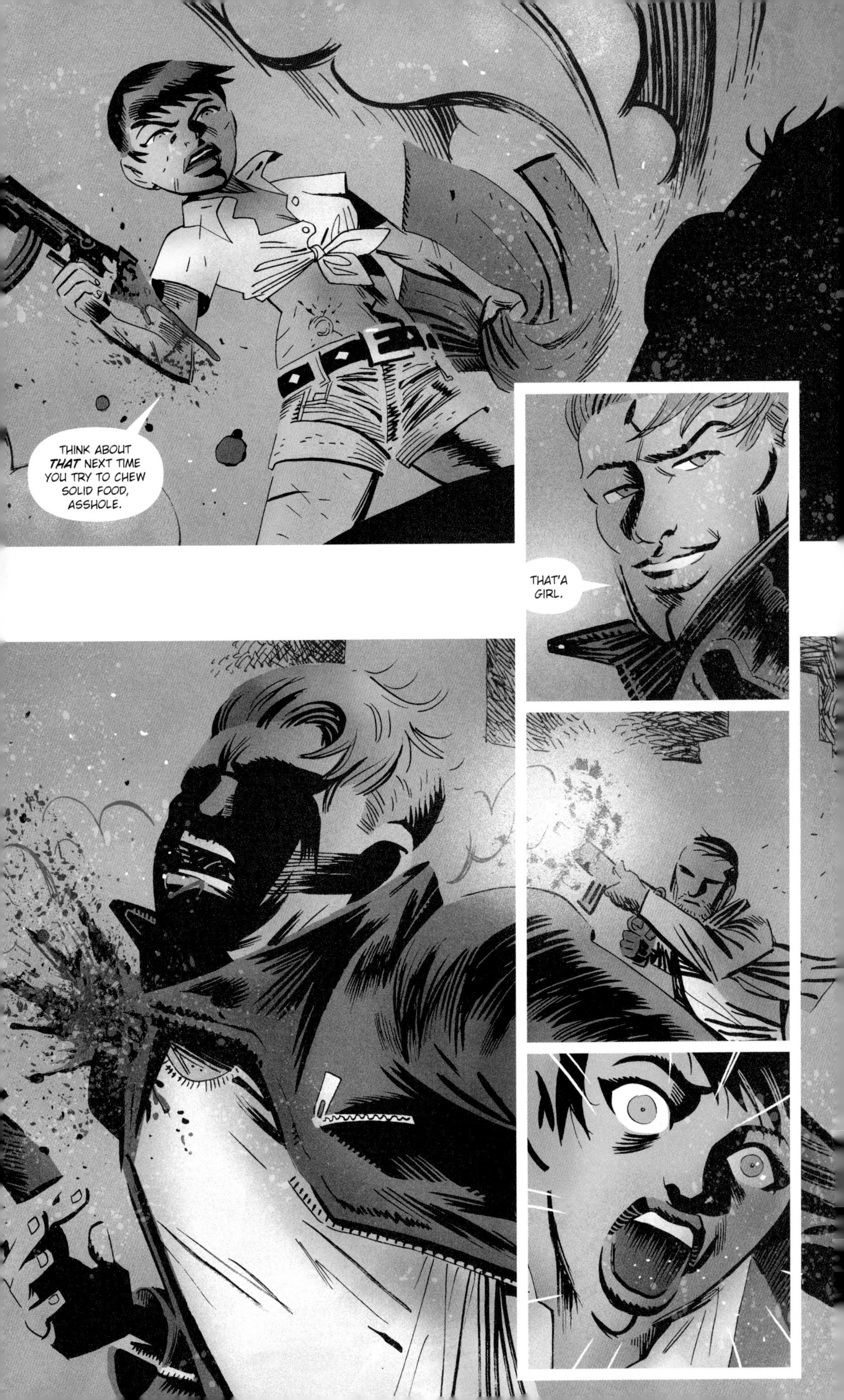
THINK ABOUT *THAT* NEXT TIME YOU TRY TO CHEW SOLID FOOD, ASSHOLE.
THAT'A GIRL.

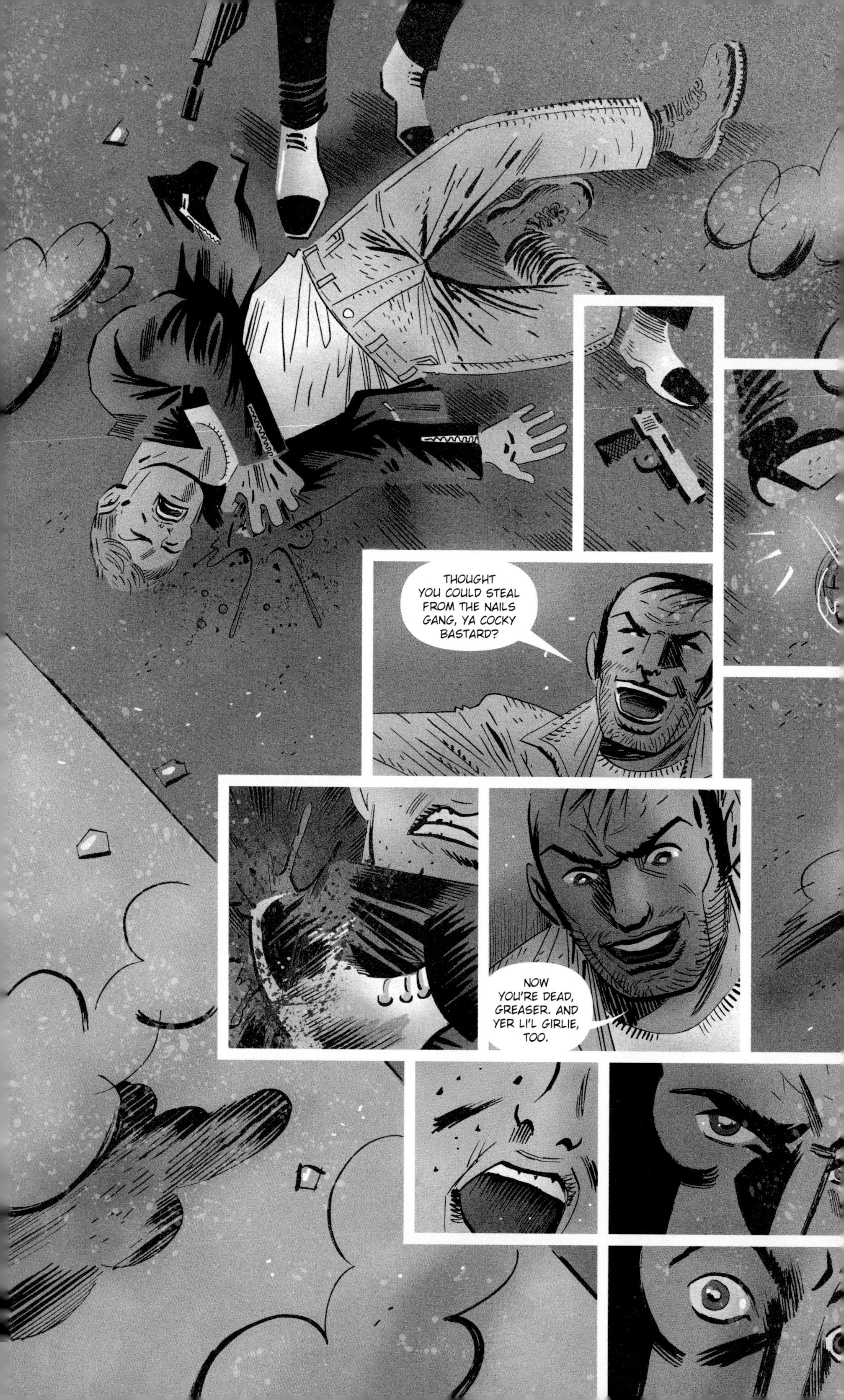
THOUGHT YOU COULD STEAL FROM THE NAILS GANG, YA COCKY BASTARD?
NOW YOU'RE DEAD, GREASER. AND YER LI'L GIRLIE, TOO.

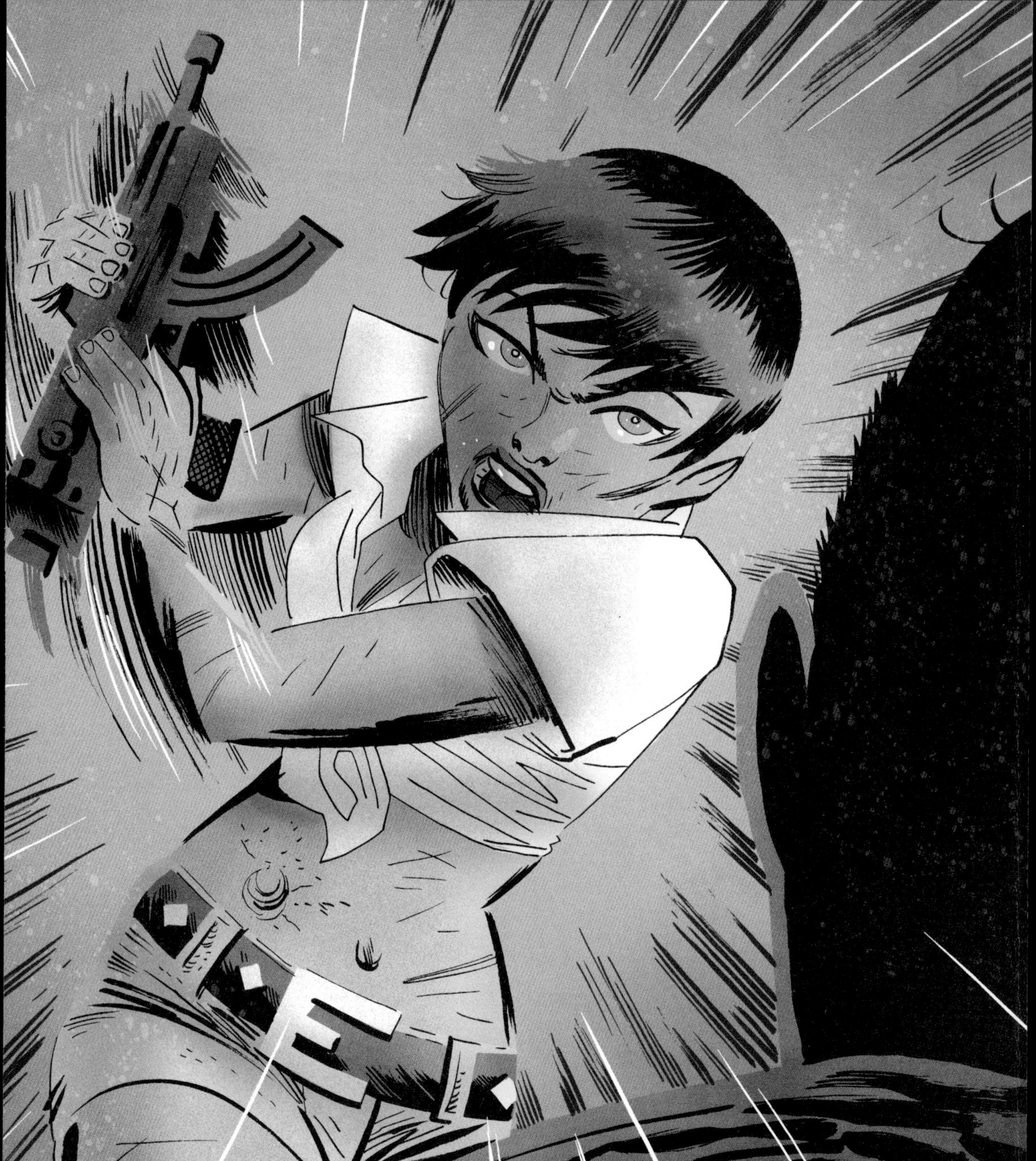
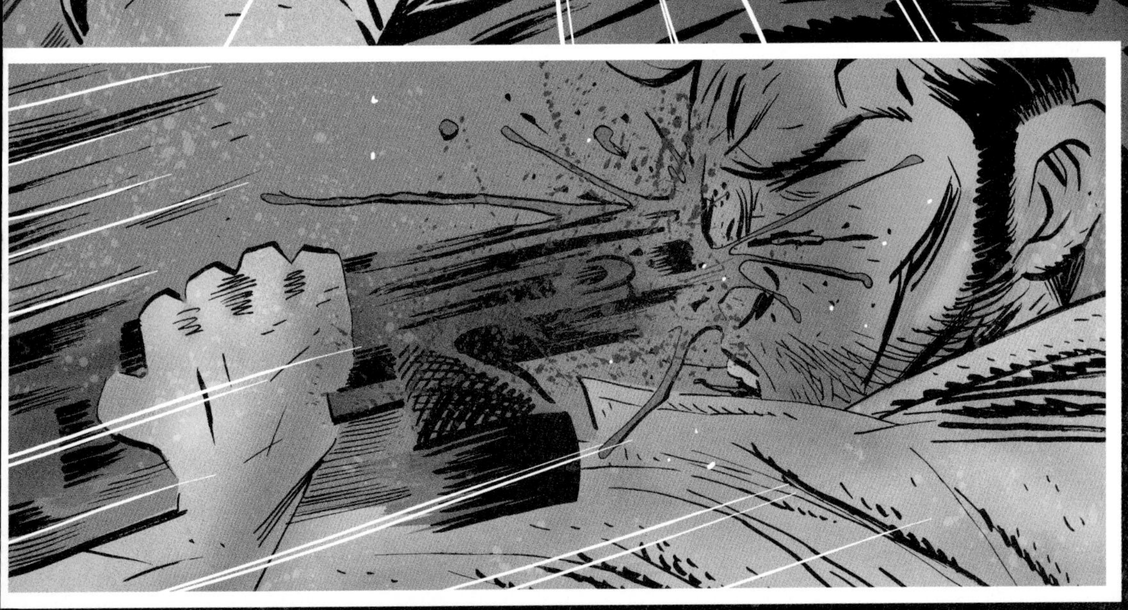

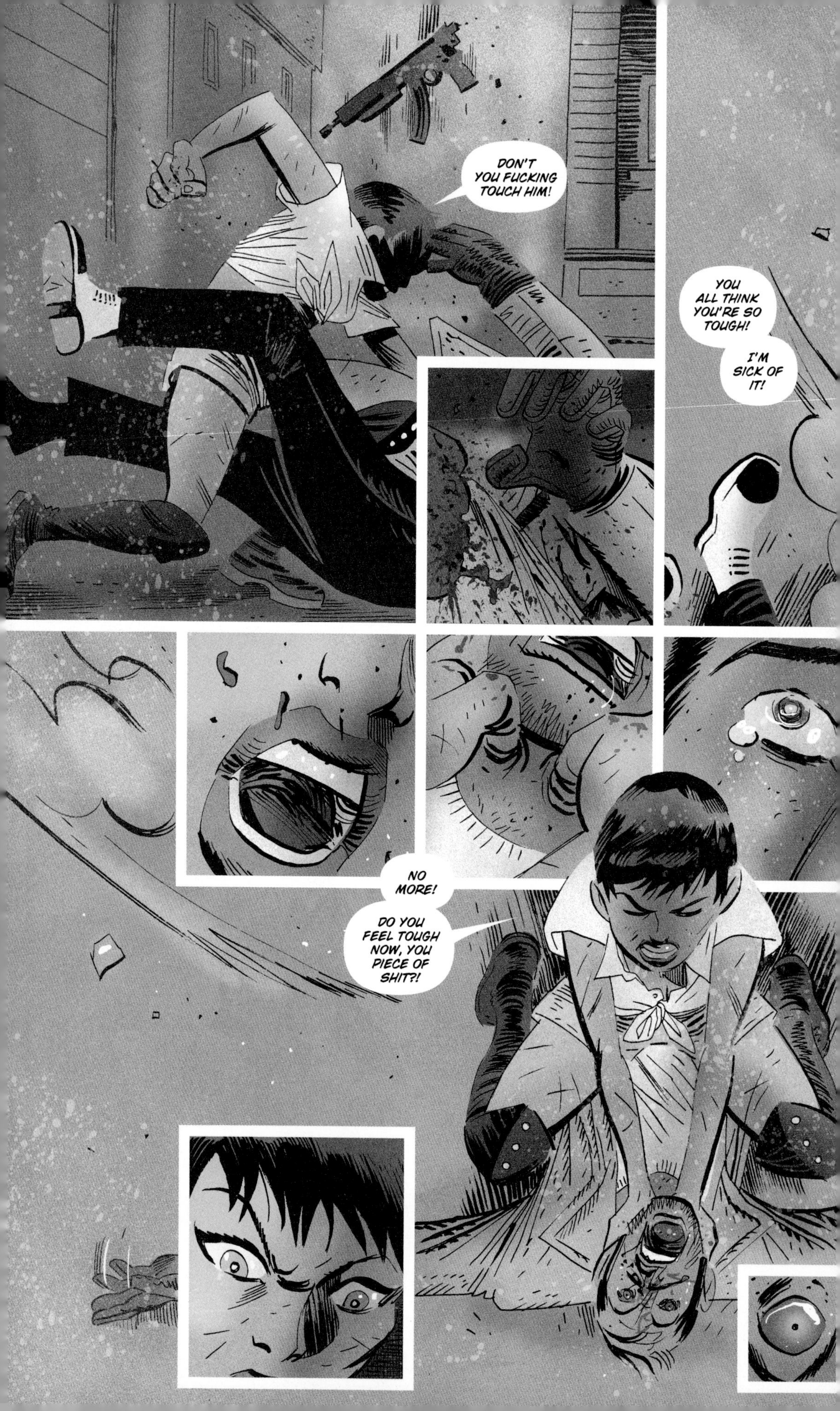
DON'T YOU FUCKING TOUCH HIM!
YOU ALL THINK YOU'RE SO TOUGH!
I'M SICK OF IT!
NO MORE!
DO YOU FEEL TOUGH NOW, YOU PIECE OF SHIT?!

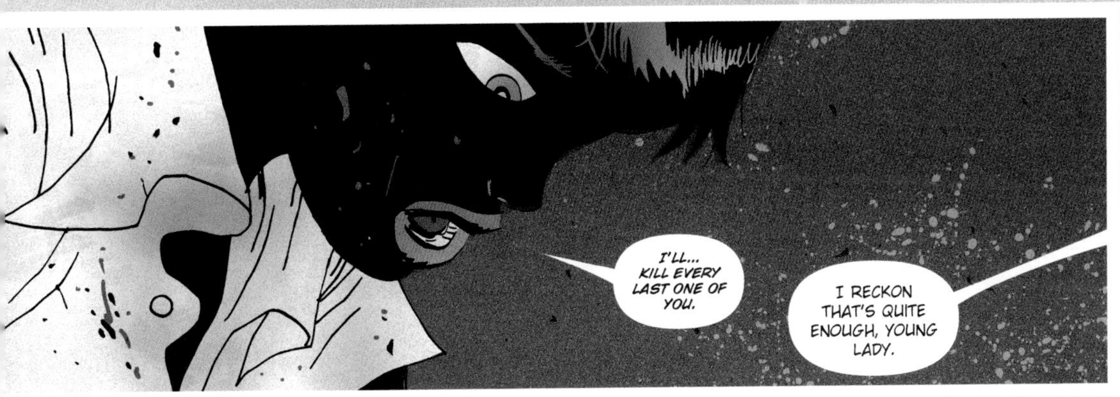
I'LL... KILL EVERY LAST ONE OF YOU.
I RECKON THAT'S QUITE ENOUGH, YOUNG LADY.

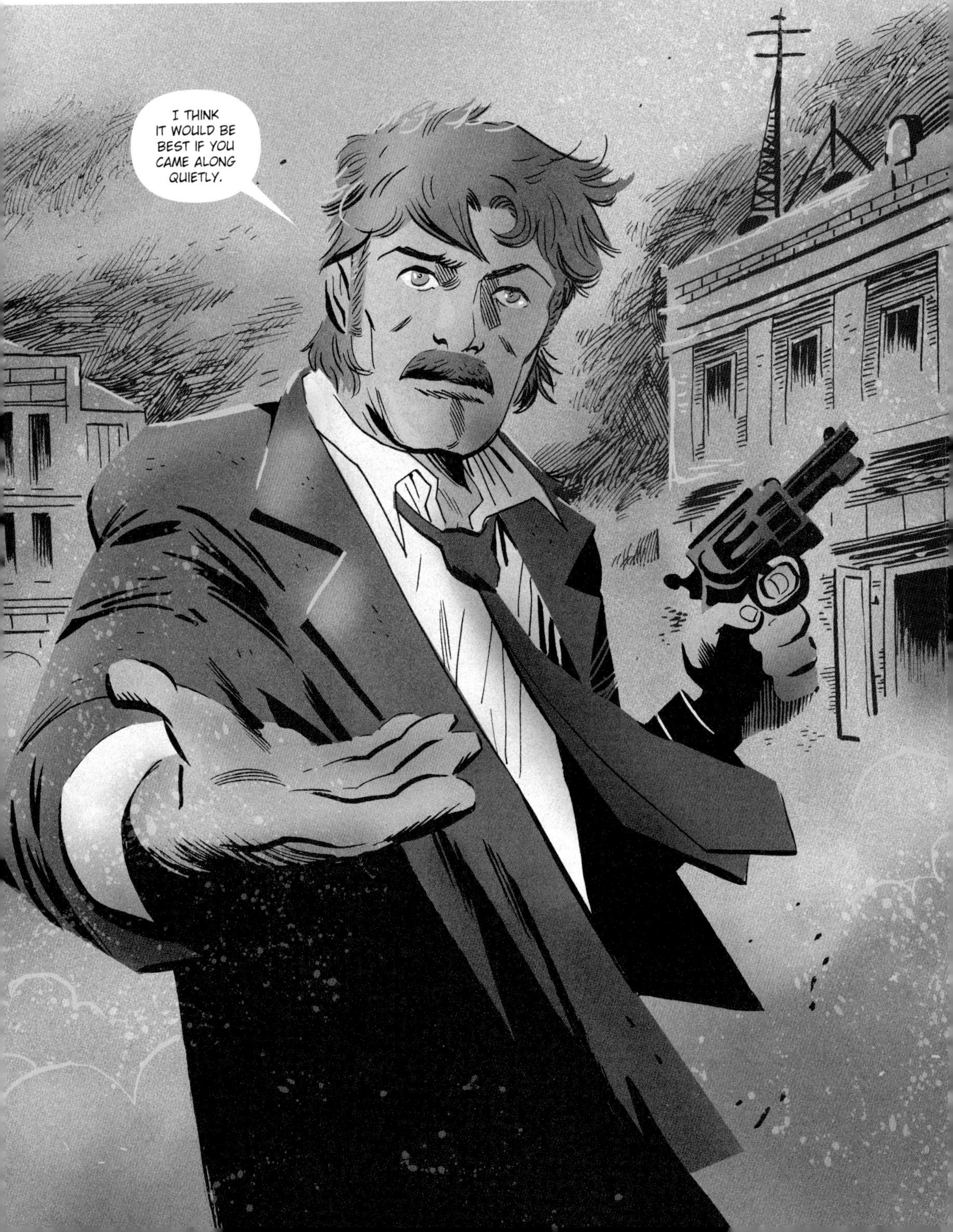
I THINK IT WOULD BE BEST IF YOU CAME ALONG QUIETLY.

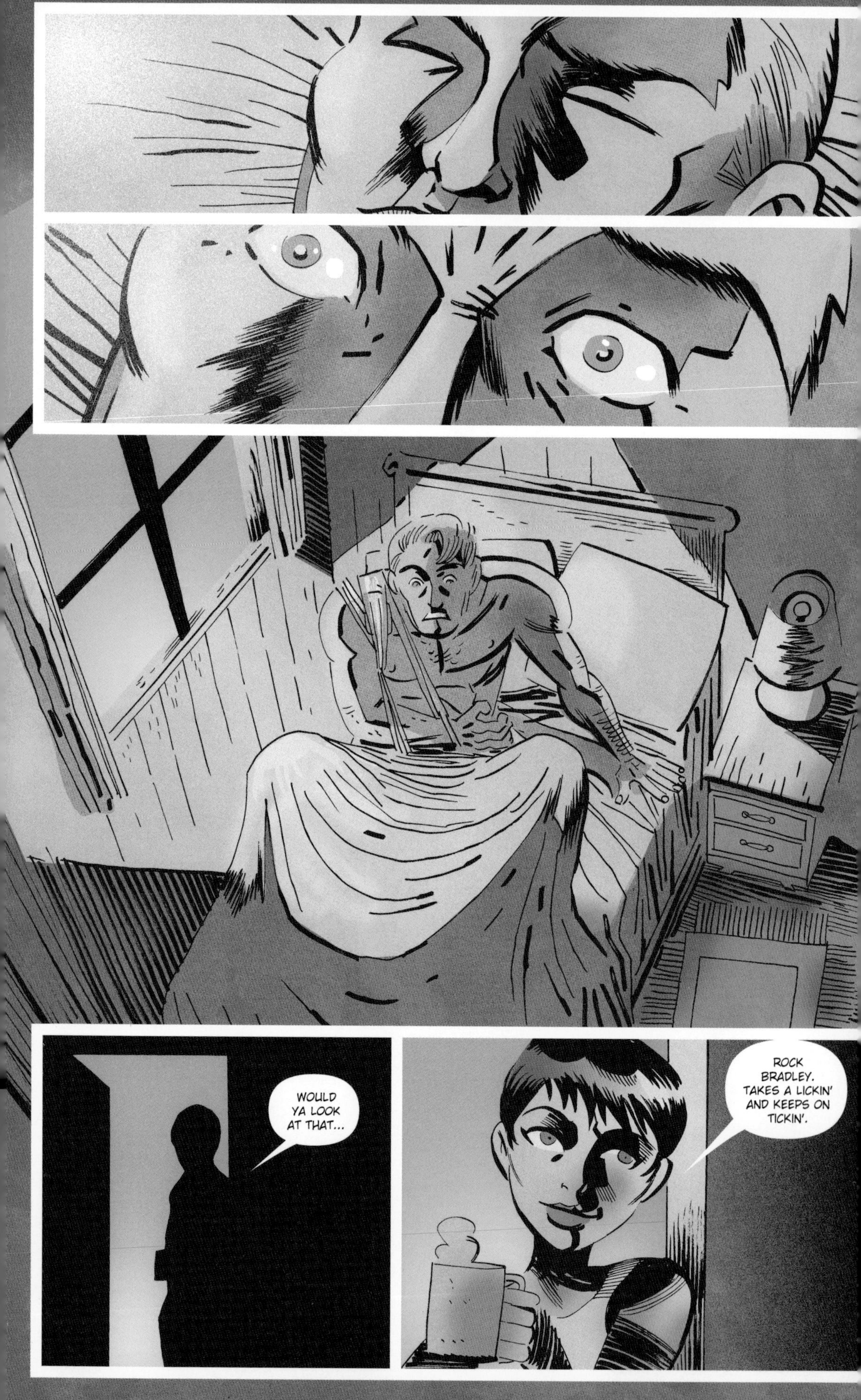
WOULD YA LOOK AT THAT...
ROCK BRADLEY. TAKES A LICKIN' AND KEEPS ON TICKIN'.

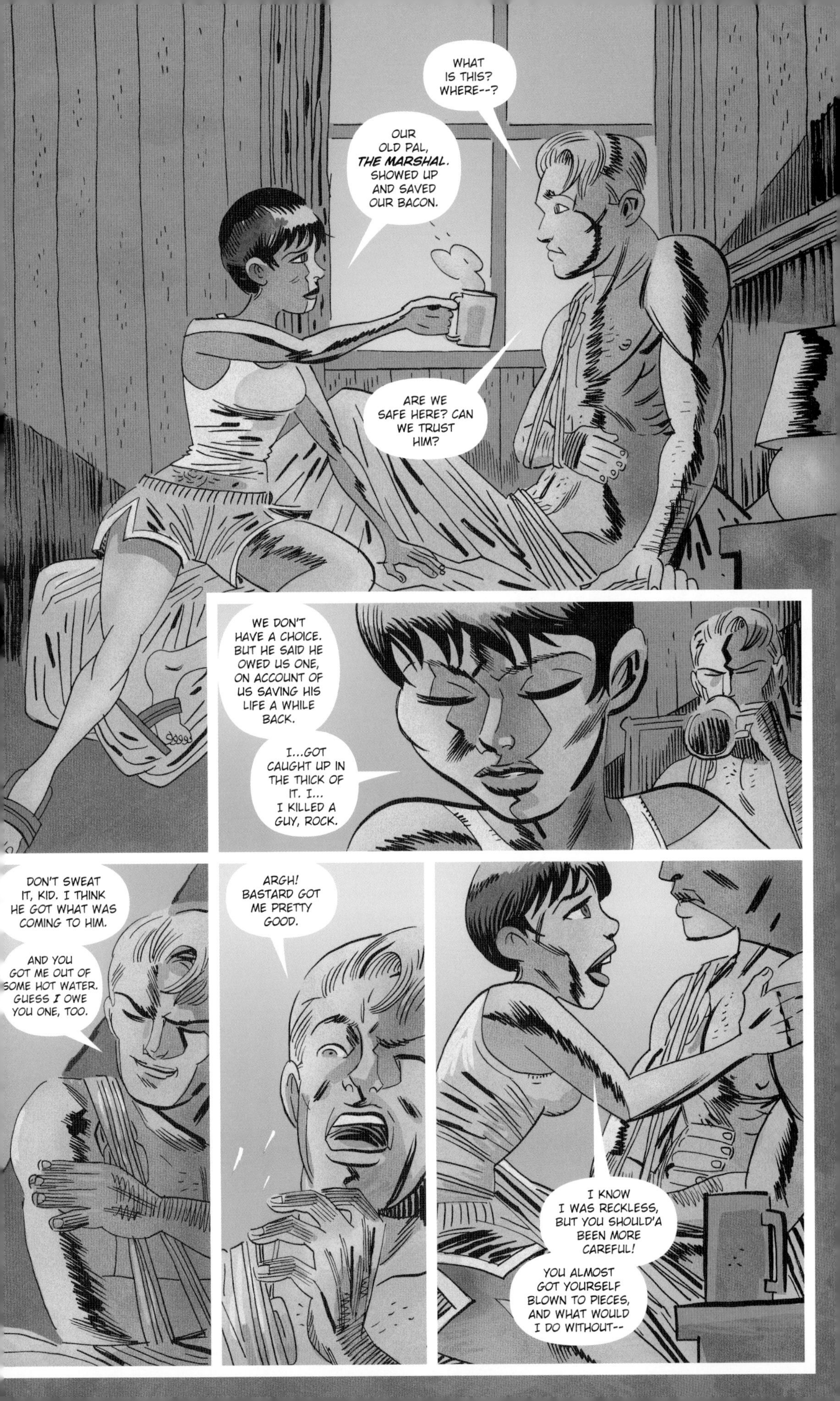
WHAT IS THIS? WHERE--?
OUR OLD PAL, THE MARSHAL. SHOWED UP AND SAVED OUR BACON.
ARE WE SAFE HERE? CAN WE TRUST HIM?
WE DON'T HAVE A CHOICE. BUT HE SAID HE OWED US ONE, ON ACCOUNT OF US SAVING HIS LIFE A WHILE BACK.
I...GOT CAUGHT UP IN THE THICK OF IT. I... I KILLED A GUY, ROCK.
DON'T SWEAT IT, KID. I THINK HE GOT WHAT WAS COMING TO HIM.
AND YOU GOT ME OUT OF SOME HOT WATER. GUESS I OWE YOU ONE, TOO.
ARGH! BASTARD GOT ME PRETTY GOOD.
I KNOW I WAS RECKLESS, BUT YOU SHOULD'A BEEN MORE CAREFUL!
YOU ALMOST GOT YOURSELF BLOWN TO PIECES, AND WHAT WOULD I DO WITHOUT--

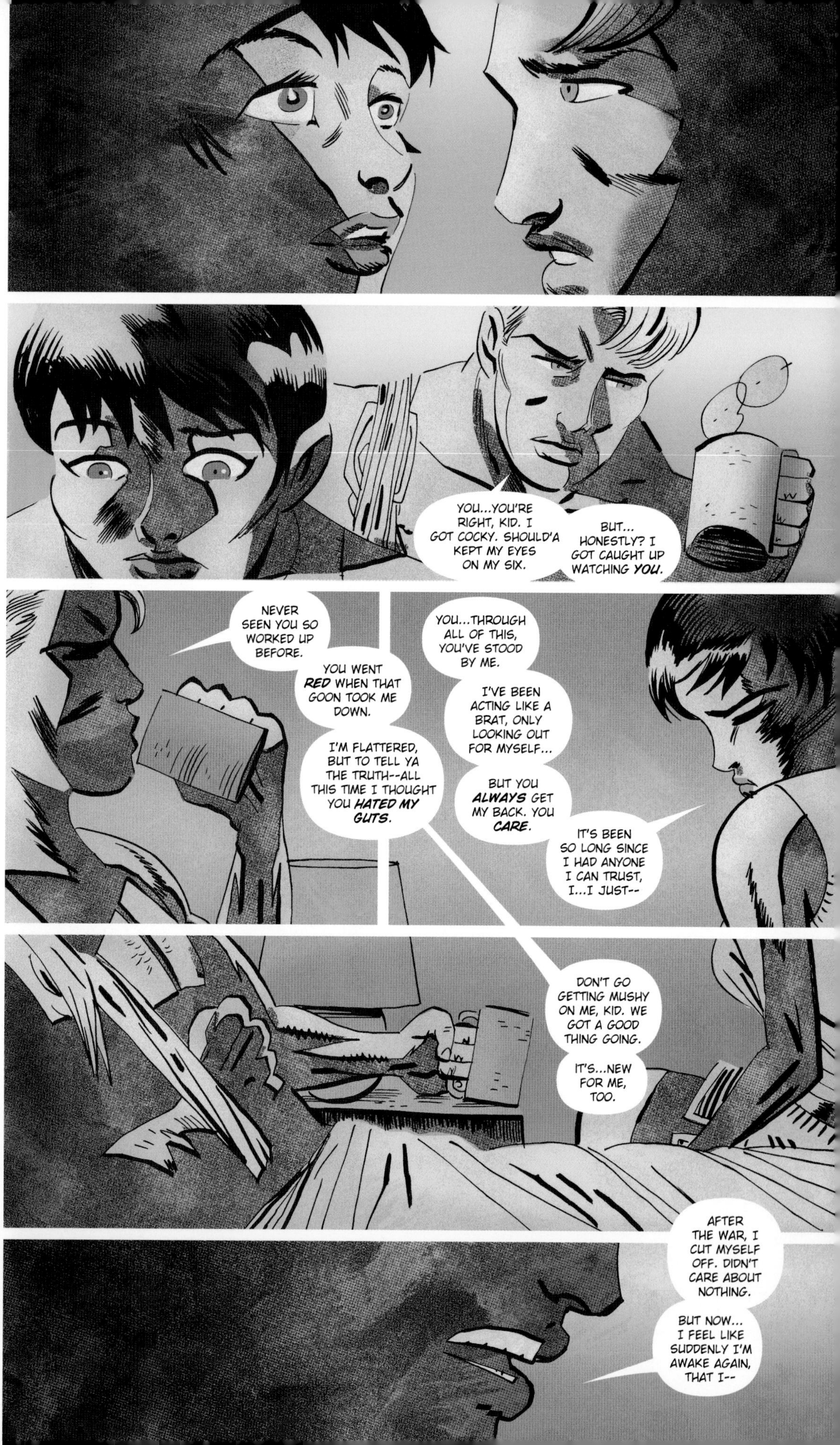
YOU...YOU'RE RIGHT, KID. I GOT COCKY. SHOULD'A KEPT MY EYES ON MY SIX.
BUT... HONESTLY? I GOT CAUGHT UP WATCHING *YOU*.
NEVER SEEN YOU SO WORKED UP BEFORE.
YOU WENT *RED* WHEN THAT GOON TOOK ME DOWN.
I'M FLATTERED, BUT TO TELL YA THE TRUTH--ALL THIS TIME I THOUGHT YOU *HATED MY GUTS*.
YOU...THROUGH ALL OF THIS, YOU'VE STOOD BY ME.
I'VE BEEN ACTING LIKE A BRAT, ONLY LOOKING OUT FOR MYSELF...
BUT YOU *ALWAYS* GET MY BACK. YOU *CARE*.
IT'S BEEN SO LONG SINCE I HAD ANYONE I CAN TRUST, I...I JUST--
DON'T GO GETTING MUSHY ON ME, KID. WE GOT A GOOD THING GOING.
IT'S...NEW FOR ME, TOO.
AFTER THE WAR, I CUT MYSELF OFF. DIDN'T CARE ABOUT NOTHING.
BUT NOW... I FEEL LIKE SUDDENLY I'M AWAKE AGAIN, THAT I--

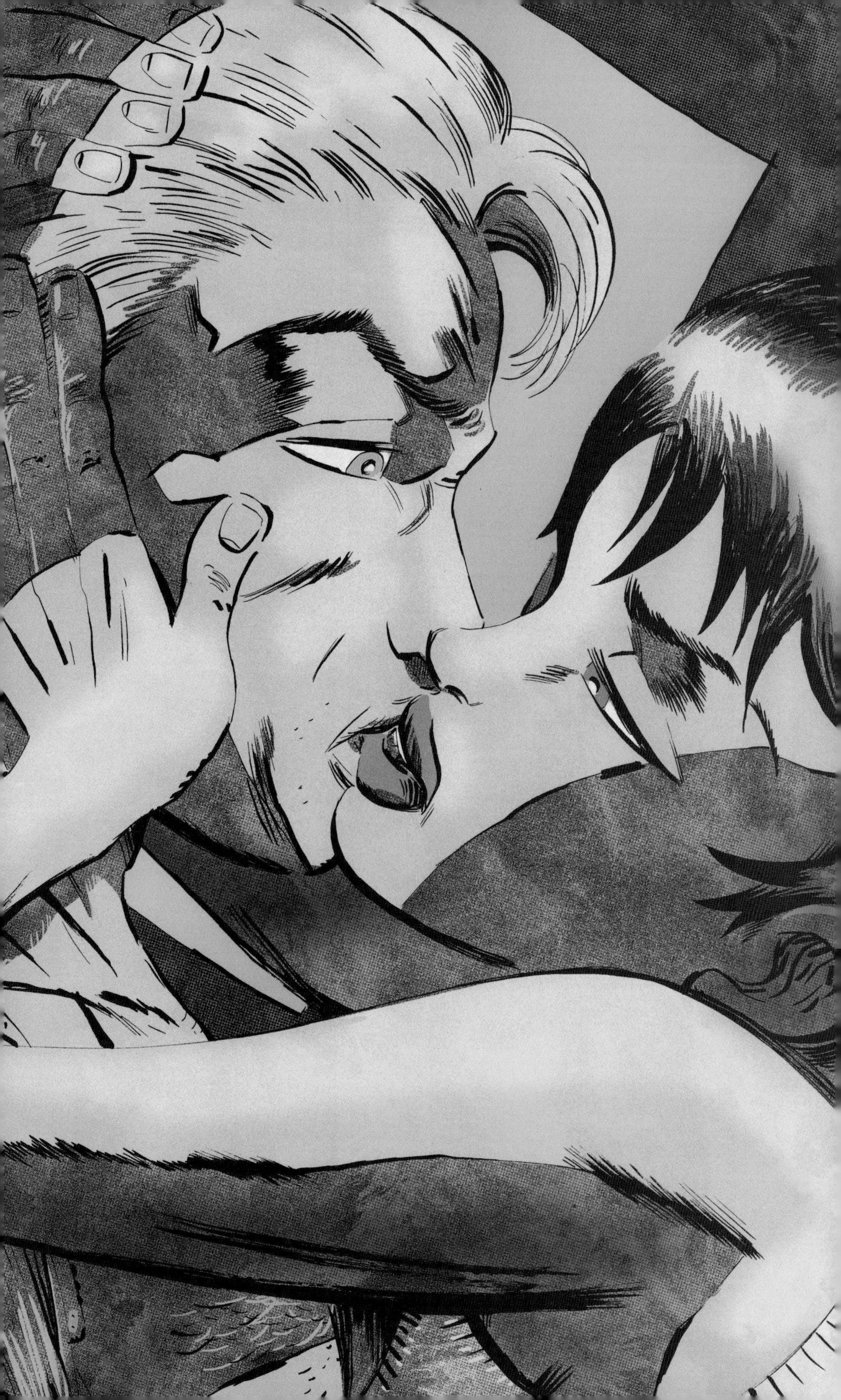

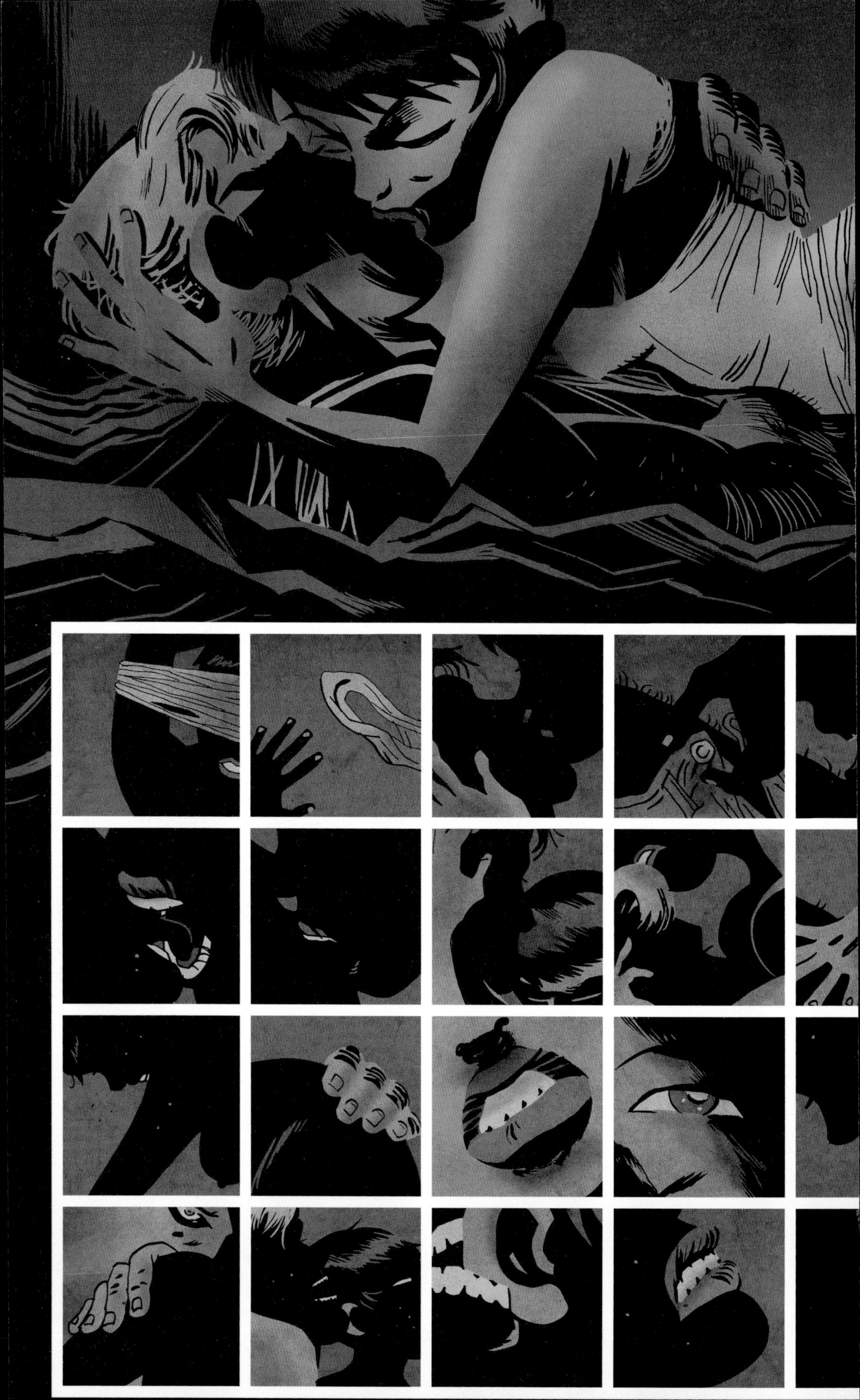

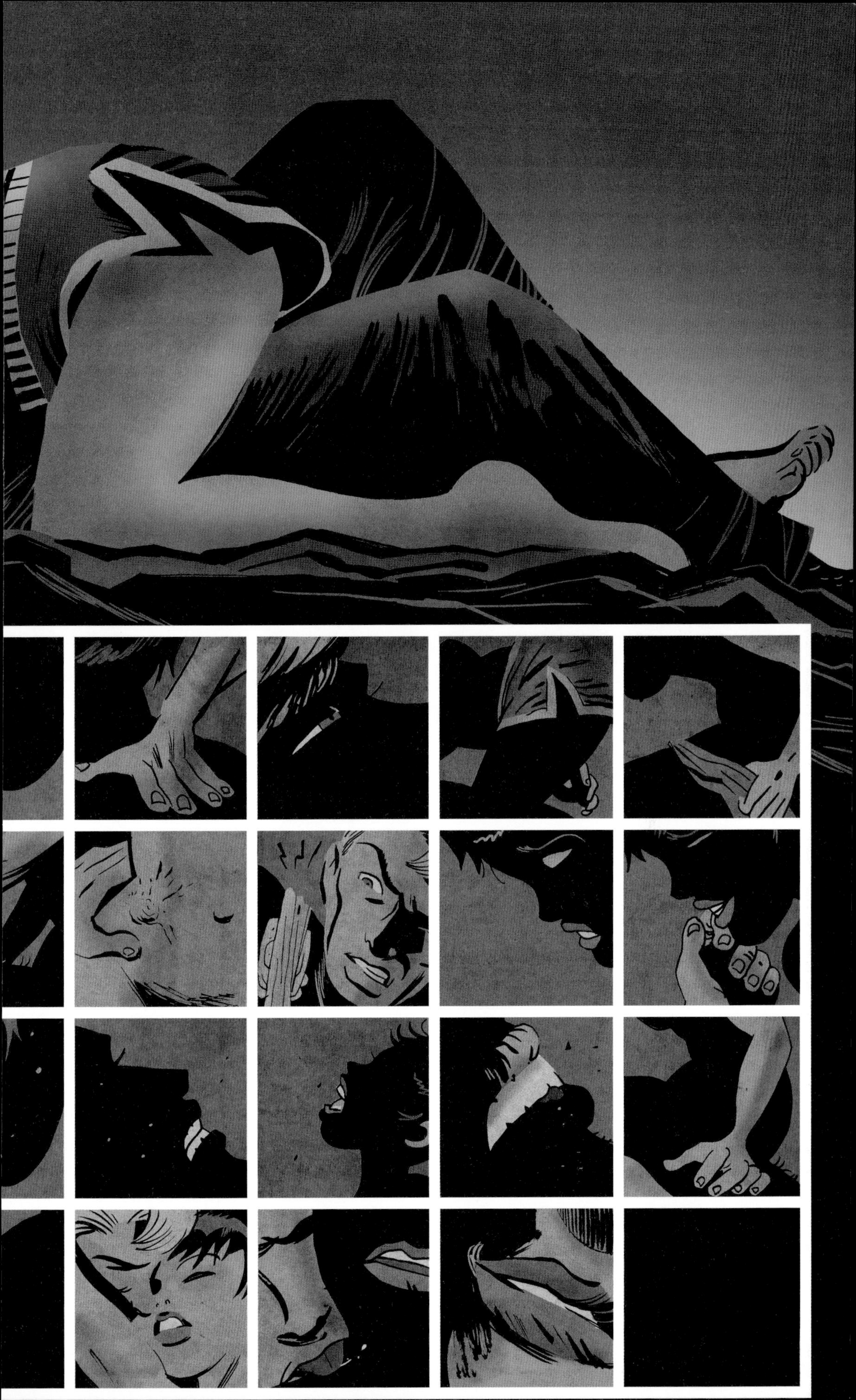

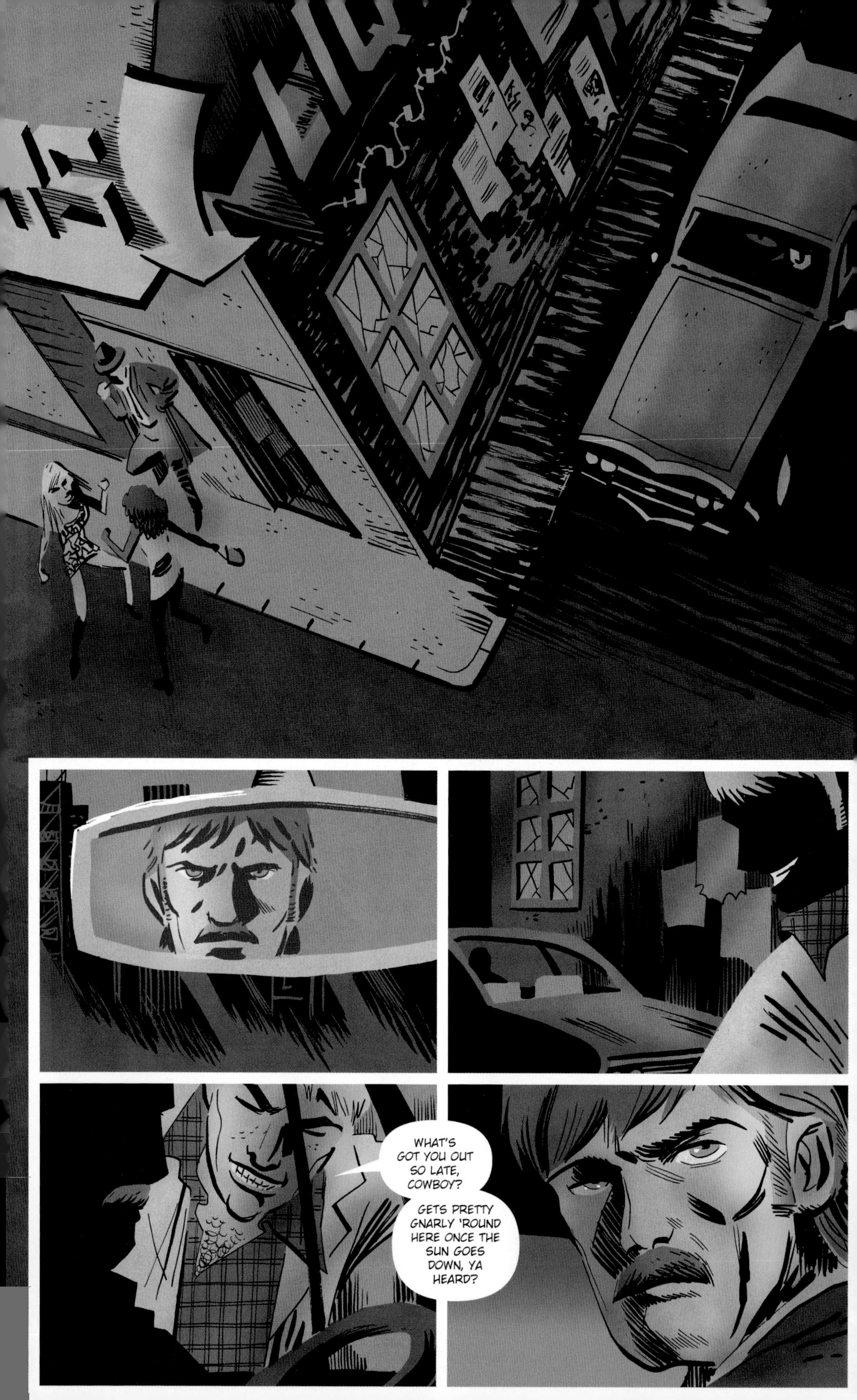
WHAT'S GOT YOU OUT SO LATE, COWBOY?
GETS PRETTY GNARLY 'ROUND HERE ONCE THE SUN GOES DOWN, YA HEARD?

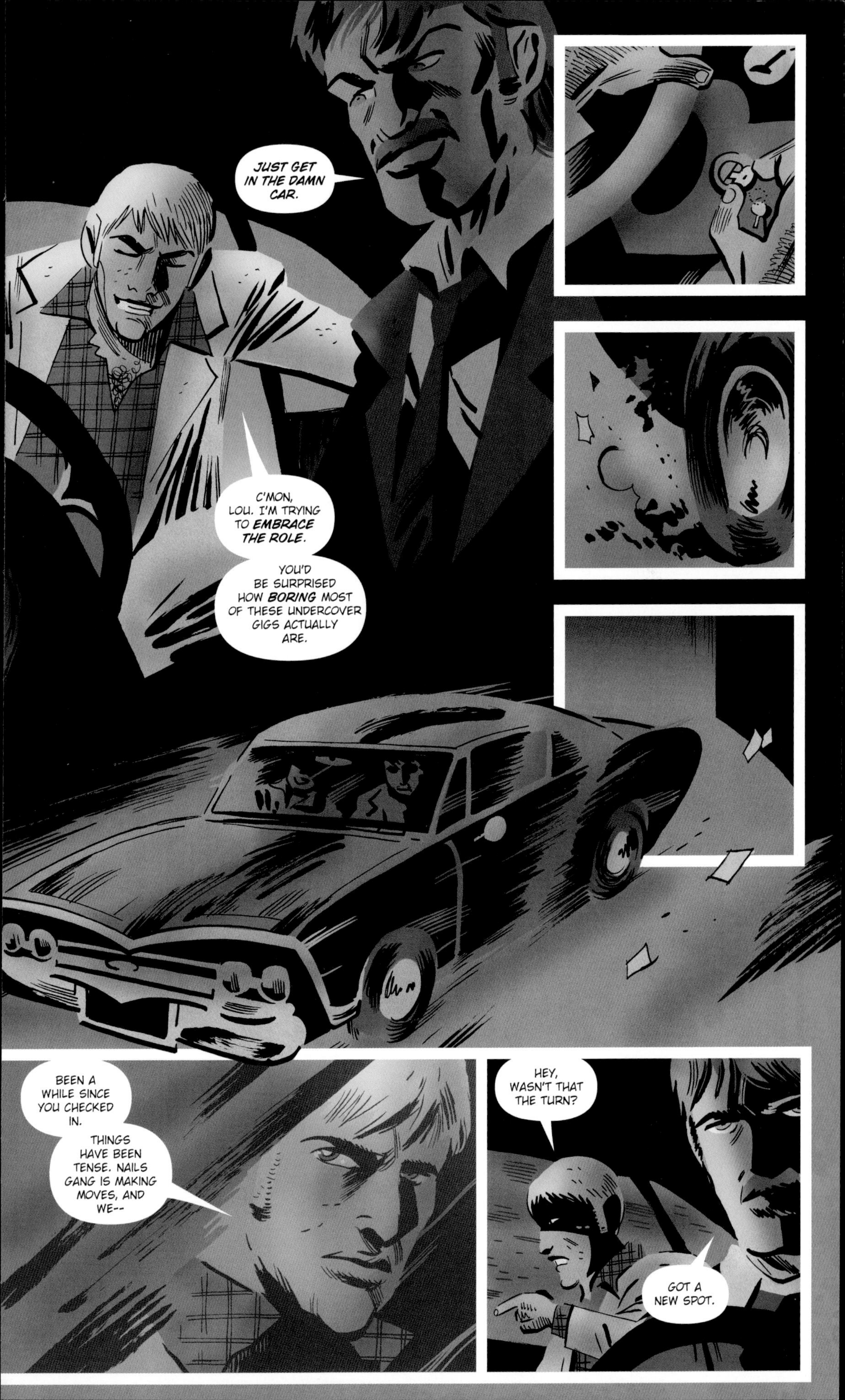
JUST GET IN THE DAMN CAR.
C'MON, LOU. I'M TRYING TO EMBRACE THE ROLE.
YOU'D BE SURPRISED HOW BORING MOST OF THESE UNDERCOVER GIGS ACTUALLY ARE.
BEEN A WHILE SINCE YOU CHECKED IN.
THINGS HAVE BEEN TENSE. NAILS GANG IS MAKING MOVES, AND WE--
HEY, WASN'T THAT THE TURN?
GOT A NEW SPOT.

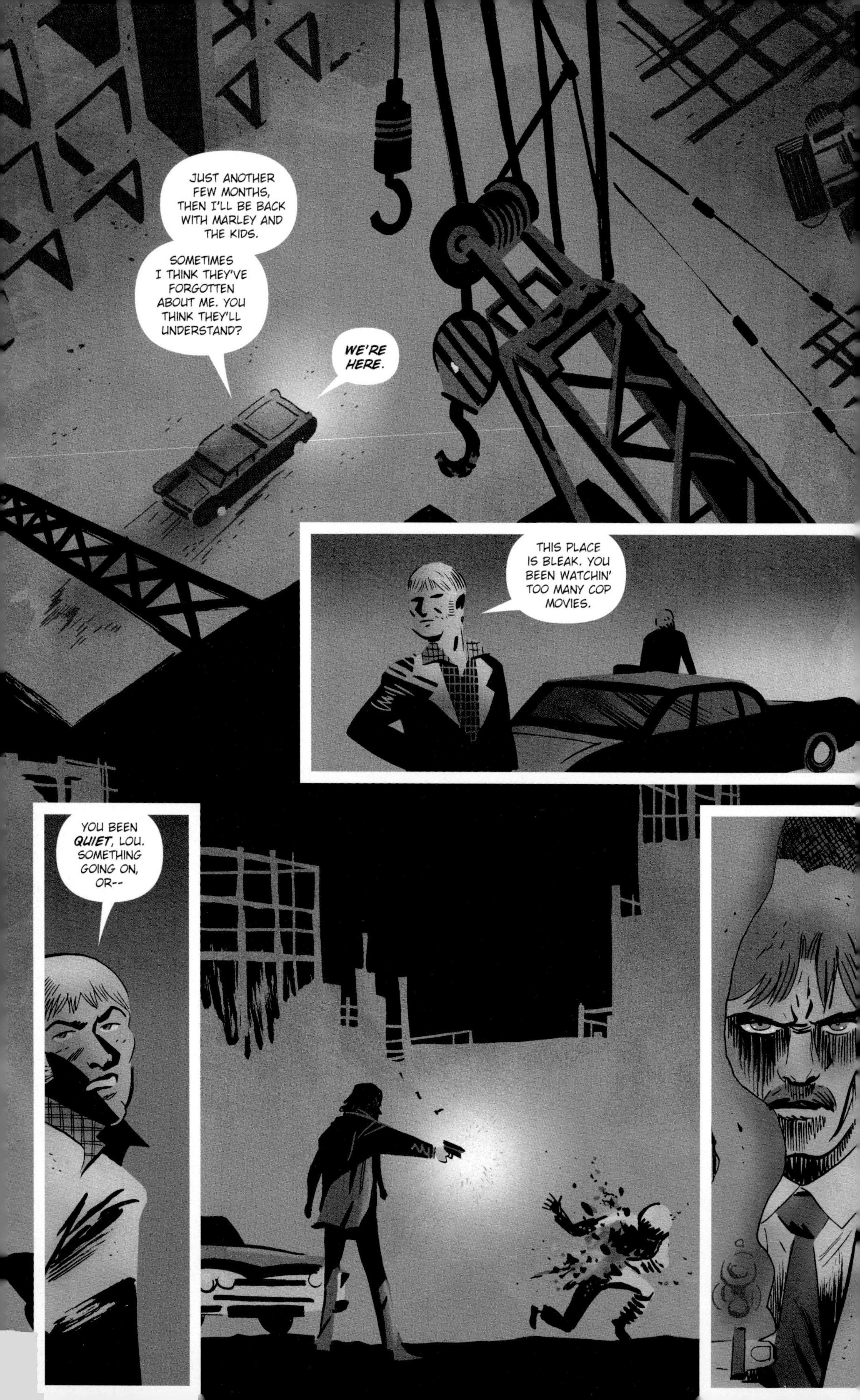
JUST ANOTHER FEW MONTHS, THEN I'LL BE BACK WITH MARLEY AND THE KIDS.
SOMETIMES I THINK THEY'VE FORGOTTEN ABOUT ME. YOU THINK THEY'LL UNDERSTAND?
WE'RE HERE.
THIS PLACE IS BLEAK. YOU BEEN WATCHIN' TOO MANY COP MOVIES.
YOU BEEN QUIET, LOU. SOMETHING GOING ON, OR--

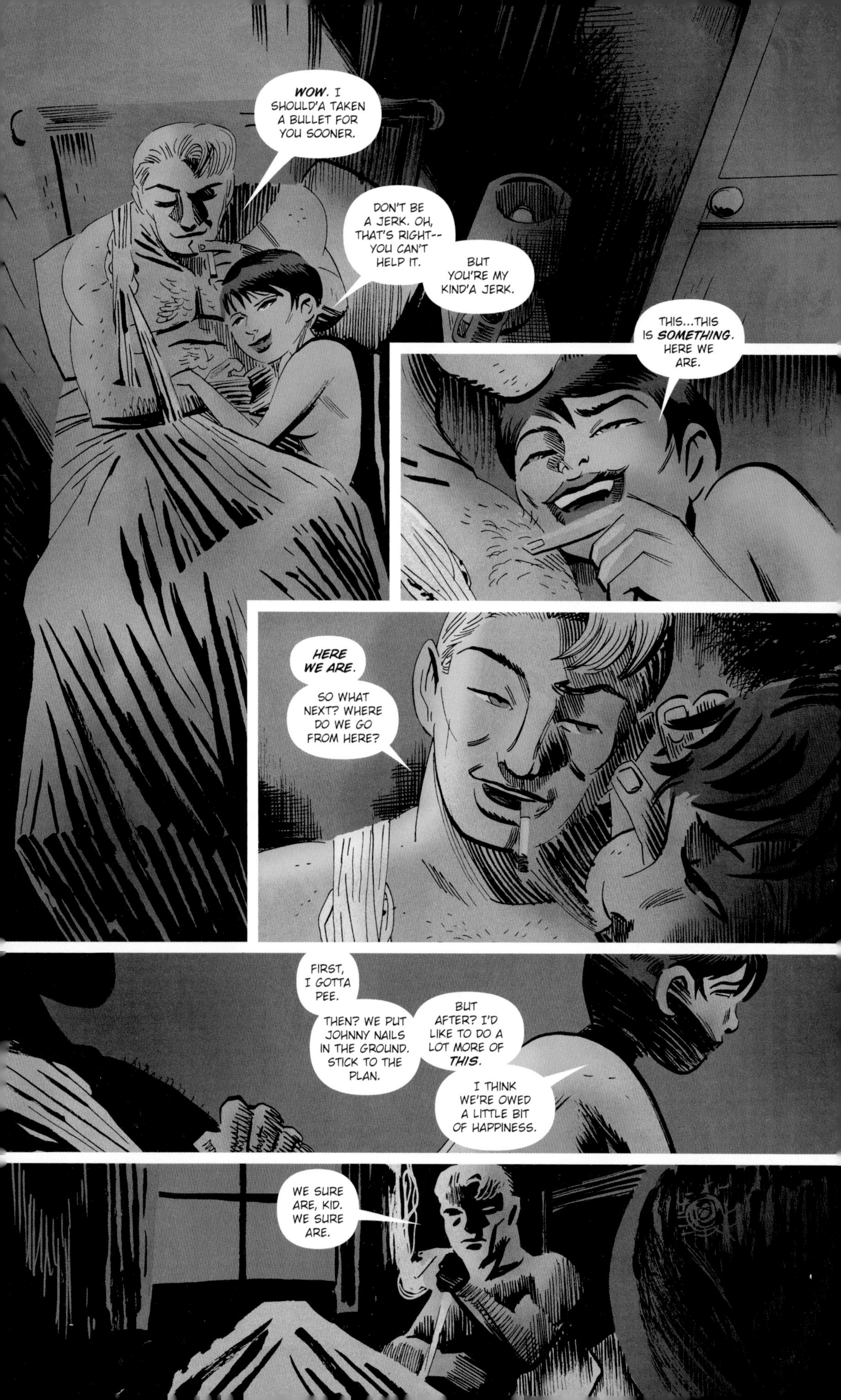
WOW. I SHOULD'A TAKEN A BULLET FOR YOU SOONER.
DON'T BE A JERK. OH, THAT'S RIGHT-- YOU CAN'T HELP IT.
BUT YOU'RE MY KIND'A JERK.
THIS...THIS IS SOMETHING. HERE WE ARE.
HERE WE ARE.
SO WHAT NEXT? WHERE DO WE GO FROM HERE?
FIRST, I GOTTA PEE.
THEN? WE PUT JOHNNY NAILS IN THE GROUND. STICK TO THE PLAN.
BUT AFTER? I'D LIKE TO DO A LOT MORE OF THIS.
I THINK WE'RE OWED A LITTLE BIT OF HAPPINESS.
WE SURE ARE, KID. WE SURE ARE.

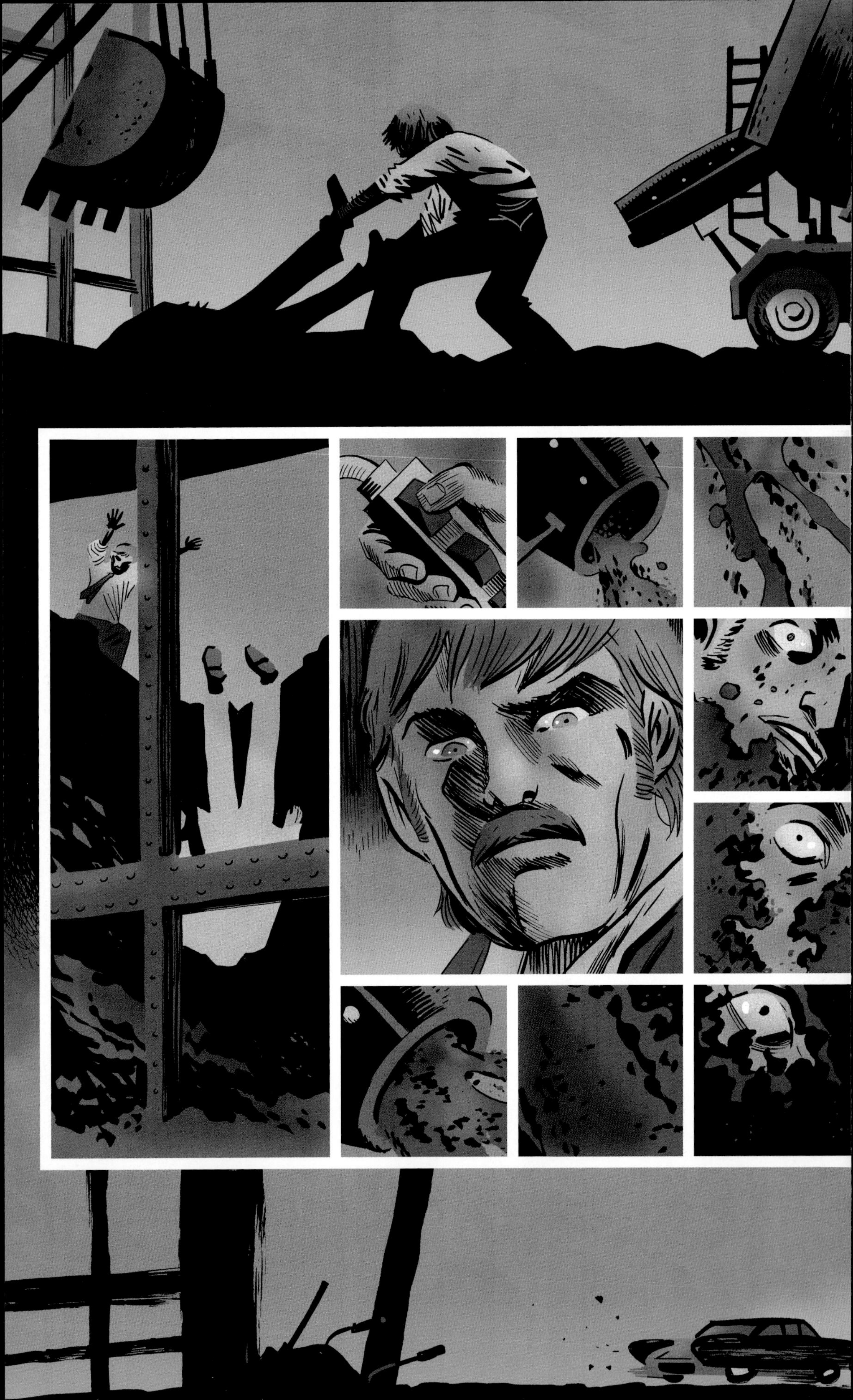

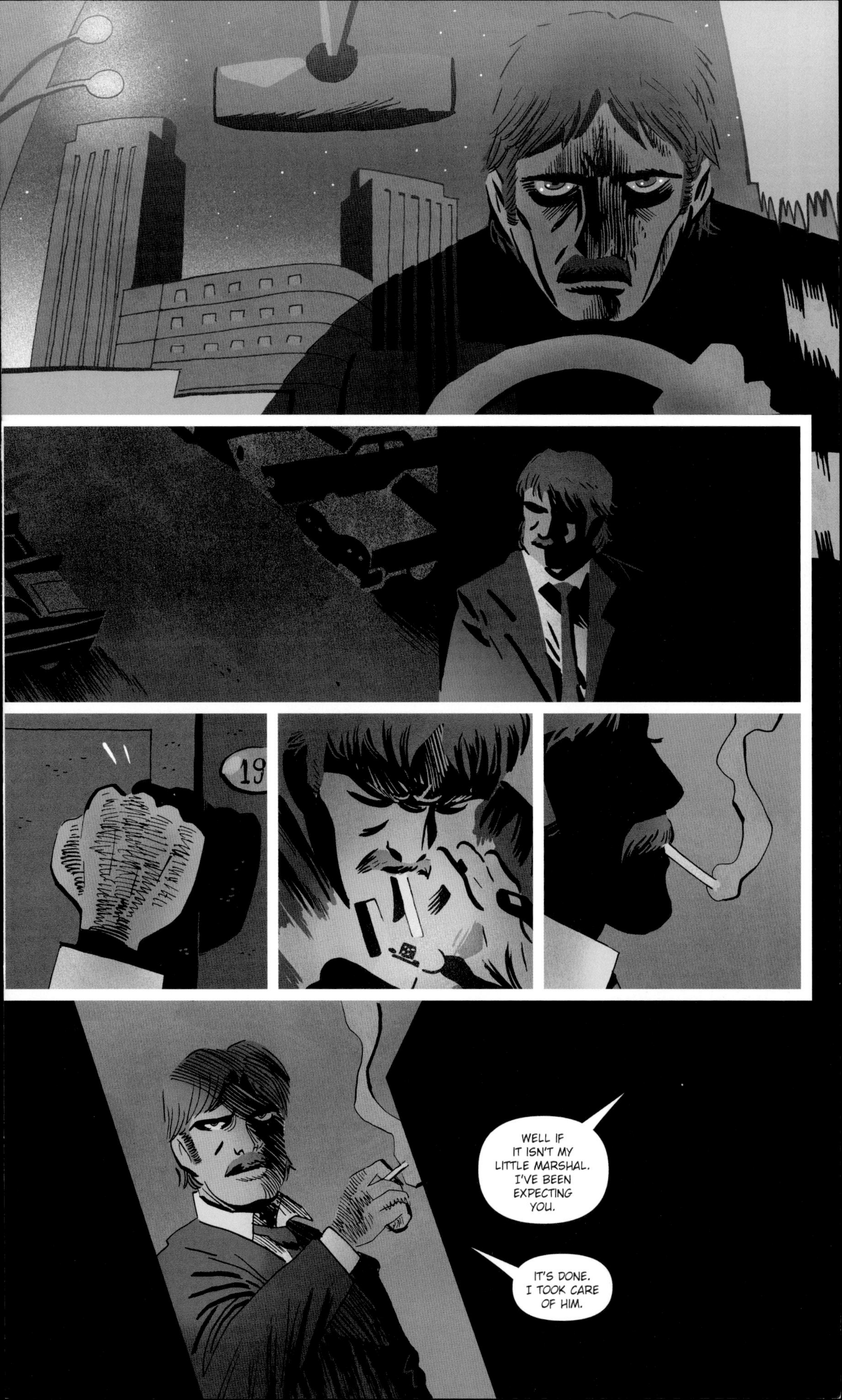
19
WELL IF IT ISN'T MY LITTLE MARSHAL. I'VE BEEN EXPECTING YOU.
IT'S DONE. I TOOK CARE OF HIM.

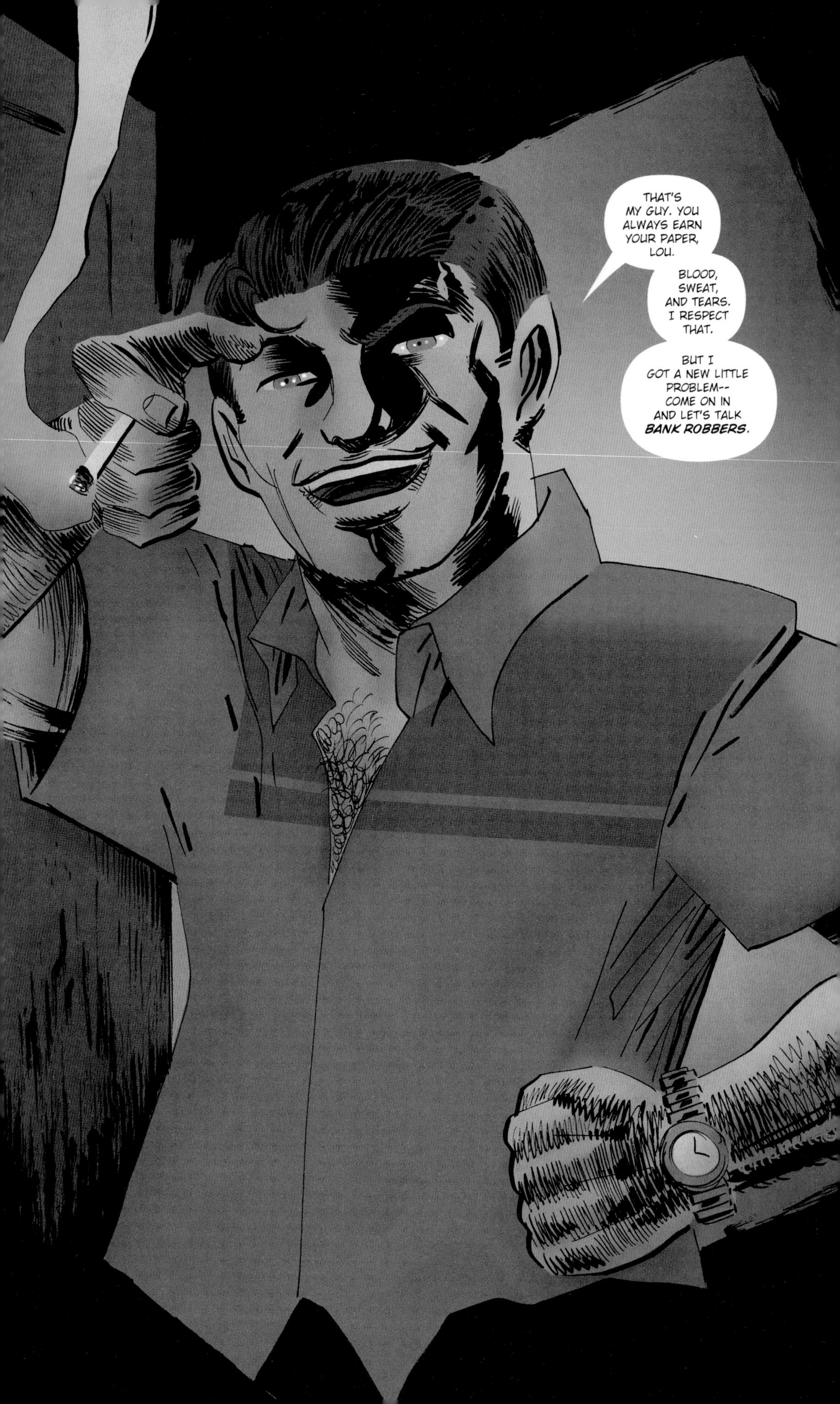
THAT'S MY GUY. YOU ALWAYS EARN YOUR PAPER, LOU.
BLOOD, SWEAT, AND TEARS. I RESPECT THAT.
BUT I GOT A NEW LITTLE PROBLEM-- COME ON IN AND LET'S TALK *BANK ROBBERS*.

CHAPTER NINE

"PRETTY LITTLE TRAGEDY"

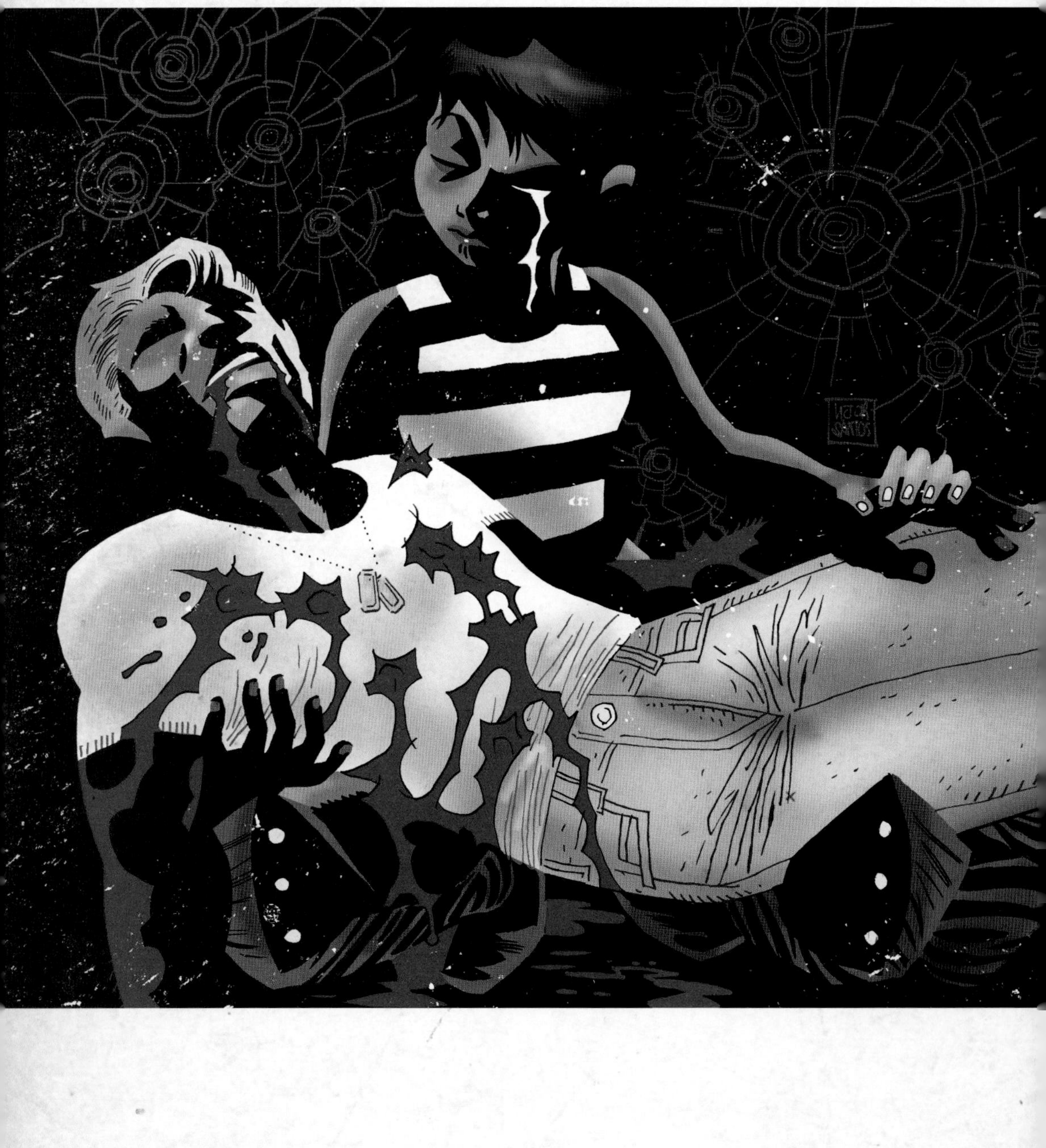

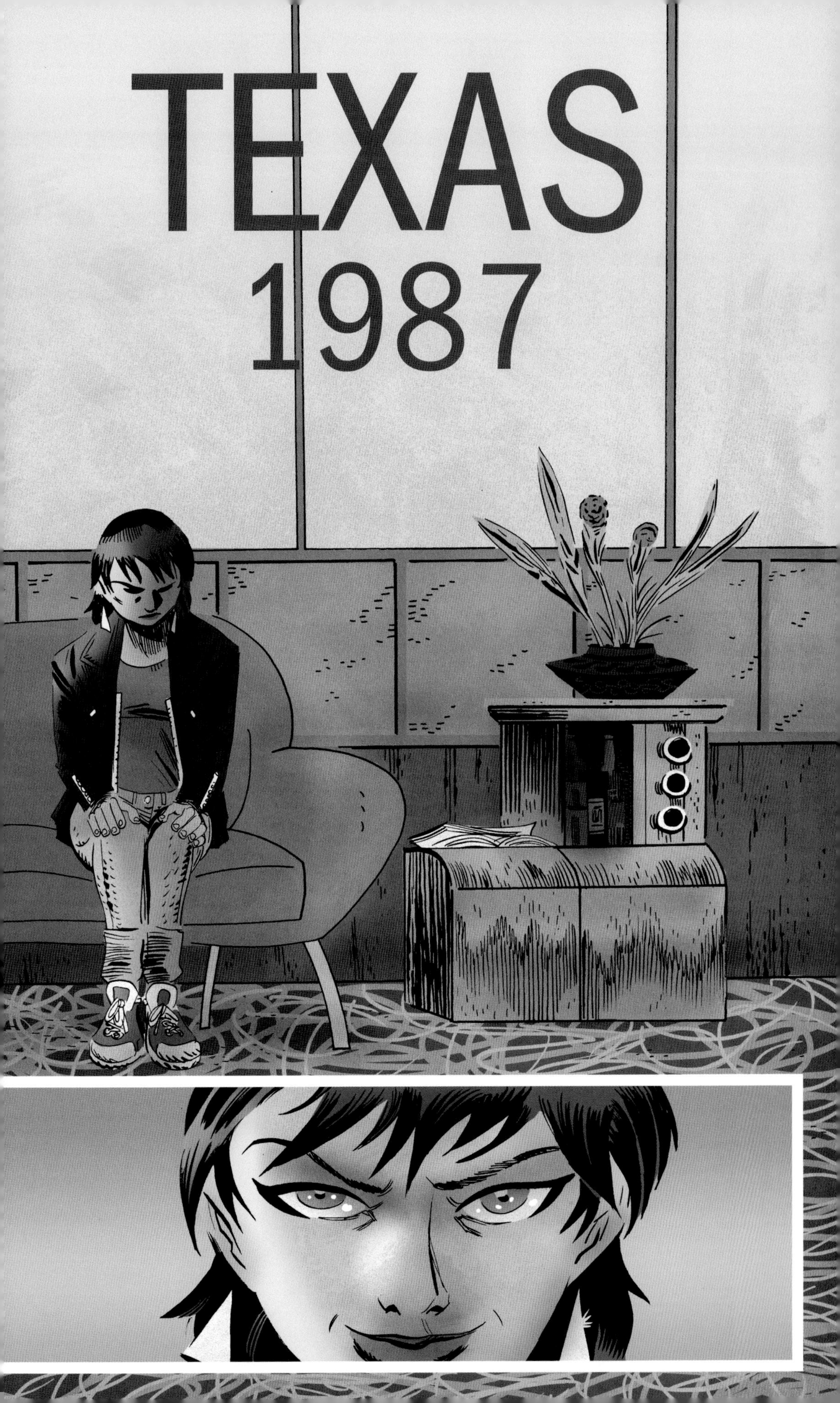
TEXAS
1987

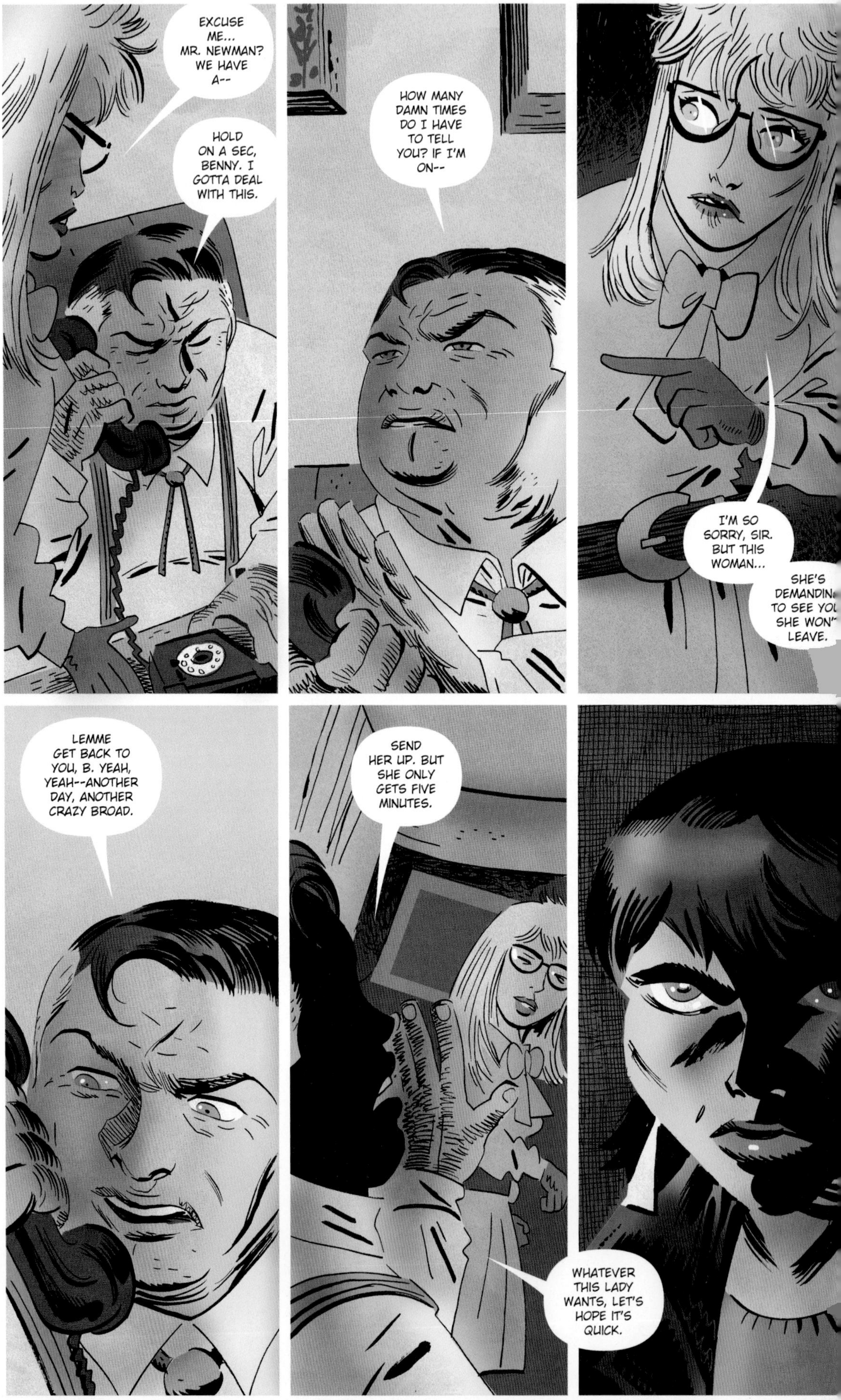
EXCUSE ME... MR. NEWMAN? WE HAVE A--
HOLD ON A SEC, BENNY. I GOTTA DEAL WITH THIS.
HOW MANY DAMN TIMES DO I HAVE TO TELL YOU? IF I'M ON--
I'M SO SORRY, SIR. BUT THIS WOMAN...
SHE'S DEMANDIN TO SEE YO SHE WON' LEAVE.
LEMME GET BACK TO YOU, B. YEAH, YEAH--ANOTHER DAY, ANOTHER CRAZY BROAD.
SEND HER UP. BUT SHE ONLY GETS FIVE MINUTES.
WHATEVER THIS LADY WANTS, LET'S HOPE IT'S QUICK.

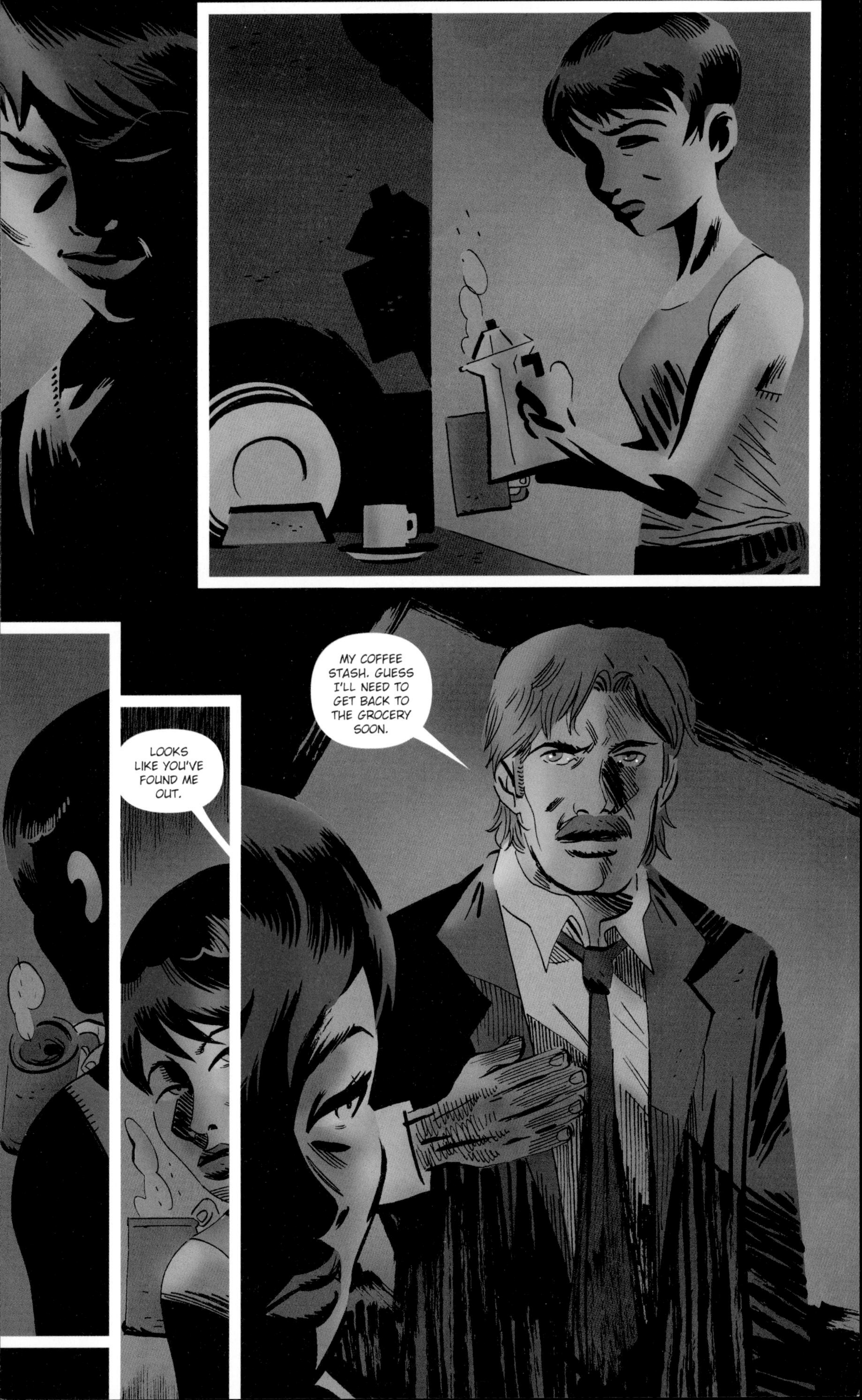
MY COFFEE STASH. GUESS I'LL NEED TO GET BACK TO THE GROCERY SOON.
LOOKS LIKE YOU'VE FOUND ME OUT.

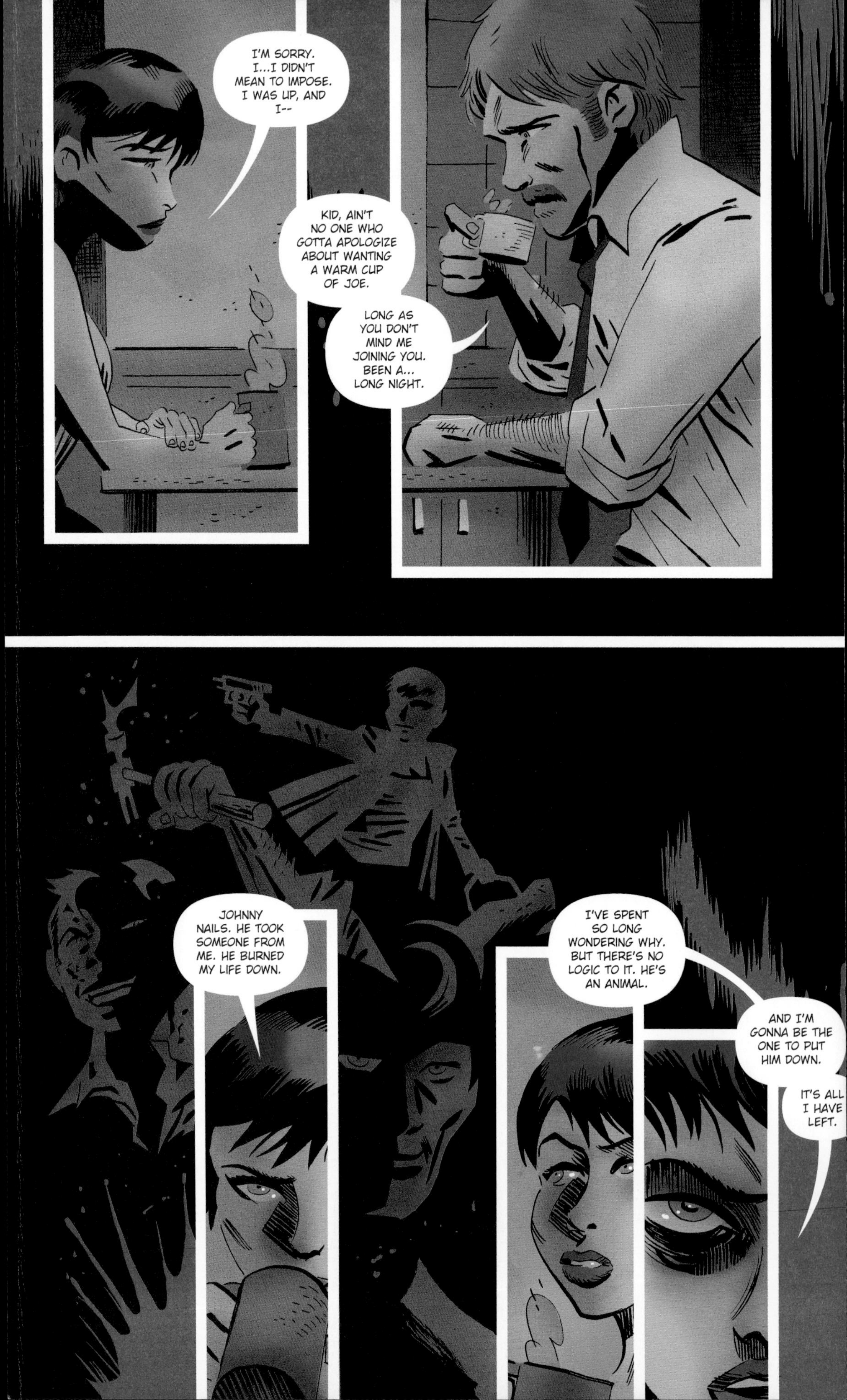
I'M SORRY. I...I DIDN'T MEAN TO IMPOSE. I WAS UP, AND I--
KID, AIN'T NO ONE WHO GOTTA APOLOGIZE ABOUT WANTING A WARM CUP OF JOE.
LONG AS YOU DON'T MIND ME JOINING YOU. BEEN A... LONG NIGHT.
JOHNNY NAILS. HE TOOK SOMEONE FROM ME. HE BURNED MY LIFE DOWN.
I'VE SPENT SO LONG WONDERING WHY. BUT THERE'S NO LOGIC TO IT. HE'S AN ANIMAL.
AND I'M GONNA BE THE ONE TO PUT HIM DOWN.
IT'S ALL I HAVE LEFT.

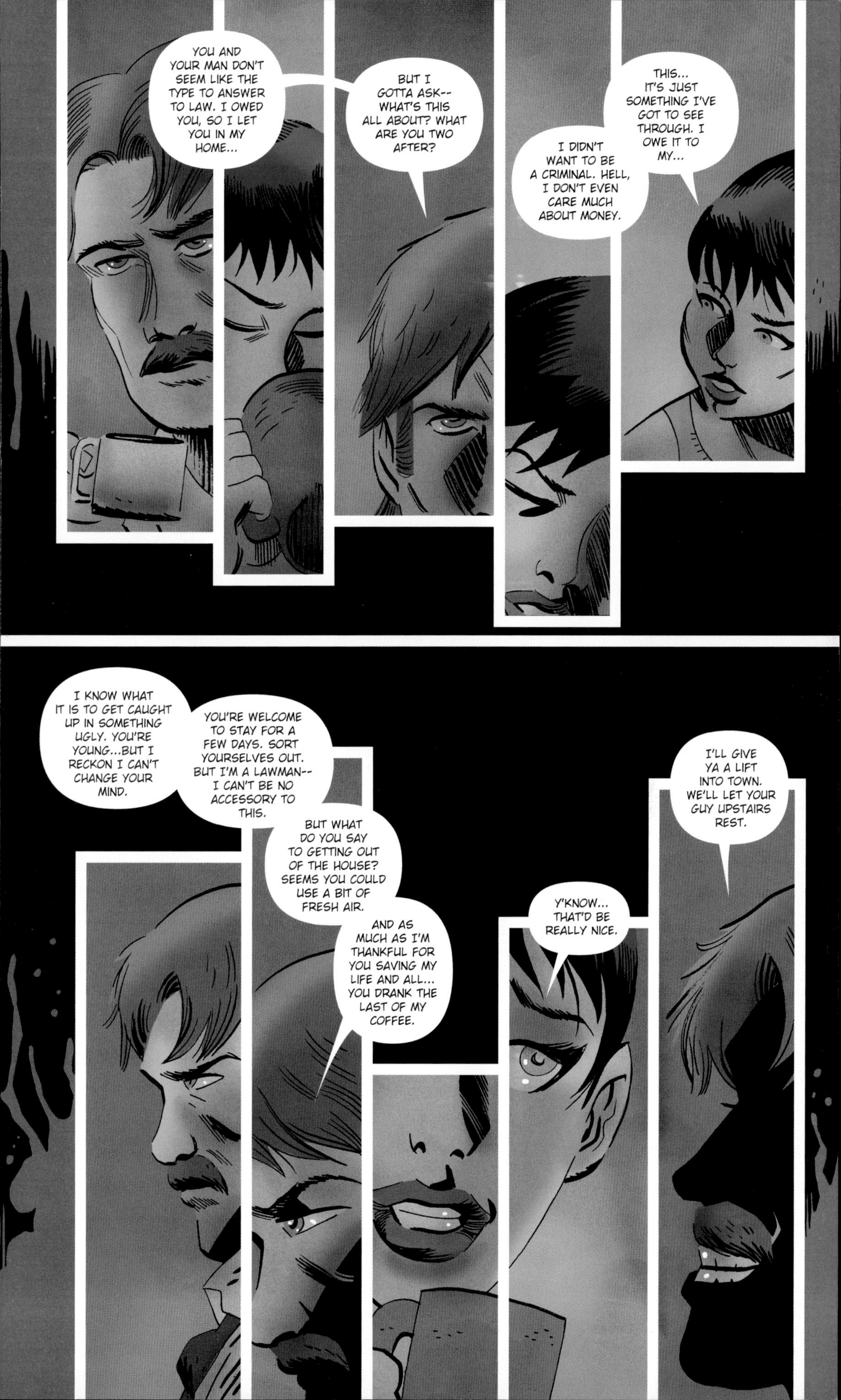

YOU AND YOUR MAN DON'T SEEM LIKE THE TYPE TO ANSWER TO LAW. I OWED YOU, SO I LET YOU IN MY HOME...
BUT I GOTTA ASK-- WHAT'S THIS ALL ABOUT? WHAT ARE YOU TWO AFTER?
I DIDN'T WANT TO BE A CRIMINAL. HELL, I DON'T EVEN CARE MUCH ABOUT MONEY.
THIS... IT'S JUST SOMETHING I'VE GOT TO SEE THROUGH. I OWE IT TO MY...
I KNOW WHAT IT IS TO GET CAUGHT UP IN SOMETHING UGLY. YOU'RE YOUNG...BUT I RECKON I CAN'T CHANGE YOUR MIND.
YOU'RE WELCOME TO STAY FOR A FEW DAYS. SORT YOURSELVES OUT. BUT I'M A LAWMAN-- I CAN'T BE NO ACCESSORY TO THIS.
BUT WHAT DO YOU SAY TO GETTING OUT OF THE HOUSE? SEEMS YOU COULD USE A BIT OF FRESH AIR.
AND AS MUCH AS I'M THANKFUL FOR YOU SAVING MY LIFE AND ALL... YOU DRANK THE LAST OF MY COFFEE.
Y'KNOW... THAT'D BE REALLY NICE.
I'LL GIVE YA A LIFT INTO TOWN. WE'LL LET YOUR GUY UPSTAIRS REST.

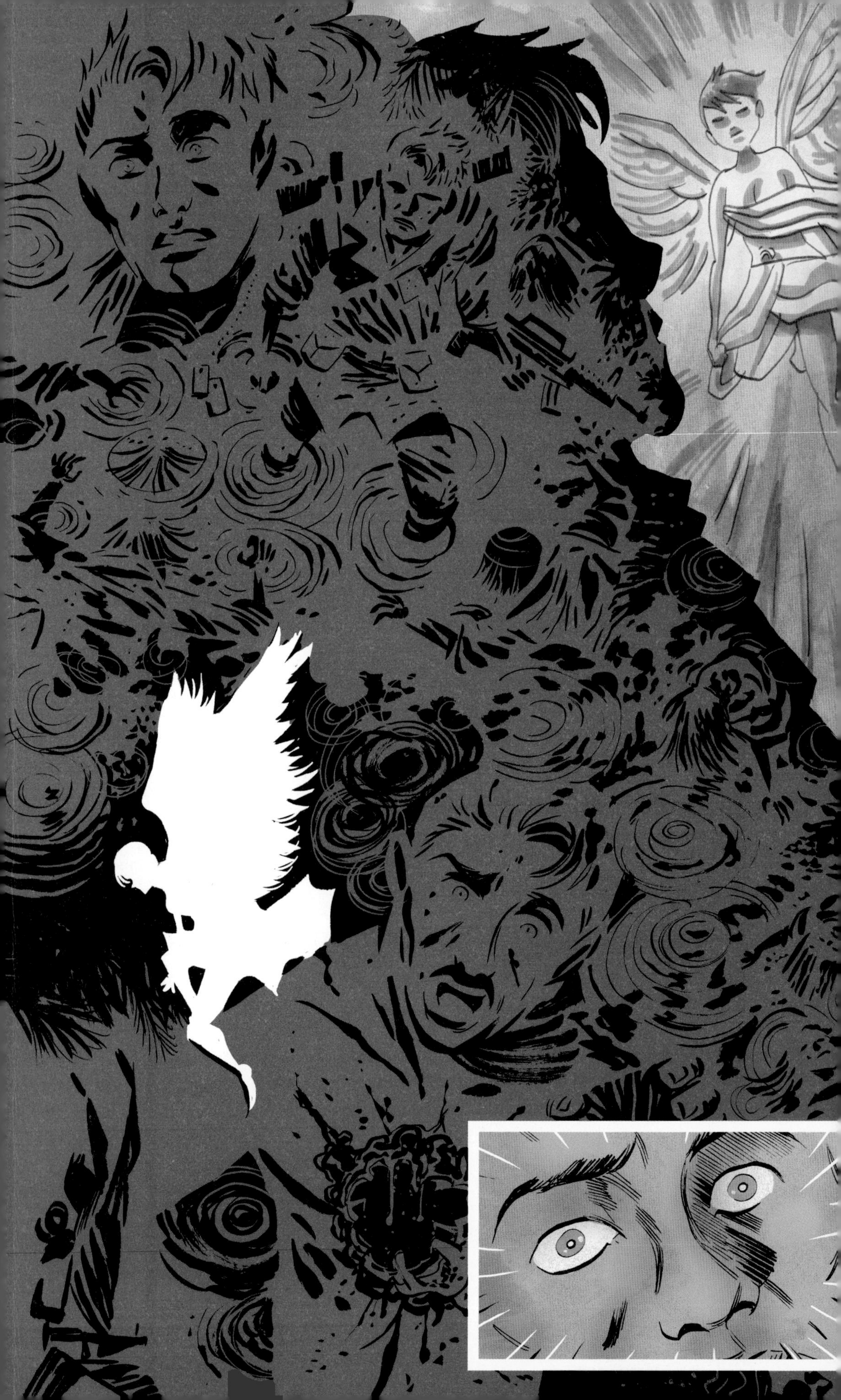

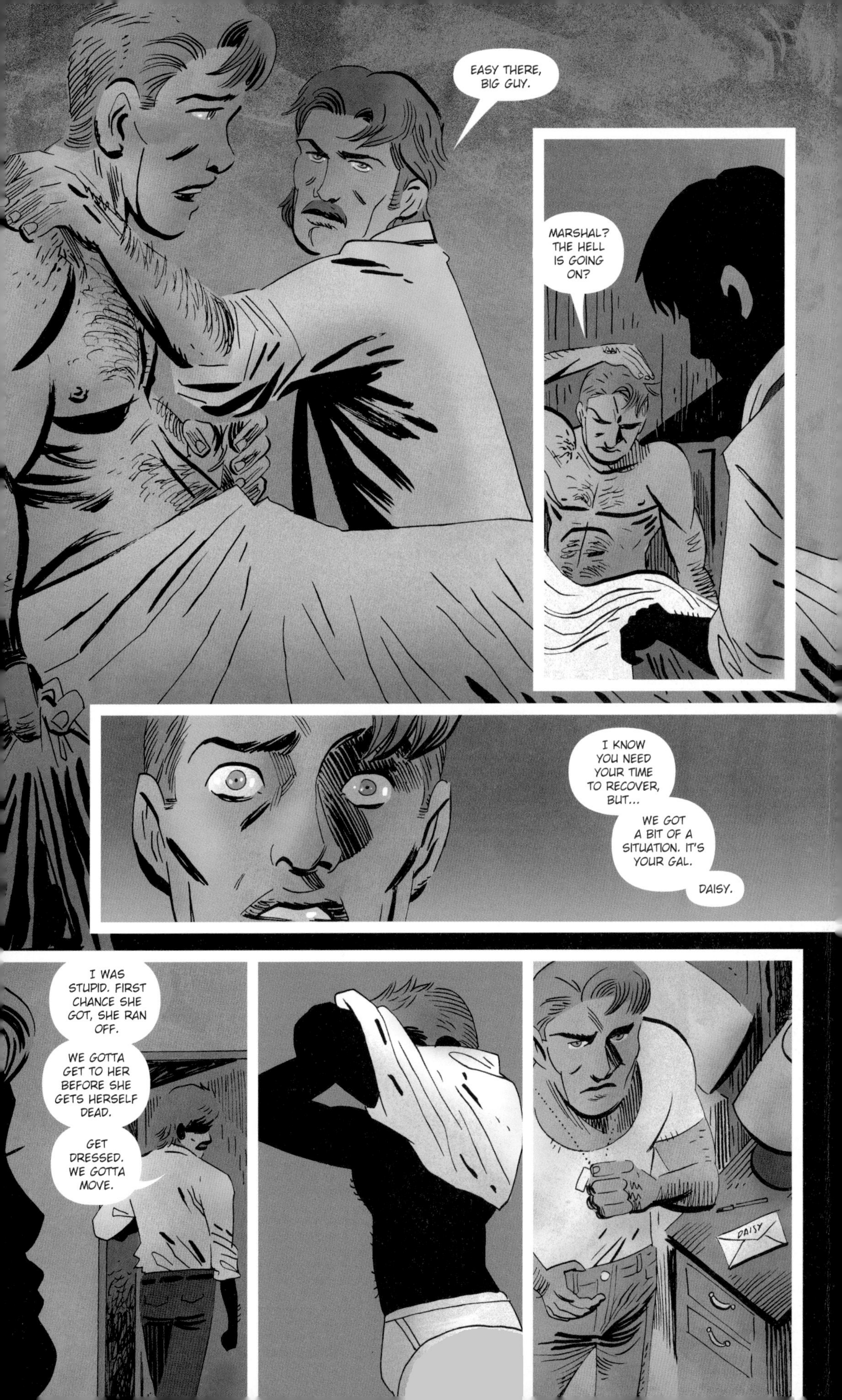
EASY THERE, BIG GUY.
MARSHAL? THE HELL IS GOING ON?
I KNOW YOU NEED YOUR TIME TO RECOVER, BUT...
WE GOT A BIT OF A SITUATION. IT'S YOUR GAL.
DAISY.
I WAS STUPID. FIRST CHANCE SHE GOT, SHE RAN OFF.
WE GOTTA GET TO HER BEFORE SHE GETS HERSELF DEAD.
GET DRESSED. WE GOTTA MOVE.
DAISY

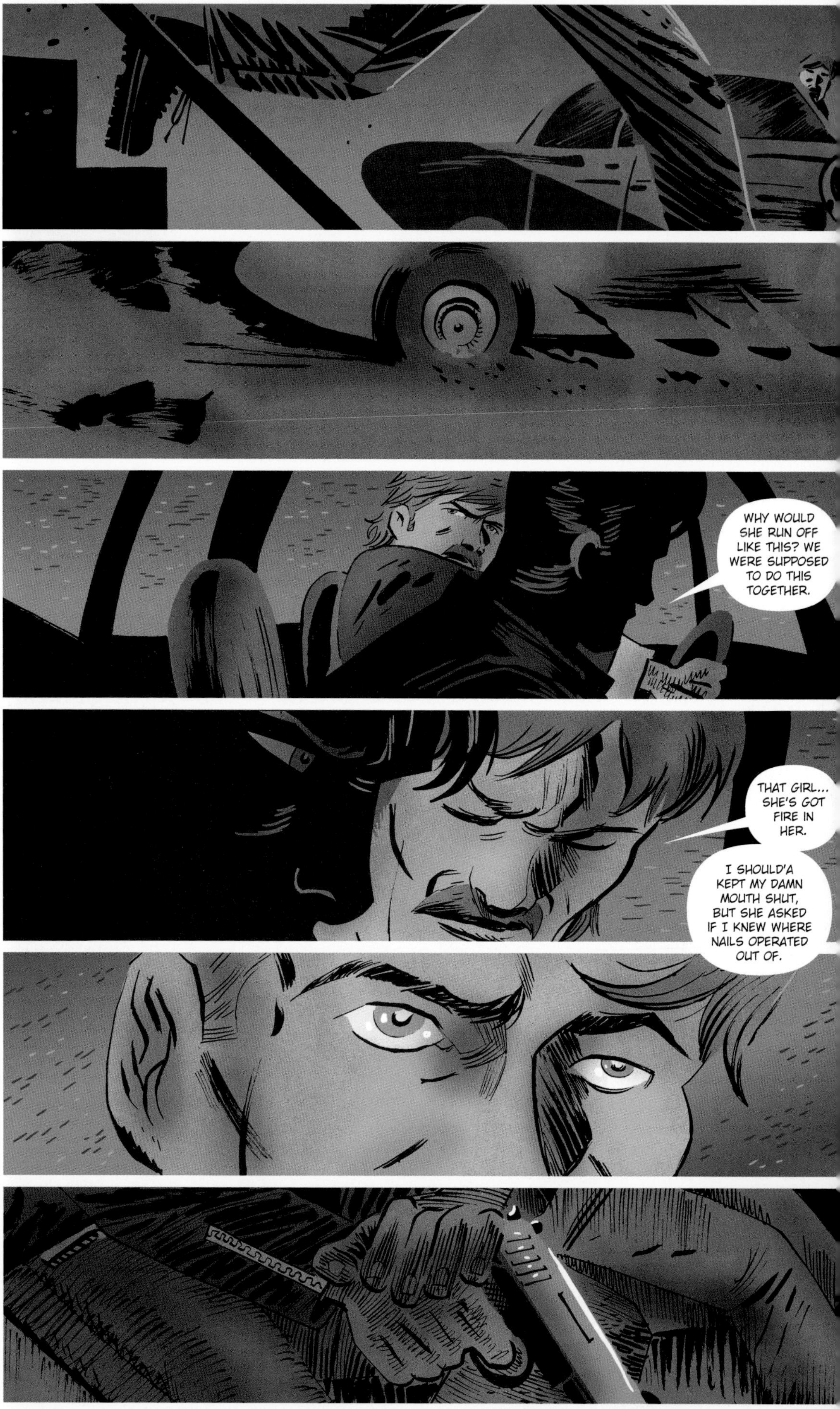
WHY WOULD SHE RUN OFF LIKE THIS? WE WERE SUPPOSED TO DO THIS TOGETHER.
THAT GIRL... SHE'S GOT FIRE IN HER.
I SHOULD'A KEPT MY DAMN MOUTH SHUT, BUT SHE ASKED IF I KNEW WHERE NAILS OPERATED OUT OF.

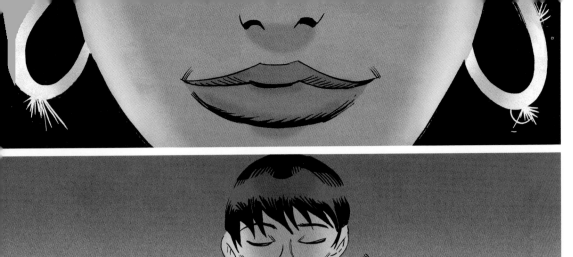
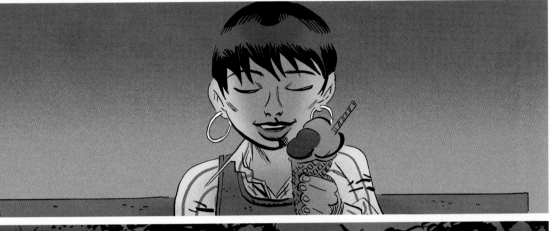

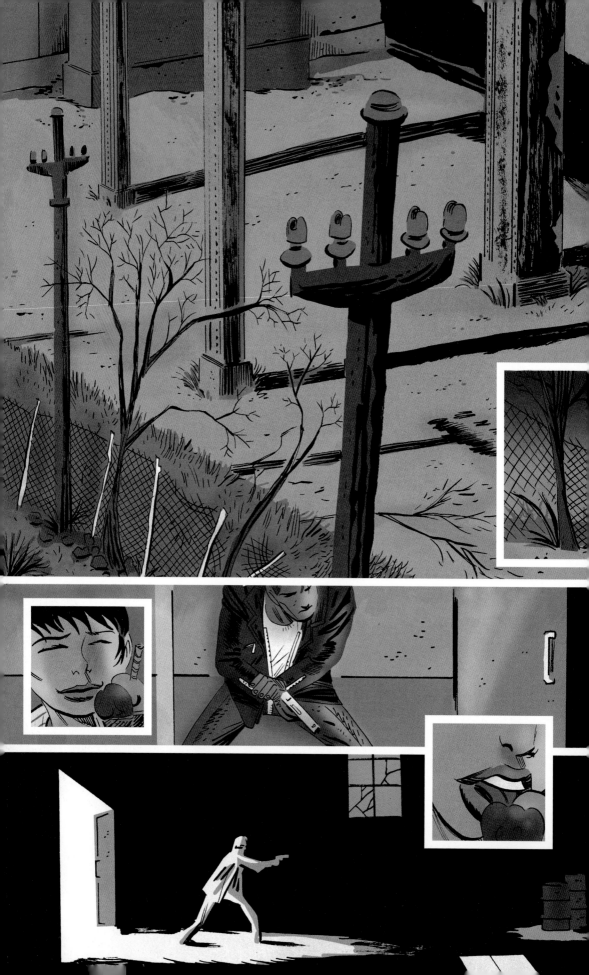

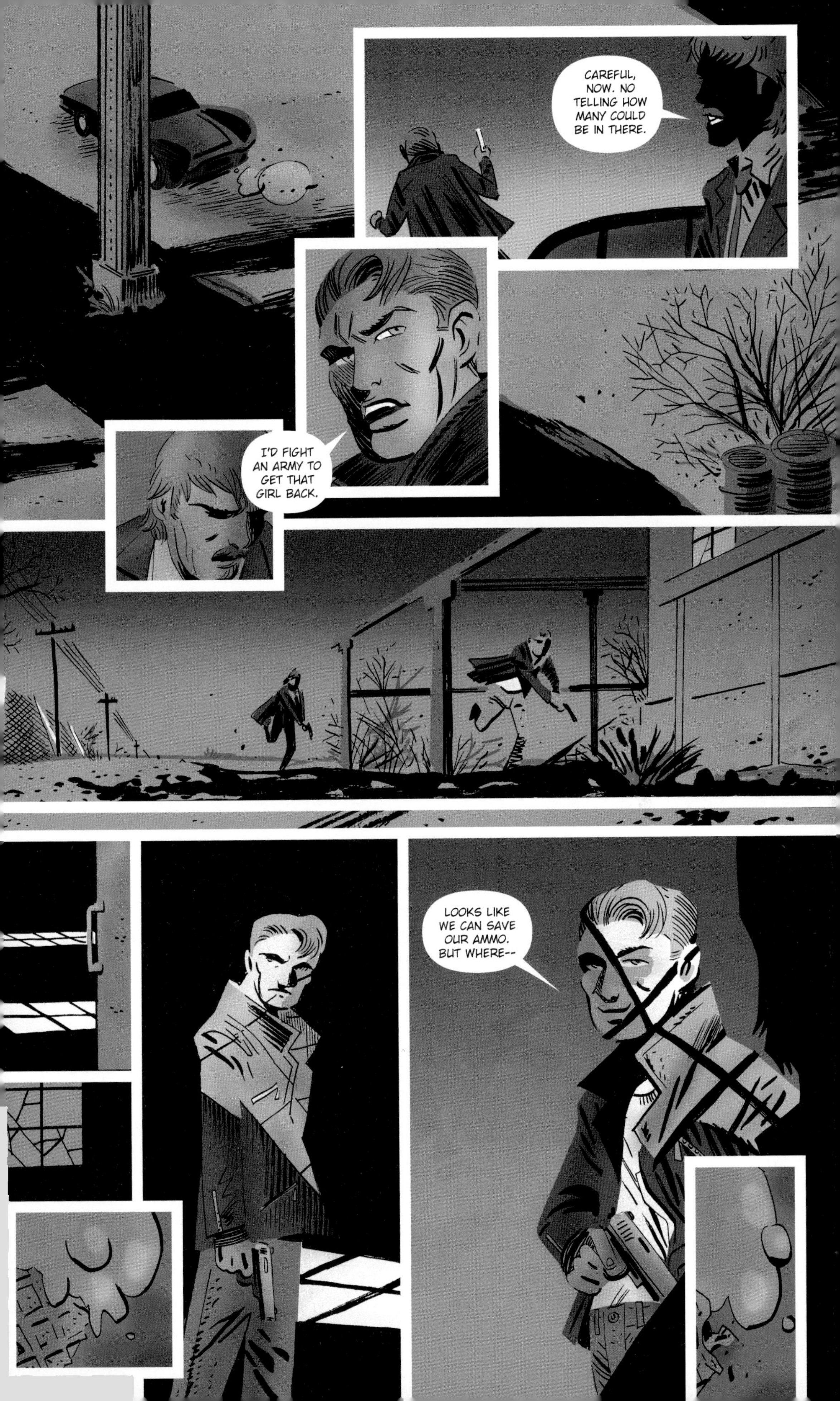
CAREFUL, NOW. NO TELLING HOW MANY COULD BE IN THERE.
I'D FIGHT AN ARMY TO GET THAT GIRL BACK.
LOOKS LIKE WE CAN SAVE OUR AMMO. BUT WHERE--

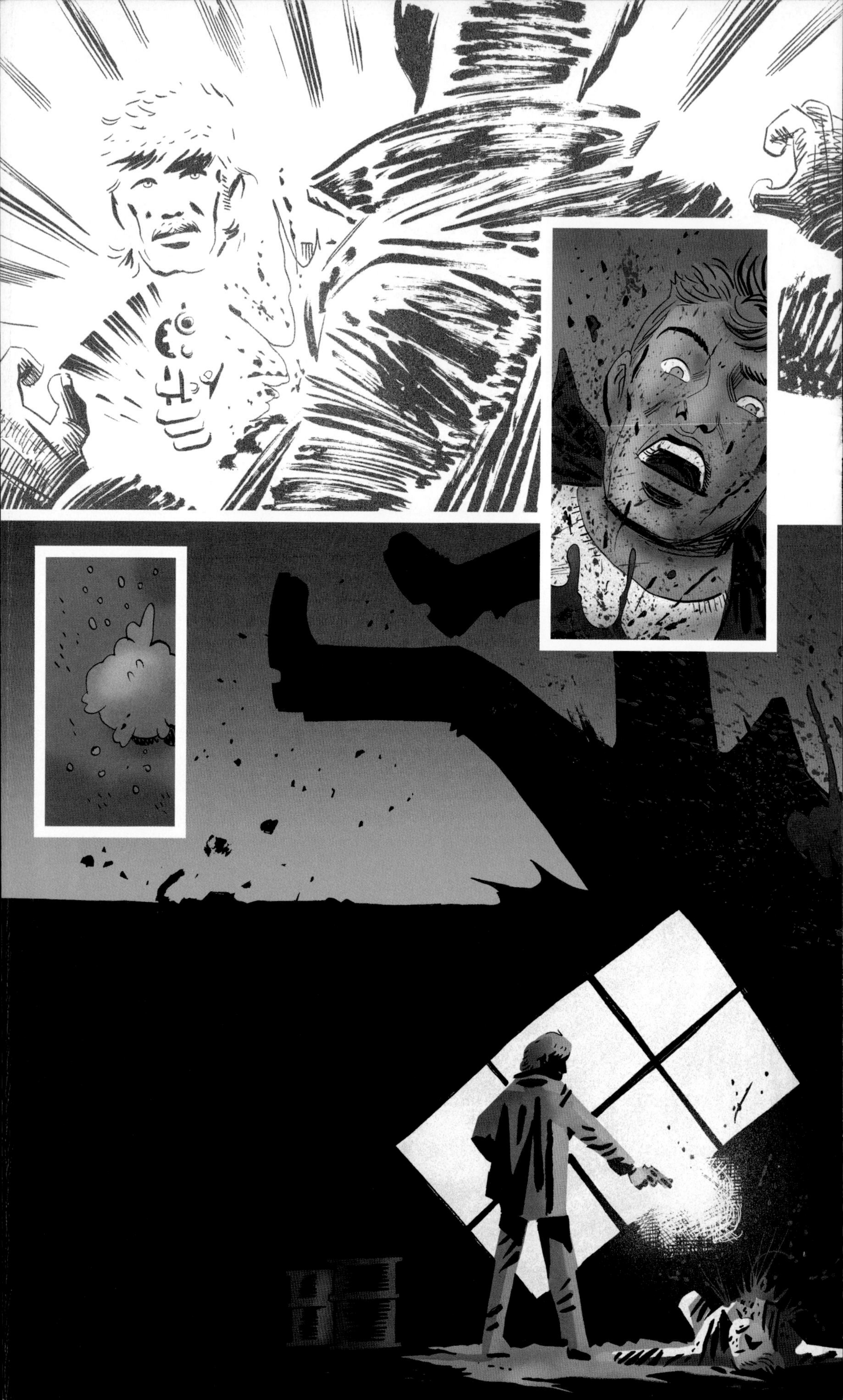

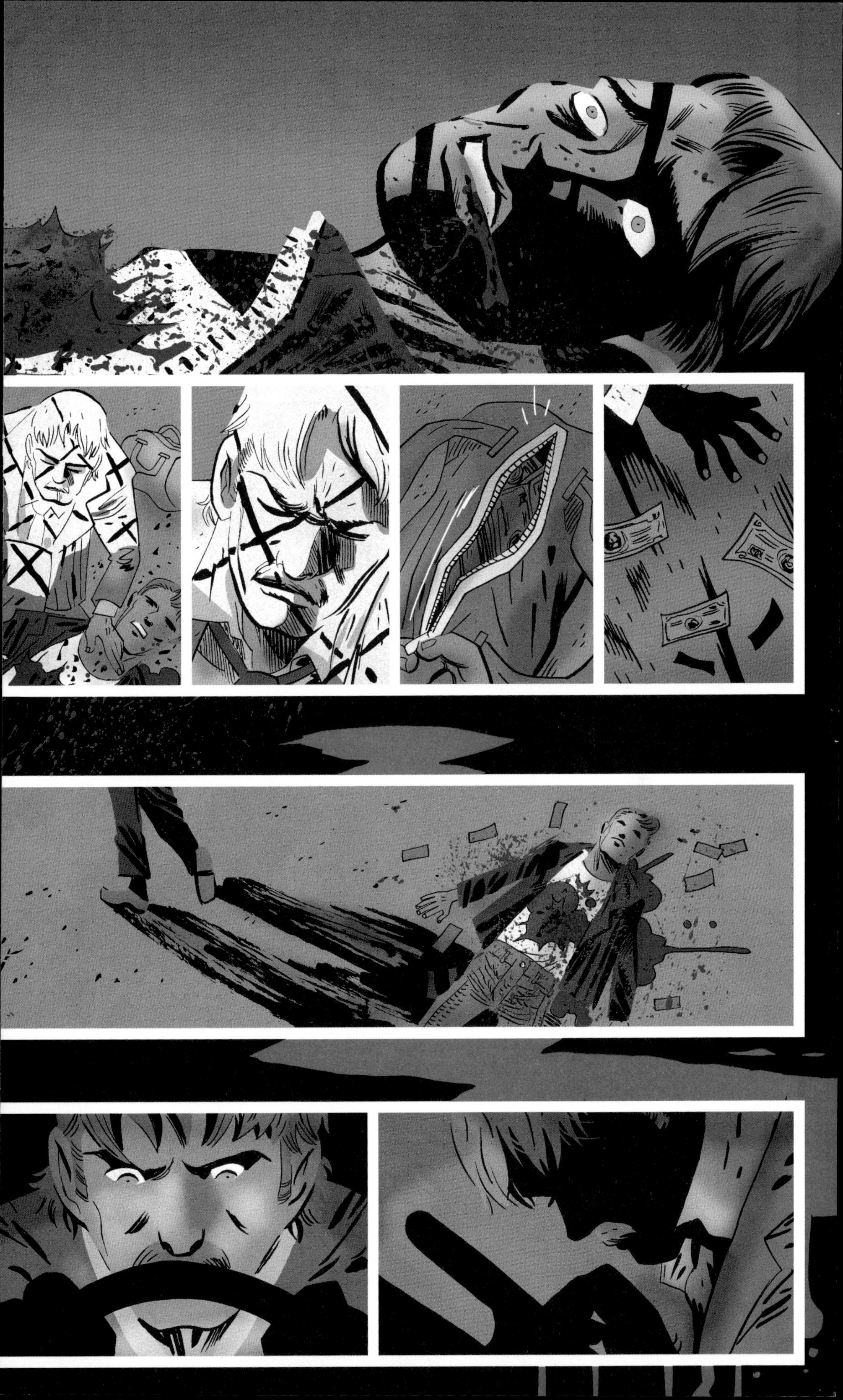

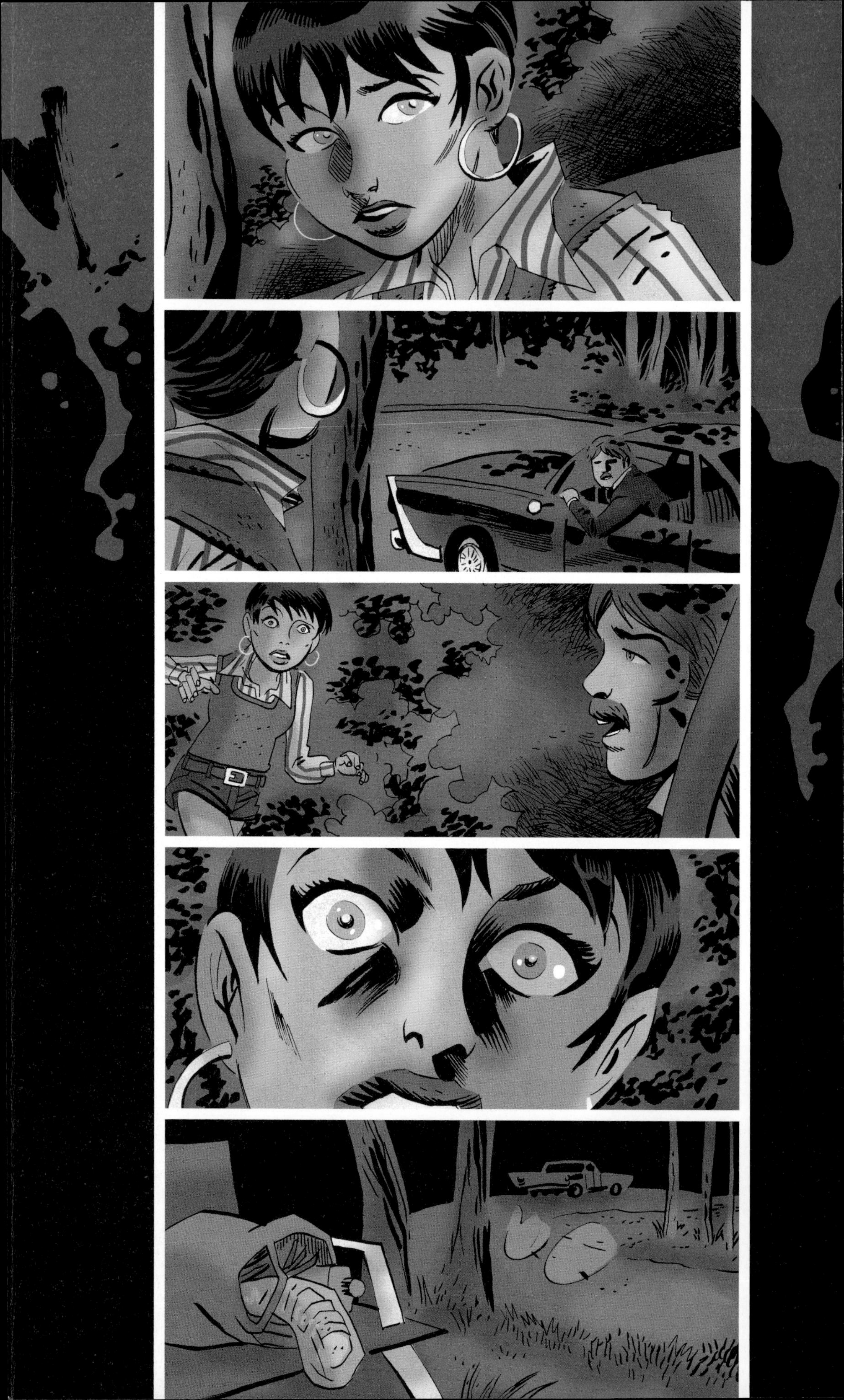

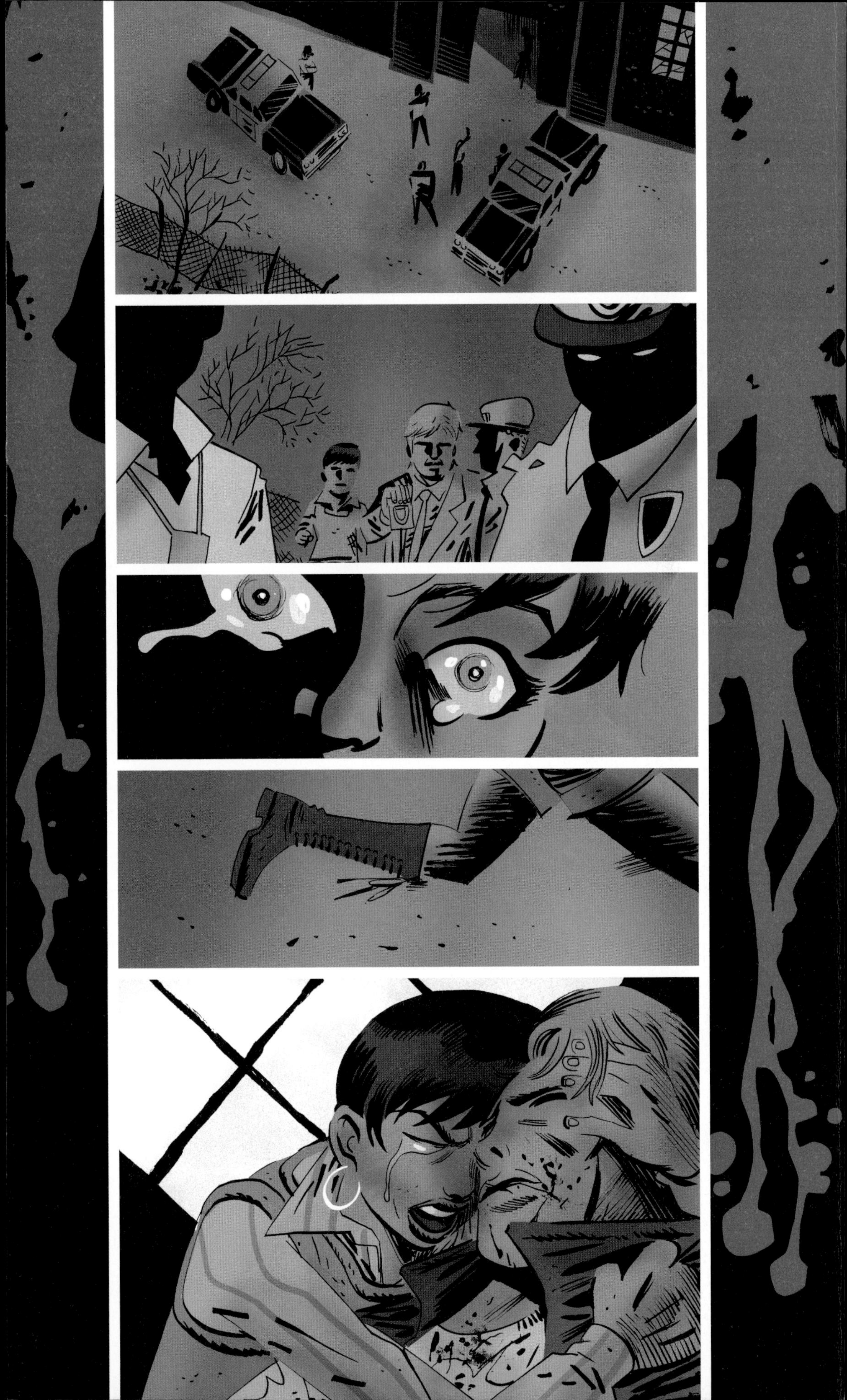

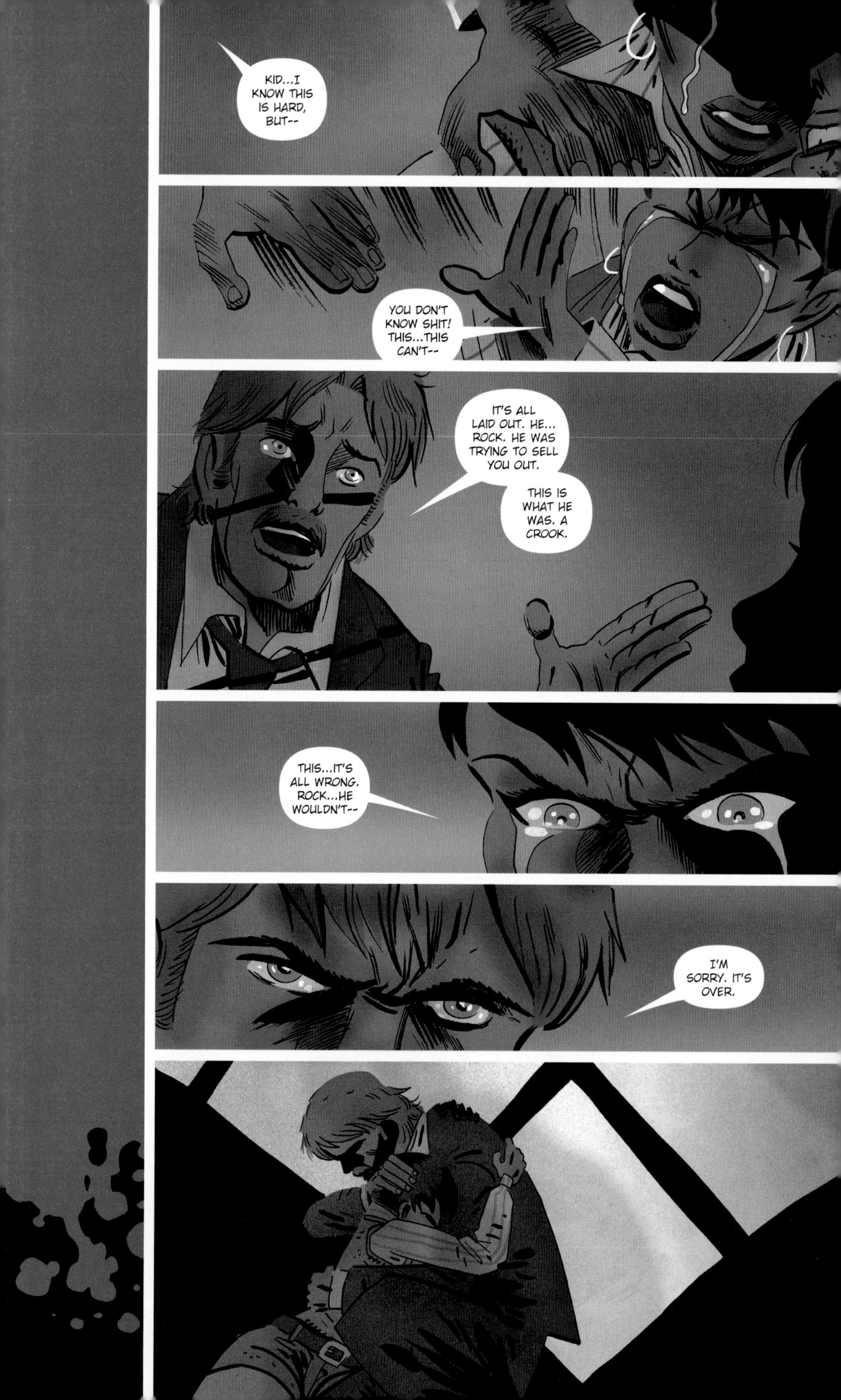

KID...I KNOW THIS IS HARD, BUT--
YOU DON'T KNOW SHIT! THIS...THIS CAN'T--
IT'S ALL LAID OUT. HE... ROCK. HE WAS TRYING TO SELL YOU OUT.
THIS IS WHAT HE WAS. A CROOK.
THIS...IT'S ALL WRONG. ROCK...HE WOULDN'T--
I'M SORRY. IT'S OVER.

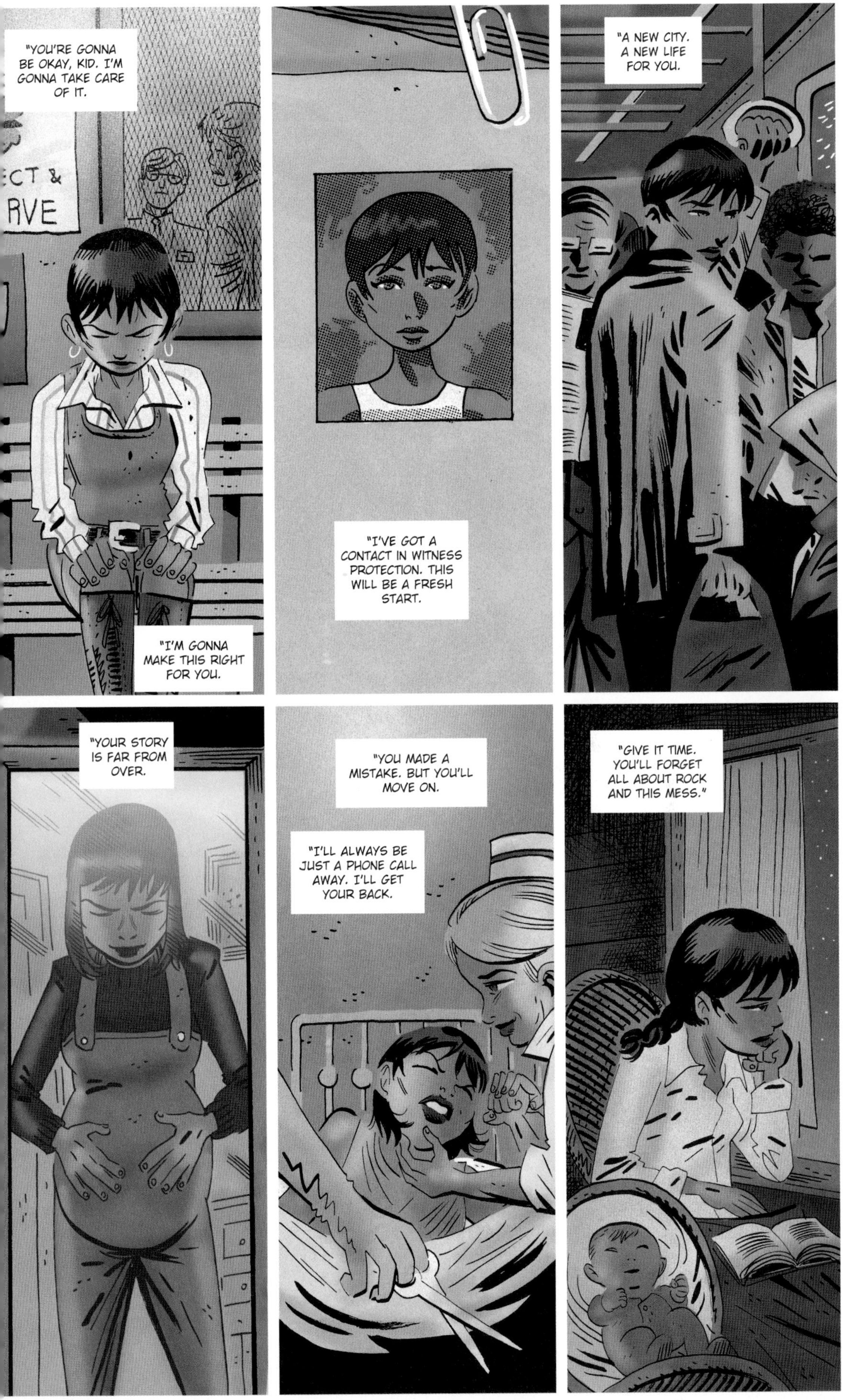
"YOU'RE GONNA BE OKAY, KID. I'M GONNA TAKE CARE OF IT.
ECT &
RVE
"I'M GONNA MAKE THIS RIGHT FOR YOU.
"I'VE GOT A CONTACT IN WITNESS PROTECTION. THIS WILL BE A FRESH START.
"A NEW CITY. A NEW LIFE FOR YOU.
"YOUR STORY IS FAR FROM OVER.
"YOU MADE A MISTAKE. BUT YOU'LL MOVE ON.
"I'LL ALWAYS BE JUST A PHONE CALL AWAY. I'LL GET YOUR BACK.
"GIVE IT TIME. YOU'LL FORGET ALL ABOUT ROCK AND THIS MESS."

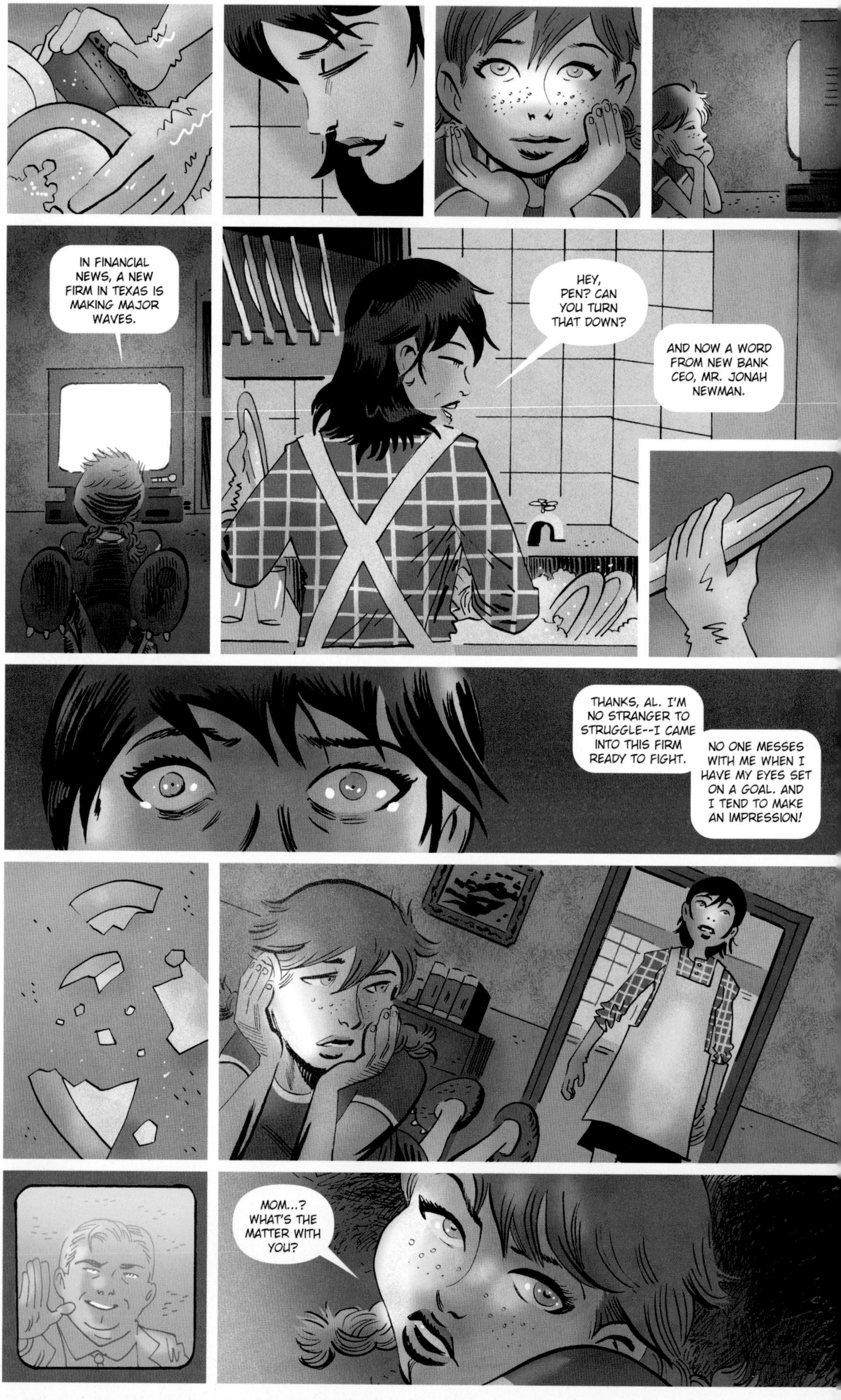

IN FINANCIAL NEWS, A NEW FIRM IN TEXAS IS MAKING MAJOR WAVES.
HEY, PEN? CAN YOU TURN THAT DOWN?
AND NOW A WORD FROM NEW BANK CEO, MR. JONAH NEWMAN.
THANKS, AL. I'M NO STRANGER TO STRUGGLE--I CAME INTO THIS FIRM READY TO FIGHT.
NO ONE MESSES WITH ME WHEN I HAVE MY EYES SET ON A GOAL. AND I TEND TO MAKE AN IMPRESSION!
MOM...? WHAT'S THE MATTER WITH YOU?

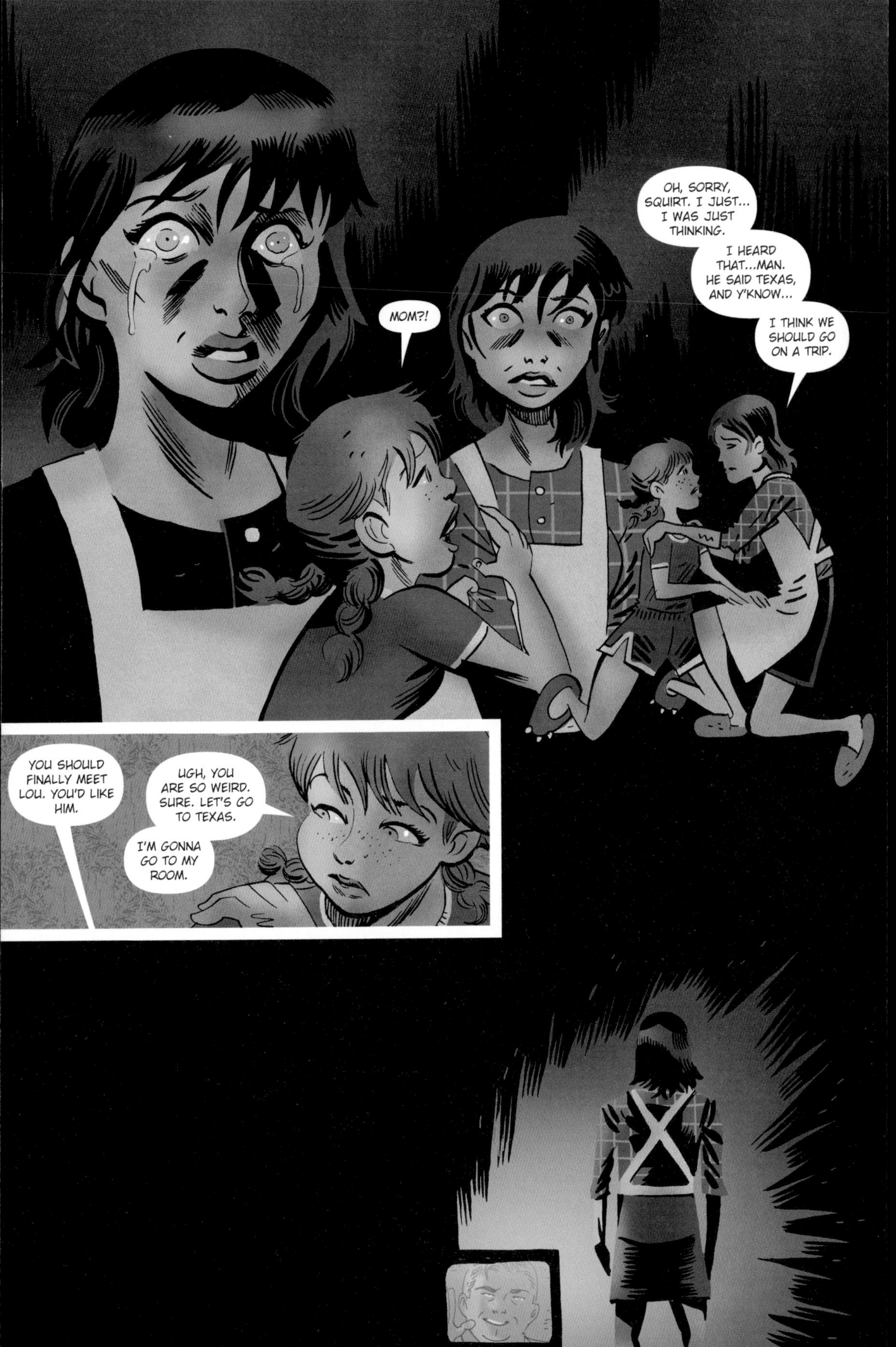
MOM?!
OH, SORRY, SQUIRT. I JUST... I WAS JUST THINKING.
I HEARD THAT...MAN. HE SAID TEXAS, AND Y'KNOW...
I THINK WE SHOULD GO ON A TRIP.
YOU SHOULD FINALLY MEET LOU. YOU'D LIKE HIM.
UGH, YOU ARE SO WEIRD. SURE. LET'S GO TO TEXAS.
I'M GONNA GO TO MY ROOM.

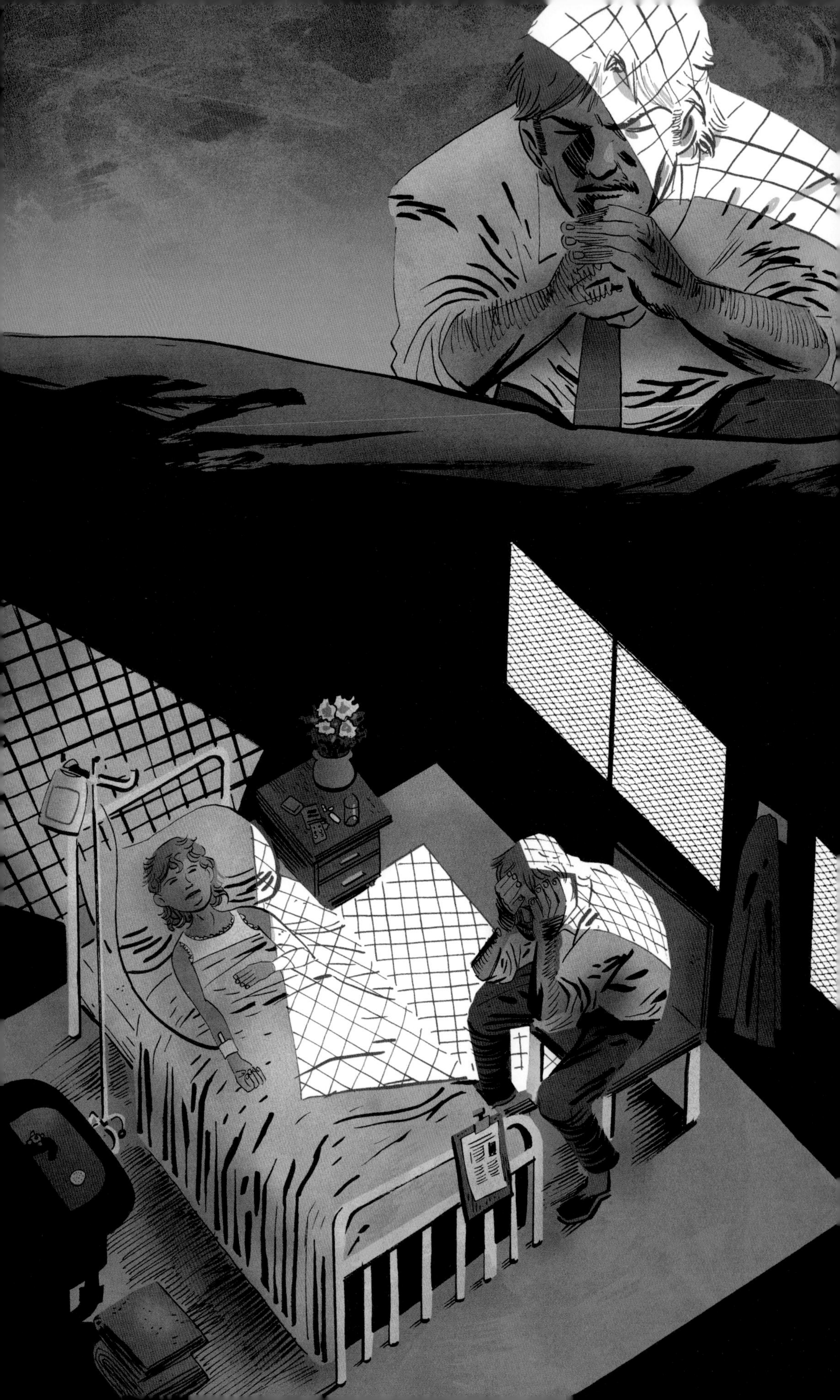

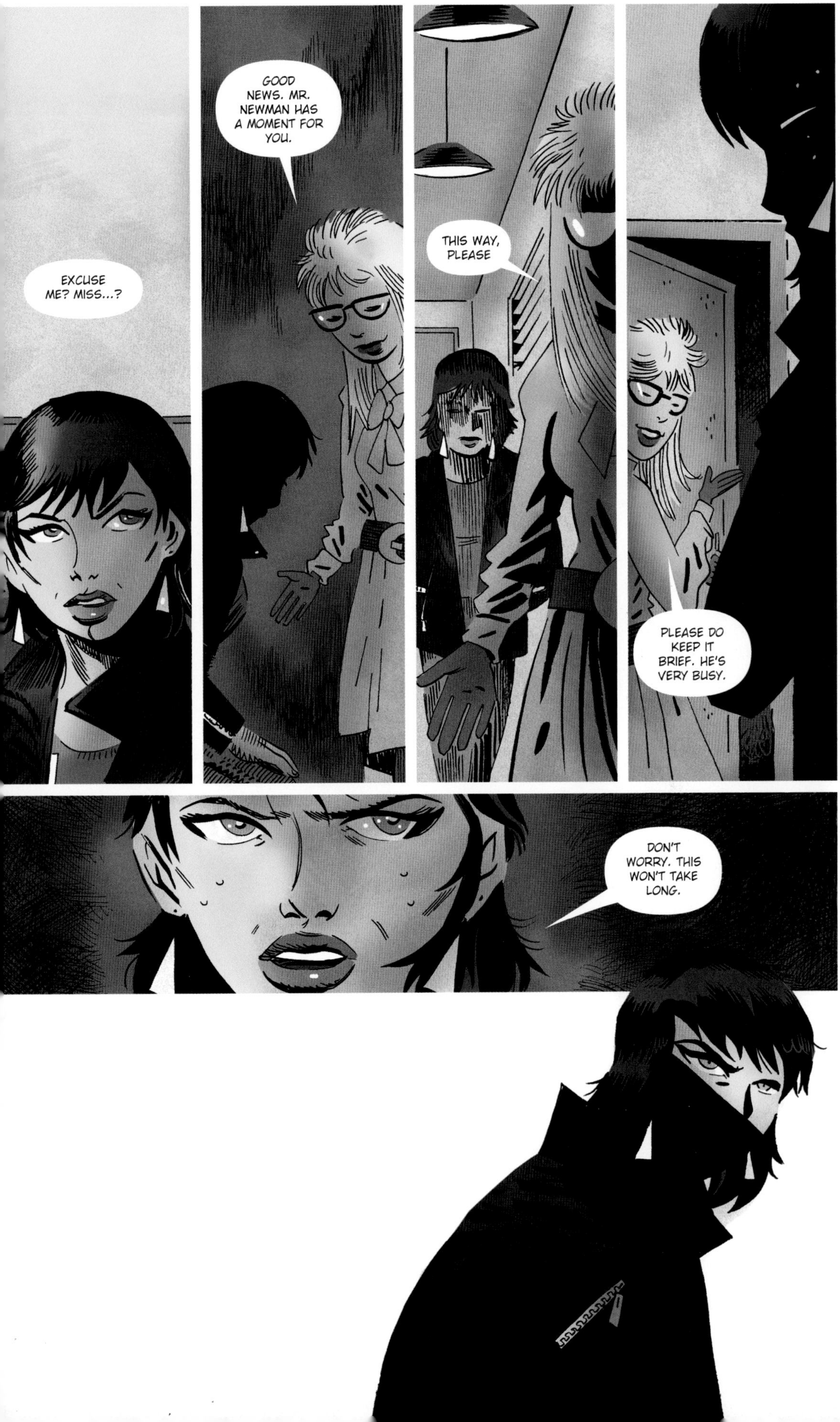
EXCUSE ME? MISS...?
GOOD NEWS. MR. NEWMAN HAS A MOMENT FOR YOU.
THIS WAY, PLEASE
PLEASE DO KEEP IT BRIEF. HE'S VERY BUSY.
DON'T WORRY. THIS WON'T TAKE LONG.

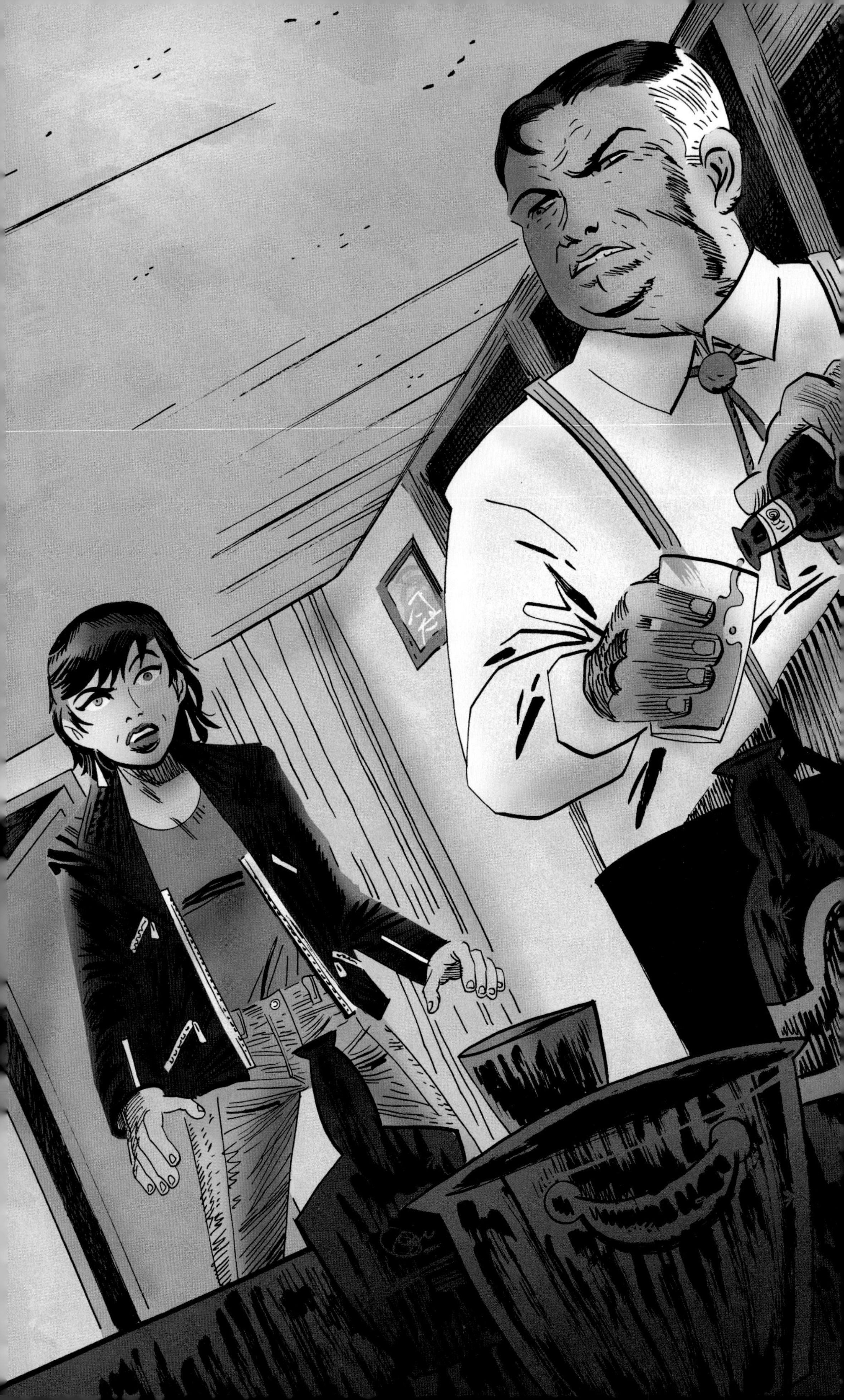

CHAPTER TEN

"MY SUNDOWN"

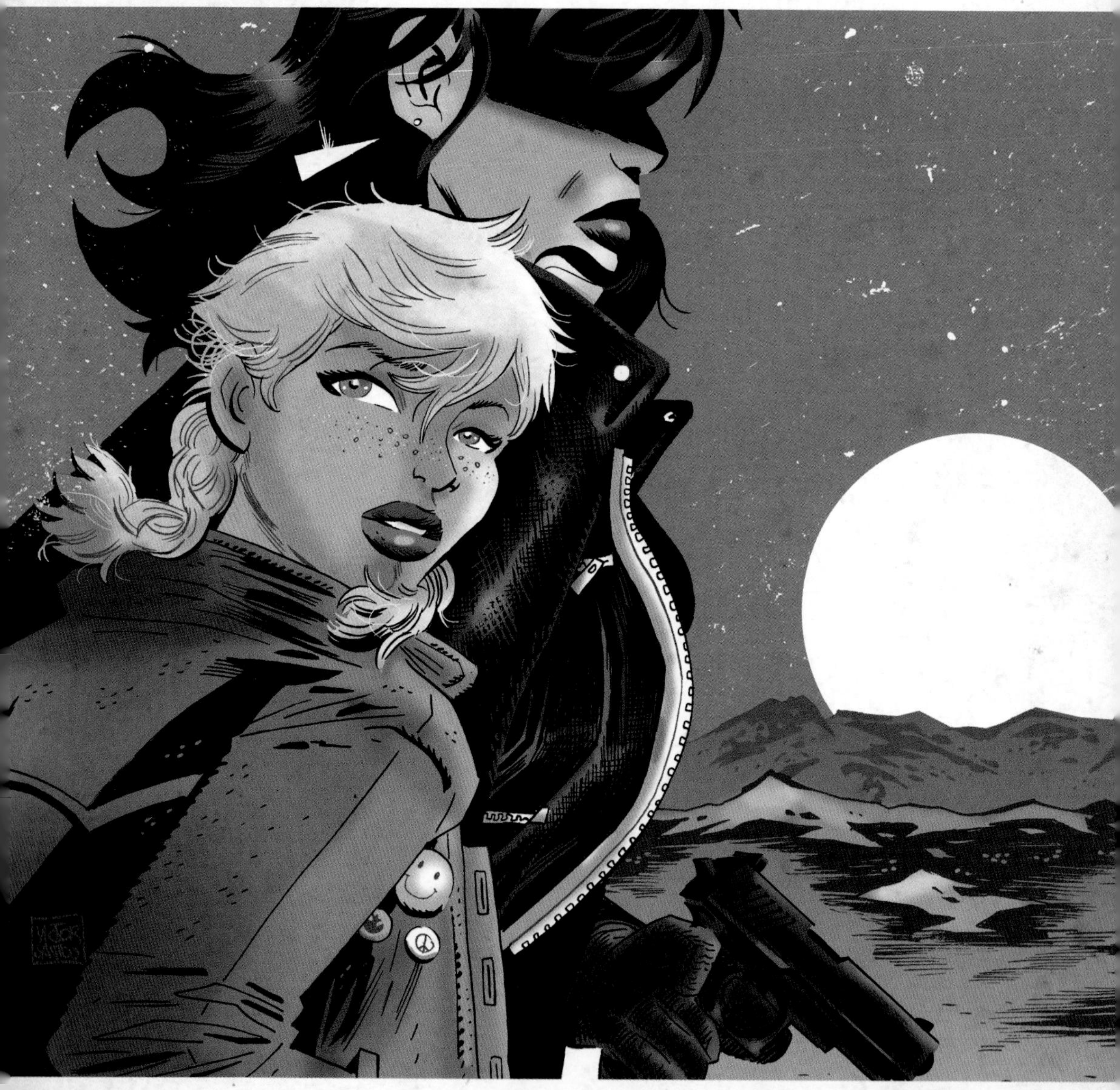

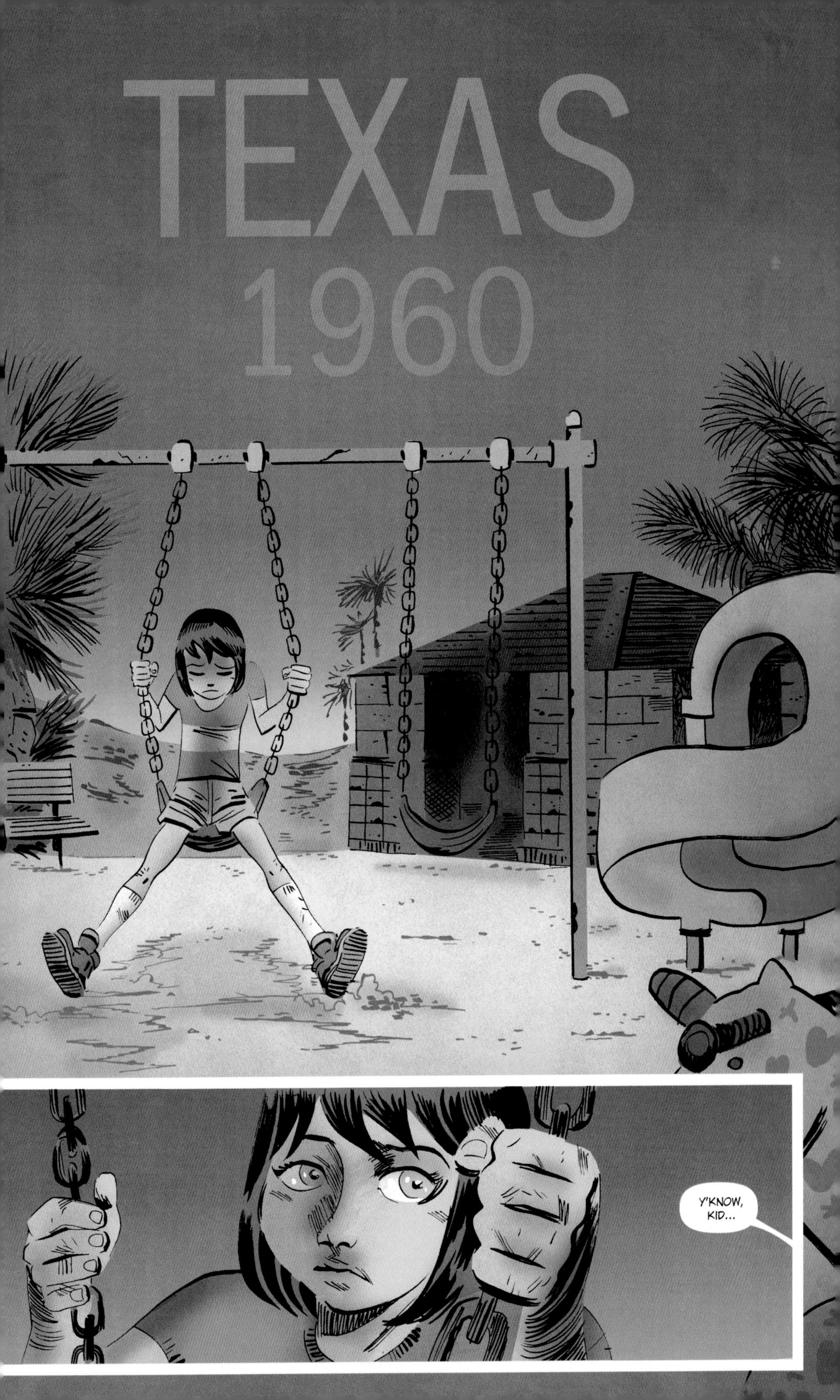
TEXAS
1960
Y'KNOW,
KID...

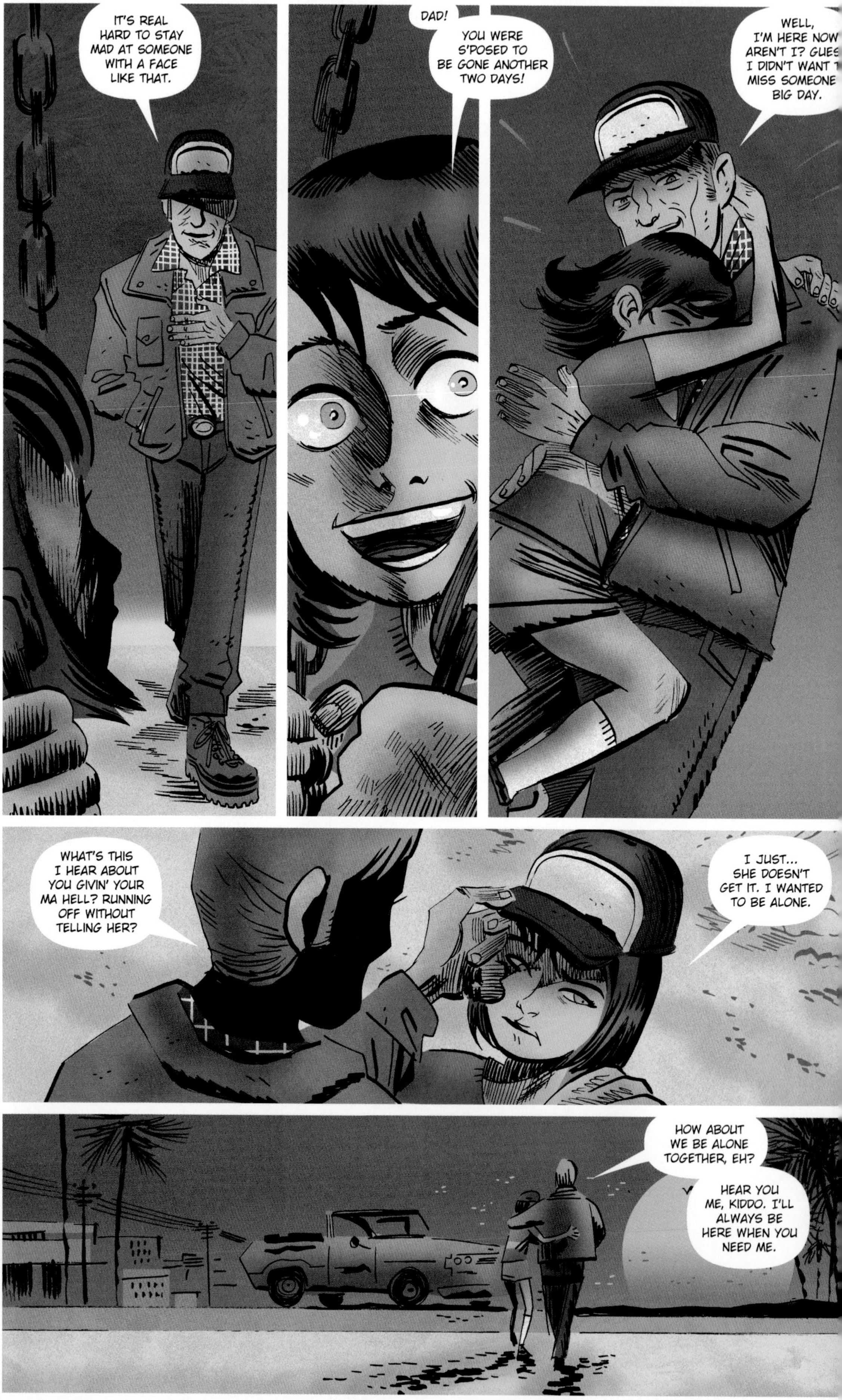
IT'S REAL HARD TO STAY MAD AT SOMEONE WITH A FACE LIKE THAT.
DAD!
YOU WERE S'POSED TO BE GONE ANOTHER TWO DAYS!
WELL, I'M HERE NOW AREN'T I? GUES I DIDN'T WANT T MISS SOMEONE BIG DAY.
WHAT'S THIS I HEAR ABOUT YOU GIVIN' YOUR MA HELL? RUNNING OFF WITHOUT TELLING HER?
I JUST... SHE DOESN'T GET IT. I WANTED TO BE ALONE.
HOW ABOUT WE BE ALONE TOGETHER, EH?
HEAR YOU ME, KIDDO. I'LL ALWAYS BE HERE WHEN YOU NEED ME.

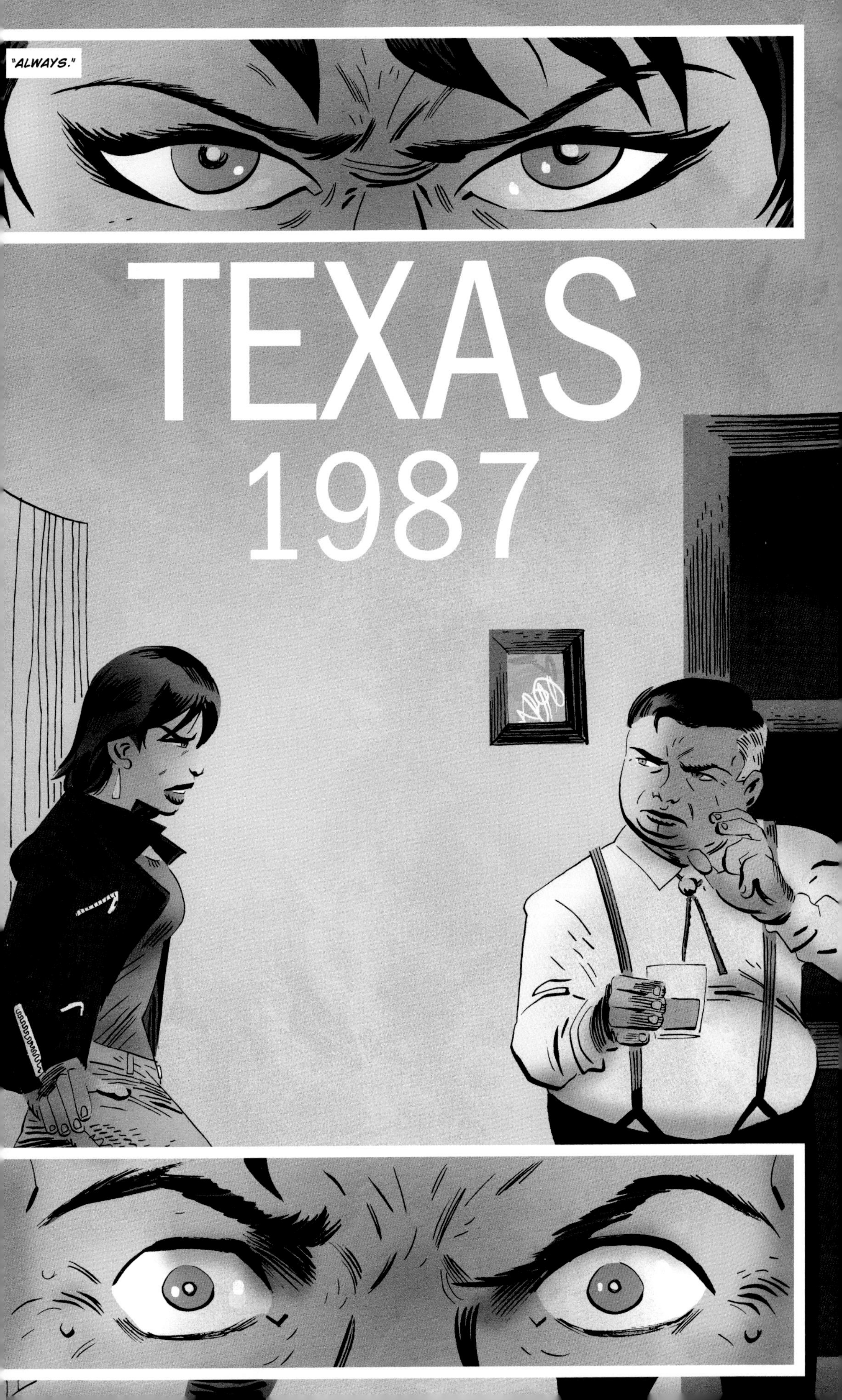
"ALWAYS."
TEXAS
1987

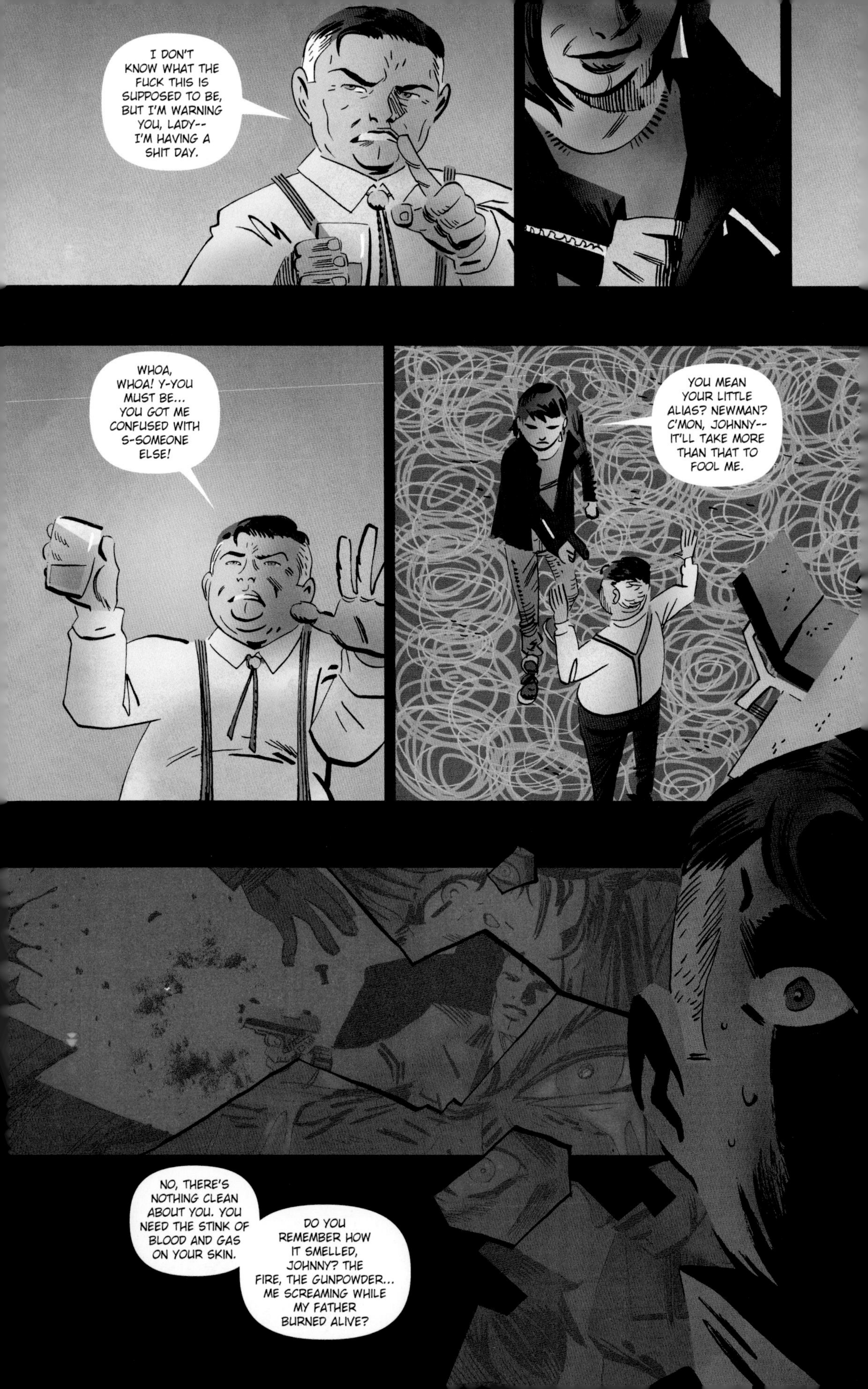
I DON'T KNOW WHAT THE FUCK THIS IS SUPPOSED TO BE, BUT I'M WARNING YOU, LADY-- I'M HAVING A SHIT DAY.
WHOA, WHOA! Y-YOU MUST BE... YOU GOT ME CONFUSED WITH S-SOMEONE ELSE!
YOU MEAN YOUR LITTLE ALIAS? NEWMAN? C'MON, JOHNNY-- IT'LL TAKE MORE THAN THAT TO FOOL ME.
NO, THERE'S NOTHING CLEAN ABOUT YOU. YOU NEED THE STINK OF BLOOD AND GAS ON YOUR SKIN.
DO YOU REMEMBER HOW IT SMELLED, JOHNNY? THE FIRE, THE GUNPOWDER... ME SCREAMING WHILE MY FATHER BURNED ALIVE?

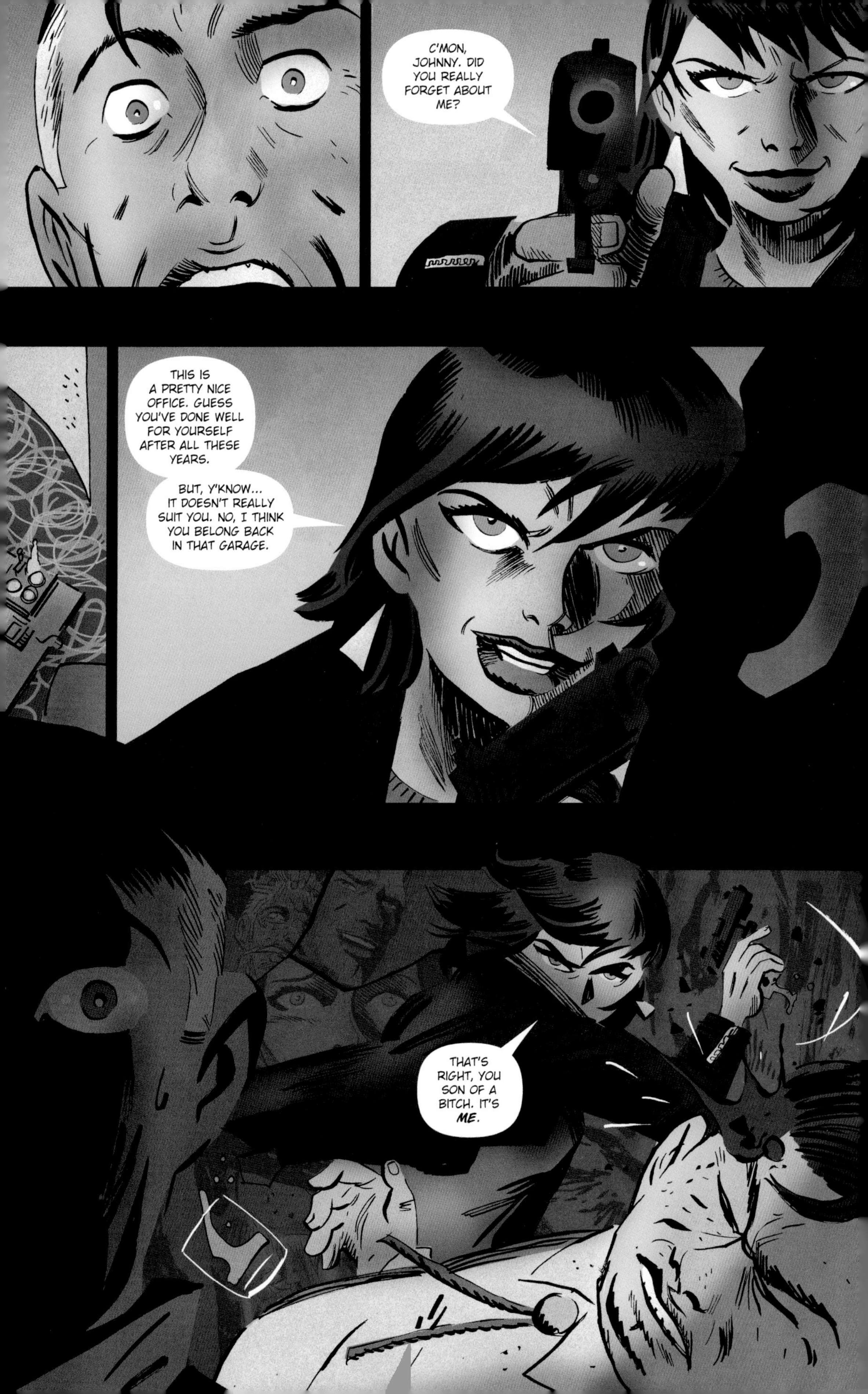
C'MON, JOHNNY. DID YOU REALLY FORGET ABOUT ME?
THIS IS A PRETTY NICE OFFICE. GUESS YOU'VE DONE WELL FOR YOURSELF AFTER ALL THESE YEARS.
BUT, Y'KNOW... IT DOESN'T REALLY SUIT YOU. NO, I THINK YOU BELONG BACK IN THAT GARAGE.
THAT'S RIGHT, YOU SON OF A BITCH. IT'S ***ME***.

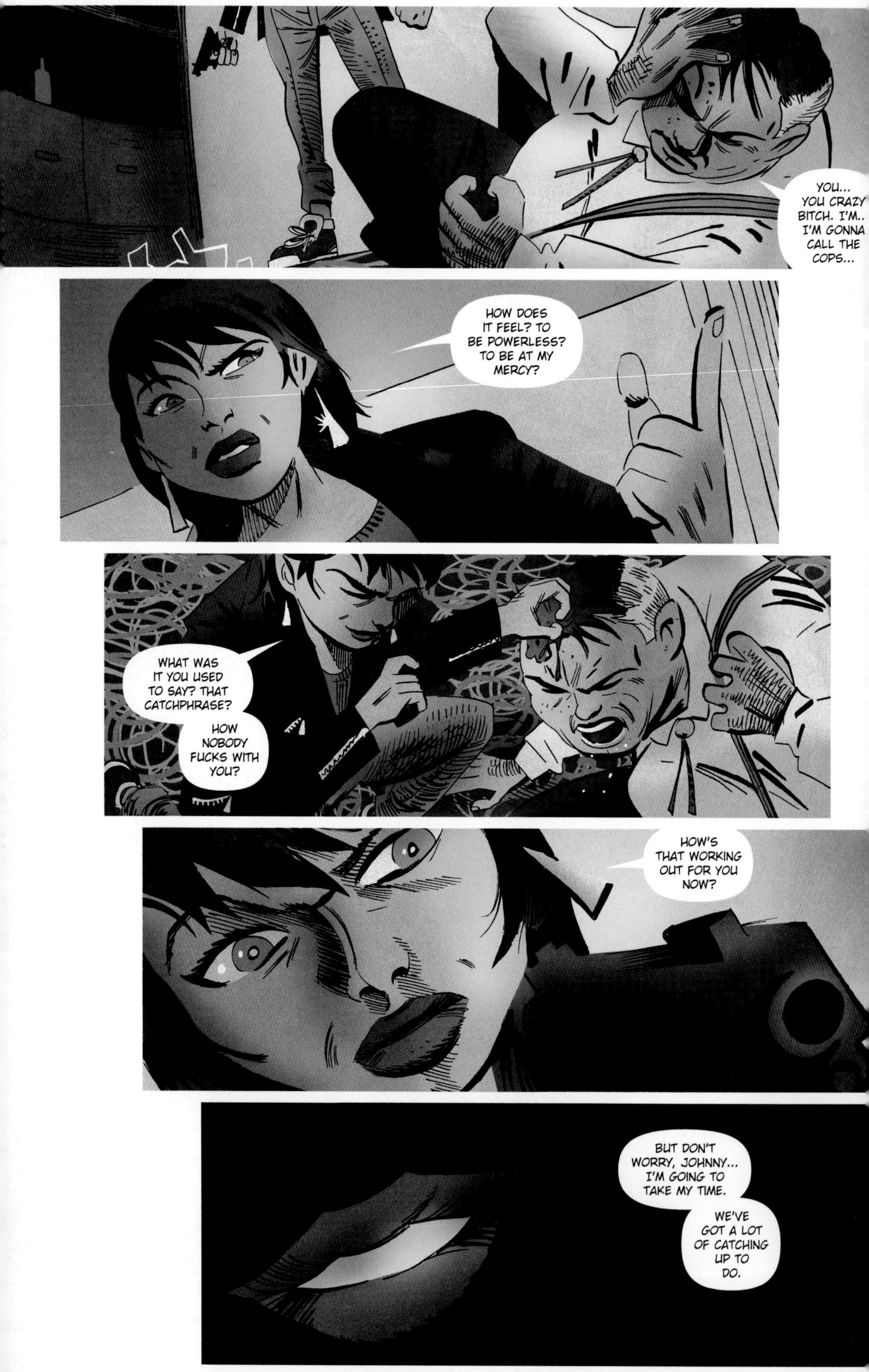
YOU... YOU CRAZY BITCH. I'M.. I'M GONNA CALL THE COPS...
HOW DOES IT FEEL? TO BE POWERLESS? TO BE AT MY MERCY?
WHAT WAS IT YOU USED TO SAY? THAT CATCHPHRASE?
HOW NOBODY FUCKS WITH YOU?
HOW'S THAT WORKING OUT FOR YOU NOW?
BUT DON'T WORRY, JOHNNY... I'M GOING TO TAKE MY TIME.
WE'VE GOT A LOT OF CATCHING UP TO DO.

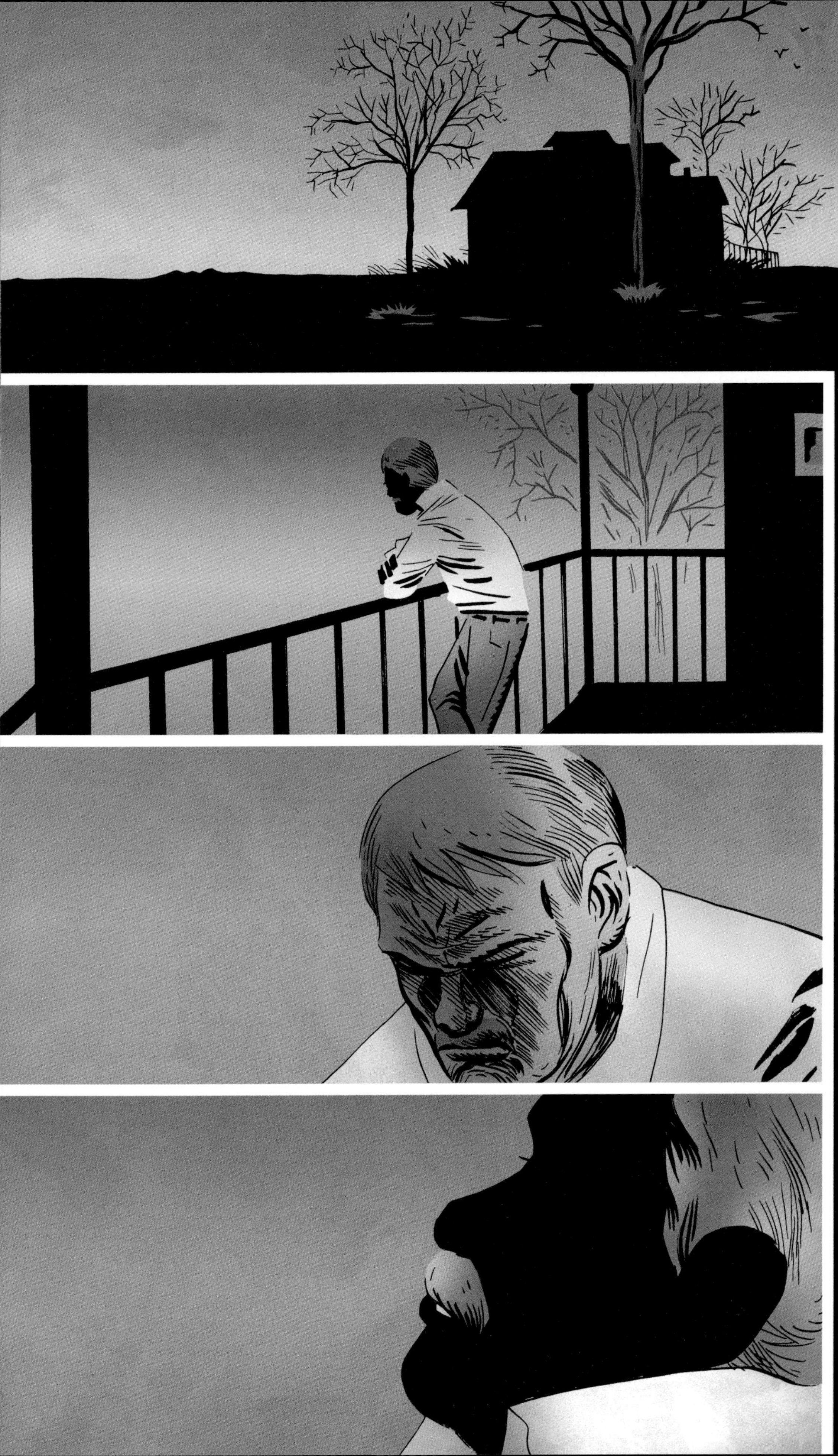

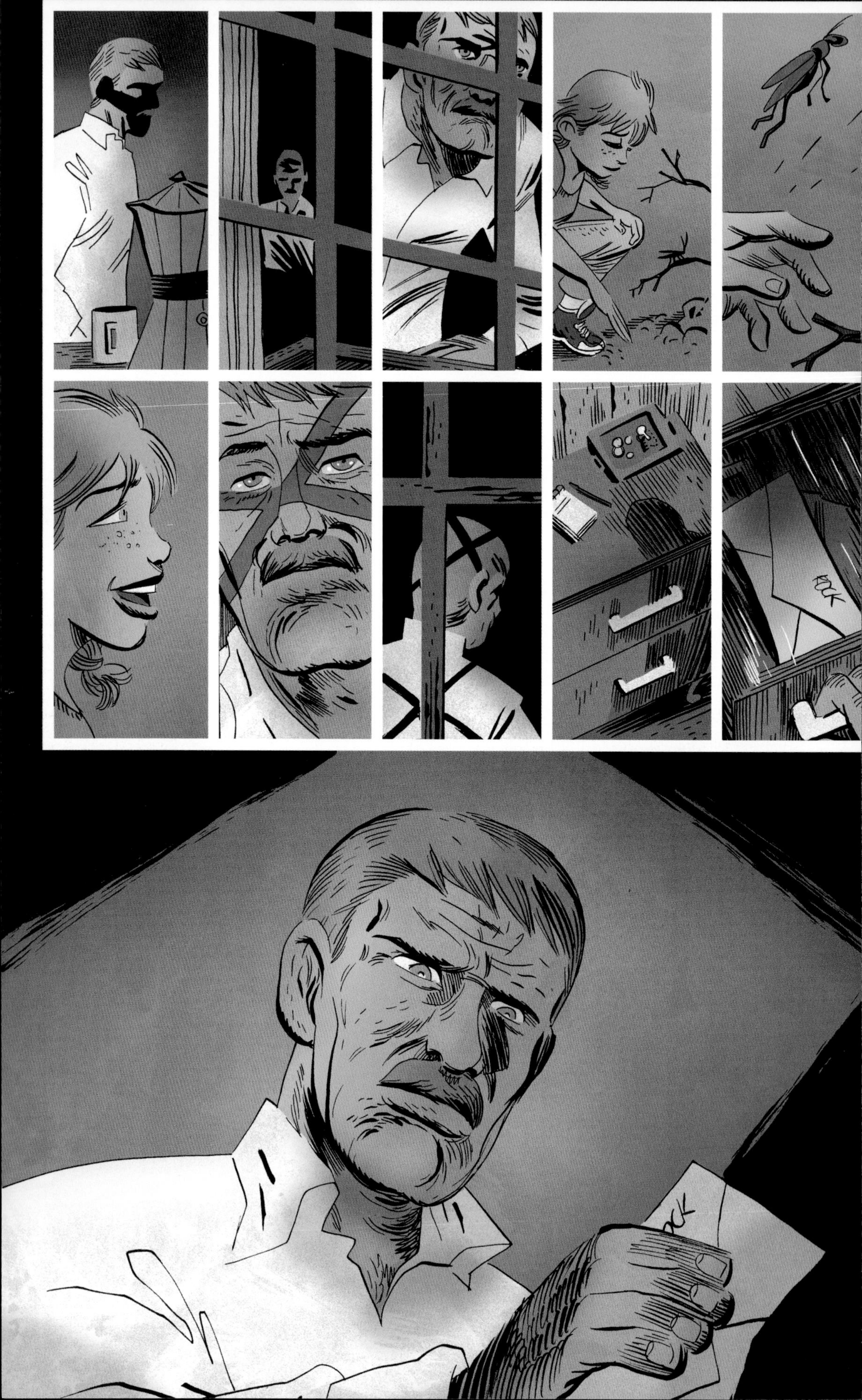

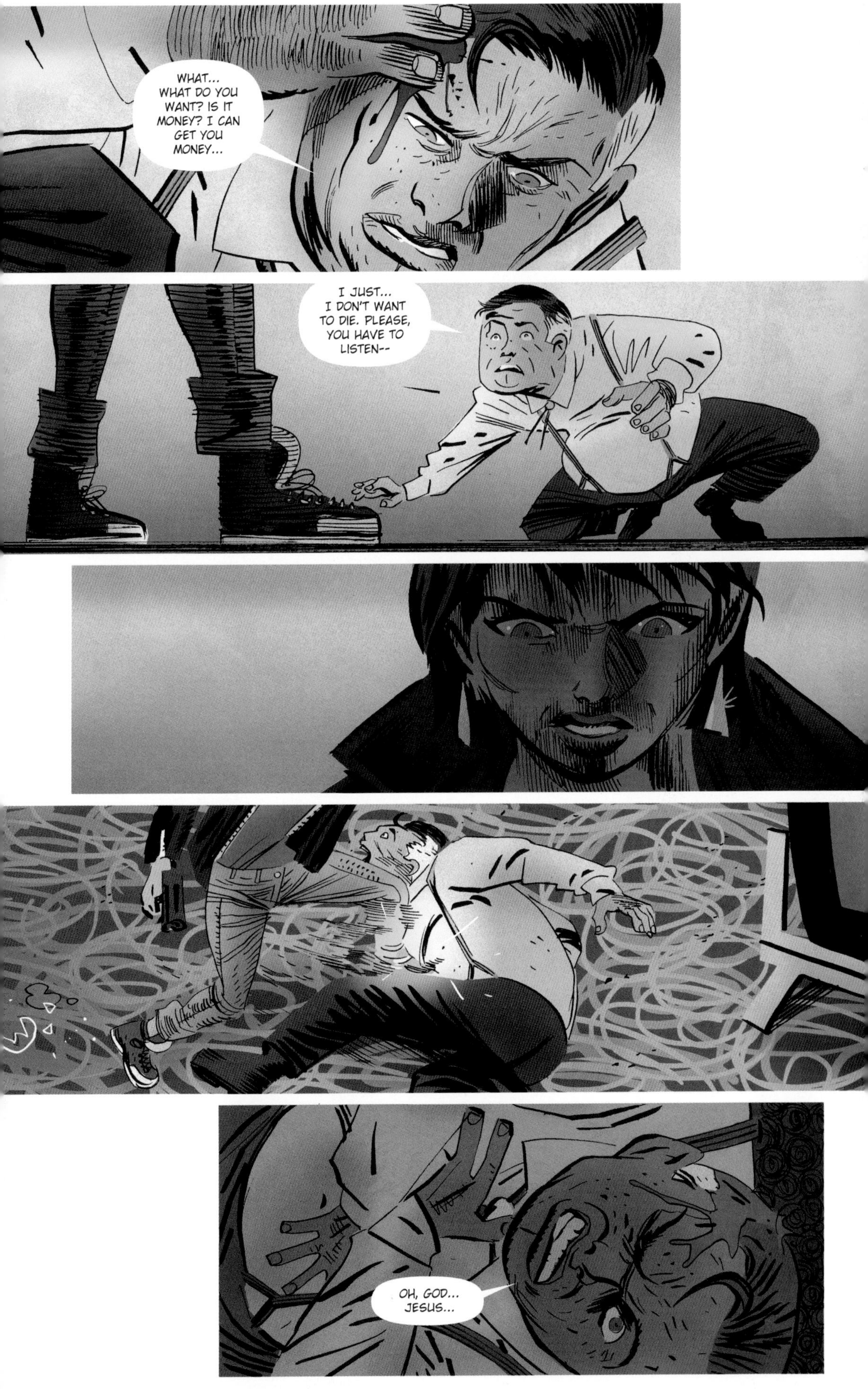
WHAT... WHAT DO YOU WANT? IS IT MONEY? I CAN GET YOU MONEY...
I JUST... I DON'T WANT TO DIE. PLEASE, YOU HAVE TO LISTEN--
OH, GOD... JESUS...

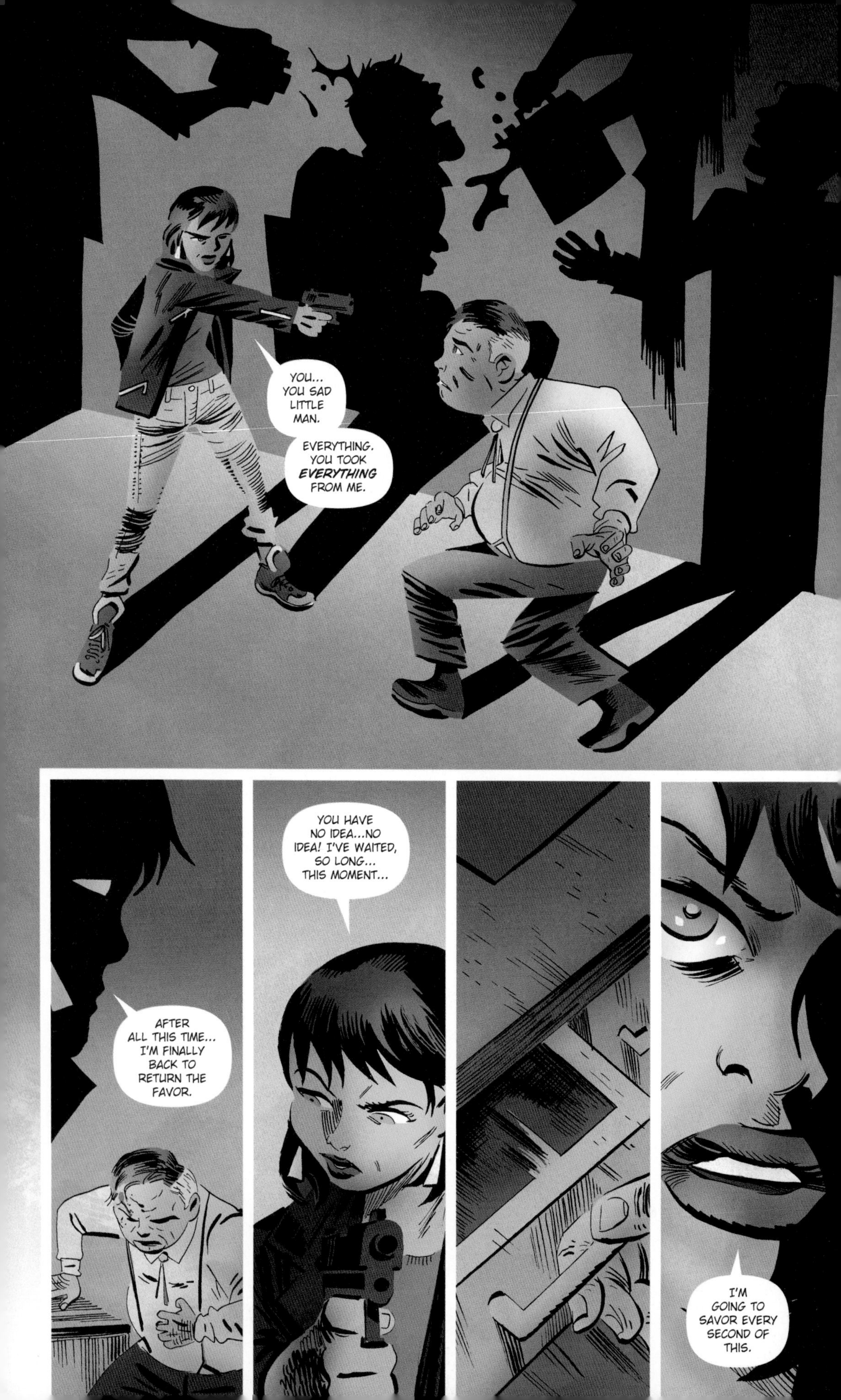

YOU... YOU SAD LITTLE MAN.
EVERYTHING. YOU TOOK **EVERYTHING** FROM ME.
AFTER ALL THIS TIME... I'M FINALLY BACK TO RETURN THE FAVOR.
YOU HAVE NO IDEA...NO IDEA! I'VE WAITED, SO LONG... THIS MOMENT...
I'M GOING TO SAVOR EVERY SECOND OF THIS.

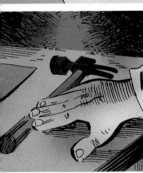

MAYBE... MAYBE THIS IS HOW IT WAS ALWAYS GOING TO END FOR ME.

MAYBE THIS IS WHAT I DESERVE.

WHAT ABOUT ME? WHAT DO I DESERVE?!

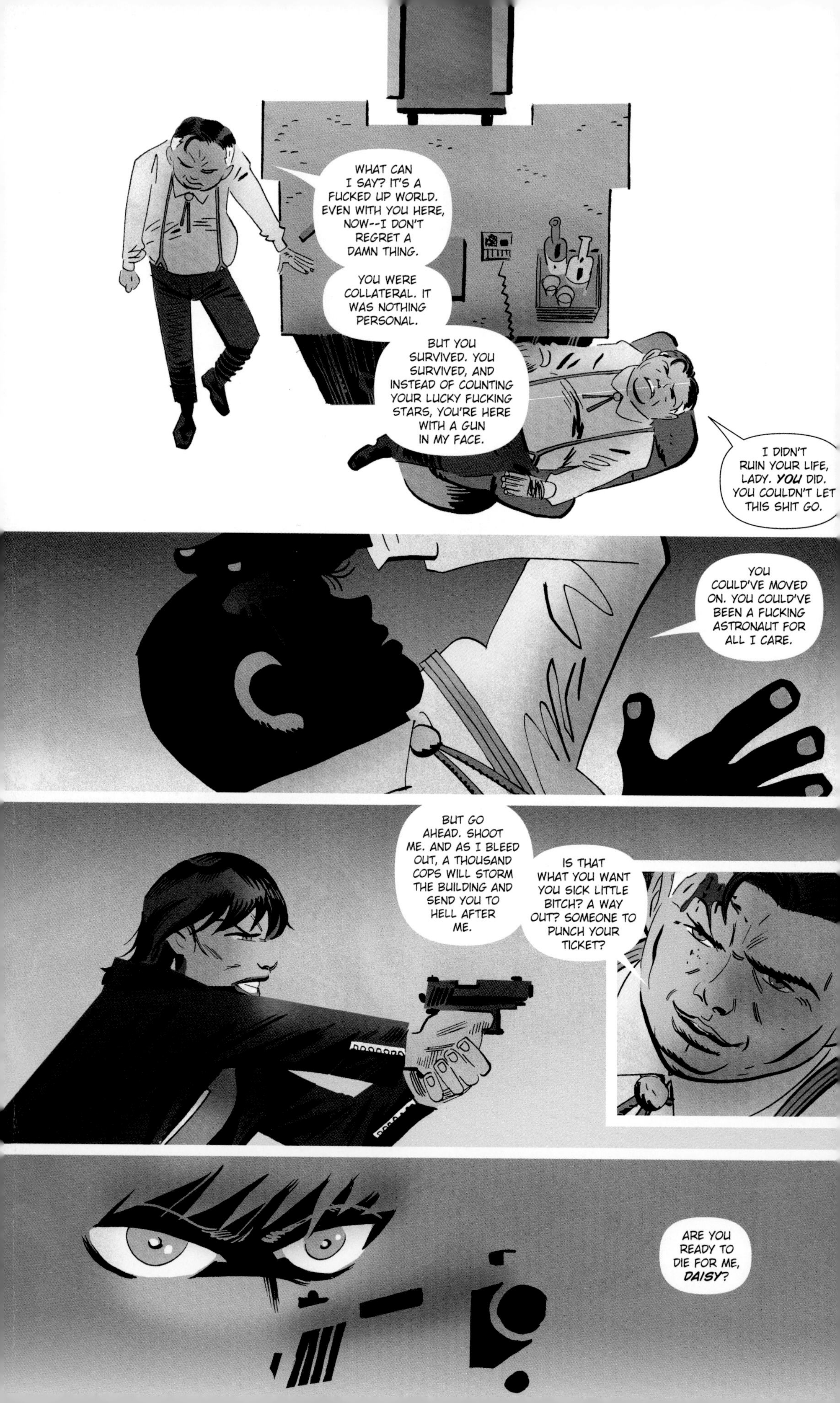
WHAT CAN I SAY? IT'S A FUCKED UP WORLD. EVEN WITH YOU HERE, NOW--I DON'T REGRET A DAMN THING.
YOU WERE COLLATERAL. IT WAS NOTHING PERSONAL.
BUT YOU SURVIVED. YOU SURVIVED, AND INSTEAD OF COUNTING YOUR LUCKY FUCKING STARS, YOU'RE HERE WITH A GUN IN MY FACE.
I DIDN'T RUIN YOUR LIFE, LADY. ***YOU*** DID. YOU COULDN'T LET THIS SHIT GO.
YOU COULD'VE MOVED ON. YOU COULD'VE BEEN A FUCKING ASTRONAUT FOR ALL I CARE.
BUT GO AHEAD. SHOOT ME. AND AS I BLEED OUT, A THOUSAND COPS WILL STORM THE BUILDING AND SEND YOU TO HELL AFTER ME.
IS THAT WHAT YOU WANT YOU SICK LITTLE BITCH? A WAY OUT? SOMEONE TO PUNCH YOUR TICKET?
ARE YOU READY TO DIE FOR ME, ***DAISY***?

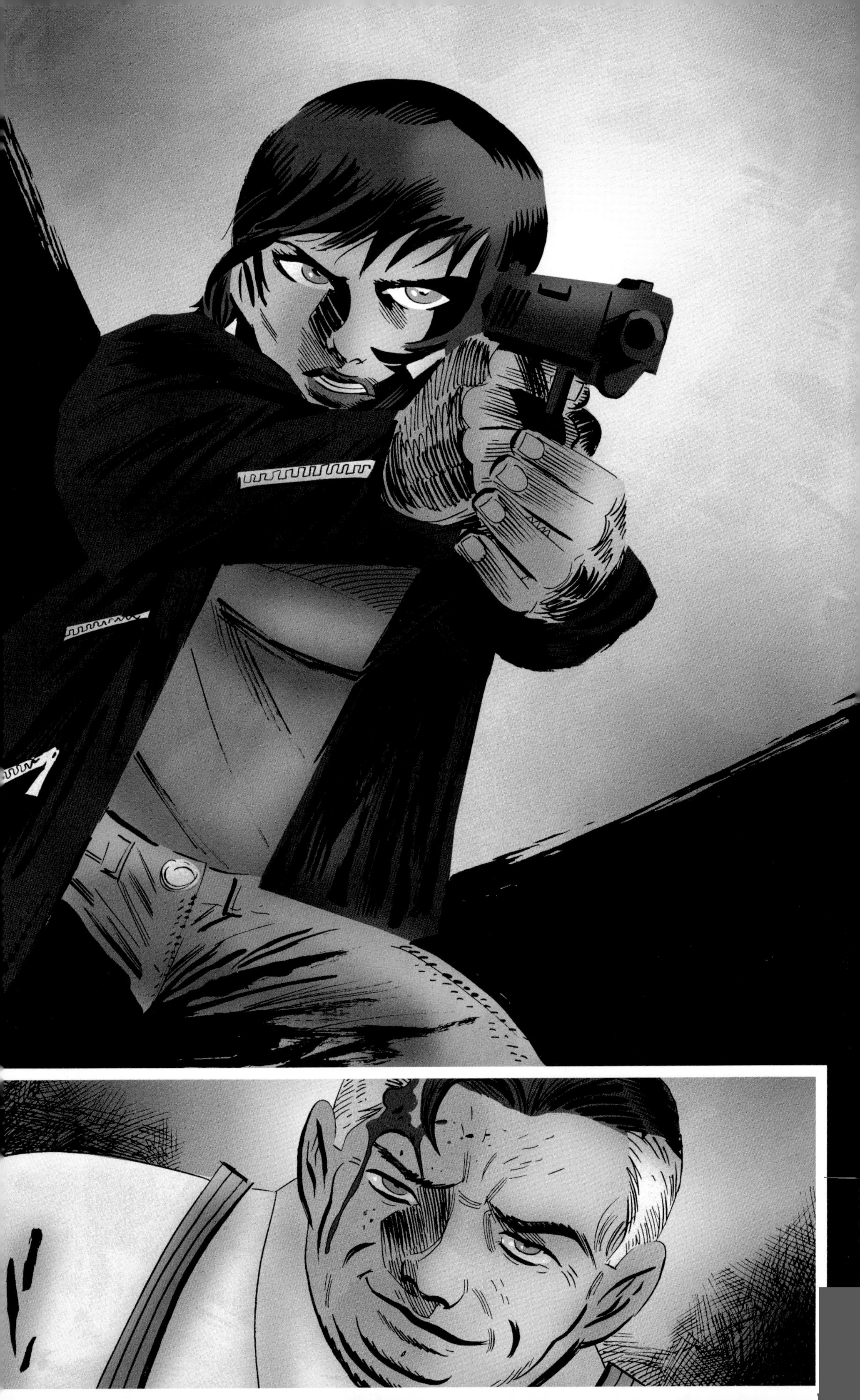

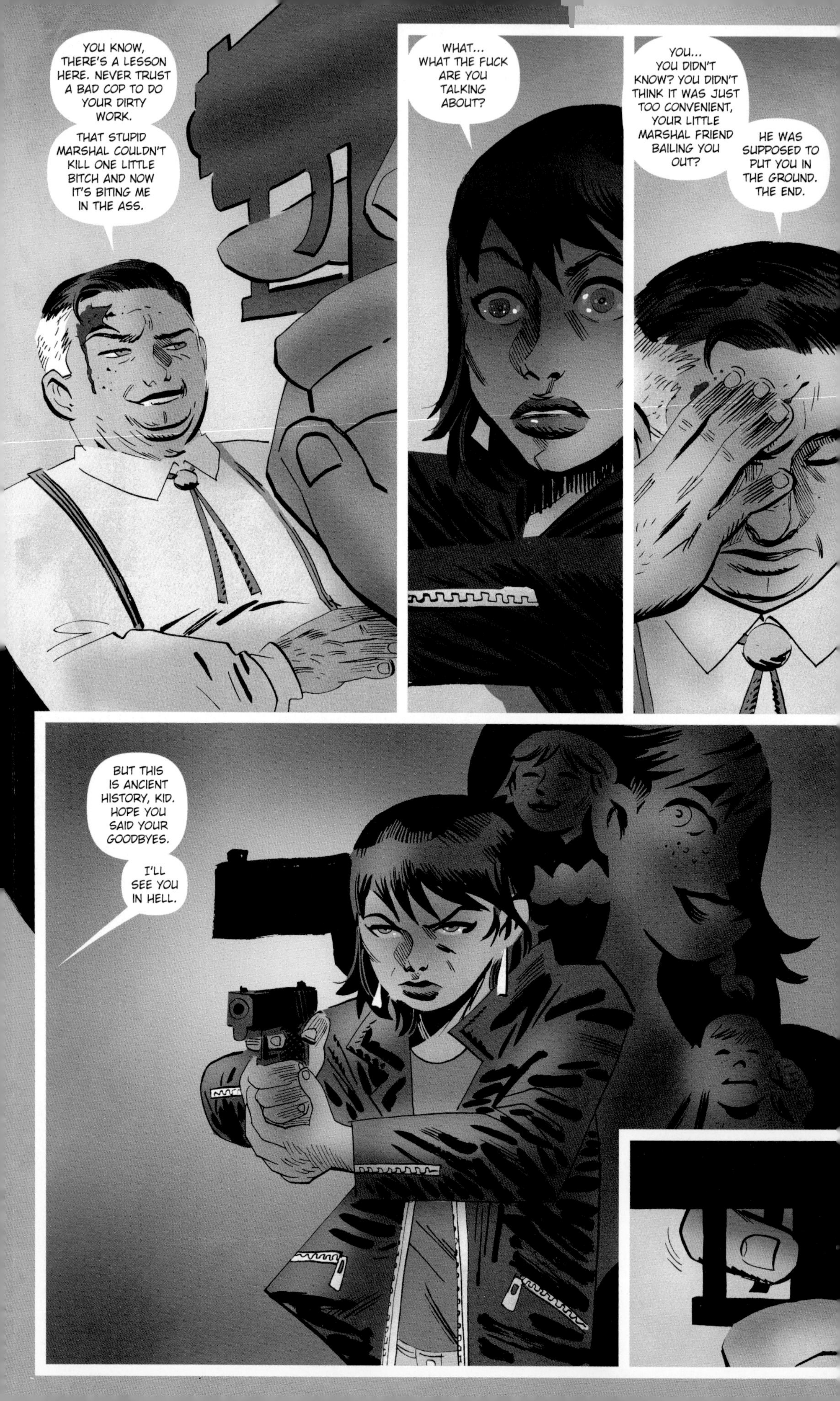
YOU KNOW, THERE'S A LESSON HERE. NEVER TRUST A BAD COP TO DO YOUR DIRTY WORK.
THAT STUPID MARSHAL COULDN'T KILL ONE LITTLE BITCH AND NOW IT'S BITING ME IN THE ASS.
WHAT... WHAT THE FUCK ARE YOU TALKING ABOUT?
YOU... YOU DIDN'T KNOW? YOU DIDN'T THINK IT WAS JUST TOO CONVENIENT, YOUR LITTLE MARSHAL FRIEND BAILING YOU OUT?
HE WAS SUPPOSED TO PUT YOU IN THE GROUND. THE END.
BUT THIS IS ANCIENT HISTORY, KID. HOPE YOU SAID YOUR GOODBYES.
I'LL SEE YOU IN HELL.

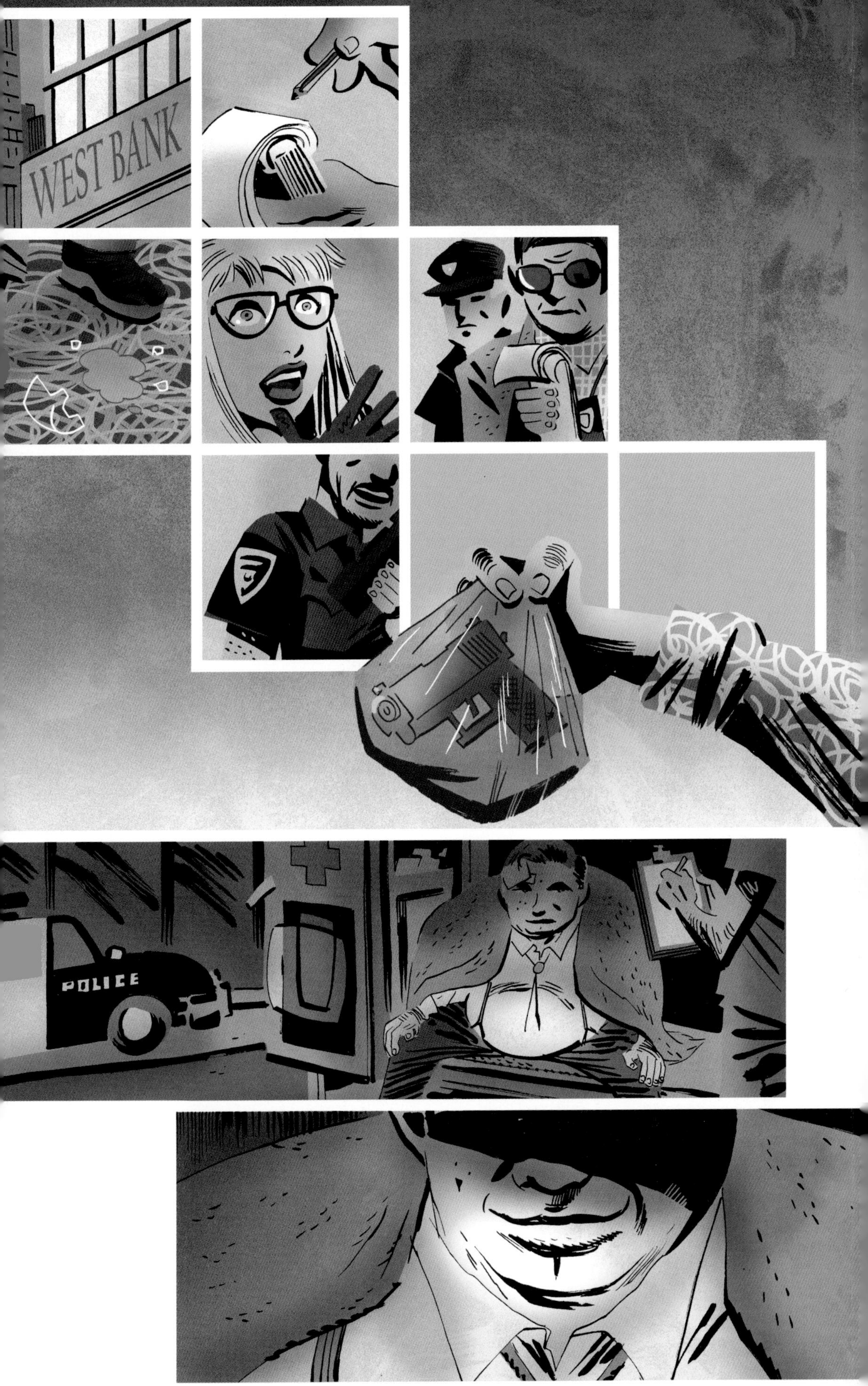
WEST BANK
POLICE

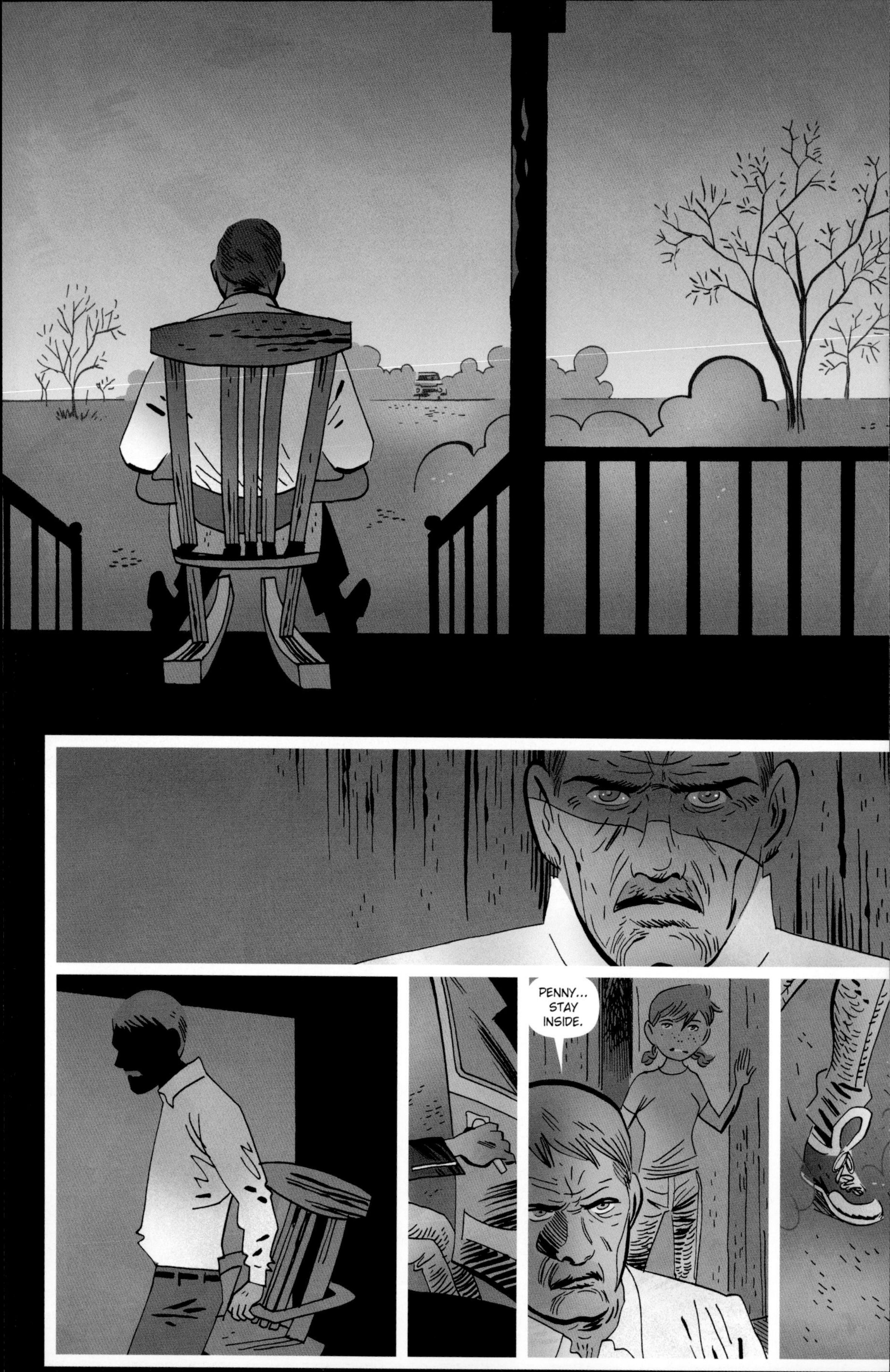
PENNY... STAY INSIDE.

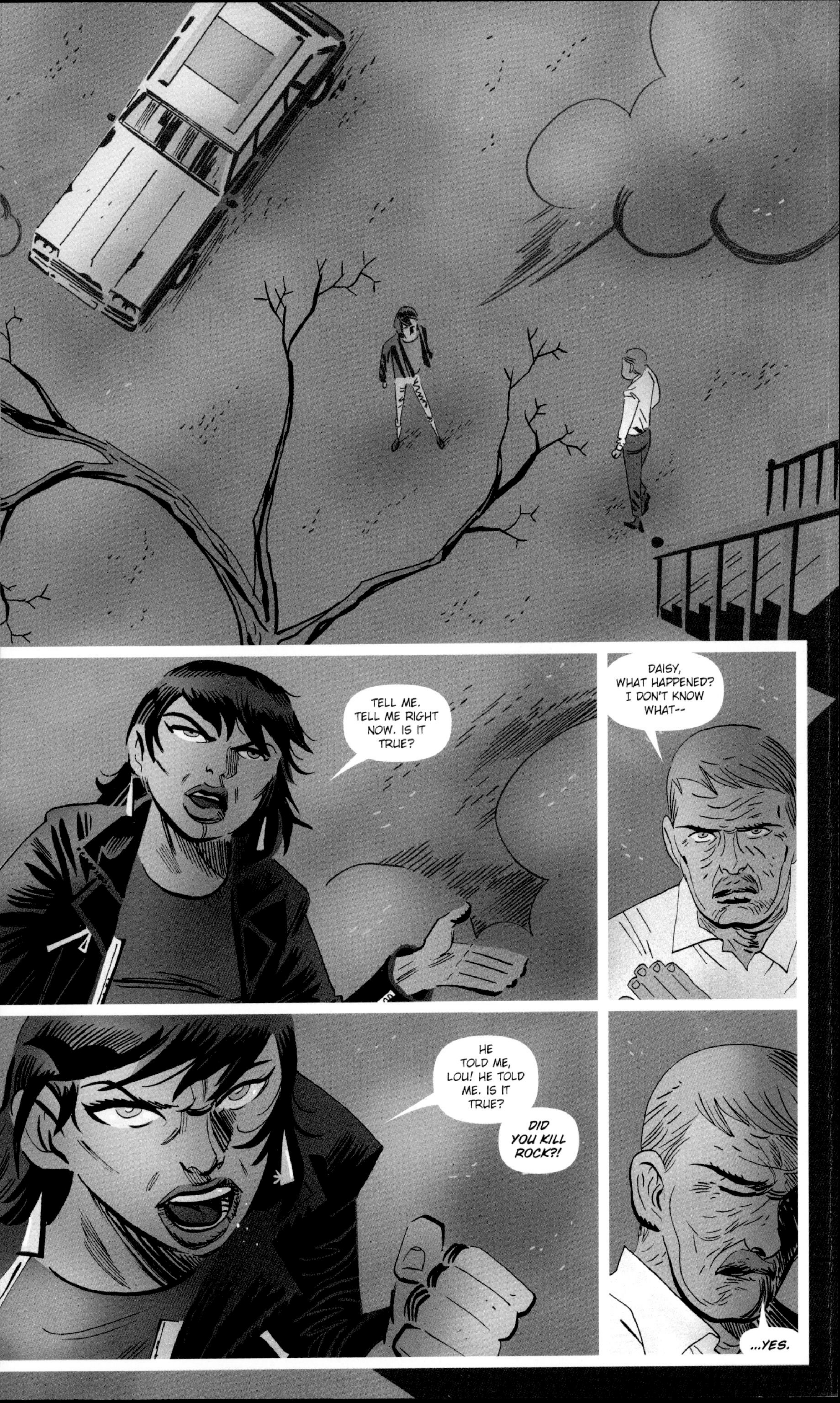
TELL ME. TELL ME RIGHT NOW. IS IT TRUE?
DAISY, WHAT HAPPENED? I DON'T KNOW WHAT--
HE TOLD ME, LOU! HE TOLD ME. IS IT TRUE?
DID YOU KILL ROCK?!
...YES.

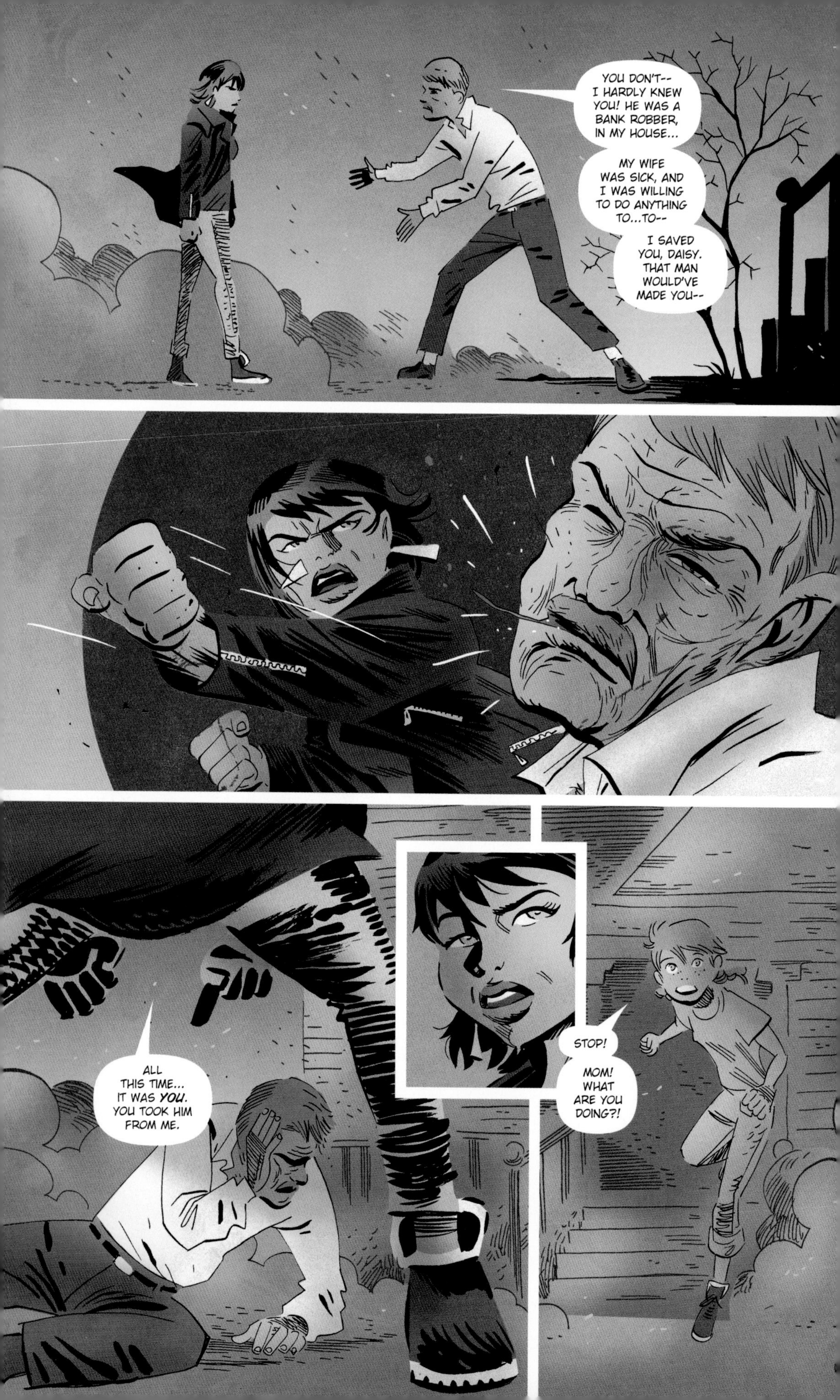
YOU DON'T-- I HARDLY KNEW YOU! HE WAS A BANK ROBBER, IN MY HOUSE...
MY WIFE WAS SICK, AND I WAS WILLING TO DO ANYTHING TO...TO--
I SAVED YOU, DAISY. THAT MAN WOULD'VE MADE YOU--
ALL THIS TIME... IT WAS *YOU*. YOU TOOK HIM FROM ME.
STOP!
MOM! WHAT ARE YOU DOING?!

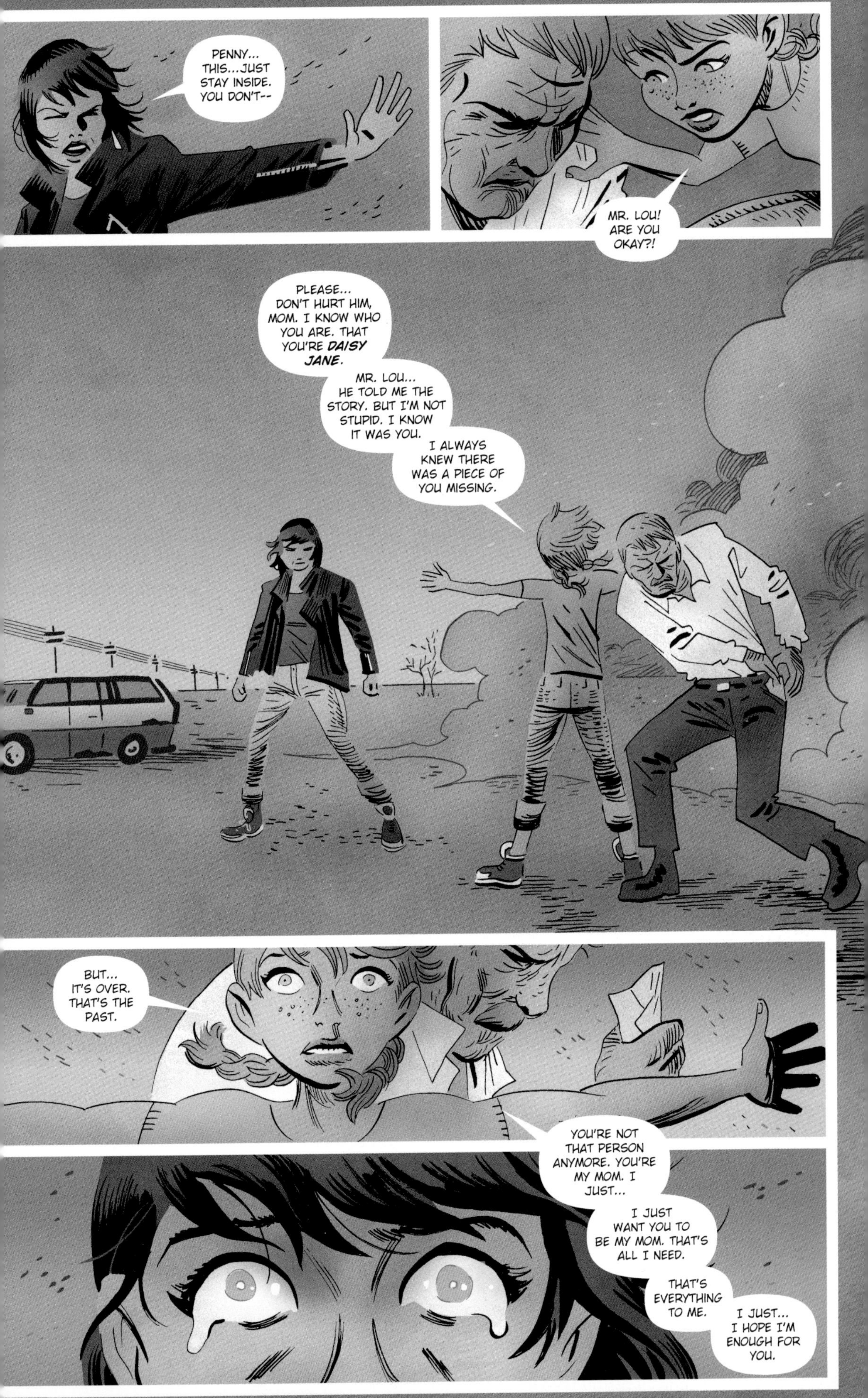

PENNY... THIS...JUST STAY INSIDE. YOU DON'T--
MR. LOU! ARE YOU OKAY?!
PLEASE... DON'T HURT HIM, MOM. I KNOW WHO YOU ARE. THAT YOU'RE ***DAISY JANE***.
MR. LOU... HE TOLD ME THE STORY. BUT I'M NOT STUPID. I KNOW IT WAS YOU.
I ALWAYS KNEW THERE WAS A PIECE OF YOU MISSING.
BUT... IT'S OVER. THAT'S THE PAST.
YOU'RE NOT THAT PERSON ANYMORE. YOU'RE MY MOM. I JUST...
I JUST WANT YOU TO BE MY MOM. THAT'S ALL I NEED.
THAT'S EVERYTHING TO ME.
I JUST... I HOPE I'M ENOUGH FOR YOU.

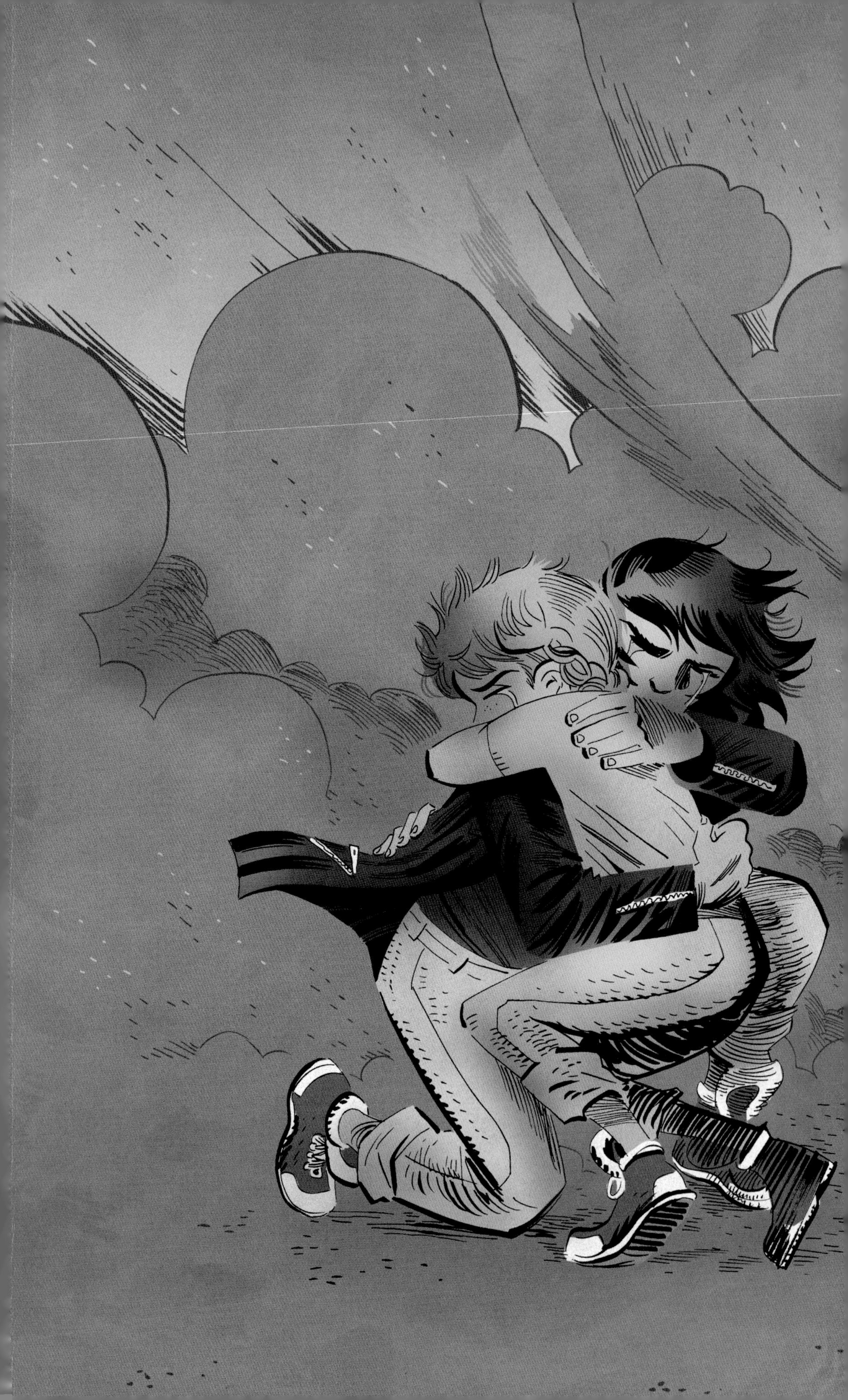

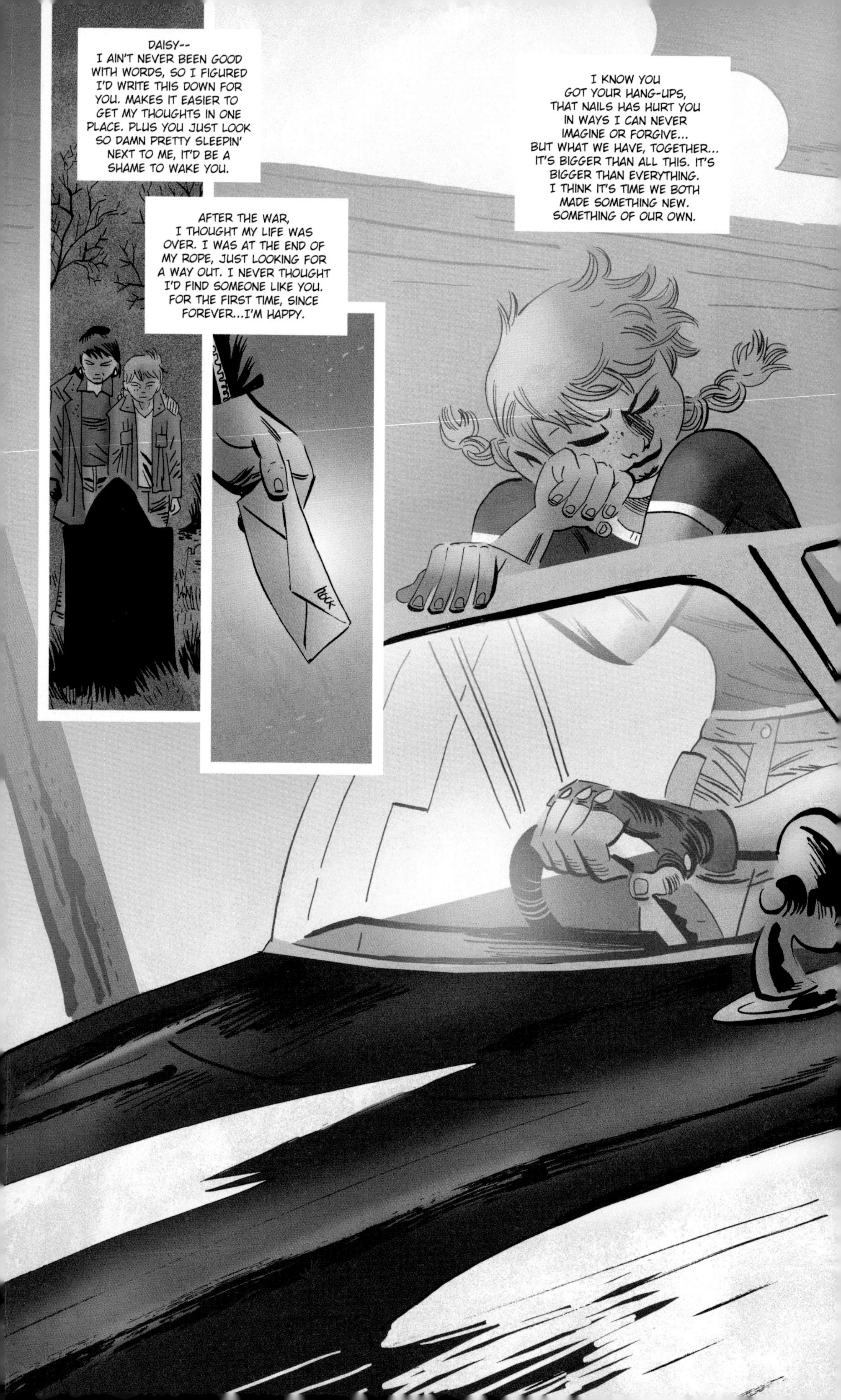
DAISY--
I AIN'T NEVER BEEN GOOD WITH WORDS, SO I FIGURED I'D WRITE THIS DOWN FOR YOU. MAKES IT EASIER TO GET MY THOUGHTS IN ONE PLACE. PLUS YOU JUST LOOK SO DAMN PRETTY SLEEPIN' NEXT TO ME, IT'D BE A SHAME TO WAKE YOU.
AFTER THE WAR, I THOUGHT MY LIFE WAS OVER. I WAS AT THE END OF MY ROPE, JUST LOOKING FOR A WAY OUT. I NEVER THOUGHT I'D FIND SOMEONE LIKE YOU. FOR THE FIRST TIME, SINCE FOREVER...I'M HAPPY.
I KNOW YOU GOT YOUR HANG-UPS, THAT NAILS HAS HURT YOU IN WAYS I CAN NEVER IMAGINE OR FORGIVE... BUT WHAT WE HAVE, TOGETHER... IT'S BIGGER THAN ALL THIS. IT'S BIGGER THAN EVERYTHING. I THINK IT'S TIME WE BOTH MADE SOMETHING NEW. SOMETHING OF OUR OWN.

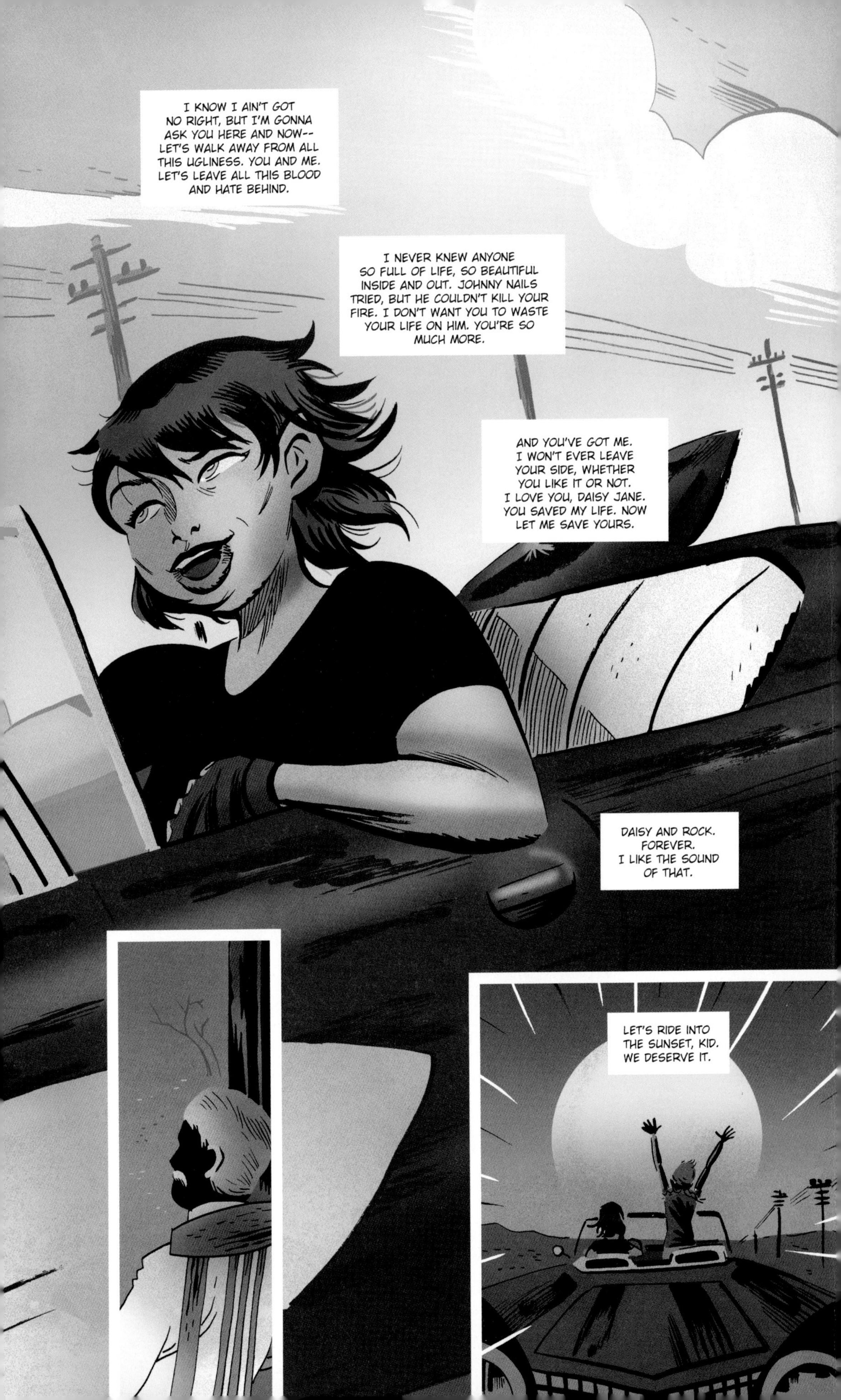
I KNOW I AIN'T GOT NO RIGHT, BUT I'M GONNA ASK YOU HERE AND NOW-- LET'S WALK AWAY FROM ALL THIS UGLINESS. YOU AND ME. LET'S LEAVE ALL THIS BLOOD AND HATE BEHIND.
I NEVER KNEW ANYONE SO FULL OF LIFE, SO BEAUTIFUL INSIDE AND OUT. JOHNNY NAILS TRIED, BUT HE COULDN'T KILL YOUR FIRE. I DON'T WANT YOU TO WASTE YOUR LIFE ON HIM. YOU'RE SO MUCH MORE.
AND YOU'VE GOT ME. I WON'T EVER LEAVE YOUR SIDE, WHETHER YOU LIKE IT OR NOT. I LOVE YOU, DAISY JANE. YOU SAVED MY LIFE. NOW LET ME SAVE YOURS.
DAISY AND ROCK. FOREVER. I LIKE THE SOUND OF THAT.
LET'S RIDE INTO THE SUNSET, KID. WE DESERVE IT.

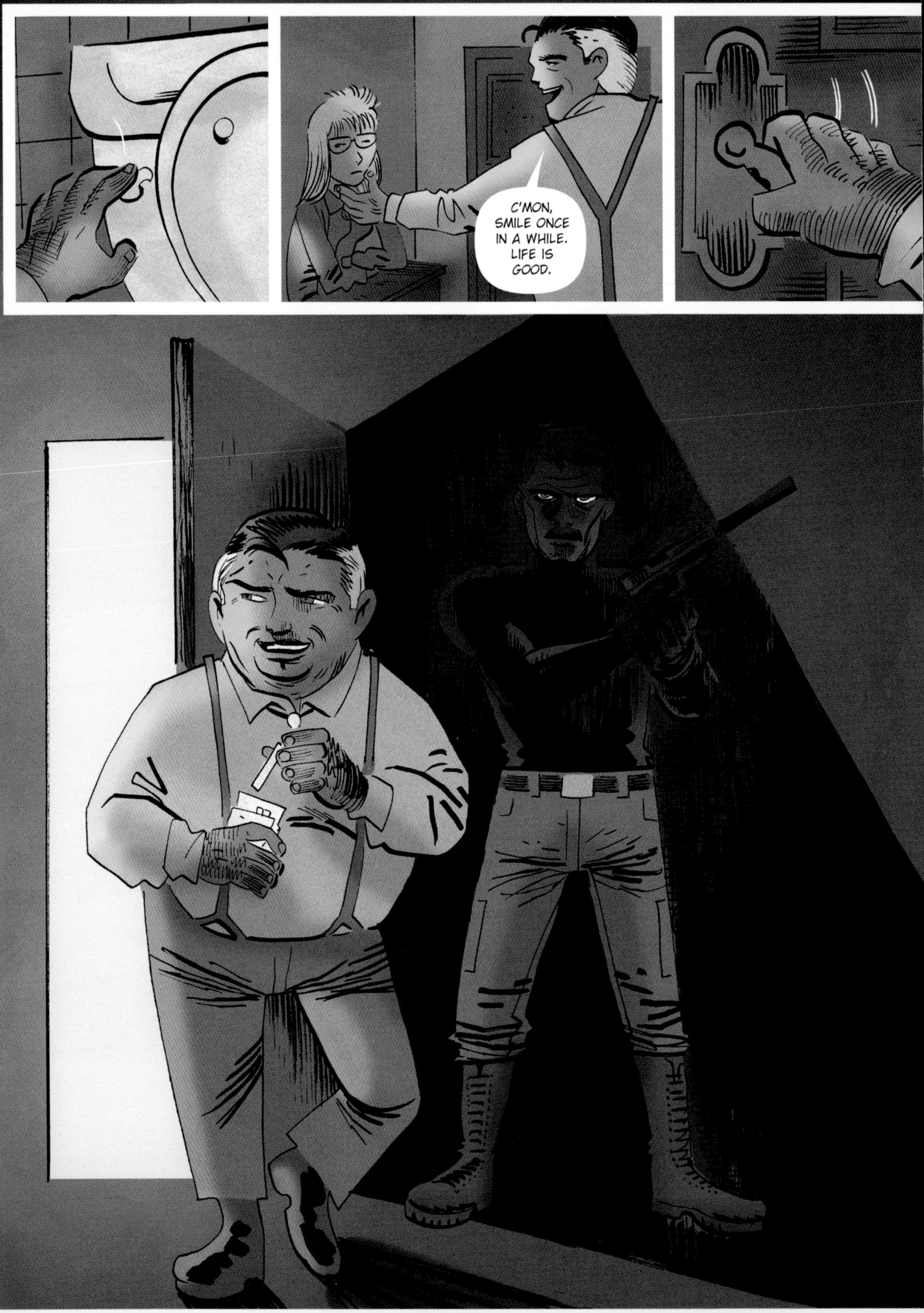
C'MON, SMILE ONCE IN A WHILE. LIFE IS GOOD.

VARIANT COVERS

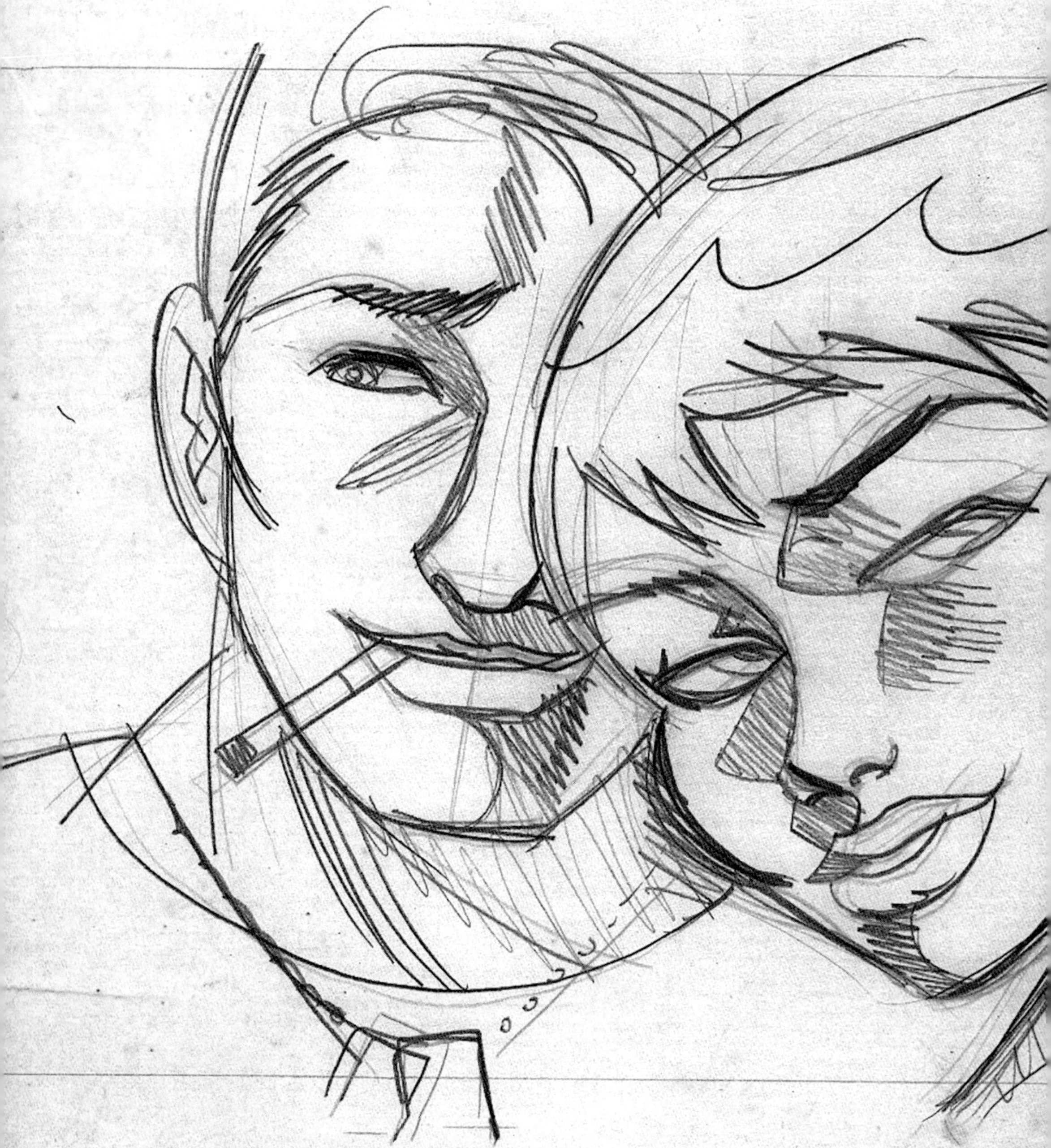

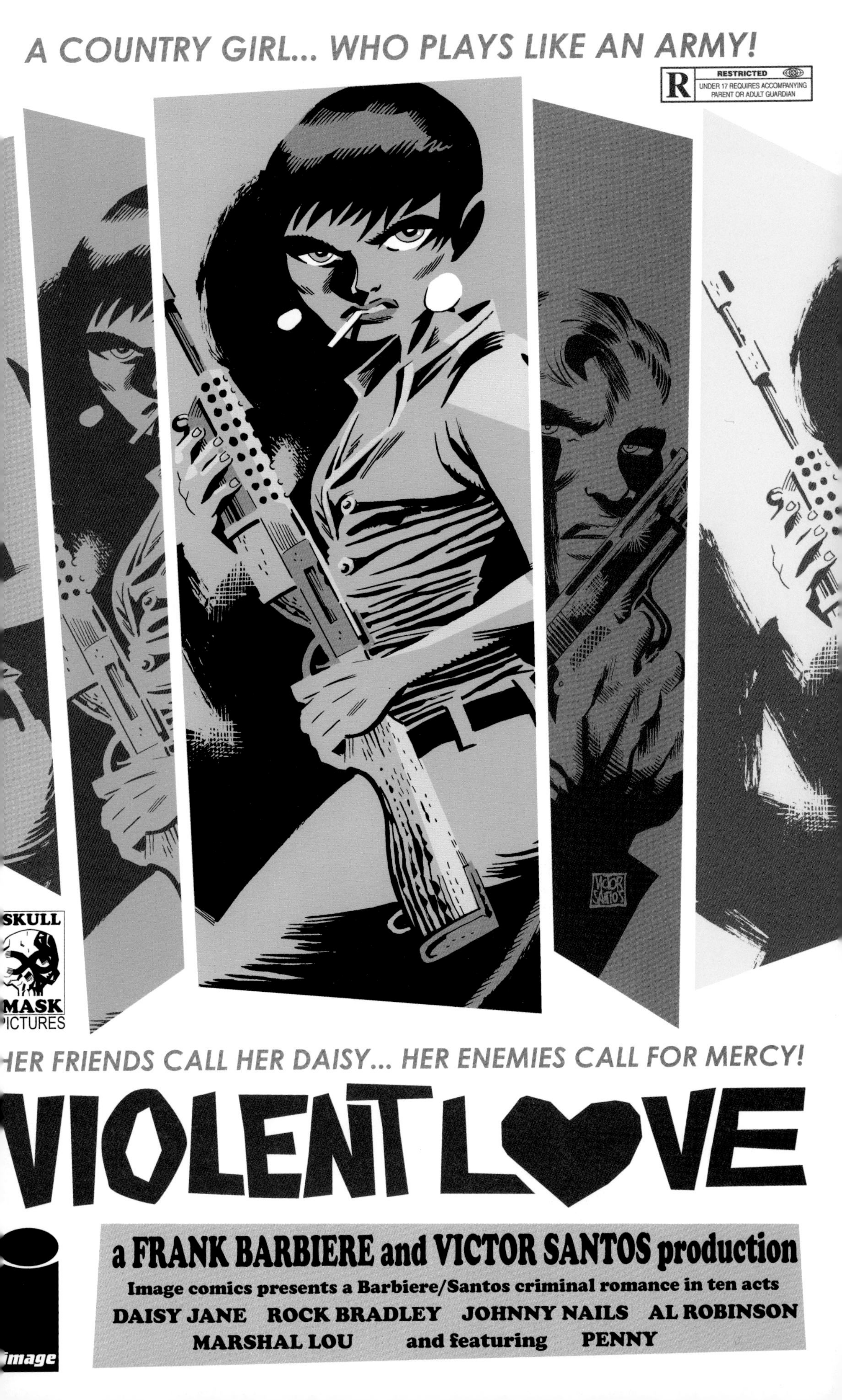
A COUNTRY GIRL... WHO PLAYS LIKE AN ARMY!
R RESTRICTED
UNDER 17 REQUIRES ACCOMPANYING PARENT OR ADULT GUARDIAN
SKULL MASK PICTURES
HER FRIENDS CALL HER DAISY... HER ENEMIES CALL FOR MERCY!
VIOLENT LOVE
a FRANK BARBIERE and VICTOR SANTOS production
Image comics presents a Barbiere/Santos criminal romance in ten acts
DAISY JANE ROCK BRADLEY JOHNNY NAILS AL ROBINSON
MARSHAL LOU and featuring PENNY
image

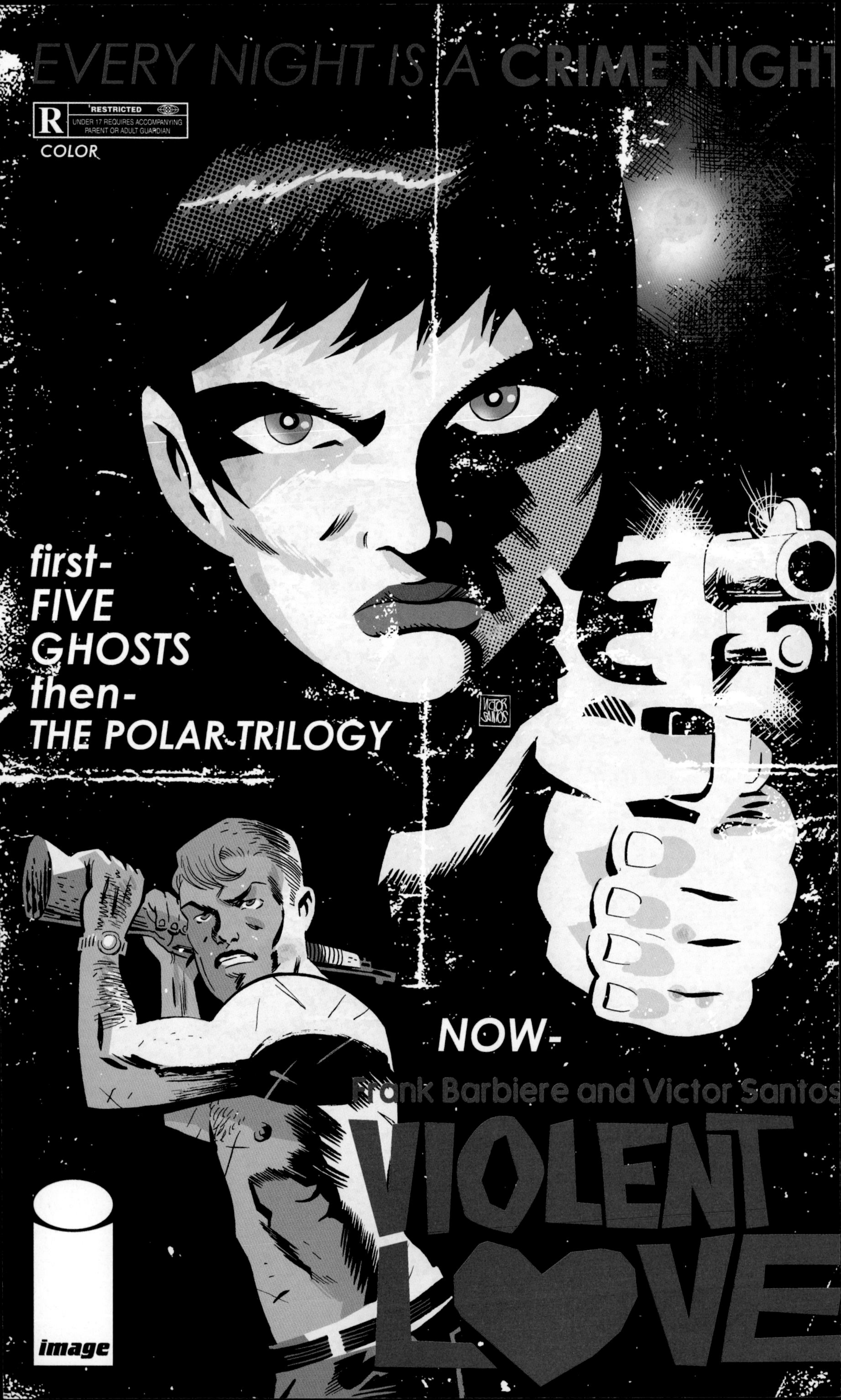

EVERY NIGHT IS A CRIME NIGHT
R RESTRICTED
UNDER 17 REQUIRES ACCOMPANYING PARENT OR ADULT GUARDIAN
COLOR
first-
FIVE
GHOSTS
then-
THE POLAR TRILOGY
VICTOR SANTOS
NOW-
Frank Barbiere and Victor Santos
VIOLENT LOVE
image

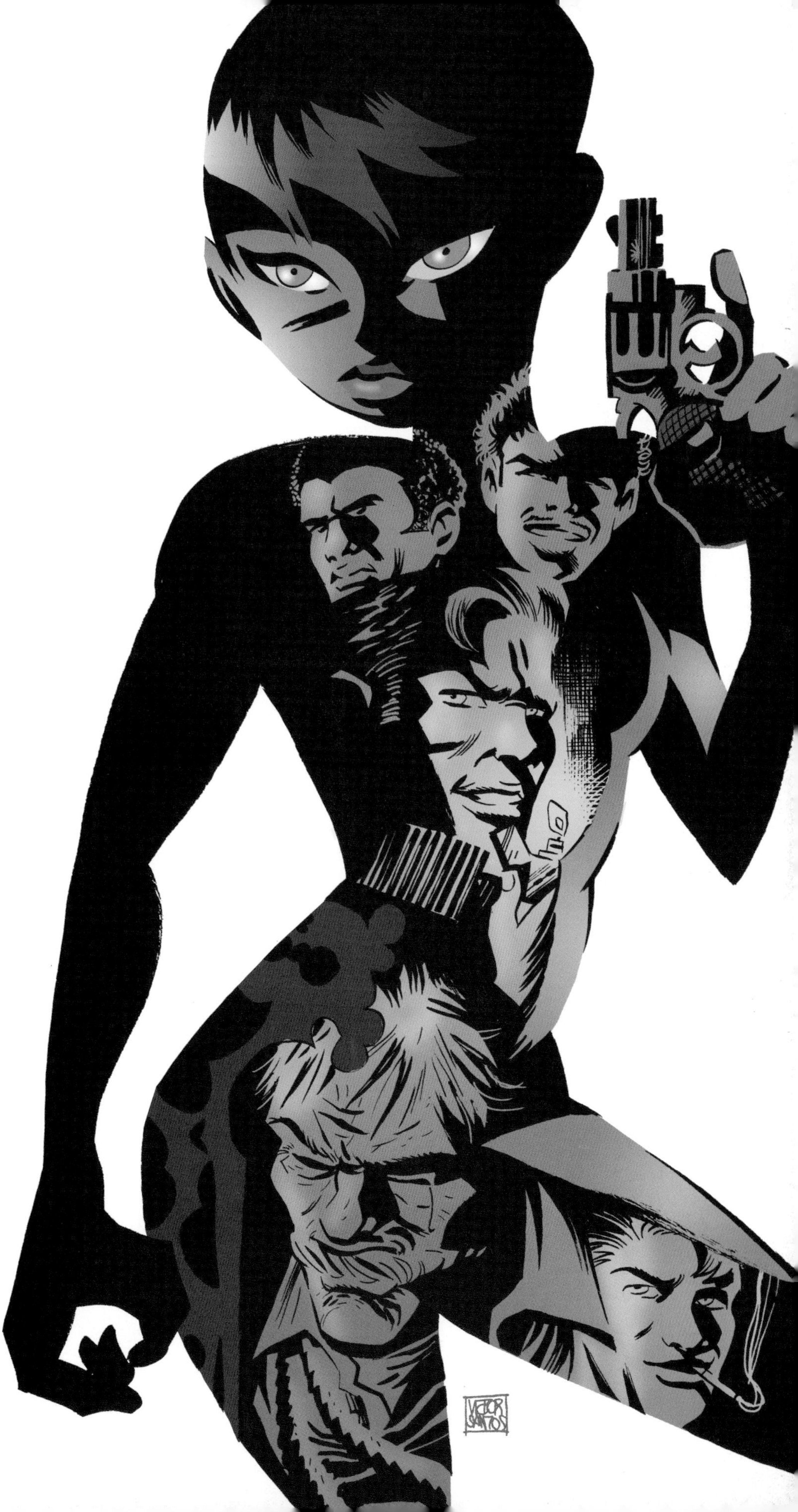

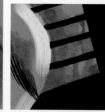

VIOLENT L♥VE

FRANK BARBIERE
VICTOR SANTOS
and **DYLAN TODD**
PRESENT

an **IMAGE COMICS** production

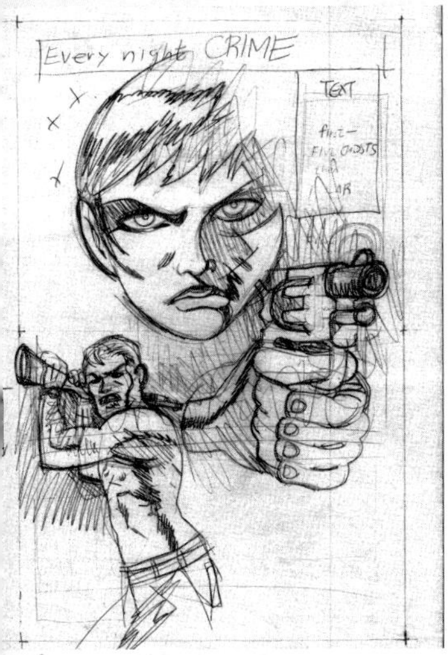
Every night CRIME
TEXT

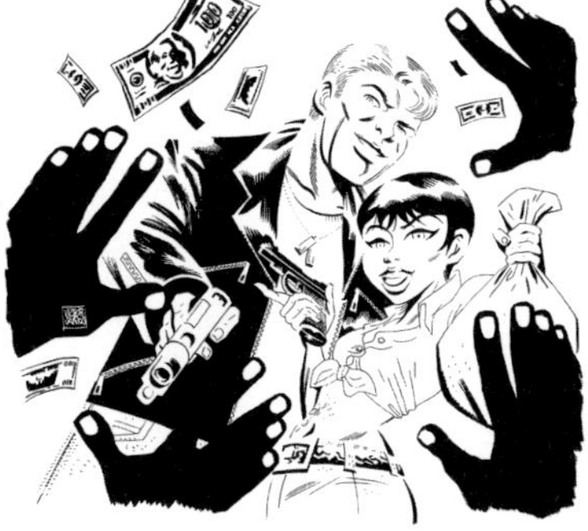

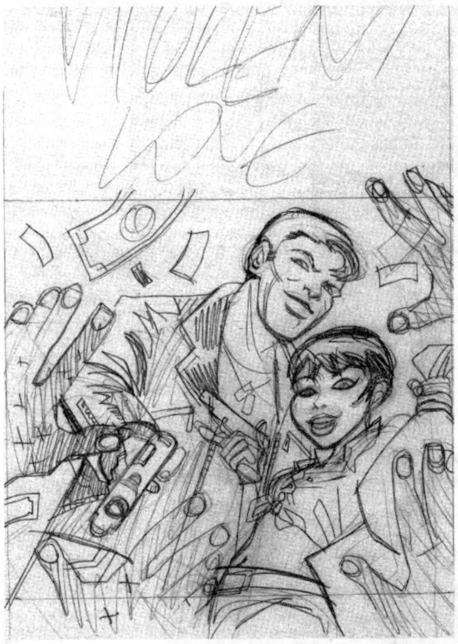

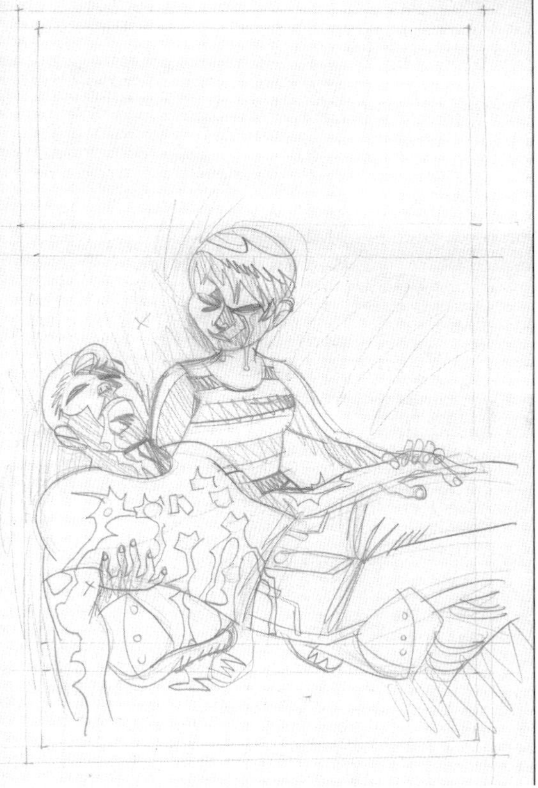

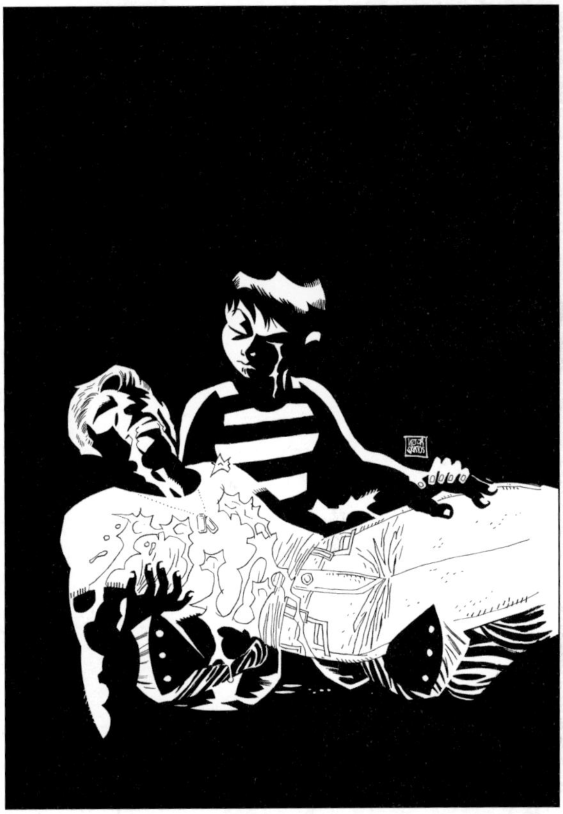

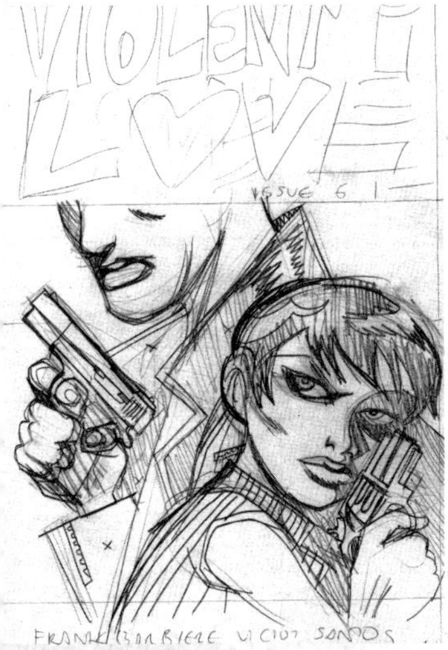
VIOLENT
LOVE
ISSUE 6
FRANK BARBIERE VICTOR SANTOS

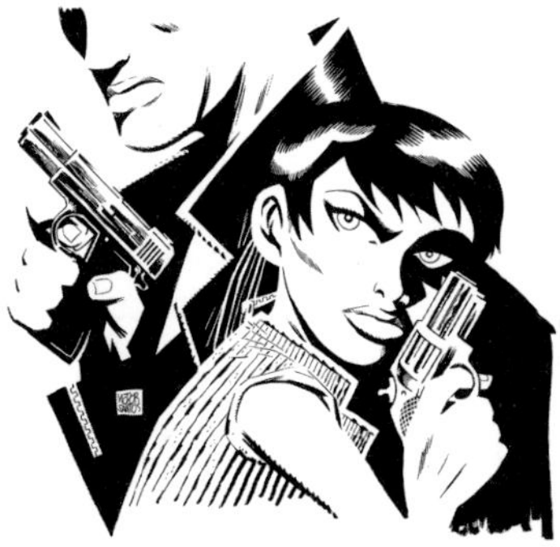

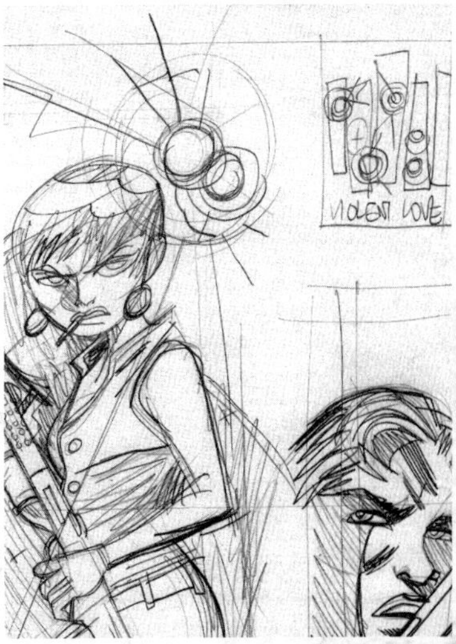
VIOLENT LOVE

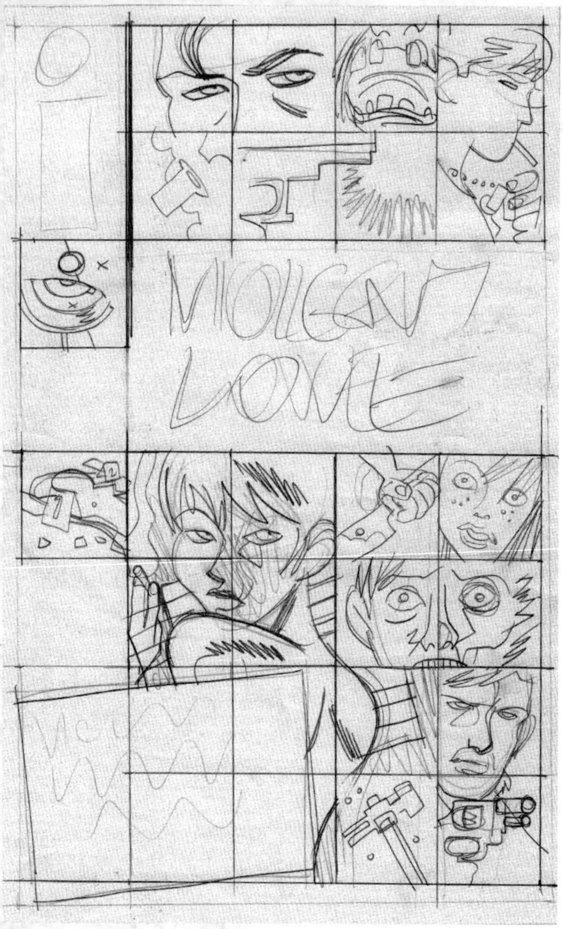
VIOLENT
LOVE

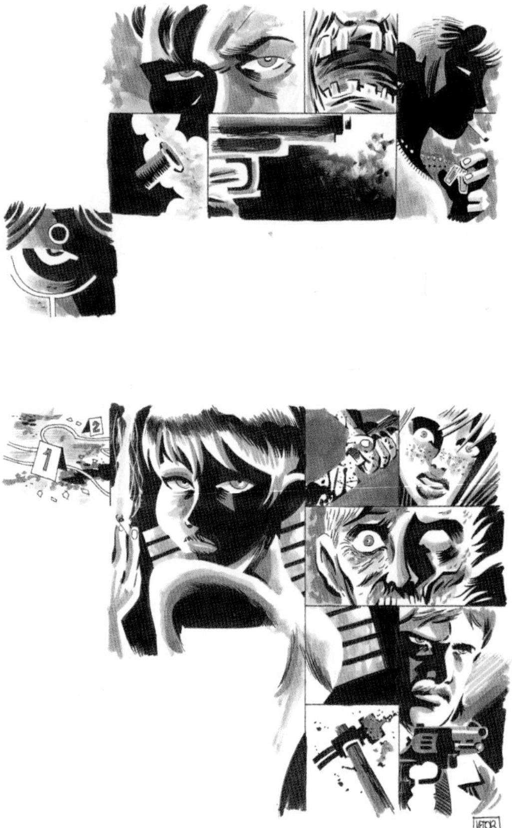

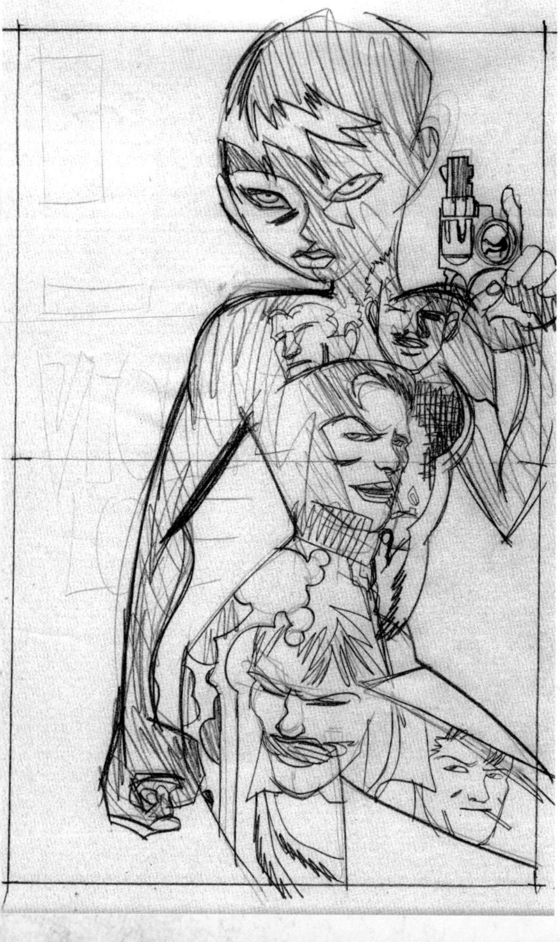

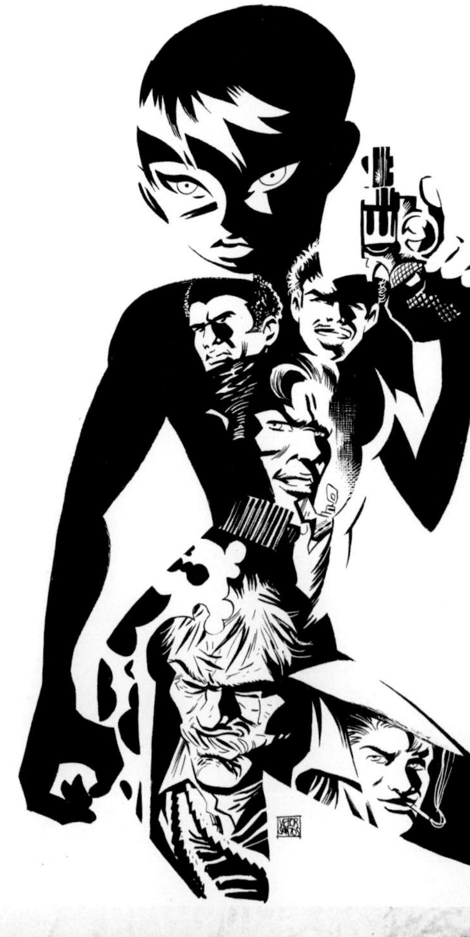

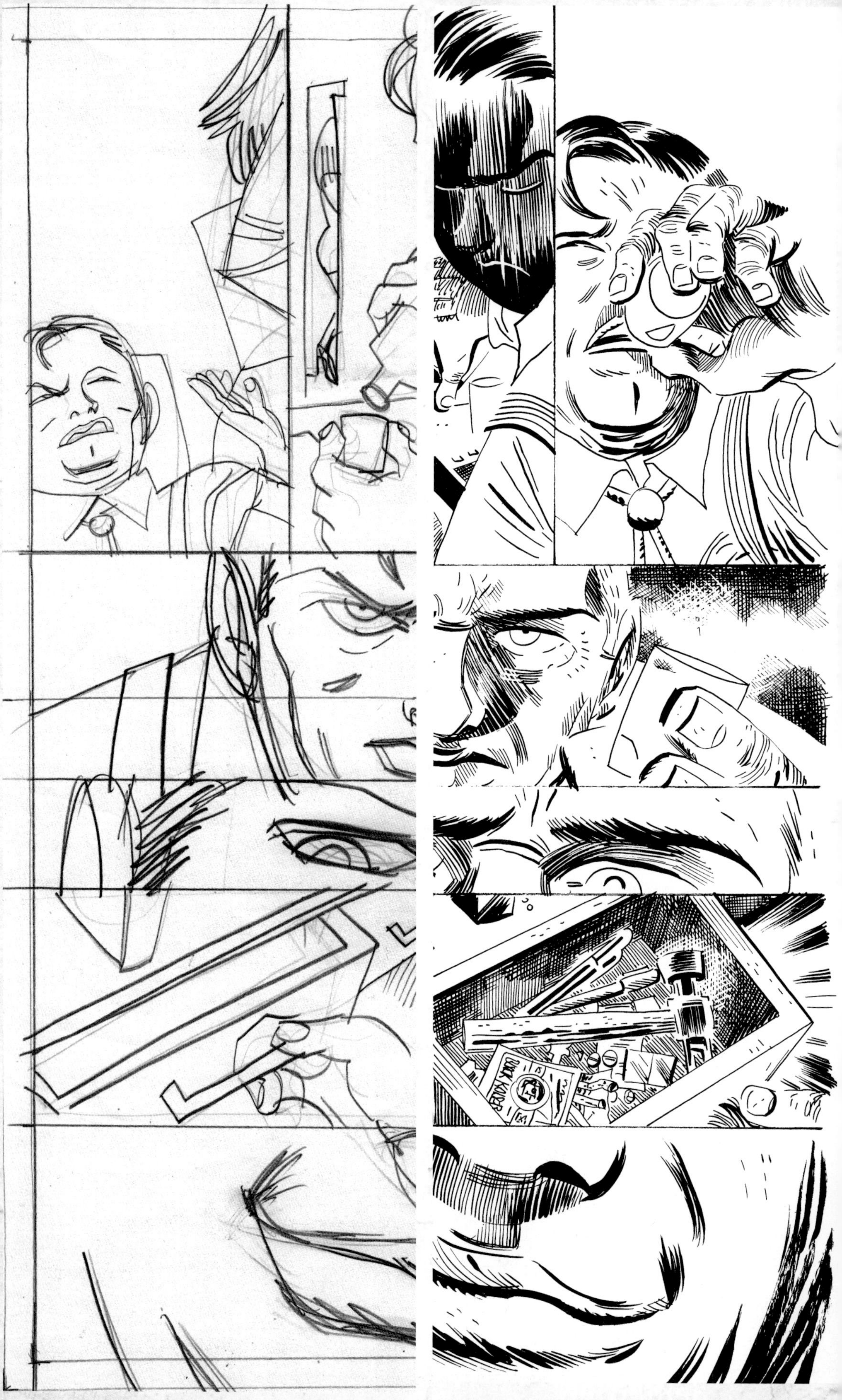

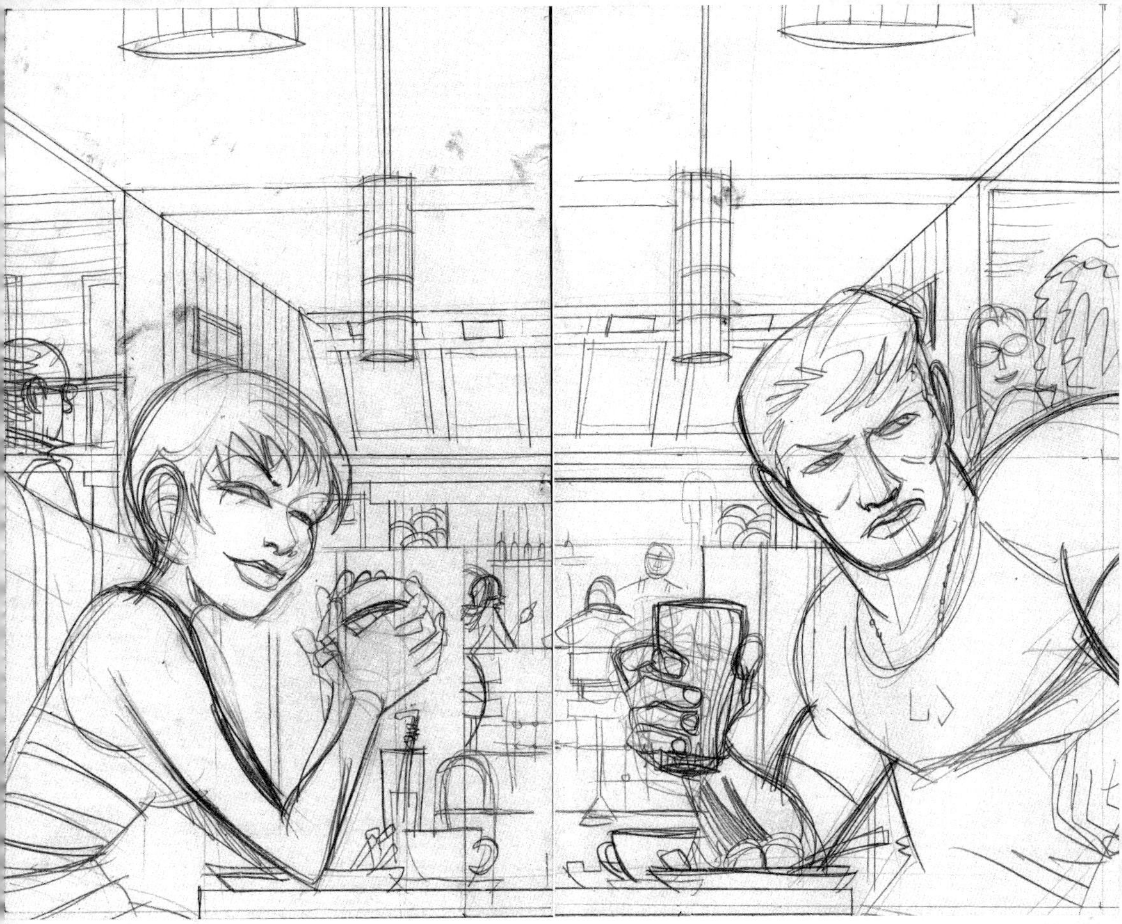

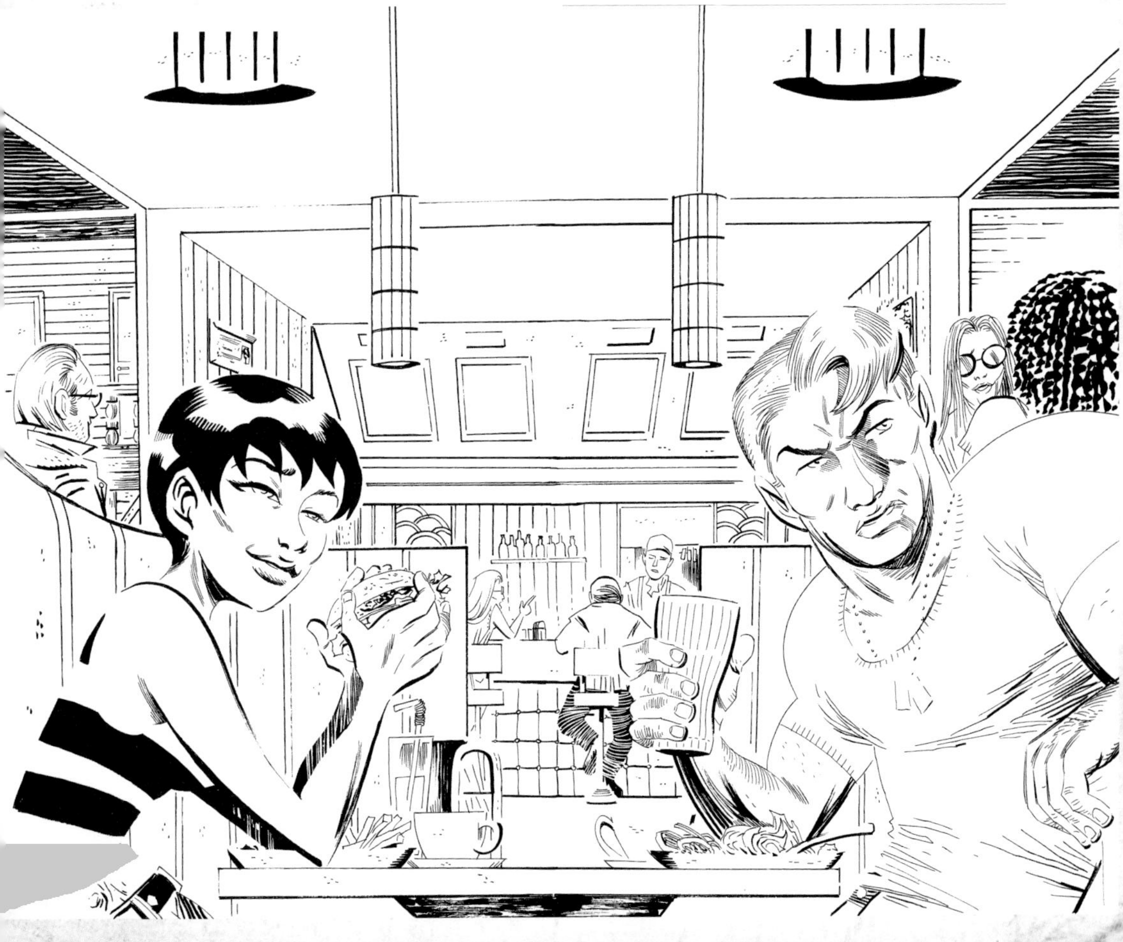

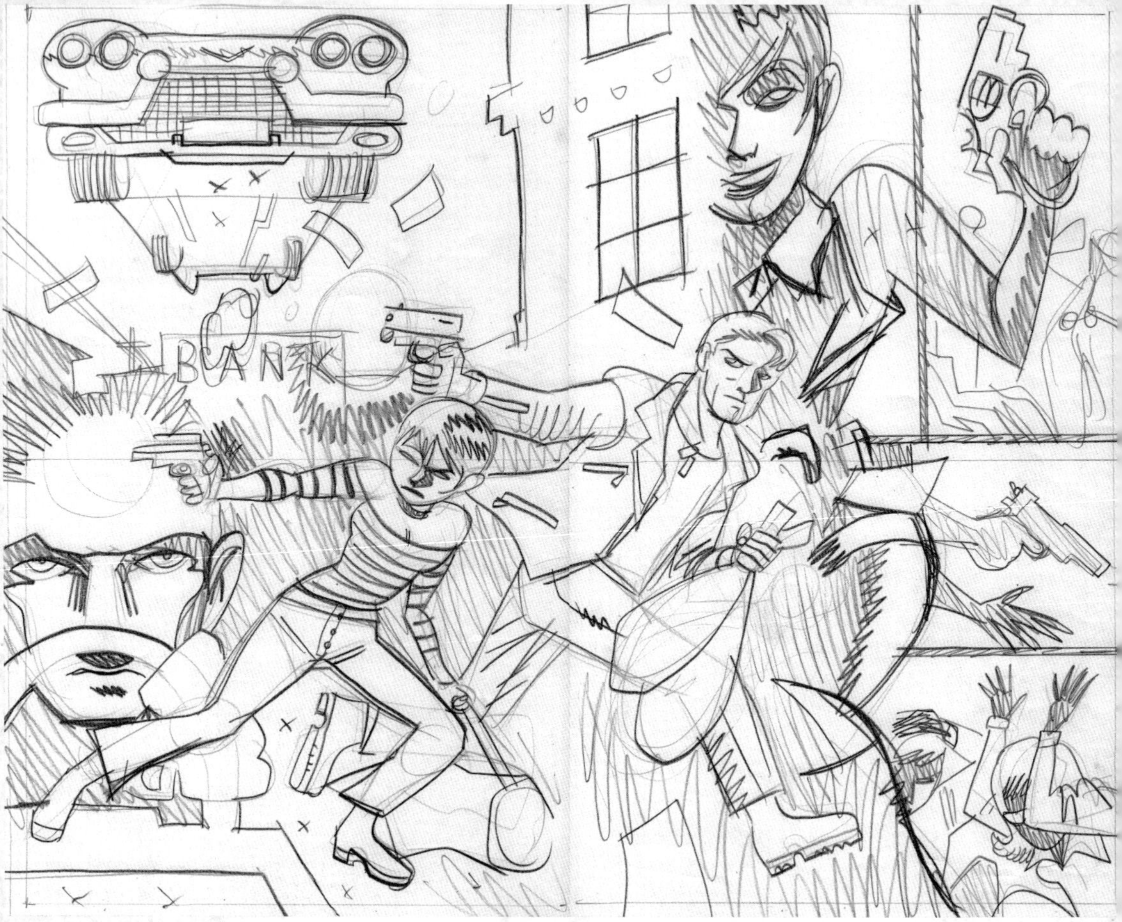
BANK

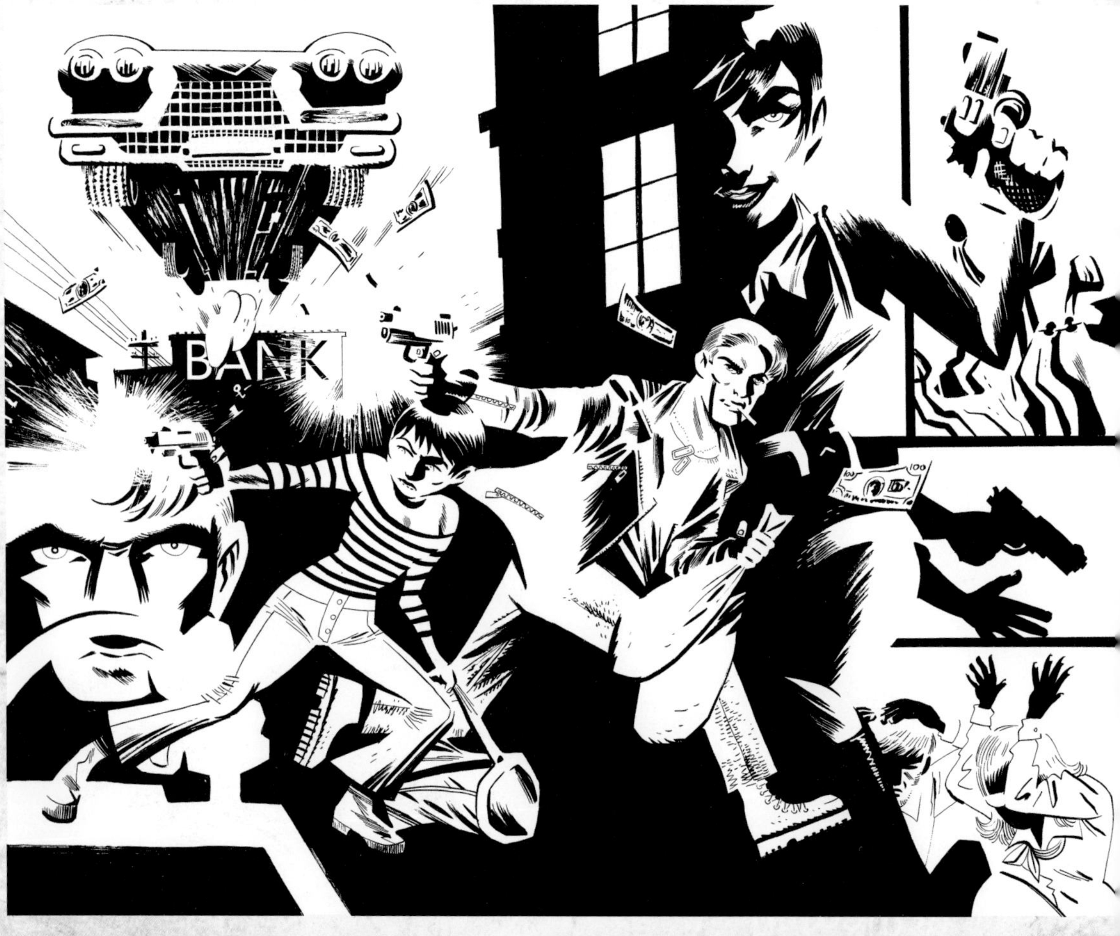
BANK

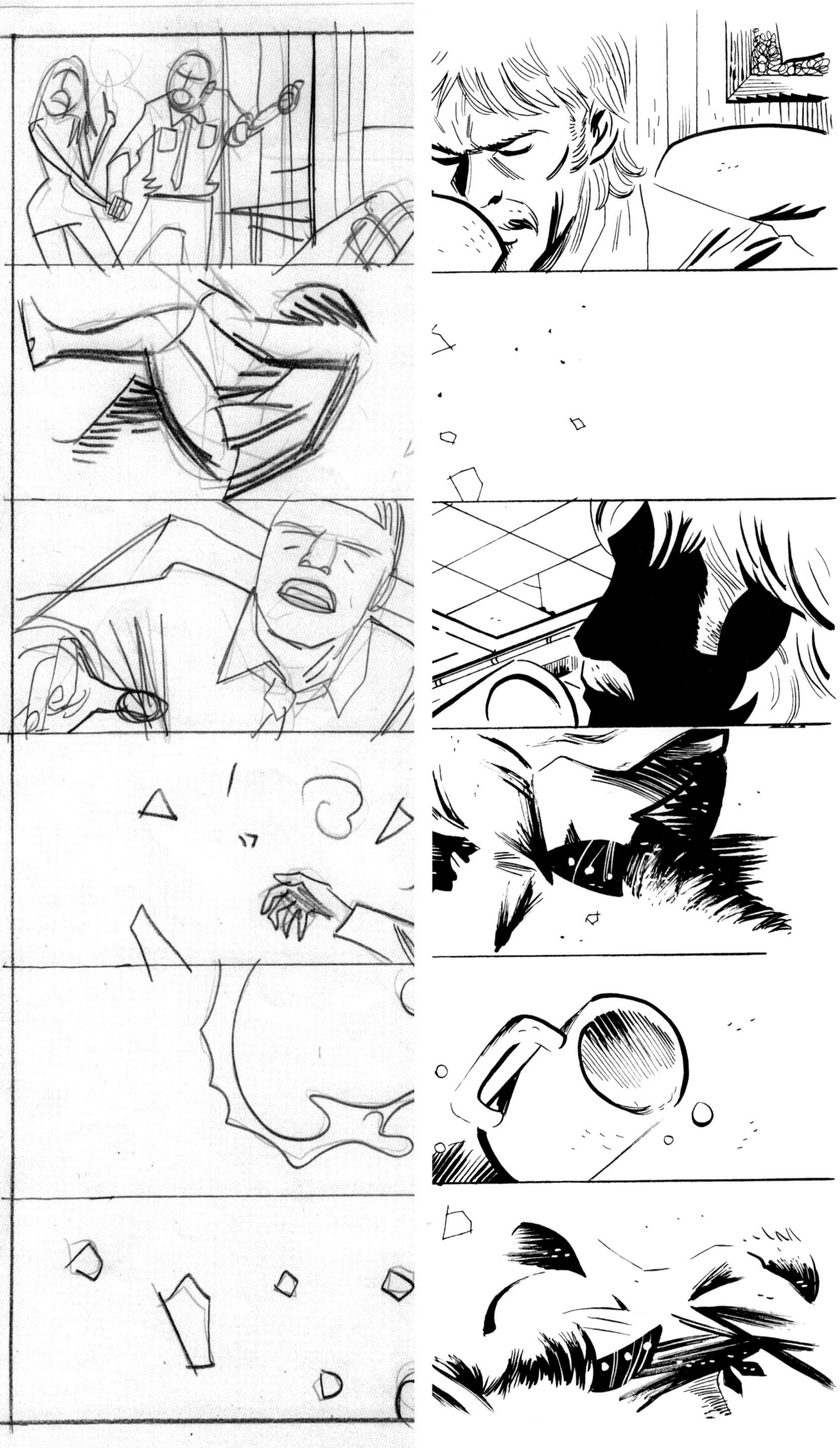

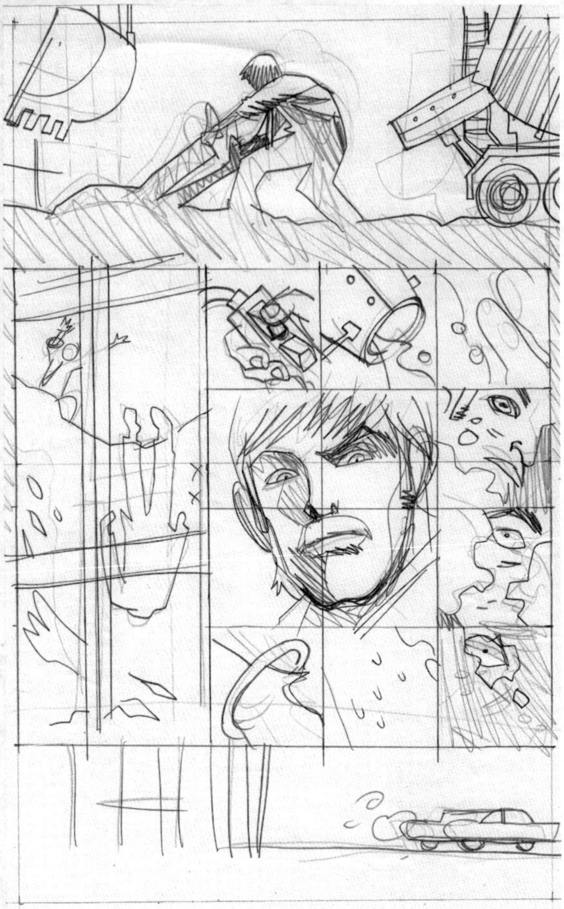
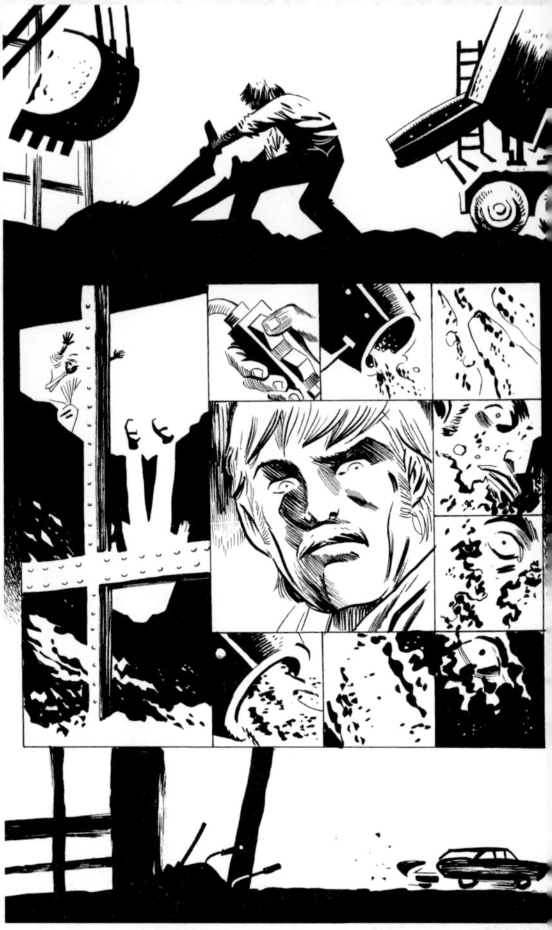
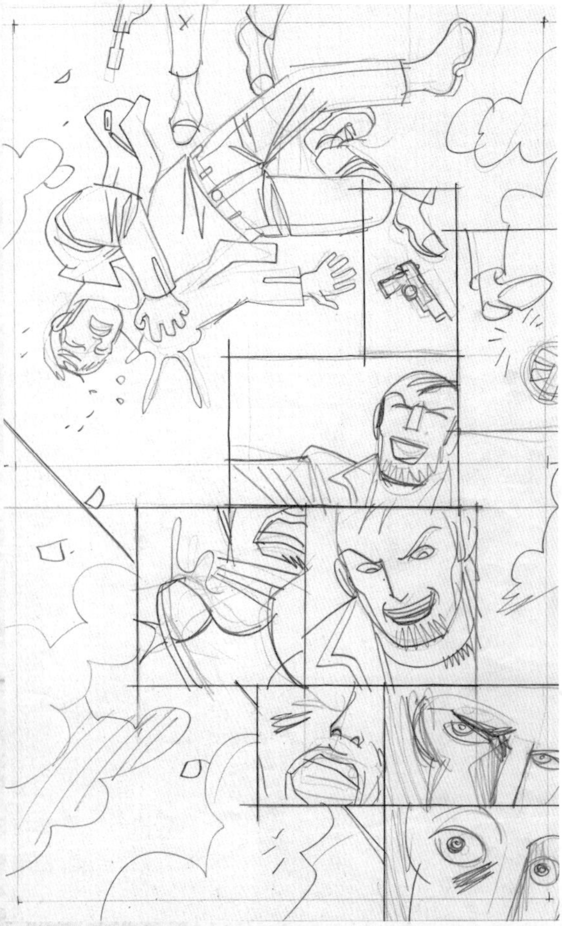
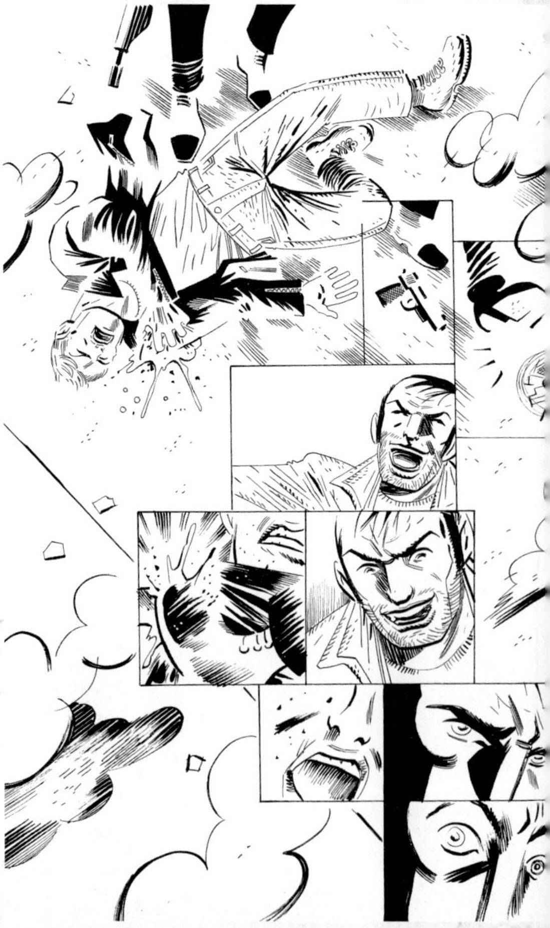

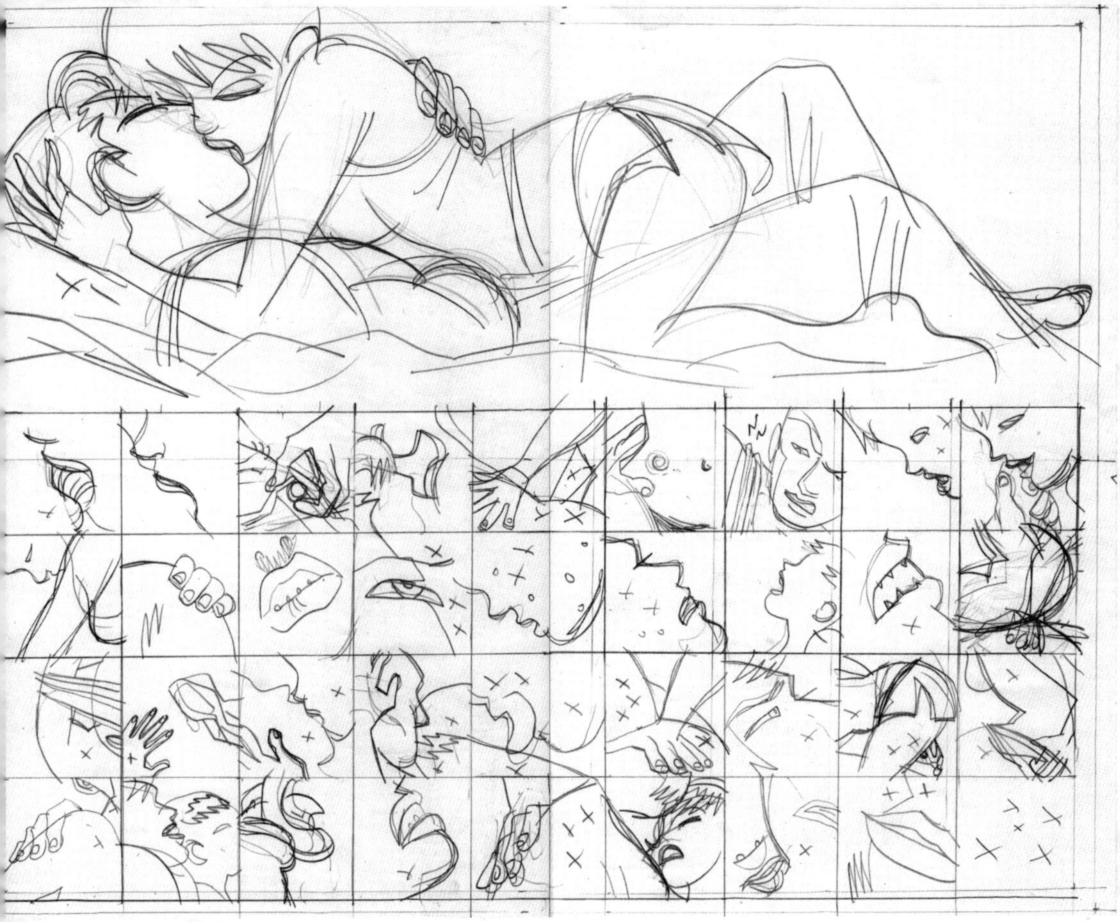

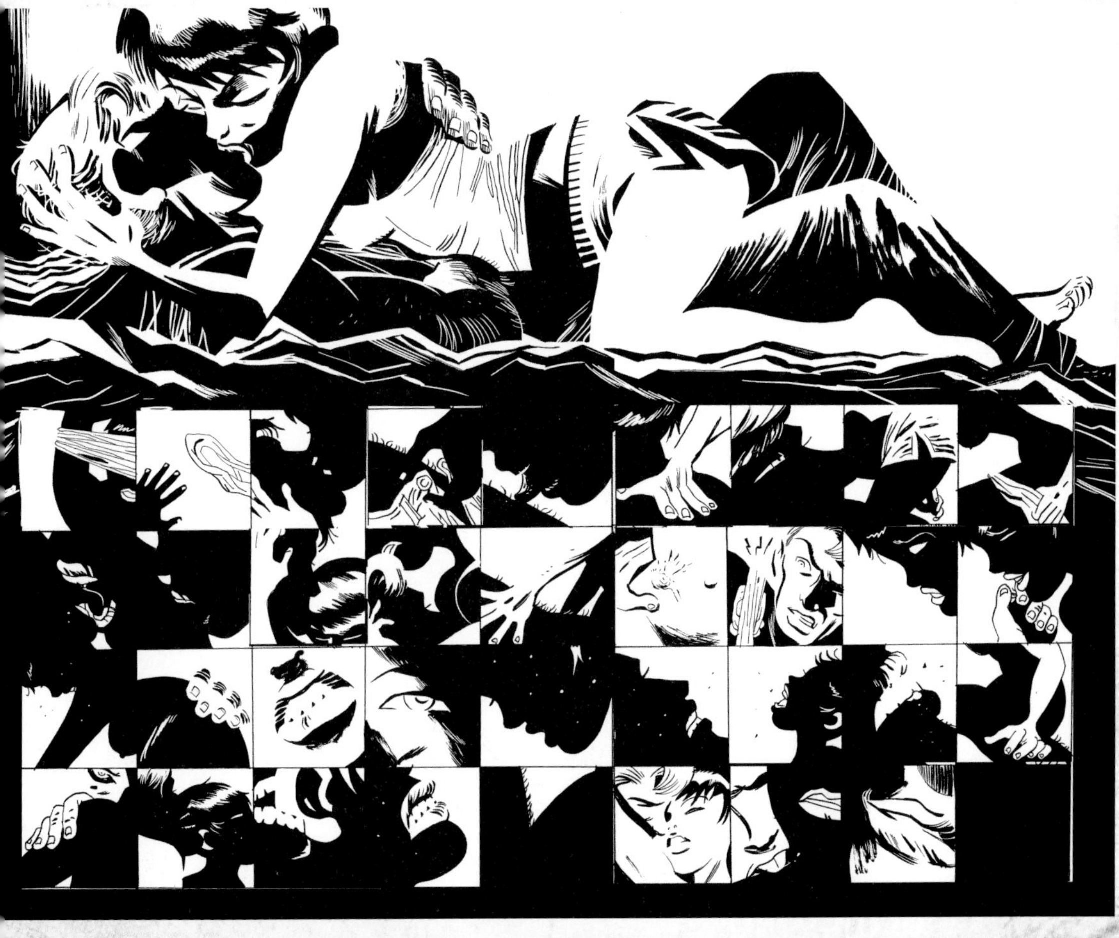

THE LAST WORD

I'm normally opposed to an afterword in my books. I don't want to feel like a magician explaining the trick, or try to justify the choices we made, but I wanted a chance to say that I'm extremely proud of **VIOLENT LOVE** and all the work that co-creator/ collaborator Victor Santos and myself have done over the last two years. This book grew out of a lot of shared interests and the joy that came from working together on a book called *Black Market* for BOOM! Studios a few years back. I've long been a fan of Victor's work, and I have to take a moment to thank my old editors Eric Harburn and Chris Rosas for having the great idea of pairing us up. Writing comics is a very unique experience and requires a lot of trust in your collaborators. With Victor, it feels like the artistic equivalent of someone finishing my sentences. He is a rare talent, one who is more than capable of writing and drawing his own books (and he does – you should check out *Rashoman* and *Polar*), so the fact I'm able to collaborate with him at all is a gift. I value his time and skill, and hence worked very hard to make sure we were telling a story I fully believed in and was important to tell.

Making comics can be an arduous, long, expensive, and thankless endeavor. There are a lot of books on the market, and it can be very difficult to stand out amongst all the great titles out there. With Violent Love, we wanted to do something different. Something that served as a love letter to the crime and noir genres we enjoy so much, but also built on them and meant something more. I'm really glad we got to experiment with romance, a frame story, and ultimately deliver a story about overcoming loss and revenge. Daisy's journey is about learning to live with the awful things that have happened and build something new. Creation in lieu of destruction. And from working in comics, one thing we know is that creation is hard. But it's always worth it. I can't thank you enough for reading our story, and I hope it sticks with you.

FRANK J. BARBIERE
DECEMBER 2017

FRANK J. BARBIERE is a writer from New Jersey. A former English teacher, Frank is a graduate of Rutgers University and the Graduate School for Education.

Frank broke into the industry with the creator-owned hit **FIVE GHOSTS** (Image Comics) and has since worked for every major publisher in the US, as well as having a global presence in France (Glenat Comics) and Italy (Cosmo Editoriale) with his creator-owned work. His body of work includes notable runs on **AVENGERS WORLD** and **HOWLING COMMANDOS OF S.H.I.E.L.D.** at Marvel Comics, as well as the creator-owned series **BLACK MARKET** & **BROKEN WORLD** (BOOM! Studios), **THE REVISIONIST** (Aftershock Comics), and **THE WHITE SUITS** (Dark Horse Comics).

In 2017, Frank began working as a narrative designer at Vicarious Visions, writing for the *Destiny* video game franchise.

www.atlasincognita.com | @atlasincognita

Born in Valencia in 1977, **VICTOR SANTOS** has written and illustrated a variety of comics in Spain and France, including **LOS REYES ELFOS**, **PULP HEROES**, **INTACHABLE** and **RASHOMON**, where he won six awards from the Barcelona international comic convention and three from the Madrid con. Since 2006, he has worked on numerous creator-owned comics in the United States including **THE MICE TEMPLAR**, written by Bryan Glass and Mike Oeming, **FILTHY RICH**, written by Brian Azzarello, **BLACK MARKET**, written by Frank J. Barbiere, and **FURIOUS**, written by Bryan Glass. He recently returned to France with the graphic novel **SUKEBAN TURBO**, written by writer Sylvain Runberg for Glenat Comics. His upcoming project is **BAD GIRLS**, a noir graphic novel with Alex de Campi for publisher Simon & Schuster.

Victor has balanced these independent works with franchise series like **GODZILLA**, **SLEEPY HOLLOW**, **AXIS**, **DEAD BOY DETECTIVES** or **BIG TROUBLE IN LITTLE CHINA** for publishers like IDW, Marvel, DC and Boom! Studios.

His most personal work as a complete creator is the **POLAR** trilogy from Dark Horse Comics, optioned by Constantin Films and in development as a motion picture. He was nominated to a Harvey Award in 2014 for his work on the first volume, **POLAR: CAME FROM THE COLD**.

victorsantoscomics.tumblr.com | @polarcomic

DYLAN TODD is a writer, art director and graphic designer. When he's not reading comics, making comics or designing stuff for comics, he can probably be found playing the *Destiny* video game franchise.

He likes Star Wars, mummies, D-Man, kaiju and 1966 Batman. He's the editor of the **2299** sci-fi comics anthology and, alongside Mathew Digges, is the co-creator of **THE CREEP CREW**, a comic about undead teen detectives.

bigredrobot.net | @bigredrobot